In Memory of
Laurel J. Ambuehl
1952-2012
Library Assistant at the Crookston Branch of LARL, 1979-2012

SCOURGE *of the* BETRAYER

SCOURGE *of the* BETRAYER

BLOODSOUNDER'S ARC BOOK ONE

JEFF SALYARDS

NIGHT SHADE BOOKS
SAN FRANCISCO

First Edition

ISBN: 978-1-59780-406-6

Night Shade Books
http://www.nightshadebooks.com

For My Mother and Father

My new patron clambered down the wagon, dark hair slicked back like wet otter fur, eyes roaming the stable yard in a measured sweep. He fixed on me briefly before continuing his survey, and it occurred to me, just as it had a hundred times since accepting the commission, that this would be unlike any other job I'd done.

Captain Braylar Killcoin beckoned me over as he spoke to a young soldier mounted on a horse. I hadn't seen the captain since the initial interview several days ago, but where he'd looked neat and well put together then, he now looked worn and road-dusty.

As I walked toward the wagon, the young soldier nodded to the captain and rode my way. Despite having ample room to go elsewhere, he headed directly for me. I backed up against the barn, but he continued angling the beast in my direction, stopping only when its muscular shoulder was rippling in my face. I clutched my satchel, trying not to flinch as the hooves nearly crushed my feet and the youth's scabbard jabbed me in the side. The soldier leaned down, face a battalion of freckles, tuft of sandy hair on his chin vaguely threatening, and said, "Bit of advice?"

I wasn't sure if he was soliciting or offering. "I'm sorry?"

He cocked his head back towards the wagon. "About riding with the captain there."

That still didn't settle who was dispensing the advice, but I assumed he meant to, so I nodded, hoping to encourage him to move his animal.

He grinned, big and toothy. "Try not to get killed." Then he flicked the reins and disappeared around the corner.

Yes, this would be a far cry from recording the tales of millers, merchants, and minor nobility. I approached Braylar as a woman led her horse around from behind the wagon, both of them short, stocky, and shaggy. She had the telltale coppery skin and inkblack hair of a Grass Dog, and wore trousers and tunic like a man. If I wondered what a nomad was doing in the company of a Syldoon commander, she wouldn't have been faulted for wondering what a scribe was doing there as well. And no one would have been faulted for wondering what the Syldoon were doing in this region in the first place, with or without nomads or scribes. All very peculiar.

She regarded me as a seasoned drover might regard a cow. Determined not to be cowed, I looked her up and down as well, stopping when I saw that the fingers and thumb on her left hand had been amputated so only the final bits nearest the base remained. I hadn't meant to stare, but certainly did, and she wiggled her nubs in my face like the death throes of a plump, brown beetle overturned on its back. I gulped and looked away.

The woman turned to the captain. "Skinny."

"I hadn't noticed."

"Skittish, too."

"That, I noticed," Captain Killcoin said. "No matter. You lack digits, he lacks fortitude, but neither absence will prove overly detrimental, Lloi. Make sure Vendurro is actually fetching Glesswik. I don't want to find them drowning in a cask."

I turned to watch her go and nearly bumped noses with the stable boy. He turned to Braylar. "Your man, inside? Told me to outfit that other wagon of yours, which I done. Waiting inside the barn. The wagon, that is. Can't say where your man got to." The boy craned his neck to look at the wagon behind Braylar. "Nice rig you got here. Why you want that other one?"

Braylar snapped his fingers to reclaim the boy's attention. "Do you know horses, boy? Or were you hired solely for your shit-shoveling prowess?"

"None better."

"With horses or shit?"

"The horses, I was meaning. Your man said to be ready when the captain rode up. What you a captain of, then? You're no Hornman, that's for certain, and the only sea around here is the big grassy one, so I'm guessing it's no ship of no kind. Unless it's a river skiff. But that's a queer thing to call yourself captain of. Small like. Are you—?"

Braylar tossed a silver coin to the boy who plucked it out of the air. He flipped it over, looked closer at the markings, and whistled, having forgotten all about captaincy.

"There's another to match it if you care for my horses half as well as you boast."

The boy's face scrunched up. "Honest?"

"Honest. But I expect the finest care. Do you have apples?" The boy nodded. "Salt lick?" Another quick nod. "Clover?"

He started to nod and stopped himself. "Think so. Have to check. Ought to."

"Very good. Unharness these horses, and unsaddle those two at the rear. Mind, though, the bay in the black saddle. Her name is Scorn, and with good reason. She likes no one, myself included, so take care she doesn't bite your face off. You find that clover, your chances improve dramatically. See to it they're treated as if they belonged to your baron himself, and you'll be rewarded."

The boy looked at the coin again. "Seen the baron, once or twice, riding past in a big party. Never stopped, nor gave no coin. Bet he wouldn't have done neither, even if he had stopped." He looked back to Braylar. "I'll treat them like the king's, I will—like the king's very own." He said this with an earnestness bordering on alarming.

When Braylar clapped him on the shoulder, the boy jumped as if stung and then ran over to the wagon. Among the horses, he moved slowly again, touching one on the neck there, talking quietly to another there, seeming far more at ease in their company.

Lloi returned with two men following. I assumed the rider that bullied me into the barn was Vendurro. The other—Glesswik, by deduction—had a long face, splotchy and deeply pocked as if it had been set on fire and put out with a pickaxe. He said, "Welcome back, Cap. Starting to wonder if your she-dog there led you astray in the grasses."

She replied, "You can be sure it was you I was leading by the nose, you would have been astrayed real good."

The corner of Braylar's mouth jumped as if caught doing something wrong, tugging small twin scars with it, and this twitch turned into a smile. Of sorts. "Move everything to the other wagon. And ensure our new… prize makes it to your room. Locked down tight. Don't dawdle, and don't draw attention to yourselves. Understood?"

Vendurro and Glesswik began to raise their right fists in unison, but Braylar waved them down, scowling. "Is that your idea of discretion, then? Have you been telling every lass you bedded that you're the Syldoon scourge as well?"

Vendurro flushed around his freckles. "Sorry, Cap. Hard habit, that one."

"See to the wagons, you sorry bastards. And give the horse boy no trouble, or I'll hear of it."

After fighting off the urge to salute again, they moved to the rear of the wagon. Captain Killcoin started towards the inn with Lloi on his heels, carrying a small trunk with a crossbow and quiver balanced on top, and I hurried to keep up.

The building was two stories, walls gray and in dire need of a new coat of whitewash. Otherwise, it seemed sturdy and in good repair—the thatched roof appeared to have been recently replaced, and the wattle and daub looked sound and well-patched.

The door to the inn was swung wide, propped open by a cask to let some air flow through. The floor was wooden, and while I wouldn't hazard a guess as to how many feet had walked across it over the years, it was worn and faded, especially just in front of the bar. There were a few unlit iron lamps on the walls, and two wide windows with the shutters thrown open above an empty fireplace. Due to the windows and the open door, the room was exceptionally sunny and motes floated in the broad shafts of light. A dozen small, round tables were scattered around the inn, as well as two long tables, all surrounded by chairs, and only a small number of them were currently occupied.

I grew up in an inn like this, though that was on the road between Blackmoss and Everdal, not in the middle of a city. But they were largely interchangeable—sticky floors, the reek of stale ale, shabby furniture, sooty smoke stains on the walls and ceiling—and I felt the same rush of ugly emotions entering every single one of them.

We headed to the bar and Braylar hailed the innkeeper, an angular man whose one soft feature was a bulbous nose.

He walked over to us and Braylar said, "Is that your boy in the yard?"

The innkeeper immediately looked defensive. "Martiss. What of it? What's he done now?"

"You're to be complimented. He seems to have a way with horses. A rare thing."

"I got nothing to do with it. Can't stand the beasts myself. But he practically lives out there—better be good with the plaguing things." He wiped his hands on his dirty apron. "Name's Hobbins. Welcome to the Three Casks. You here for food? Drink? We got no more rooms, but there might be a space or three on the common floor if you got intent to stay."

Lloi said, "Won't be needing no new rooms. Arranged already. Bristly bastard, been here a few days, sure you seen him."

Hobbins rolled his tongue across his lower teeth, bulging his lip out. "Built like a boar? Half as agreeable?" Lloi nodded. "Ayyup. I seen him." He turned back to Braylar. "Told him I didn't like renting rooms to them that weren't there; liked to see who I got under my roof. But I thought he was about to draw that big cleaver of his, so I made an exception." He glanced at Lloi, and despite noticing her blade and the crossbow, he said, "Can't say I like making exceptions for the likes of her, though. Her kind makes the other patrons right uneasy."

Lloi started to respond but Braylar cut her off. "She makes me uneasy as well. But never fear—she won't sleep under this roof."

If Hobbins was mollified, he didn't show it. After looking like he was chewing on another comment, he finally said, "Guessing you'll be needing food and drink, then."

"Indeed. Do you by chance have a tub to wash away the dust from the road?"

"No tubs. Got no time to heat them. Small family, big inn. We got some barrels in the back, though, full of water. But don't you be trying to climb in them. Got no time to be fixing broken barrels."

"And soap?"

"Course we got soap. Like to scour your skin clean off, and no perfumery of no kind, but it's soap, just the same. When you're ready to eat, you'll be needing to do it at one of them tables. No eating at the bar. I keep my bar clean as a priest's bunghole."

"Fastidious," Braylar replied.

Hobbins either failed to recognize the word or the sarcasm, as he was nonplussed as he pulled a key from behind the bar and handed it to Braylar. "Room's top of the stairs, last on the left. Just grab a table when you're clean and settled and Syrie'll be by, take your orders."

"Very good. And those barrels, that I'll be careful not to mistake for tubs?"

Hobbins pointed a bony finger. "Only one back. Opposite the front."

We walked up the stairs and unlocked the room. It was hardly extravagant—two bowed beds, a table and bench—but when Braylar looked at Lloi, you would have thought we were bedding down in a leper colony. "No window? The second floor, and no window?"

She set the chest down and glanced around to be sure he hadn't missed a small window hiding in a corner somewhere, then shrugged. "I was riding with you, you recollect, not renting out rooms. You got issue, take it up with that whoreson, Mulldoos."

"As someone much misliked in these parts, you'd do well not to tweak the nose of the only one inclined to protect you."

"I protect myself plenty fine. What's more, if anyone's doing any protecting around here, it's—"

"Enough, Lloi." His words were placid enough, but his expression stopped her short.

She looked at me, and then back to him. "Right. Less tweaking. You be needing me for anything else just now, Captain Noose?"

"Yes. I meant what I said. Keep a tight rein on your tongue tonight."

She gave him a look that was impenetrable, at least to me, and said nothing.

"You've ridden with us for some time now. Too long not to have reached an understanding with him."

"Oh, we understand each other real good. He wouldn't mind seeing my guts on the floor, and I wouldn't weep overmuch to see his. Real easy relationship we got."

Sighing, Braylar grabbed another tunic out of the chest. "Make certain my horse hasn't killed the boy." Lloi headed out to the stables and we headed out to the barrels. When the door shut behind us, Braylar began unlacing his ankle boots and said, "Stop anyone who attempts to come out."

I was unarmed and had a bookish quality that rarely stops anyone from doing anything, so I asked how exactly he expected me to accomplish that.

He replied, "Tell them your patron is particularly shy. And violent."

So I stood near the door and watched as Braylar unbuckled his weapon belts; on the right hip, a very long dagger, and on the left, a steel buckler and his wicked-looking flail. I noted something odd about the weapon during our initial interview, but now I got a closer look. The two flail heads resembled monstrous visages, though stylized—each had a mouth clenched tight in fury or horrible pain, a nose of sorts, but above that, neither eyes nor ears. Where they should have been, there was simply a ring of spikes continuing around the crown of the head. The heads weren't large, each about the size of a child's fist, but I was sure they hit a great deal harder.

Though those visages were rarely seen anymore—they were outlawed, reviled, or largely forgotten, depending where you were from—it was clear the spiked heads represented the Deserter Gods. Which was strange. Not so much that a Syldoon would have a weapon with holy images designed to cause unease—causing discomfort presumably came naturally to them—but that one would have something with holy images on it at all. The Syldoon were rarely accused of being pious. It was said they'd pay to have twelve temples built without setting foot in a single one.

The captain unwound his scarf and it was immediately clear why he wanted a guard—the Syldonian black rope tattoo around his neck was on prominent display. When he pulled his tunic over his head, there was perhaps another reason for privacy as well. His torso was an overworked map of scars of all kinds, long and pale, short and puckered. Having already made the mistake of staring too long once today, I quickly looked back to the door.

Being only a chronicler, and never to rich patrons, I wasn't accustomed to perfumed soap or copper tubs—it was usually the public baths for me, and often the end of the line to get in—but at least I'd never had to resort to a barrel. I wondered why a Syldonian captain opted to stay in such an establishment; surely, *he* could have afforded the finer stuff. If anything, they were known for being ostentatious and extravagant; even if he was clearly trying to hide his affiliations, he still could have roomed at a place with a proper tub, copper or not. It was curious.

As I watched the water blacken, I also wondered what he'd been doing in the days since our interview—he looked to have taken to the road, and ridden it hard—but opted to hold my tongue on that count as well. The captain didn't seem the kind of man to tolerate intrusive questions. Or even nonintrusive ones for that matter.

When he finished scrubbing and rinsing, he dressed and led me back to the room. As we entered, I was surprised to see two people waiting for us. I assumed they were Syldoon as well, though they both had small hoods covering their necks and inked nooses around them.

One was standing, leaning against a support beam, his dark skin barely contrasting with the wood behind him. He was incredibly tall and not lean, and he looked over at me, his upper lip bare above a multi-braided beard that tumbled down his chest, and regarded me coolly for a moment. Then he tilted his head and gave me a long, slow nod that, if not openly warm or welcoming, was at the very least cordial. I'm not sure, but a small smile seemed to be playing on his lips. Compared to the other two men clothed in muted, earthy colors and modest cut, his outfit was nearly outlandish. His trousers, striped black and white, wouldn't have drawn undue attention on their own, but they fed into leather riding boots folded over above his knees that were almost impossibly red. His hood, bright red as well, was noteworthy for the elaborate dags like broken teeth all along its edge, and the extreme length of the tail that was looped through his belt behind him. The flanged mace hanging on his hip was also overly ornate for something designed to bludgeon someone to death.

The other man was seated and equally well-armed—a trait common to all Syldoon, no doubt, even when battle doesn't seem imminent—with a nasty-looking falchion on his hip. He apparently had been speaking, and acknowledged my interruption with an expression normally reserved for hated enemies or piles of manure. He had close-cropped hair, so blonde it was nearly white, pale skin, and judging by his frame—wide and thick with muscle—I assumed he was Mulldoos. Everything about him looked hard, except for thin eyebrows that would've been more at home on a petite woman. He turned to Braylar and said something in a tongue I didn't understand.

Braylar replied, "In Anjurian, if you would. No need to be rude."

His eyes narrowed as he looked me over again, then he said to his comrade, "What do you figure? Longer or shorter? I'm going with shorter."

The other man saw my puzzled expression and laughed. "I wager this one outdistances them by a fair amount. I have a good feeling."

Braylar looked at me and said, "You might have deduced as much already, but these are my two lieutenants. The pale boar is Mulldoos Smallwash. He doesn't believe we have need of a chronicler, but—"

Mulldoos broke in, "The Emperor mandates we need one, we need one. Thing I object to is the choice. I still say we could use a Syldoon. Retired, injured maybe—"

Braylar ignored the interruption. "You might try to win him over, but do so at your peril. The tall laconic one is Vatinios of Stoneoak, called Hewspear. You have an equal chance to earn his affection or contempt. Hewspear handles logistics. Which, admittedly, has proven an easier task since our company has been winnowed down to handle more... subtle affairs. And Mulldoos maintains the discipline and readiness of our small band. Both advise me on matters of strategy."

Mulldoos said, "Which you promptly ignore."

"The perks of being captain. And as you two have obviously surmised, this is our new resident scribe, Arkamondos."

Hewspear nodded. Mulldoos didn't. I took a seat on a bench and Braylar addressed his lieutenants. "Are we ready to move, then?"

Mulldoos leaned back in his chair and closed his eyes. "Sounds logistical to me."

Hewspear said, "We've only been awaiting your arrival, Captain. Did you..." He paused, eyes flicking to me for the briefest instant before returning to Braylar, "accomplish all you hoped to on your journey?"

"I did, indeed. Vendurro and Glesswik are securing our new cargo. See to it they do a good job." He gave Mulldoos a pointed look. "That encompasses logistics and discipline. We'll be down shortly."

Mulldoos stood, rolled his head around on his monstrous neck, and Hewspear followed him out.

Braylar sat on the bed, wood groaning as the ropes under the mattress were pulled tight. I wasn't quite sure what to do, so sat waiting. He folded his arms behind his head and looked over at me. "You have your quills and parchment, yes?"

I nodded and he said, freighted heavy with irony, "I'm not certain I should like you, Arkamondos—you're too impertinent by half—but I can't seem to help myself. Still, we should reestablish something here. I didn't solicit you because you're the most sublime scribe, and I didn't hire you because you're the most lyrical; the bargain was struck because you reputedly miss nothing. It's said you're perceptive and quick. I want you to get it all, and you claim you can do this thing. So… miss nothing. Record everything. No matter how contrary or nonsensical it might seem to you at the time. Digressions, tangents, observations. All of it. But you aren't to pollute it with poetry. This is our bargain. This is our understanding. You've been hired to record everything. So get out your pens and ink and record what you will of our meeting today."

He closed his eyes and fell asleep faster than I believed possible, even before I had even gathered my writing supplies. And some time later, when my quill finished scratching across the page, linking and inking my brief account together, his eyes opened back up and he immediately sat upright. "Very good. And with that, Arki, my young scribe, we should quit and fill our bellies with the local fare, such as it is. Tomorrow, we continue on the road."

I looked at him, probably blinked stupidly a few times, and then asked, "The road?"

"Yes," he replied. "Leave. Trek. Depart. Journey rather than sojourney. Tomorrow after breaking fast."

"But… but you didn't say anything about this. Our contract—"

"You're right. I didn't. I also disclosed no information about where our interviews would be conducted. You assumed, I assume, they'd take place in Rivermost. How unfortunate. But if you've been misled, you're at least partially to blame for not asking more astute questions. You're wifeless and childless, yes? With few friends, I imagine."

Harsh, but I didn't protest as he continued, "Whatever it is you think you leave behind, consider what you stand to gain: while you'll be paid well enough for your services, I can give you something much grander than coin. Fame. Fame for having been the archivist of an amazing tale. I could've chosen any scribe to record this, but I chose you. Among many. And you'll have the rarest of opportunities to record something exceptional firsthand. For now, I'll tell you this much. All empires crumble. All borders change. All kingdoms die. Where I'm taking you, you'll witness the death of a body politic, the expiration of a way of life, the redrawing of a map. Something singular and priceless. So put away your bleak looks and let's eat some of Hobbins' slop. My belly grumbles."

The captain had chosen well, even if his tone and phrasing were on the hurtful side. Whatever reticence I had about leaving Rivermost, he was spot on—I had no family, or none that had claimed me as such for years, and no friendships of any lasting duration. The promise of being part of something larger than my life—which, admittedly, up to this point hadn't exactly been consequential or noteworthy—was exciting, even if my involvement was restricted to observing and recording. At least it would presumably be something *worth* setting to parchment for once. And there was no denying the draw to that. If I had to scribble down another ledger report or the history of one more self-satisfied grain merchant, I might jab a quill in my eye.

Captain Killcoin started towards the door. This discussion was clearly at an end, so I stowed my supplies and started after him.

I was in a daze as I followed my new patron down the stairs. I'd been in Rivermost for some time, and I fully expected that if I ever left, it would be because I'd run out of work, not because I was accompanying a Syldoon commander on a mysterious assignment. After all, no one accompanied them anywhere on purpose if they could help it. And yet there I was, trailing behind one. He had his scarf tight around the tattoo again—clearly, he was cloaking his origins. But part of me wanted to yell to everyone in the inn, "I'm traveling with the Syldoon!"

I'd been around soldiers on a few occasions, on rare instances as a boy at the Noisy Jackal when I was actually allowed in the common room, and occasionally in my travels since, but I'd never had cause to really share their company—violence always seemed to be both the question and the answer with their kind, which made me decidedly nervous. And given that my nerves were delicate enough as it was, I avoided them whenever possible.

What's more, the Syldoon were no ordinary soldiers. The prospect of spending a long period of time working with this man and his company was equally exciting and discomfiting. Exciting, because it was a unique opportunity—even if he wasn't especially forthcoming about the particulars, it was clear we would be on a venture of some import. And what better way to establish myself as a chronicler worth following than by following a patron who intended great things?

Discomfiting, because he was a Syldoon, after all. While I wasn't a native Anjurian and didn't have any direct experience with the Syldoon, the tales of their atrocities and treachery were well known. I suspected they were exaggerated, as these things usually are, growing more horrifying with each retelling. But there must have been some truth there, too. And even a little of it was enough to cause pause. A lot of pause, really.

My mother always said that Syldoon were best to be avoided, and if that failed, placated. Of course, despite serving at the Jackal on one of the busiest highways in Vulmyria, she never traveled farther than five miles from the hovel she was born in, so it's unlikely she had first- or even secondhand knowledge of their kind. And no one would have accused her of being brilliant, even on the handful of things she had experience with.

Still, while her wisdom had been suspect about most things, the Syldoon were regarded by practically everyone with fear, hatred, or at least hot suspicion. Even if she only parroted what she heard, my mother probably stumbled onto the truth with that single warning. But here I was, the newest member of a Syldoon retinue, willing rather than conscripted. It was difficult to believe.

I almost wished she could have seen me now.

While chronicling the staid sagas of grain merchants and overstuffed burghers was undeniably tedious, it was at least safe. There was next to no chance of any physical danger to myself. But that was also the problem—it was so incredibly… safe. The "death of a body politic" might have been something best recorded from far away or well after the fact. In fact, I was certain of it. But the chance to witness something of real historical significance unfolding before me, to attach my name as scribe, to perhaps achieve some measure of fame because of it… there was no denying the draw—it was loaded with intoxicating possibility.

Most chroniclers led the life I had—penning away the vastly uninteresting details of men, or occasionally women, of no lasting significance. Tales flat and turgid, dusty and without meaning except to close family or sycophantic friends. Maybe not even them. At least with those from the middle or lower castes. And even those archivists with noble benefactors often secretly complained that nothing really ever happened.

But now, for reasons I didn't really understand, I'd secured the patronage of a Syldoon commander. And not one in his dotage relating glories from days gone, but one promising adventure, action, consequence. Perhaps it wasn't wise of me to accept so quickly. Perhaps I should have deliberated, weighed the draw against the potential drawbacks more carefully, judiciously…

But reservations or not, the choice was made. If it proved too dangerous down the road, I would simply extricate myself from the arrangement. I wasn't doing anything that couldn't be undone. I hoped.

Though the inn was crowded with the expected miners, masons, river sailors, and the most meager fieflords, it wasn't especially large, so even in the low light of oil lamps, spotting Mulldoos and Hewspear wasn't difficult. They were at a long table next to the empty fireplace, along with Vendurro and Glesswik. I didn't expect Lloi to join us, but she was there as well.

As we walked towards them, Braylar's flail rattled and clinked at his side, and more than one patron looked up to see the source of the noise, though most returned to their conversations quickly enough, it being too dark to make out the Deserters on the end of the chains. The one exception was the table of Hornmen we passed. Another weapon in the room always earned more than a cursory glance from them, no matter what the weapon looked like. Especially when the owner was heading towards a table where every occupant was armed. Mulldoos a falchion, Hewspear a flanged mace, Vendurro and Glesswik swords, and Lloi a sword as well, though curved and shorter, in the fashion of the Grass Dogs. And each member of Braylar's retinue also had a mug in hand. Ale and armament. Yes, soldiers did make me nervous.

Braylar took a seat alongside Hewspear, and while there was an opening near Mulldoos, I thought it prudent to choose one between Vendurro and Lloi. As Hobbins promised, Syrie was there almost immediately. She dropped off four mugs of ale with the Hornmen and made her way to us. It was obvious she was her father's daughter. She had the same height and angles, with just enough womanly cushion to pad the straight lines. Her arms were bare, shoulders rounded with small muscles from a lifetime of carrying trays. Luckily, her nose must have come from her mother.

She set her tray down on the table and tucked a strand of hair behind an ear. "You two look thirsty enough, am I right? What can I get you?" She smiled, and while she wasn't the kind of girl to immediately excite the loins, I could see someone forgetting she was forgettable, especially if she kept smiling like that. I wondered if my mother had ever had a smile that did the same; if so, she never used it on me.

Braylar said, "We are thirsty indeed, lass. What would you suggest?"

"Going to a different inn. But seeing as you're here, I'd say the ruddy ale. It's no good, but better than anything else the Canker brews."

I asked, "Who is the Canker?"

She tilted her head back toward her father. "Called on account of his cheery disposition. So, two ruddy ales then?"

Braylar nodded. I nearly asked if they had any casks of wine, but I doubted someone lovingly called Canker knew how to discern good grapes from bad. I inquired after cider, which elicited a laugh from Mulldoos, but Syrie's smile never wavered. "It's as thick as oil, and half as tasty, but it's there if you'll have it."

I opted for the ale.

Braylar asked, "Is the fare as fine as the drink? If so, I don't think we could miss an opportunity to sample some."

"The Canker cooks as well as he brews, true enough. But tonight my brother's in back, and he's a fair hand. We're serving some capon brewet or civet of hare. The ale compliments neither, so you can't go wrong."

"Then some of both, yes?"

"Both it is. Back soon enough." She headed into the kitchen, skirts swishing.

Mulldoos bit off the corner of his thumbnail and spit it onto the floor, glaring at me the whole time. "Bad enough we got to deal with your dog at the table, but now your scribbler, too? Almost enough to put me off my drink."

Hewspear laughed. "The largest army assembled would fail in the attempt. I doubt very much a crippled girl and a reedy scribe are up to the task."

Lloi leaned over to me. "Don't take no offense, bookmaster. The boar's got no love for man nor beast, so you're in fulsome company."

I wasn't sure if she intended Mulldoos to hear, but he clearly did. "Your savage folk should have cut the tongue in place of the fingers, done us all a favor."

Lloi was about to respond when Braylar held his hand up. Syrie arrived with our mugs and set them on the table. "You're free to spend your money as you please, but if you'll be drinking for long, I'd recommend the pitchers. Cheaper on the whole. The Canker would just as soon I served empty mugs and charged twice as much, but that won't stop me from speaking my piece."

Braylar replied, "Honesty, integrity, and beauty, all in one girl."

The prettying smile again. "You repay my truth with lies, but I can't fault you for the exchange." She winked and moved off to another table.

After taking another swig, Braylar wrinkled his nose. "It might actually be worth paying twice as much for an empty mug."

I took a drink, and the ale was like bitter silt. Ruddy indeed. But that didn't stop Vendurro—he tipped his mug up as if it contained the finest elixir on earth, then elbowed me in the ribs. "Guessing you never had cause to ride with the likes of us before, huh?"

I nodded and he said, "The bloodletting, well, that will tweak your dreams some, until you stop noticing. And the cursing and farting, no shortage of that, and that's no kind of pleasant to deal with. But the hardest thing to get used to is ale that tastes like it came straight from a donkey's cock. But that's soldier swill, son. So best get accustomed." He wiped some foam off his lip and said, "Guessing, too, you haven't seen Cap put that nasty flail of his to good use yet then either?"

Hewspear flashed him a look brimming with warning and wrath, but Mulldoos went one better. "Best shut your hole right quick. Son."

Vendurro held his hands up, supplicant. "Easy, easy. I wasn't going to go on about the... unnatural bit. Just talking about the captain and his flail spinning bloody circles around someone, is all. That's all I was getting at. No need to go hostile." He looked at Glesswik. "Remember Vortnall, Gless? Remember that?" He rapped on the table. "That was some kind of something, eh?"

"Graymoor."

"What?"

"Wasn't Vortnall at all, but Graymoor."

Vendurro was drunkenly dubious. "You sure?"

"Graymoor."

"Huh. Could have sworn it was Vortnall." He elbowed me again. "We were at a tavern—good one, too, with some of the plumpest barmaids you ever seen—and the captain there, well, he took to his drink like a man dying of thirst. Drank his share and mine and yours and more besides. Our rooms were all at an inn, other quarter of the city." Vendurro stopped, looked at Glesswik. "You sure it was Graymoor? Vortnall had those really narrow streets, and I seem to recall—"

Glesswik hit him on the arm and almost sent him off the bench. "Tell the bloody story."

"Whoreson." Vendurro steadied himself and laughed. "So, we all left to go back to the inn, all save the captain. Mulldoos and Hewspear, the rest too, they were already there, bunking down. Mulldoos here, he sees me come into the inn, charges up to me, saying, 'Where's the captain?' I say, 'Drinking, I'm thinking.' Mulldoos, getting real angry like he does, says, 'You left the captain alone? Drinking? Go fetch him.' I protest that the good captain wasn't one to be fetched by the likes of me, nor no man, when it came to it. But Mulldoos spins me around by the shoulders and kicks my backside, saying, 'Go fetch him or spend the next tenday digging latrines.' Now, seeing as how we were in a city, I almost asked if he got permission from the mayor for those new latrines, but I kept that to myself."

Glesswik burped and added, "Good thing, too. You'd still be digging them."

"True enough. So off I went. But I wasn't about to go fetch the captain by my lonesome, so I pull Glesswik with me. It was late then, after curfew, and the streets were mostly deserted. Watch should have been out patrolling, but if they were, we saw no sign. We round a corner, getting near the tavern, and not too far ahead of us, we see four street toughs barring the captain's way. Now, not sure how it is where you're from, but in Graymoor and most cities like them in these parts, the street toughs like to arm themselves with lash balls. Long piece of leather, one end looped around the wrist, the other tied to a weight of some sort. Sometimes iron in the shape of an egg, sometimes a small bag full of lead pellets, sometimes a little stone wheel, like a tiny millstone. Quick, quiet, easy to hide, and more than capable of cracking a bone or three. Handy in a street fight, not handy for much else.

"Now, these toughs, they drop their lash balls, practically in unison, like they been practicing the move for effect half their years, thinking they got themselves an easy mark, lone man staggering. The captain, though, he starts to laughing, looking at the weights and the leather lashes, laughing like they popped daisies out of their sleeves. Hand on his knee to steady himself, he's laughing so hard. Then he straightens and says something we can't hear. Gless and me, we start sprinting, but before we even make it halfway there to help, the captain rips that wicked flail off his belt. Flips the handle up with one hand, snatches it out of the air with the other. Most nights, he does that smoother than silk, but that night, he caught it on the belt hook some.

"But the closest tough, he hadn't been expecting much in the way of resistance, he's slow to react. He whips his own weight around on the end of his lash, but the captain's already slipping left, takes the weight a glancing blow on the temple. Then he whips his flail around, taking off the top half of the tough's head. Another tough moves in, lash ball coming down, but the captain steps into the blow, catches the leather with his free forearm, ball spinning around, and the captain's flail is on the move again, coming down hard. Snaps the tough's collar bone like an old broomstick. Drops him like a stone. But the lash was still wound around the tough's wrist, pulled the captain off balance some before he wrenched if off the tough's arm. The other two, if there was any time to bludgeon the captain bloody, that was it. But they seen enough. Both tear off into the dark, lash balls trailing behind them like tails, not looking so tough after all.

"Now Gless and me reach the captain. The boy he broke is sitting in the dirt, cradling his busted shoulder, spit bubbling on his lips, saying please over and over like it might do some good, eyes full of the wide fear of one about to be murdered. The captain is staring down at him, flail in one hand, a look in his eyes I couldn't quite read. Gless asks if he wants us to kill this one, or give chase to the others, clearly expecting to hear yes to one or the other, maybe both. The captain ponders for a moment, then says, 'No. Let them run. Let them run.'" Vendurro did a fair imitation of Braylar. "'And as for this one…' he leans over, the wicked heads of his flail dangling just in front of the not-so-tough, who closes his eyes and sets to mumbling some prayer or other. Then the captain tosses the lash ball into his face; he cries out as if struck a mortal blow.

"When he finally opens his eyes, the captain is already striding toward the inn, Gless moving fast to keep pace. I look down at the dumb prick, can't resist saying, 'You got more luck than any low bastard deserves. It was me you tried thieving, you'd be as dead as dirt.'

"I catch up, Gless and me flanking Cap, looking into the shadows for anything else that might want to tussle, but it's quiet. Halfway to the inn, Gless asks the captain what he said to the toughs, just before pulling his flail, and I admit curiosity got me to wondering too. Cap was wiping the blood off the cut on his temple, stops and looks at Gless like he's daft, then says, remembering—well, why don't I let the captain here tell it?"

Glesswik rolled his eyes. "Awfully big of you."

"Remember what you said, Cap?"

Braylar swallowed before replying, "I told them I'd never seen such tiny flails before."

"That's right. Just like that!"

The whole table laughed, and after the merriment died down, Glesswik looked at the captain. "I never did understand why you let that one live. The one on the ground, that is. Seemed... out of character, if you don't mind my saying."

"Uncharitable, Sergeant Glesswik. Most uncharitable."

"Oh, I mean no offense, Captain. None at all. Fact being, it's actually a compliment of sorts. You're the hardest plaguer I ever met. Not so much nasty as just... hard, like I said. Half the reason we follow you, I'm thinking. Anyone in this company would die twice for you, if they could, because they know that if anyone crosses us, that'll be the last thing they do, maybe their whole family, too."

Hewspear ran a finger around the rim of his mug. "I believe what the good sergeant is getting at is that it isn't your affable demeanor or endless ribaldry that endear you to the men, but your absence of mercy for those who oppose you."

Mulldoos laugh-snorted. "Ribaldry, he says."

"My apologies, Mulldoos. I'd forgotten your intolerance for weighty words."

"Only intolerance I have is for windmills like yourself."

"A windmill doesn't spin simply to hear itself spin. It performs a service."

Mulldoos said, "Then I stand corrected. You and the windmill got nothing in common."

While Lloi remained generally quiet, the Syldoon continued telling tales, often punctuated by a curse or a shove or some expectorating. I looked over at the Hornmen a few tables a way, and their behavior wasn't much different, and might actually have been worse. These exchanges must be what passes for friendship among the soldiering kind, at least when primed with ale.

One Hornman in particular seemed to have upended more cups than the others. His speech was slurred around the edges, and his cheeks and nose looked almost painted red. Earlier, I noticed that he nearly came to blows with one of his own. Now, returning from relieving himself, he brushed shoulders with a man heading in the opposite direction. This seemed inconsequential enough, but the Hornmen grabbed the other patron by the shoulders and slammed him into the wall.

Another Hornman jumped up and pulled his comrade off, though it took some prolonged and intense encouragement to persuade him to return to the table.

The scene nearly convinced me to wait, but my bladder couldn't have been more full, so I planned as circuitous a route as possible around the Hornmen table and made my way outside. After returning a short time later much relieved (again skirting the Hornmen table with due care), I discovered the Syldoon in the middle of another... lively discussion.

Drawing on a disquieting wealth of experience with death and dying, they were arguing the worst way to go. Vendurro volunteered drowning, especially under ice. Mulldoos countered that burning trumped it, and described a corpse he'd seen with blackened skin broken open in fissures, revealing the pink flesh beneath, like a hog that had been roasting too long. Lovely. Glesswik described a man he'd seen pressed to death in a public square, the administrators turning the screws of the device extra slow, screams carrying on for half a day before the end.

After a pause, as everyone at the table was imaging that awful ending, Vendurro said, "Oh, that's rough. To be certain. But seems like we ought to be excluding torture and the like. Not really in the spirit."

"In the spirit? Gods be drunk! What are you going on about? Why should we exclude them?"

Vendurro looked up from his mug. "Those are designed to cause damage. Usually slow. Got no other end."

"And weapons do?" Glesswik asked. "No, the captain mentioned dying slow from a spear in the gut, you didn't say nothing about that. You whoreseon—you're just bitter yours wasn't worse, is all. You're a bitter little bastard, you are."

"Battle wounds is something different," Vendurro maintained.

"How? You tell me how, I'll buy your next drink."

Vendurro thought for a moment before responding, "Torture, the dying bastard's got no say, no chance. Can't defend hisself at all. No hope. Any battle, a man's got some say in the finality of the thing. And if he doesn't, gets struck when he's looking the wrong way, well, he knew that was something possible when he set to marching. But torture, it's not, that is, I can't rightly say, it's just…"

Glesswik smiled broad, victorious. "Nope. No drink for you. We said death. Worst death. Nothing at all about cause."

Hewspear had remained silent through this exchange, but he leaned forward and said, "You lads are thinking small. While those are without question poor ways to die, they're too brief by half to be truly considered."

Mulldoos shook his head. "Here we go. This ought to be good. Go on, go on, can't wait."

Hewspear ignored him and continued, "You're sons of the plague—every one of you has seen its ravages. But the last plague was nothing compared to the one that preceded it. I'm guessing not a one of you is old enough to remember that one. When I was a boy, half my village buried the other. Elders and babes were taken in equal measure, and all those in between too. Oh, make no mistake, I'm confident that burning and pressing are painful. Intensely. But they don't last for days or weeks. My father and I outlived my brother and mother. My brother was young, so he didn't last as long as most in the village. Fevers, boils that rupture, phlegmatic poisons spilling from the wounds. Vomiting. Coughing fits, so long and hard that blood vessels burst in his throat, to give the watery bile a bit of color. His whole body itching, as if he'd rolled in nettles or rashleaf—we had to bind his arms, so he didn't tear at his flesh, which was already a mess of pus and blood. This went on for eight days, each worst than the last. My mother lasted twice as long. There are countless awful ways to go. But I would take any of them over a bad plague. Truth be good, I won't see another in my lifetime. You young pups won't be so lucky."

Our table sat silent while conversation hummed all around us, large and drunken. Finally, Glesswik muttered, "Leave it to Lieutenant Driz-zlethorn over there to take the fun out of death." He seemed genuinely disappointed that the macabre topic was at an end.

Mulldoos banged his mug on the table. "All you whoresons have the wrong of it, even old venerable father plague, there. Worst death? Seems you all are forgetting about that skeezy bastard, Rokliss."

It took a moment for everyone to react, but when it happened, there was a raucous explosion of laughter. Vendurro slapped the table. "Oh, Rokliss. Now there was a twisted son of a whore. Oh, gods, I'd forgotten about him."

The laughter rolled on, all save Lloi, who looked at the Syldoon soldiery around her like a mother ready to scold impertinent children. Clearly, everyone knew the tale but me.

Vendurro didn't wait for me to ask. "Rokliss was in our company. Good soldier. Better than Glesswik, not so fine as me." Glesswik shoved him and Vendurro nearly toppled off the bench, laughed, and contin-ued. "Patron of the arts, he was. Real somber. Pious as a priest most days. But he had a thing for whores. Nothing peculiar there—soldiers have appetites, most have dipped their wicks in a whore a time or ten. Even them that's married."

Glesswik added, "Especially them that's married."

"So, no judgment on whoring. But the thing of it was, Rokliss had a peculiar hunger. Liked his whores big. We're not talking a little extra stuff-ing or padding, neither, but busting the seams big. The fatter the better. Plenty of ugly whores in the world, but not many big enough to satisfy the appetite of Rokliss. So when he found one he had a preference for, he became a right regular."

Mulldoos raised his mug in mock solemnity. "Andurva."

The others hoisted their mugs as well. Vendurro said, "We ribbed him something fierce, but Rokliss never minded. Seemed to take a queer pride in his amorosity. We asked him why he didn't rent a grain cart and pull her along behind us on campaigns, but old Rokliss, he said that he might have been a deviant, but he had limits. He'd only visit Andurva when we was stationed close. And so he did. But besides loving his swollen whores, he also loved his strong wine. Big appetites, Rokliss had, but bad combination."

The laughter carried around the table again, and Vendurro let it run its course, a huge smile on his face. With a true storyteller's patience, he waited for it to quiet enough for him to go on. "Well, one night, Rokliss didn't come back to the barracks. And that just wasn't like him at all. Like I said, real proper soldier. So we set off to track him. Checked a few taverns on the way to be sure, but we pretty much knew where we'd find him holed up. Case you hadn't guessed, Andurva's room at the Golden Griffin. Thing of it was, we had no idea at all how we'd find him."

More snorts and chuckles. Vendurro rapped his knuckles on the table three times. "Whoremaster knocked on Andurva's door. No answer. So he apologized to us, over and over as he sought the key, getting more agitated by the second. Finally finding it, he let us in. And there they were. Andurva slumped over him like a pale mountain, her hands wrapped around his ankles, snoring as loud as three men. And underneath was poor Rokliss. Head buried under her massive thighs, most of him hidden under the avalanche, except for his skinny legs. For his own sake, I'm hoping Rokliss went black first. Or at least at the same time. However it played out, passing out while licking the nether regions of the fattest whore you ever laid eyes on is a mighty bad thing to do. His last breath had to be the worst ever drawn."

The table exploded again, and even Lloi couldn't stifle a laugh. When the chance presented itself, I asked what became of Andurva.

Glesswik replied, "The captain's generosity, that's what."

I feared the worst, but Hewspear added, eyes twinkling, "The whoremaster was horrified that one of his girls had taken the life of a Syldoon, however inadvertent. He summoned the bailiff, and was intent on having her hanged."

"Would have taken a ballista rope," Mulldoos said. "And that might have broke."

"True enough. Vendurro sent another soldier back to summon the captain, Mulldoos, and me, and we arrived just a few moments after the bailiff. The flummoxed whoremaster was screaming at Andurva, who, as you might imagine, was weeping, now that she'd been sufficiently roused to discover she was being charged with the murder of her finest patron. But, upon hearing the story, and the condition the pair had been found in, it was clear Rokliss had obviously brought this upon himself. Captain

Killcoin assured the whoremaster that Andurva's life wasn't required to satisfy us, and would in fact displease us greatly if he insisted. The whore-master argued she shouldn't have been so drunk, and accident or no, the death of a Syldoon was on her hands."

Vendurro amended, "Thighs."

"Indeed." Hewspear continued, "We convinced the whoremaster that we wouldn't hold her nor himself responsible. Once his fear and anger were assuaged, he calmed, but still discharged the poor girl immediately and told her to quit the city. Which she did. The captain paid for her passage by cart to the next closest city, advising her to sleep more lightly."

"Must have been a big cart," Glesswik said, "pulled by a lot of oxen."

Mulldoos raised his mug again and lead the toast. "To Rokliss, then. Dumb whorelicker that he was."

Everyone else joined even, even Lloi, though with less enthusiasm. "To Rokliss."

The Syldoon really did seem to have an unhealthy fixation on all things whorish. Their breed of camaraderie was crude, coarse, callous, and what-ever other alliterative pejorative I could summon. Cruel? Perhaps. But there was another quality there as well. Or lack of one. There was no preening or pretension at the table. Their rough humor made no excuses for itself.

Most of the patrons I'd penned for were doing their best to elevate themselves, to impress, to solicit the attention of the caste above. And though it was difficult to admit, even to myself, but my own experience was little different—growing up a bastard, I was always conscious of what others thought, and did my best to overcome any prejudice and earn as much approval as possible, especially since my own livelihood depended on me pleasing and placating my benefactors.

The Syldoon couldn't care less what anyone thought of them, and that was refreshing. If gross.

Perhaps with a patron like the captain, I could focus on events for once, on history unfolding, on something truly significant.

I was thinking on that when I heard some commotion to my right. The curly-haired Hornman who got into a scuffle earlier was banging on a table, yelling, "Gods and devils, man, you think I want to throw my life away for that bastard? And we don't have to. That's what I'm telling you. Incompetent, cockless bastard."

I jumped at the word, though he clearly hadn't been talking about me.

The Hornman next to him looked around, and realizing his friend was attracting quite a bit of attention, laid his hand on the man's shoulder to try to quiet him down. The curly-haired soldier slapped it away. "Lay off." He looked around the inn, eyes red with drink. "You think I give a horse's shit what any of these bastards think? I don't. They can rot. The lot of them. The whole lot."

A woman nearby whispered angrily to one of the men at her table, who promptly shook his head no.

The surly soldier noticed this silent exchange. "Your skinny bitch there got a problem?"

The man ignored the glaring woman. "No, Hornman, no. No one here has a problem."

"Good. That's good." He tapped the hilt of his sword. "That kind of problem only got one kind of solution."

A tall soldier with wild yellow hair said, "Our friend is drunk, he means no harm. Didn't mean no offense to the woman nor yourself. Our apologies."

The curly-haired man turned on his companion. "Apologies? Don't you apologize for me, Scolin, you whoreson." He started to rise out of his chair but Hornmen on either side restrained him.

He tried unsuccessfully to pull free. "Off me, you poxy bastards! Nobody tells me when to, who to… when to speak. You hear me? Not you, not no man, and for certain, not no uppity wife of no cuckolded prick like this weasel." To the woman again, "That your problem, skinny bitch? Not getting enough good cock?" He grabbed his crotch. "That problem I use the other sword for."

So much for refreshing.

Syrie appeared at their table. "Now then, now then, what's the problem here? Mugs empty again, that it?"

The curly-haired soldier grabbed a mug off the table and turned it upside down, emptying half a mug of ale onto the floor. Syrie jumped back to avoid the splash as he said, "That's right, you ugly calf, empty again. Fill it." One of the other soldiers laughed.

Scolin said, "Don't pay him no mind, missy. None at all."

She grabbed her skirts in one hand and knelt down, pulling a rag from her apron. "Not the first time these boards have tasted ale." Her voice was pleasant enough, but her eyes were narrow and her jaw tight. She finished wiping up what she could and stood up. "Now then, maybe some hot food would help soak up some of this ale, eh? Would you gentlemen be needing some supper then?"

The curly-haired soldier said, "We'll be needing some more ale to soak up the ale," and he laughed.

The other soldiers joined him, all but Scolin, who said, "Food would be fine. Another round as well."

"Short enough." She turned and headed back to the kitchen. She emerged a short time later, tray laden with steaming food, and her father handed her two fresh mugs of ale. Another boy who I assumed was a brother trailed behind her, and it became immediately clear why he remained out of sight most of the time. All of his features were horribly asymmetrical. The left side of his face was several inches higher than the right; eyebrow, nostril, lips, ear—all horribly aligned. Body as well. Both his left arm and leg were shorter than the right, and he walked with a noticeable hitch.

He stopped by the bar after Syrie, and his father placed four fresh mugs on his tray as well, scowling at him. The brother limped over to the table of soldiers and set their mugs down. All of the soldiers look at him with the same expression I must have worn, one of awe and revulsion. But when the curly-haired soldier saw him, he immediately let out a loud laugh. "Gods and demons, we got a monster serving us. What hobgoblin buggered your mother, boy?"

The poor boy set the bowls and spoons on the table as quickly as he could as Syrie made her way to our table. She heard the mocking but tried to ignore it as she sets our bowls and mugs before us, smile nowhere in sight.

The brother bowed quickly and turned to head back to the kitchen, but the curly-haired soldier stuck a leg out and tripped him. He fell face first, tray sliding across the floor. The soldier jerked out of his chair and stood over him. "Who said you was going anywheres, goblin boy? We were just getting started conversing."

Several of the other patrons stood up as well, though I wasn't sure why. Clearly, no one was going to contest the actions of a table of drunk Hornmen. Hobbins and Syrie rushed over to the boy. Hobbins grabbed the back of his son's tunic and hoisted him to his feet. "Up, up with you. Back to the kitchen, boy."

Scolin had the curly-haired soldier by the elbow and was trying to guide him back down to his seat. Syrie grabbed some mugs off the table and said, "No worries—you won't be charged for these."

She started to leave but the curly-haired soldier grabbed her hair and pulled her back, saying, "Whoa there, calfling. We got use for those yet." Scolin tried to restrain him but the drunken soldier shoved him away and pulled her hair again. She tripped over a chair leg and fell to the ground, mugs of ale overturning in all directions. The drunk soldier kicked her backside and she slid forward in a puddle of ale. "You stupid bitch." He reared back to kick her again and found a blade next to his throat. Braylar's.

I'd been so transfixed, I didn't even see him approach. But Braylar had his long dagger across the soldier's throat, a full mug of ale in his other hand. Braylar lifted the mug very slowly to his lips, blew some foam onto the floor, and took a long, slow swig, eyes never leaving the Hornman. After he swallowed, Braylar smiled and said, loud enough for the innkeeper to hear, "Your ale tastes like ox piss, Hobbins. Truly it does. And you know what they say of pissy ale, yes? It makes patrons irritable. Of course, if a patron doesn't like the drink or atmosphere, he's free to move on. The city has many inns to choose from. Myself, I don't mind a little pissy ale, makes you appreciate the finer brew. So I'll stay." He took another measured swig, licked his lips, and asked the soldier, "How about you? Are you going to ride on, or are you going to stay and enjoy the ale?"

The Hornmen behind curly-hair suddenly appeared more sober than they had all evening, and their hands were one and all wrapped around the hilts of their swords. I glanced at Braylar's retinue, and they seemed equally poised to spring out of their seats.

As Syrie gathered the mugs and ran off to the kitchen, Mulldoos whispered, "Easy, lads. Let it play out a bit. Nothing rash now."

Hobbins was there then, nervously wiping his hands on his apron. "It is pissy ale. Can't deny that. And my daughter, she's a clumsy cow. But neither's reason to spill blood. No, no reason at all. Been no blood spilled here in… some time. So why don't you—"

"Ride or drink?" Braylar put a little more pressure on the dagger. "What's it to be then?"

There was a long pause. I was sure the Hornmen and Syldoon would clash any moment, and Hobbins would be mopping up blood for days. But in a quiet, croaky voice, the curly-haired soldier said, "Drink."

Braylar pulled the dagger away and slid it back in the scabbard. "Very good. Hobbins, fetch another tray of ales, yes? These boys seem thirsty yet. I'll pay for those that spilled and the coming round as well."

Hobbins mumbled something to himself and started back to the bar. Braylar was walking back to our table when the curly-haired soldier drew his sword and tried to stab him. I thought the captain a dead man for certain, but he must've heard the sword clear the scabbard, because he pivoted and spun to his left. The blade slid past him and Braylar swung the mug, a spray of ale trailing behind. It cracked across the drunken soldier's face, splitting his lip, and from the sounds of it, breaking his nose as well. Then Braylar cracked him in the back of the head, just above his neck. The soldier started to slump forward, and Braylar hit him again on the way down for good measure. The mug broke with a loud crack and the cylinder landed on the man's back and rolled to the floor.

The other Hornmen had their swords out now, all of them pointing in Braylar's direction. The retinue were on their feet as well, weapons drawn. Braylar looked at the handle in his hand and called out, "Your mugs are weaker than your ale, innkeeper. I regret I have to pay for either. Still…" He reached into a pouch and tossed a silver coin over his shoulder. "That ought to make amends."

A soldier with thick ropy hair said, "You just struck a Hornman, dungeater." He was younger than the rest, but now that the first man was unconscious, clearly the drunkest man standing.

Braylar turned and examined the swords. "A Hornman?" he asked. "Truly? I'm a stranger to these parts—is that some kind of musician?"

"You watch your filthy dungeating tongue, dungeater. I'll cut it out and… and… I'll cut it out of your filthy mouth, I will."

"Bold words when facing a man armed with a mug handle. Are all Hornmen so fearless, or are you one of the elite?"

The boy took a step forward but Scolin put a hand on his shoulder. He gave Braylar a hard look. "What he means to say is, striking a Hornman is a bad idea. Bad as striking at the law itself. Usually, a man strikes a Hornman, we just throw him in the stockade, and if he got no friends, he'll stay there a good long while. But generosity's a lean commodity these days. So maybe we hack off the offending limb. Or, we got the time and a good tree, we just hang the dumb bastard until the life stretches out of him. Just not a good idea, striking a Hornman. If you take my meaning. Now, you look like a traveler, maybe you just didn't notice our surcoats and baldrics. That right, stranger? You just didn't realize who you was striking? Didn't see our surcoats? Or our horns hanging on our sides?"

Braylar replied, "No, I didn't immediately notice your surcoats. What I did see was a drunken lout abusing a cripple and beating a girl. That must not be a hanging offense, or any offense at all, no?"

The ropy-haired soldier said, "Let's cut him open, Red. Open him cock to nose."

Braylar fixed him with a stare. "Surely you would find naught but dung, Hornling, but I welcome you to try."

Scolin, who for mysterious reasons was called Red despite the light locks, looked down at the unconscious soldier. A small puddle of blood was pooling around his head, mixing with the ale. Red Scolin nudged the man with his foot, and he moaned. Red Scolin sighed. "Lunter's as big an ass as you'll find when he's got ale in his belly. Truth is, you done us a favor by shutting him up." He sheathed his sword and took a step forward. "But you see these surcoats now, stranger, and you'll mind that tongue of yours, or I'll have it out and fry it with our morning bacon. You hear?"

Braylar chose his next words carefully. "No doubt it would be finer than anything Hobbins has planned for us, but I'm rather fond of my tongue and would hate to see it in a pan. So I'll mind myself, particularly when addressing those bearing horns. At least, so long as they aren't musicians, who are naught but scoundrels."

Red Scolin laughed, and though the other soldiers didn't, they reluctantly put their blades away. Braylar slid the mug handle in his belt. "Unarmed and amiable again, you see? In fact, I'd do even more to make amends for my uncouth behavior." He turned to Hobbins. "Two pitchers for the Hornmen, innkeeper, and one for myself, yes?"

Hobbins looked at Braylar and back to the soldiers. He licked his lips and left to fetch the ale. The other soldiers moved back to their chairs, but the ropy-haired soldier was still peevish. "That it, Red? Lunt's bleeding like a, like a butchered hog, and all you gonna do is warn him?"

Red Scolin sat back down at the table. "No. I'm going to drink his ale and be glad to hear no more from Lunt tonight. Take him upstairs."

"The dungeater?"

"Lunter, you ass. Take Lunter upstairs. Clean him up, put him in bed."

"You ought not to let him go like that."

Red Scolin asked, smiling, "Lunter?"

Ropy-hair looked confused. "The dungeater, Red. He struck a Horn-man. We all saw. Struck him in the face, and in the head. He hit him with his mug, across the face and mug. I mean head. He—"

"Right enough. Struck him with his mug. Right after Lunter tried to stab him."

"But the dungeater, he drew blade first, he—"

"Enough. I gave an order, soldier. Get him upstairs, now, or maybe it'll be you seeing the inside of a stockade, you hear me?"

Ropy-hair gave Braylar a hateful look before bending down and sliding his hands under Lunter's armpits. "Give me a hand here, Looris."

Another soldier started to rise, but Red Scolin replied, "Just you, Barlin. Don't forget to clean him up, neither. Basin's by the bed. I want to see it full o' red when we come up later. No blood on Lunter, no blood on the bed. You got that? Clean him good before you come back down. Go."

Barlin cursed. He hefted Lunter up, almost slipping in the puddle of blood, grunting with exertion. "Lunter… you sack of guts… nothing but a…" but the rest of his declaration was unintelligible. Barlin slung the larger man over his shoulders. He wobbled as he walked, from the ale and the weight, and he tottered dangerously up the stairs, swearing the entire time. I expected the two to come rolling back down at any moment in a wild tangle of limbs—but somehow he completed his task and disappeared down the hallway.

The conversation resumed in the room, hushed at first, but gradually regaining its boisterous volume. Ale makes for short memories.

Braylar nodded to Red Scolin and returned to our table. Mulldoos laughed. "Got a real special way with people, you do, Cap. Should have been an emissary, diplomat maybe."

"We all have talents."

Syrie brought a pitcher and new mug and filled it for Braylar.

When she finished, he lifted it to his lips and drained it top to bottom.

He tapped the brim and she filled it again. "We try to keep him in back, my brother. Easier that way. For everyone, but especially him. He doesn't like it when people stare, and people are always staring. Likes it less when people abuse him, and they do that often enough as well." She sets the pitcher down. "So what I'm saying, trying to say, is thank you. For stepping in like you did. You didn't need to. We would have handled it. Always do. But thank you, just the same."

Braylar drained most of the rest of his mug and wiped his sweaty forehead with the back of his hand. "Sweet, sweet Syrie, I'd happily break a thousand mugs over a thousand skulls if only to see you smile again."

And with that she did. "Now, they'll be no more of that, you can have the smile for free. I got enough to clean up without worrying about no thousand mugs and thousand skulls. But I thank you kindly just the same. For the rescue and the compliment. Now, I'll be back straight away with your food."

Vendurro said, "Cap, I got to say, if I'd have known that's what you meant by discretion, that would have clarified things right quick. See, I had a whole different idea in mind."

Syrie arrived with our food a few moments later. "And will you be needing anything else this evening?"

"One more pitcher, Sweet Syrie," Braylar said. "Perhaps a tumble or two in your bed. Nothing more."

Syrie laughed. "The ale you shall have, but I won't be tumbled so easy."

"No? Pity. I suppose I'll have to settle for the smiles alone then. And the ale. Please, please, don't forget the ale."

She laughed again and spun off with her platter to the next table. I couldn't help wondering how many times my mother had been propositioned like that. Or more to the point, how many times she had rebuffed someone when she had.

The other Syldoon continued their talk, mostly of seductions or failed attempts, and Lloi stood up to go.

Mulldoos said, "Not leaving now, are you, dog? We'd all love to hear of the maids you've stuck your filthy nubs into."

Lloi replied, "Betting you would. Only difference is, mine would be true whereas yours are all drunken lies swelled up like a cow bladder."

"You got a mouth like a rasp and a cunt full of nettles. Even that fat sow

Andurva knew enough to talk sweet once in a while. Guessing that silk house rued the day they paid for you."

I wondered what he meant when Lloi started walked around the table toward Mulldoos, taking her time. I watched her hand, afraid it might drift to her blade, but it stayed clear. She laid her good hand on Mulldoos's shoulder and leaned down, mouth close to his ear. "You nailed it true. I should be sweet as honey, especially to them that show such kindness like yourself. Starting now. Let's say we go up to your room, you and me, and I file the rasp down some, give that massive cock of yours a good tongue bath? Or—"

Mulldoos knocked her hand off his shoulder and glared at her, but she continued undaunted, "Maybe prune the nettles some and drop my slippery nest down on your horsedick, show you what a good little—"

He shouted, "Enough!" And when some of the other patrons looked at the commotion, he quieted, if a little, "Enough. By the gods, you're a filthy beast. Go to barn with the rest of them. Leave the men to their drink."

"And bloated boasts. You're welcome to them." She nodded to Braylar and headed out the door.

The rest of the Syldoon struggled not to laugh, and ultimately failed. Vendurro spit out, "Could have had yourself a free one there, Mulldoos." That set the table to near hysterics.

Mulldoos nodded in exaggerated fashion, clearly not amused at all. "That's right, you whoresons, that's right. Have your fun." He took a huge swig of ale and turned to Braylar. "I swear to Truth, Cap, you didn't need her so awful bad..."

He left the thought unfinished, but Hewspear didn't. "You'd take her for your very own?"

That set off another raucous round of laughter.

"Leper lesions, the whole stinking lot of you." Mulldoos slammed his mug on the table.

With the latest potential bloodshed diverted, I finally settled in to eat.

After we finished our meals, Syrie collected our plates and dropped off more ale, and before I knew it, my mug was again empty and in need of refilling. Unaccustomed to drinking at a soldier's pace, my head was truly beginning to swim. I excused myself and returned to the room.

I woke several hours later. My bladder was full and my head was pounding, so I suspected one or both being the cause of my rousing. But then I realized I heard a muffled laugh and low voices. Disoriented, and my head still clouded from the ale, I thought for a moment it must have been one of the patrons in the next room. But when I heard the voices again, I realized they were coming from within my room. Braylar and a woman. A giggling woman. They spoke again, but low and soft, and I couldn't make out the words.

Without a window the room was near pitch, and I couldn't see anything either. I didn't know what to do. I didn't want them to know I was awake, but wondered if the woman knew I was in the room. It occurred to me she must have, for the entire inn saw that Braylar and I were sharing the room. I doubted a patron had arrived in the middle of the night, and doubted even more that even if she had she would've immediately made her way into a strange man's bed. Presuming then that it was a woman already in the inn, I began to wonder who it could be when the answer struck me like cold water. Syrie.

Would my mother have cared about a man being in the room? Probably not. Why should Syrie have been different?

I felt my cheeks grow hot and wondered how I could excuse myself. Perhaps I should have simply cleared my throat and gotten up with a blanket, heading downstairs to join the others on the common floor. That would've been awkward, but so was staying put. Deprived of all sight and now fully alert with my anxiety, I heard the rest of the noises with an almost inhuman clarity. And really wished I hadn't.

There were some soft sounds and movement—what I assumed was them slipping out of whatever remained of their clothing—and a giggle from who I was certain then must have been Syrie. There was a sharp wooden sound—the slats of the bed adjusting to the weight shifting above them—followed by another giggle. Braylar said something, though, trying as hard as I could despite my paralyzed embarrassment, I couldn't discern individual words. I heard nothing for some time, save my own breathing mixed with theirs, and while much of me hoped they'd fallen asleep, I'm shamed beyond my ability to express that there was a part of me that yearned to hear more. I tried to comfort myself by thinking that it was a common enough human curiosity, nothing more—a fascination with what people do in the dark when they're alone (or believe they aren't being spied on)—but I wasn't certain I believed that.

Their breathing became slightly more rapid, and I tried very hard to maintain my own, wondering how it had sounded before my waking and trying to approximate the breathing of a sleeping man as best I could. I heard Syrie moan as their bodies shifted, a small sound that seemed to originate from the back of her throat and exit through a closed mouth. I closed my eyes, hoping to block out what was occurring on the next bed for a moment or two and fill my mind with some other, more pure thought, but in doing so, I found myself imagining more keenly what they were doing. Was she spreading her legs for him? Was his hand on her thigh or small breasts that had caused her to moan so, or had it traveled to the core of her sex? I felt filthy with such questions and visions in my head, but the more disgusted I became, the more I found I couldn't think of anything. I was horrified to discover that I was becoming physically aroused myself, listening to them couple in the dark alongside me.

And my horror only increased when, unbidden, I began to wonder how many men my mother must have lain with like this. It wasn't even her father who ran the Jackal, so there was even less reason to be chaste or selective. I remembered far too many nights when she hadn't returned to our room until dawn, and even at a young age I knew it wasn't because she'd been cleaning as she so often claimed, but only vaguely guessed at what the real reason was. At least she hadn't brought them to our bed. There was that small mercy.

Syrie moaned again, slightly louder this time—I pictured her mouth opening, her head thrown back, perhaps turning to the side—and then Braylar began whispering unintelligible words again. I tried to remember the last time I'd whispered words to a lover, to recall exactly what it was I might have said, but I couldn't focus. The whispering ended, and I heard his lips on her body—I pictured his mouth moving down from her ear, traveling along the course of her neck, her head twisting again as he did, kiss by kiss down her shoulder, her arm. I might have been correct, but if I was, judging from the sucking sound I heard next, the lips had detoured off an arm and made their way quickly to a breast.

She exhaled sharply as he sucked, and the slats creaked again as they changed position on the bed. I imagined him, mouth on her breast, one hand in her hair, rubbing the nape of her neck, the other traveling up her thigh, her legs spreading farther. And with each sound, and each instance I interpreted those sounds, I found myself becoming increasingly more aroused as well as disgusted with my arousal. I felt the urge to touch myself, and an equally strong urge to roll over and press my stomach to the mattress, to prohibit my perversion from growing further.

I could tell Syrie was trying to muffle her sounds, and I was sure her head was turned, her mouth in her pillow. I imagined her pulling the edge of it up with one hand in an attempt to stifle the growing intensity of her passion. If so, she removed the pillow long enough to whisper something to him. I couldn't understand much, but from the tone, she was concerned about waking me. Braylar responded, and I heard him clearly this time, "Fear not—he sleeps like the dead tonight." She whispered something else in return, and he replied, "He's sotted, I swear." There was another movement, and I heard her cry out sharply, whatever momentary concern she might have had overcome with lust.

Still, her small show of modesty and consideration for what she believed to a sleeping man shamed me still further. But it still didn't cool my heated blood. The slats groaned, and I heard him shift his weight— was he mounting her now? had she succumbed and spread her legs to accept him?—she moaned her muffled moans anew and I was sure I had my answer. Feeling torn in my two directions, I twisted my blanket in my hands and balled it into my fists, closing my eyes as tightly as I could, trying to think of the look of pain on Syrie's brother's face as he was mocked by the soldiers, the look on the soldier's face as Braylar had a blade to his throat. But these were fleeting, and couldn't distract me from the two bodies joining only a few feet away from me. I simultaneously wanted to touch myself to release the growing ache in my stomach and to scream, "I'm here!"

But I did neither and then something surprising occurred. I heard Syrie say "No." Braylar continued groaning—was his head buried in her hair? were his hands locked in hers? was he kneading her flesh?—and she repeated herself more loudly, "No, I can't do this."

I still heard their bodies slapping together with the same pace, and

Braylar replied through gritted teeth, "You can, Syrie, yes, yes, yes you can."

She said "I won't," loud enough that if I hadn't already been awake her protests would've changed that. The slapping of skin on skin stopped then, and I heard nothing more but their heavy breathing for a few moments. I was afraid the captain was going to force himself on her, but the next thing I heard was feet hitting the wooden floor soundly. Braylar said, "Get out." Followed by silence. Then, more loudly, "Out with you! Get dressed and go. Now."

I imagined her holding the blanket up to her chin, her face flushed with fleeting lust and confusion. Barely above a whisper, she said, "Please. Don't be angry. It's just, well, were we alone and all, I'd—"

He laughed, "You grow suddenly shy in the middle of fucking a stranger because there's an audience? No. Get out."

I heard her shift her weight, perhaps rolling onto one elbow, touching his shoulder or his elbow, saying, "This doesn't mean—"

But again, he didn't let her finish. "It's a simple word. There's no mistaking its meaning. Much like the word 'no.' Out." Whatever fire she might have still felt went out as surely as if he'd pissed on it. Which was ironic, considering what happened next. I heard him stand and take a few hesitant steps. The sound of metal rattling on the wood. A few seconds later, the sound of liquid hitting the metal. In the silence, it sounded like thunder or battle.

She felt around for her nightclothes and slipped into them. Braylar remained standing where he was, clearly waiting for her to leave. After a few more seconds he kicked the chamber pot and said, "I'd ask you to take this on your way out, but that would be discourteous to the other guest in the room, no?"

I heard Syrie sigh and the floorboards told me she moved toward the door. I imagined her hand feeling its way down the frame to the handle, then I saw a space of black slightly less black than our own as she opened the door and slipped out, pushing it closed behind her.

Syrie was a better woman than my mother. I felt equally awful for having judged her so harshly and for allowing my own lust to rise up.

Braylar stumbled back to his bed, threw back the blanket, slid in, and said, "Would that I'd rescued a whore." I listened as his breathing quickly grew heavier, woollier, and some time later, sure he was asleep, I walked over to the chamber pot as quietly as I could and emptied my own over-full bladder.

After I lay back down, my mind was ablaze with everything that transpired that night, and I felt like my chance for more slumber had disappeared completely. But as it often does, sleep snuck up and ambushed me again.

I was shaken awake, bladder somehow full again and head pounding. The room was still dark, and I was completely disoriented. Was it morning? Braylar was standing next to the bed. He shook me harder. "Get up. Now. Up."

"What is it?"

"Get your things."

Half asleep, I didn't understand. "But it's dark. What's happening?"

I heard him move across the room. A few moments later, the lantern bloomed and I blinked and covered my eyes. When I adjusted to the brightness I saw Braylar pull on a boot, his weapon belts already buckled around his waist.

I sat up and put my feet on the floor. "It's not yet dawn. Why must we—"

"They're coming. We don't have much time."

I pulled my tunic and trousers on. "Who? Who's coming?"

"I don't know," he replied, pulling on the other boot as he hopped to maintain his balance, adding, "I wish I had time to shit."

"If you don't know who it is, how do you know we need to go? I don't—"

"Violence is coming, Arki, coming fast. I don't mean to be here when it arrives."

My mouth was desert dry and my head felt like it had been run over by an ox and a heavy wagon behind. I wanted dearly to use the chamber pot, but he clearly wasn't in a mood to tolerate any delays. I got dressed as quickly as I could and threw my satchel over my shoulder.

"Good, then—" He stopped to cock his head, listening.

I listened as well. There it was. A creak. And another. And then muffled voices coming from the downstairs common room.

Braylar said, with much bitterness, "A room without a window. You deserve to be caught and hung."

"But, but you said you didn't know. Didn't you? You don't know they're here for us, or who they are even, isn't that right?"

He ignored me, circling one last time like a bear staked to a post, waiting for the dogs to descend, and then he shoved me roughly back toward the bed. "They'll be here in a moment. It's likely they'd sooner kill us as not. And I won't be taken alive. I'll take out as many as I can, and then—"

"But why? Even... even if they are here for you, why not surrender? So long as you live, there's a chance to—"

"To what? Escape? Be rescued?" He laughed. "You've read too many romances, Arki. I doubt they'll take me prisoner, but if they do, it will only be to hang me on the morrow. That's the good scenario."

"The good? To be hung? What's the bad?"

"They ask questions. Questions lead to more questions, none of which I'll answer truthfully. That will lead to torture. Then I'll answer very truthfully. All men do in time. So, I kill as many as I can before they cut me down. And then they'll turn on you—"

He broke off and listened. I heard it, too. The stairs were creaking. Men were ascending.

"Surrender if you like. However, I wouldn't advise it. Torture is very unpleasant." He pulled his dagger out, spun it, and held it out to me hilt first. "I suggest you slit your throat first. Cleaner." He nodded. "Quicker."

I refused the dagger and held my satchel to my chest. "They could be anyone. They, they might not be here to kill us, or arrest us. And I've done nothing wrong! They—"

He snatched his dagger back. "We all make choices." And then he moved to the left side of the door so it wouldn't hit him when it swung in, his flail and buckler at the ready.

There was more creaking, the floorboards now. Whoever they were, they were close, coming down the hall, almost to our door. I clutched my satchel and wondered for a brief instant if I should have taken the dagger, before reminding myself that I was innocent. I just hoped whoever it was cared about such things.

We waited. I looked at the door, sure someone was right in front of it, equally sure I'd be the first thing anyone saw if they broke through. But I couldn't move. My body didn't respond, even as my mind screamed danger was on the other side of the door. And then I heard another creak, and almost emptied my bloated bladder. This creak was followed by another, and another still, as whoever had been in front of our door moved further down the hallway.

I looked at Braylar, and there was confusion in his eyes, and for the briefest moment, I thought doubt as well. I don't remember doing it, but I'd begun holding my breath at some point, because I exhaled then, and felt faint.

A few more moments went by, in which I heard nothing at all, and then there was a horrendous crack, the splintering of wood down the hall. And then chaos erupted. Shouting, a man screaming, ordering someone else to surrender peacefully, more shouting, all of it running together, several voices at once, made incoherent.

I sat against the wall as the source of the commotion made its way back down the hall again. From the sounds of it, men fought other men, some shouting that an injustice was being done, others shouting for silence. There were collisions, the prisoners no doubt struggling against their captors as they were ushered past us, slamming into walls and doors as they went.

Braylar waited until he was certain danger had moved down the stairs, and then he cracked his door, just enough to look out and gauge the situation.

I whispered, "Who is it? Who did they apprehend?"

He tilted his head and opened the door an inch or two more. "I don't know."

"What's happening?"

He didn't respond, but opened our door entirely and stepped out into the hall. Poking my head out, I saw Braylar wasn't alone. In fact, I'm sure there wasn't a sleeping soul left under the roof. Most had come out of their rooms, but there were a few peering out from behind doors. That seemed prudent.

Braylar was standing alongside a wagon driver, leaning out over the railing. I walked over quickly and stood behind him. The common room below was a flurry of activity. Those who had slept on the floor between the benches were being pressed out of the way at spearpoint, pushed

toward the walls to make room for the prisoners who were being es-
corted down the stairs. A few grumbled complaints, but that ended the
moment the spears got too close. Reluctantly or not, everyone moved
back, leaving a clear path to the door.

Hobbins was on the floor below, looking none too happy. I glanced
down the rail and saw the Hornmen (all save Lunter) in their nightclothes
as well, though a few had grabbed their swords. The same held true for the
Syldoon as well, Mulldoos and Hewspear on our level, and Vendurro and
Glesswik below—underdressed but hands on weapons. It struck me that,
other than the men conducting this raid, Braylar and I were the only other
people in the inn who were fully dressed. I wasn't sure if anyone would
notice, but my regret at leaving the room was growing by the moment.

The men who had woken everyone were dressed plainly and without
indication of their position or rank. They wore blackened mail over dark
gambesons, but no surcoats, livery, or badges. At a glance it was impossible
to determine anything about them besides the fact they were abducting
two very frightened-looking patrons whose faces I dimly recalled from the
crowd the night before. There were at least ten soldiers, most armed with
short spears and round shields, but some had swords drawn, and there
was a man at the foot of the stairs with his sword still in the scabbard.
He had brown-and-gray hair receding sharply above his temples, and he
appeared to be the only man not doing anything. I supposed that made
him the leader.

Red Scolin looked remarkably alert as he called down over the railing,
"There are Hornmen under this roof. Unhand those men and explain
yourselves. Now." Despite the fact that he had no armor and his small
group was badly outnumbered by the soldiers below, he issued this command as if there wasn't any chance it would be ignored.

The leader looked up. "Ahh, yes. Thought you might still be here."
He unrolled a scroll and handed it to another soldier who started up the
stairs with it. "Baronial writ. We are to apprehend these men and deliver
them urgently."

Red Scolin replied, "Maybe you didn't notice, but this is an inn. Full
of travelers. And subject to the laws of the road. Our jurisdiction, none
other. Any arresting needs to be done here, we're the ones doing it, and
if not us, then the city watch." The soldier handed Red Scolin the scroll.

The leader below said, "Peruse at your leisure. You'll find it a binding document. We have authority in matters of sedition, from now going forward. On the road or off. In an inn or not. Your jurisdiction has been superseded."

The rest of the Hornmen cursed and one or two called out insults as Red Scolin examined the scroll. When he looked up, he seemed less certain, but still said, "I heard nothing of this from my commander. Until I do—"

"We're leaving. If you attempt to interfere, you'll be arrested as well, on grounds of interfering with the baron's business. Mayhap sedition as well."

Red Scolin threw the scroll at the soldier. "You're making an awful error here, Brunesman. Our order isn't beholden to your baron, nor no other. Even the king himself—"

"Is likely abed. As should you all be."

The leader turned towards the door and the soldiers began herding the prisoners across the common room.

One of them, no doubt in a moment of panic, elbowed a soldier in the jaw and ran toward the door. The spearmen in the room were more concerned with keeping everyone out of the way, and they didn't turn right away, even as they heard shouting, and the swordsmen could do little but pursue and shout as he ran. For an instant, it looked like the patron was going to win his freedom, or at least access to the door and the world beyond, but two soldiers who'd been stationed just outside entered the inn, and the patron's legs almost went out from beneath him as he changed direction, heading towards the kitchen. However, he'd taken only a few steps when a spearmen stepped in his path.

Apparently realizing all escapes were closed off, and having no other idea what to do, he jumped on a bench, and from there onto a long table, waving his bound hands before him. He looked up at the Hornmen in desperation, hoping for some kind of reprieve.

He opened his mouth, but whatever he was going to say was snuffed out. A spear flew across the room and the prisoner doubled over when it sunk into his stomach, dropping to his knees. His nightshirt protruded in back, the spearhead having gone through him entirely but not quite through the fabric. The prisoner grabbed at the haft of the spear, mouth moving silently, but with his hands bound he wasn't able to do much with it, and then he fell forward. He jerked like a fish yanked from the sea, his body convulsing, head rising and slamming back onto the table, finally letting out a low moan that seemed to carry on forever. The leader stepped forward, glaring at the man who threw the spear as he did. He pulled the prisoner up by the hair, who finally let out a shrill scream, as if the hair pulling were more painful than the spear sticking through him. The leader drew a dagger across his throat, covering the table with a fresh coat of blood.

We all watched silently as the red pooled on the table and began to run onto the floor. Hobbins stepped forward, incensed, which temporarily made him bold. "I said you could come in, take who you wanted—but this blood here, this blood is a different story. You told me you wouldn't be spilling no blood, but here you are, spilling plenty all over my good wood. I got a reputation in Rivermost, a good one—this here is a clean establishment, clean as you find anywhere. But this—" He looked around the inn with his arms spread wide—"this here is a mess, no two ways of looking at it. People hear about something like this, it's bad for me, see? People ride on by if they think there's murder in the night here. Do you see my problem? I said you could come in, take who you wanted, so long as you was clean about it, but what do I see here, but blood. Blood, blood, and more blood—"

"Count yourself lucky it's not yours. Perhaps next time you'll think twice about sheltering traitors under your roof." The leader wiped his dagger on the dead prisoner's back and turned to face Hobbins as he sheathed it.

The soldiers prodded the other prisoner out the door. This one, not surprisingly, offered no resistance at all.

Hobbins gulped, his thin neck bobbing, but he found some small reservoir of courage to continue talking. "Traitors? Now, you didn't say nothing about no traitors here. You said criminals. I know nothing and less about no traitors."

"Then you best learn how to tell, and learn quickly. Dangerous times, old man. These are certainly not the last." He walked toward Hobbins, who took two quick steps back. "Pray we have no cause to visit your inn again."

Hobbins nodded weakly and looked around the room at the rest of us suspiciously, as if the Brunesmen might have left a traitor or two behind as some kind of test. He looked at the blood again and yelled for Syrie. She came out from the kitchen, having anticipated his order, carrying a pail of water and a thick-bristled brush.

He grabbed her by the arm and pulled her to the puddle of blood. "Hurry up now, it's soaking in." Then he looked around the common room again. "You people, I'm sorry you had to be woken like that. But a man can't account for all those that sleep under his roof, can he?" No one answered. "No, no he can't. I knew nothing about no traitors, same as you good folk. We got nothing to do with them, they got nothing to do with us. And that's all there is. So you go on back to sleep. Few hours left in the night, and you paid for the roof, so use it." He turned to go, but something passed across his face—so blatantly it might have been a curtain being pulled back, revealing a mind calculating all things against silver made or lost—and he no doubt considered the damage word of mouth might have on his future patrons. He stopped and added, "I got no use for breaking fast myself, least not until the sun's in the middle of the sky. Don't serve it neither. That is, most days. But tomorrow, I'll rustle up something first thing, and those that partake will get it at half cost."

I looked down the railing, but the Hornmen had disappeared back into their rooms. Hewspear and Mulldoos walked over. Braylar turned to them, and twitch-smiled. "You see? Our timing will be perfect."

I had no idea what he was talking about, but clearly the other two did. Hewspear said, "The baron does seem to be ferreting out treachery in all corners."

Mulldoos yawned. "Who says those two were traitors? Besides the baron's ferret boys, that is?"

"That's all that matters," Braylar replied. "The baron's predisposed to see treachery, whether traitors exist or no. Appearances, Mulldoos. That's what we trade in."

Mulldoos scratched at his testicles and said, "Going back to bed. Long ride tomorrow." Then he burped and returned to his room.

Hewspear watched him go and turned back to Braylar. "He does have a pronounced lack of imagination. But he might also have a point, however blunted. Who's to say the baron isn't playing at something less obvious than traitor hunting?"

Braylar started back towards our door. "We shall see."

After closing and locking the door behind us, he started undressing. I asked, "What were you discussing on the balcony? What—"

"You've been in my company for less than a day. Do you really suppose that makes you a confidant? Trusted adviser?"

Of course I didn't. But how could I avoid asking? After I emptied my bladder and stripped down to my nightshirt, I kept thinking about the man dying on the table in the common room. So much blood. So much struggling ended so abruptly with the quick swipe of a dagger.

As a boy at the Jackal, they generally kept me in the back, scouring spoons and plates, emptying chamber pots, so I rarely even saw the patrons, let alone any attacking each other.

Since then, I'd seen brawls in a few taverns—though I typically tried not to frequent the places those were likely to occur, sometimes it was unavoidable. And once I saw a drunkard actually pull a knife and stab someone, but the blade was short, and he'd caused only a small wound before the innkeep clubbed him to the ground.

But this… tonight… this was something much different, and much more disturbing.

Braylar laid back on his bed, arms folded behind his head, staring at the ceiling.

I said, "When you woke me up, you said you knew violence was coming. And it did. What woke you? Did you hear horses outside? And why were you sure the baron's men were intent on violence?"

He didn't answer right away, long enough that I sat up to see that his eyes were still very much open. His left hand drifted down to his flail, fingertips absently running up and down the handle. I was about to say his name when he responded, eyes still fixed upwards. "There are many things to be explained when the time is right. You can be sure I'll know when that is." He looked at me for another moment or two and then reclined again. "Turn out the lamp, Arki."

He closed his eyes. Mine stayed open long after it was dark.

The next morning, I woke up to find myself alone in the room, Braylar and his gear gone. I felt like I'd been subjected to the press—my head pounded fiercely, and the room tilted as if I were on the deck of a ship on a rough sea. I promised myself I would never try to match the drinking pace of a Syldoon again.

Gathering my supplies, I headed downstairs. Many who'd been sleeping in the common room were already gone, no doubt at first light, perhaps before, given the sequence of events in the night, and the inn was surprisingly empty. The Syldoon were seated around a table.

Vendurro saw me and waved me over, which elicited a groan from Mulldoos. Most of the bowls in front of them were nearly empty, clotted with the remains of whatever Hobbins had thrown together on such short notice.

I passed the table the prisoner had been killed on, and while Syrie had done what she could to clean it, there was no disguising the bloodstain, and the entire contents of my stomach nearly came rushing up.

I sat down next to Vendurro. He whistled, which seemed to be the most piercing noise ever made by man. When Syrie showed, he said, "We're about through here, but the scribe could use a bowl and some bread, I'm thinking."

She looked at me quickly and nodded, her cheeks flushed, and then headed to the kitchen without a word.

Glesswik said, "Touchy little bird, ain't she? Think she'd never seen a man's throat cut before."

I wondered at the conversations they must have had that morning. Had they seen Syrie creep into Braylar's room? If so, had they pressed Braylar for details of his conquest? Had he lied about what a wild minx she was? Or admitted that some belated modesty got the better of her?

In retrospect, I'm glad I wasn't privy. The whole episode would have only mortified me further.

The Syldoon pushed their chairs back and rose from the table. Braylar turned to me and said, "Eat something. But don't dawdle."

I nodded and watched them walk out the open front door. Syrie arrived a few moments later her tray laden with a bowl of steaming slop with a heel of bread half-submerged on one side and a spoon on the other, and a mug of watery-looking ale. My stomach wrenched and I took a deep breath.

She set the bowl and mug down in front of me and asked, "Anything else you be needing, just now?" This seemed more perfunctory than pleasant.

I looked up at her and immediately regretted it. Had she known I was awake while Braylar slid inside her? Was she repulsed? Or perhaps ashamed? My cheeks were inflamed, and hers no less so.

"No," I mumbled. "Thank you, Syrie. No."

She looked away quickly. "Safe journeys then." A moment later she was back in the kitchen. I felt as if I should have said something, but had absolutely no idea what.

I was sure I'd been born after my mother tumbled into a patron's bed, just as Syrie had. Though I couldn't possibly imagine she was overcome with any sudden bout of modesty. Where Syrie struggled to smile in the face of circumstances designed to prevent it, I remembered my mother as a tough, calculating woman possessing some low cunning and little enough else. She was intent on changing her lot in life but grew increasing bitter as it failed to happen.

Perhaps she'd given herself over to those men in the hopes of winning a heart attached to a loose purse string. Had she imagined someone might rescue her? Sweep her out of the Jackal and into some better life? Or had she simply been trying to distract herself from just how few real options she actually possessed by slipping into as many different men's arms as possible?

I stared at my food for some time before taking a bite, until I remembered Braylar's warning about dallying. I forced myself to eat what I could and made my way to the stables.

Lloi appeared to be in the final stages of packing Braylar's new wagon. The wood was painted a faded green, and the canvas that was pulled tight across the frames was dyed blue. Four horses pulling, with his other two tethered to the side, as before.

The other Syldoon were mounted near the front of the wagon. As I approached, I heard Braylar addressing Mulldoos, "I've heard your reservations, weighed them, and found them too slight to burden me just now."

Mulldoos looked about as pleased as a man who rolled around in rashleaf. "Course you did, Cap. That's what you do. But it's not just me thinking this here. The gray goat, the other two, we all of us think the same. Maybe you didn't need guard detail coming to Rivermost—though, when it comes to it, I'm sure you did there too—but you sure as shit need detail going out."

Braylar shook his head. "We've discussed this. And now we're done discussing. You ride ahead. Lloi will accompany me. We'll take a different route. No detail is necessary. You're needed ahead. I must get there undetected. It isn't so very complicated."

"Me and Hew can handle what's ahead. At least keep Ven and Gless with you. Not much, but you get in a scrap, even two more—"

"I need stealth. You need speed. Every moment you delay puts the entire enterprise at risk. This discussion is over. Ride out."

Mulldoos spit in the dirt. "Going on record—this idea stinks worse than a dead leper whore."

"So noted. We'll meet up in five days time at the Grieving Dog."

Mulldoos looked ready to argue or spit some more, but spun his horse in a circle instead and spurred it off to the street. Vendurro and Glesswik followed. Hewspear rode over to the bench and looked at Braylar. "You know it pains me to say it, but Mulldoos might have the right of it on this point. Traveling with a scribe and crippled girl for protection isn't especially safe." He lowered his voice. "Not with the cargo you carry."

Captain Killcoin watched the others head out of the yard. "I value your input, Lieutenant, as always. Now safe journeys to you as well. Five days time." He nodded, and Hewspear did the same, though with a small smile playing on his lips.

After Hewspear rode off, Braylar looked down at me and arched a dark eyebrow. "You don't look particularly well rested."

I replied, "It wasn't the most restful night."

"At least your belly is full, yes?"

I said, "It was fine, if you like a little peas and grain with your oil."

"There's a basket of plums behind your seat. They're a very nice plum color, although not having tried one I can't vouch for their taste. Beside the basket there's some dried goatmeat, and beside the goat, flasks of coppery water and watery wine. They're indistinguishable. Flasks and taste."

Balancing my satchel as best I could, I climbed up into the back of the wagon and made my way inside. I wasn't certain how long our journey was going to be, but if the supplies were any indication, it was meant to last half of forever. There was what passed for a narrow path between miscellaneous boxes, barrels, buckets, sacks of grain, and a large chest.

Hanging from a variety of hooks, large and small, were copper pots, a shovel and a hand axe, as well as several curious bunches of dried herbs and plants that smelled of mint and lemons. I wondered if they were for cooking or keeping insects at bay.

I set my satchel and bedroll alongside a barrel and was about to settle down when the wagon started forward and I nearly fell on my face. I regained my balance, moved to the front, pulled the flap aside, and took my seat alongside him, just as we came to a stop again. Syrie's brother Martiss was standing below us and Braylar said, "You kept your face intact. You must have done something right."

The boy patted the flank of one of the harnessed horses. "That one tethered, nasty as could be, just like you said, but after a time she and me worked something out. Others were easy enough."

Braylar opened his pouch. "You can be sure I've looked them over, nose to tail, and true to your word, the care appears to have been exemplary."

The boy wasn't quite sure what to do with that, but when Braylar tossed him two coins instead of the promised one, his face lit up. "You're a fair dealer, by my account. I'll tell anybody that asks, too, maybe a few that don't."

"And I'll be sure to tell anyone that travels this way, a stay at the Three Casks will involve bad food, bad drink, and good horse care." Braylar flicked the reins and we were off.

I noticed a package alongside Braylar, wrapped in felt. He saw me eyeing it and said, "It's a gift." And when I didn't respond, or move, he added, "For you. Meaning, you should open it."

I picked the package up, finding it surprisingly heavy, and slipped the small cords off the cloth and unwrapped the object. I didn't have a particular thing in mind, but what I found would have exceeded even the greediest expectations. It was a large brass box, inlaid with fantastic scenes of silver and niello. On the top, two horsemen carrying crossbows and a pack of hounds bringing down a huge stag. On one side panel, a unicorn lying down, legs folded serenely beneath it, and on the other, a gryphon at rest in much the same position, with its wings down across its back and a large collar around its neck. The box (or case, as it turned out to be) was a metalsmithing masterwork of exquisite and elaborate detail, the likes of which I'd seen only in the inventories of some of the highest of nobles who had interviewed (but never retained) me.

I tried thanking Braylar, but he interrupted me before I said two words. "Do you know what this is?"

After examining the case again, I said, "No. I can't say that I do."

He pointed to finely worked clasp on the front. "Open it. Your gratitude should double."

Freeing the clasp, I lifted the lid. There were several small holes along the upper right side, perfect for holding sharpened quills. Below those were two rectangular openings with small hinged lids, one for sand and another for a container of ink. Alongside the small compartments for ink, a polished smooth writing surface flashed in the sun, with a small lip running along the bottom to keep pages from sliding off. Then I saw the small clasps on the inside of the lid, designed to hold any finished pages as they dried. I turned back to Braylar again, but he indicated that my inspection wasn't complete. Turning the brass box around, I noticed the gryphon panel was actually a cleverly disguised drawer that held extra sheets of vellum, some quills, and a small knife for keeping them sharp.

I also noticed two knobby legs that popped out from the rear of the pen and parchment case that enabled the whole station to sit at a slight incline, perfect for writing. Braylar had been wrong—my gratitude more than doubled. The generosity was almost appalling. I said, "Thank you, Captain Killcoin. But this is much too fine."

"You're not wrong," he replied. "It's a lordly gift so I expect you to perform well enough to warrant its gifting. Fill it with whatever supplies you need."

Having thanked him again, and retrieved the necessary supplies, I reclaimed my seat at the front of the wagon. I was fiddling with the case, trying to set it on my legs to eliminate as much movement as possible, when Braylar said, "Perhaps I've not thought of everything, but what is the category just beneath everything? That's what I've thought of."

He handed me a thin board and I set it under my writing case. I was sure I'd be remiss if I didn't thank him again, so I did, and then set to recording.

⊕

Braylar took us out of the alley and into the traffic on the thoroughfare. Even with the board, it wasn't like writing on a secure table or desk. The quill tip made countless unseemly scratches with every small bump and shift of the wagon, skipping across the page in small jumps as of its own volition.

I noticed that Lloi had ridden off as well. "I thought you said she'd be accompanying us."

Braylar replied, "She won't ride with us. Or seldom enough to count as a passenger. As you can see, Rivermost is crowded, even at this early hour. She moves among those strangers, looking for any that might show any... unusual interest in my passing. If it sounds as if I have a good many enemies, you can be sure there are a good many reasons. So, if you happen to see her ride past, don't hail her, don't address her, and do your best to pretend that you haven't noticed her at all. Do you understand?"

I nodded, not understanding. We rode down narrow dirt streets, the stone and timber keep shouldered against the river to the east, looming behind us, its tall towers stark in the new morning light. Even at that early hour, the city was awake. Odors were everywhere: fish and a heavy mud smell from the river, urine a sharp undernote, excrement sometimes mingling with the mud, bread baking, horses, the poor and unwashed. Shops opening, small wagons of apples and oranges rolled out by sleepy merchants, awnings raised, tables of furs and spices and ceramic pots and bolts of cloth set up. Hammers striking steel in smithies. A courier ran by in a crisp court tunic, a cylindrical pack of summons and missives bouncing on his back. Three feral cats darted between boots and hooves, their fur matted and muddy. Guards leaned lazily against the walls, waiting for their shift to end. A heavy wagon pulled by a team of tired-looking oxen rolled by, creaking with its burden of barreled ale. The last patrons left whorehouses and returned to their work, caravan guards, miners, magistrates.

Once we joined the flow of traffic, I asked, "We are obviously leaving. As you said. But you never said where we were going. Exactly."

"I didn't even say vaguely, did I?"

I laughed, mostly forced. "So, where are we headed?"

He pointed straight ahead in exaggerated fashion. "That way."

Seeing the look on my face, he added, "A destination doesn't matter until you get there, yes?"

I didn't understand the need for this secrecy—was there a practical purpose or was he doing it simply to torment me?—but it was clear I wouldn't accomplish anything by protesting further.

He drank some weak wine or strong water and flicked the reins, and we turned down another street in the city, the dirt turning to cobblestones beneath our wheels. It was obvious we were traveling through a newer section of the city. On our left masons began ascending what looked to be a rickety scaffold on the north facade of a monastery, their heads wrapped with dirty cotton cloth or covered in floppy straw hats to protect them from what promised to be an unrelenting sun. The monastery was several hundred years old, but all the buildings around it—a hospital alongside the monastery, a glassblower's shop alongside that, a grain silo a little further down, the curtain wall behind the silo—were of newer construction.

We rode only a few more streets, once nearly running over a man leading a mule laden with baskets. I thought I saw Lloi walking her shaggy mount down a street running parallel, but it was only for an instant before the person disappeared from view as we passed the connecting street, so I couldn't be certain.

We turned down another street, closing in on the gates, and traffic was thickening. Men bent over with bundles and baskets of all manner of things on their backs, small carts and large wagons, most laden with goods, some leaving empty, shoeless dirty children chasing each other or fleeing their mothers, women hawking trays of sweetmeats, beggars begging, guards in quilted jerkins ushering them off and generally looking disinterested in anything else. I looked at Braylar, examined him in the sunlight, and little had changed since the previous night. A new tunic, though of the same cut and ash color as the previous one. The same scarf around his neck, hiding the inked noose. The same tics around the corner of his mouth. I noticed his eyes—gray-green like mossy stones, and about as friendly or revealing. Much like they'd been when he arrived at the Three Casks, they were constantly moving, like a predator's. Subtly, to be sure, but moving nonetheless, a measured sweep past every face without any noticeable stop, although I'm sure he was registering more than the casual air admitted. Perhaps dreading to see a look of recognition. Perhaps hoping to.

I glanced up to see the city gates growing before us. It struck me with finality that we were leaving a place I'd hoped to settle in for some time, heading to a destination I knew nothing about. Growing up a bastard son in a small inn, I thought I'd live and die as my mother had, never dreaming I'd travel anywhere. Even after attending university, my ambitions were still modest, constrained. Secure a decent patron, live a life of letters, obtain some level of steady comfort.

Rivermost wasn't the largest city in the world, but bigger than anything I'd ever experienced or expected, and already farther than I envisioned traveling. So even if the limited range of patrons there wasn't inspiring, I'd already gone farther than I'd ever imagined. I was content. Or at least thought so. Until Captain Killcoin approached me, presenting an enterprise so unlike anything I'd ever conceived of.

And there I was, suddenly on the move again, the scope of my life again growing in completely unfathomable ways. I tried telling myself that this was a good thing, even if I didn't have much in the way of detail. It was growth. And growth was good. But the company I'd chosen, or that had chosen me, was enough to dampen that enthusiasm.

There was some congestion, one wagon entering, another leaving, neither allowing the other to move, but the guards cursed and threatened and one gave way and then suddenly we rumbled beneath the portcullis and over the open bridge, and I found myself looking back through the wagon, the opening behind us like a window, wondering if I'd ever see this city again.

Journeying with a destination in mind and small distances between was fine. That was all that I'd known since receiving my schooling, moving from one small city to the next, hoping to find a patron who wouldn't dismiss me. Travel was necessary, and I accepted that, or at least tolerated it with minor grumbling. I knew where I was going, how to get there, and roughly how long it might take.

But this journey was secretive, and even the necessity for that was opaque. If I at least knew why I was kept in the dark, I wouldn't have minded. As much. But the captain didn't seem inclined to reveal much of anything. And that left me feeling more than unsettled.

My nerves, already tight, were being ratcheted even tighter. At the outskirts of Rivermost, I felt it across my chest, up my back, through my neck, taut with tension.

"Don't look so melancholy, Arki. Travel is good for the constitution."

We crossed over the dry moat, made our way through the shanties around the outskirts of the city. This was my second summer in Rivermost, and each spring the shanties had appeared almost overnight, like persistent weeds. The hovels and patchwork tents were populated by dirty, thin musicians and street performers, religious zealots, those peasants and low-enders who couldn't afford the wares or entertainments of the city, and a menagerie of diseased prostitutes who serviced them all. My mother might have been a loose barmaid, and heartless besides, but at least she wasn't a full-fledged prostitute. Though some might contend that was only a matter of semantics and economics. Why the guildmasters didn't burn the shanties to the ground or drive off their occupants, I'll never know, but I was happy there was an armed and somewhat nefarious man in the wagon with me. Those places tended to attract only the worst sort of clientele.

Braylar remained silent as the countryside rolled past, and he was motionless for the most part, only occasionally flexing his right hand or twitching a bit. Farms began to spread out in all directions, and the road became rougher.

We sat in silence for a time when Lloi fell back alongside us. She kept pace next to the wagon bench and Braylar looked down at her, finally asking, "I assume if you spotted any following us, you wouldn't be waiting for me to ask, no?"

Lloi arched her back and replied, "Go back far enough, plenty of folks following. Don't call them roads for nothing. Can't vouch for intent, but if any had harm in them, didn't seem to be aimed your way none."

Braylar stopped the wagon and Lloi halted her horse, neither looking at the other. Finally, Braylar said, "You could tether up and ride awhile, if it suits you. Or not. They don't call it a wagon for nothing."

Lloi shrugged her shoulders and then did as he suggested; after securing her shaggy horse to the side of the wagon, she climbed in the rear and settled inside.

Braylar flicked the reins and we started forward again. He took a swig of what must have been very warm wine. We had the road largely to ourselves, and so he untied the scarf and used the end to wipe the sweat from his brow.

"There's no reason for us both to bake. Take a respite beneath the canvas, if you wish, as Lloi has done already. You'll lose the breeze, but at least you'll be out of the sun."

As the sun was high and scouring, I decided to follow his advice and move inside the wagon. Lloi was sitting cross-legged near the back, leaning back against a box, lazily swatting at flies.

The indecision must have been inscribed on my face, but she waved me in with her half-hand, which was surely the most disconcerting invitation I'd ever received.

I found a space against a barrel and, after folding my blanket over and placing it behind me as a cushion, sat down as well, though I shifted and tried again, as nothing I did seemed to make any position remotely comfortable.

Lloi smiled, but had the good grace not to laugh outright. After letting me settle in, she held out a pouch balanced in her palm filled with some sort of seeds.

I'd never eaten seeds before, and assuredly not when offered in a fingerless hand, but uncertain how she'd take a refusal, I reached into the pouch and grabbed a few. She pulled out some with her other hand, popped them in her mouth, and began working them around. A few seconds later, she spit some shells out the back of the wagon.

I did my best to mimic her, but breaking the seeds open in my mouth without swallowing the shells proved more difficult than I imagined. I managed to work a few open with my teeth and then promptly swallowed the shells, choking and sputtering as I did, and this time Lloi did laugh. However, hers seemed less prone to mockery than Braylar's, and it wasn't harsh on the ear, so I smiled in return.

I broke a few more open and managed to dislodge the contents without swallowing the shells this time. The meat of the seeds, tiny though they might be, was surprisingly tart, but not unpleasant. Still, not being near the rear of the wagon and not wanting to spit them onto Braylar's back on the front, I had no idea what to do with the shells. Having no alternative but trying to swallow the tiny husks again, I spit them into my hand and dropped them on my lap.

Lloi spit a few more shells out the back, still smiling. "Bought them in the city. Good?"

I nodded, but when she offered me the pouch again, I said, "Many thanks, but I'm fine."

Lloi withdrew the pouch, pulled a few more out. "As you like." She popped them in her mouth and turned to look out the back of the wagon.

Worrying that this would be the full extent of our conversation, and reluctant to return to Braylar's side until requested, I said, "Forgive me if this is too brusque, but it strikes me as, well, a little odd that you're with a Syldoon commander. What exactly do you do for him?"

She turned back to me. "I do what needs doing. That's what I do. Got nothing to do with the Syldoon, except by incident. Captain the only one that got my loyalty, and him only just barely." She smiled broadly, discovered a shell in her teeth, worked the tip of her tongue around to dislodge it, then spit it out. "Syldoon the same as all men—greedy, crafty devils that use you when they got appetite, spit your husk out when they're done. A lot like these." Out came another shell. "No, I'm not tethered to them nor theirs. Just Captain Noose. Him and me, we got some sort of…" she searched for the word and stumbled across the wrong one, "affiliatory thing betwixt us." The words "Captain Noose" conflated, with the rugged "t" dropping out entirely.

I said, "So, you have some kind of history or bond, is that it?"

"You asking if he mounts me?" She cackled, spitting out shells. "No, none of that. No mounting going on."

That wasn't quite where I was going with that. "How is it you came to share each other's company?"

"Same as any two people, I guess. One day, we were strangers. The next, we weren't."

I could see I'd need to be exceptionally specific. "Where did you meet?"

"Captain Noose was right—you got more questions than a leper got sores. Met in a whorehouse."

I coughed and tried to hide my shock.

She laughed again. "You got a lot of red in the face for not being the one there. Wasn't you whoring or being whored, was it? Or maybe that's it, maybe you was wondering which it was I was doing there? Maybe that's what coloring you up like an apple, eh? Well, I'll tell you straight, I wasn't fucking of my own volition, and that's as factful a thing as ever's been said. Clear it up some?" Seeing my hot cheeks, she added, "All bookmasters as delicate as you, or you that glass-fragile all on your lonesome? Or maybe you're just struck dumb because you're wondering how a beauty like me came to be a whore, that it?" She cawed a rough laugh and continued, "Like I said, wasn't no choice of mine. Didn't wake up one day and say, 'Lloi, I think today's the day you go whore.'" Another few seeds in, another few shells out. "Sold off before my thirteenth summer." She said all of this with the complete nonchalance of someone talking about porridge. "That's right. My tribe gave me a trim first," she wiggled her nubs, "something nice to remember them by, then they sold me to the first slave company that come by. Turns out, these slavers were on the coin for a silk station, edge of the Green Sea. So that was that. Until it wasn't."

"Why... why would they do such a thing?"

"Expect they didn't want nobody thinking it was on accident. A missing hand, well, that could be just about anything, couldn't it? Crushed under a wagon wheel, eaten by a ripper, a souvenir of battle. Lots of ways to go getting a hand lopped off. But the fingers, all of them but the little bit by the meaty part of the hand proper? Well, hard to mistake that for much else but a real deliberate chopping, one by one. Not many accidents happen that particular."

I'm sure I blanched before clarifying, "Why did they mutilate you at all, I mean?"

"On account of what I was, of course. No mistaking that for much else, neither. Some tribes, they send my kind through the Godveil." Lloi shivered a bit, though I couldn't tell if it was genuine or done for my benefit. "Ought to count myself lucky they just cut me up some and turned me whore. Silk house would've done me in, time enough, weren't for the captain coming along, but the Veil... well, that would've done it straight away, sure as wind is windy. Seen it happen. No kind of way to go at all."

She looked at me blankly, gauging my reaction, then continued, "Guessing they do something different to my kind where you from, eh? Can't guess it's six shades of nicer, though. Might even be worse, though can't imagine how. Still, people got a whole lot of creativity when it comes to maiming and killing."

She pulled the drawstring on the pouch shut, tucked it into a sturdier leather pouch hanging from her belt and looked ready to close the conversation off. But she was right about one thing—I did have questions, and I wanted to hear more, so I tried a different tack. "I'm sorry to hear that happened to you. I certainly have nothing in my experience that compares. But we're not all that different, for that."

Her hands fell into her lap and she leaned against a barrel, looking me up and down in that quiet, disconcerting way she had. "Do tell."

"Well," I tried to frame the words carefully to avoid being disingenuous, "I might not have been a nomad, or a girl, or mutilated and sold off exactly, but I do know what it's like to have no family to speak of."

She nodded slowly, still seeming less than convinced. "You do, do you?"

I debated backing away from the statement all together, leaving the conversation where it was. I wasn't sure how revealing I really wanted to be—but if that's what it took to keep her talking, I supposed it was worth it. "My mother worked at an inn, a lot like the Three Casks, but it was on a road. I was born there, grew up there. I never knew who my father was, and my mother refused to discuss him at all. Even bringing up his name earned me a wooden spoon across the backside, so I learned to avoid the topic.

"When I was young, not eight nor nine, a man showed up at The Noisy Jackal—that was the name of the inn, and he—"

"Good name."

I stopped and looked at her.

"For a tavern. Good name. Better than the Three Casks. No kind of character at all in a name like that. Might as well call it The Three Boards, or The Three Drunks, be done with it. Come to think of it, though, that wouldn't be half bad. The Three Drunks, I was meaning. Says there's some kind of story behind the name, which there ought to be. Otherwise no sense naming a thing at all."

I waited until I was sure she was done and tried again. "Yes. Well. This man appeared, and—"

"Was it your da?"

"Oddly enough, I was just about to tell you who it was."

She smiled. "Course you were. Go on."

"No, he wasn't my father. But he was his retainer."

"What's that, then?"

I felt we were nearing an impasse. "What's what?"

"Retainer, you said, was it? What's that?"

I nearly rolled my eyes before remembering that Anjurian wasn't her first language and she'd had no formal schooling besides. "His man. My father's man. Like Vendurro and Glesswik are the captain's men. His retainers."

She started to nod, accepting that, and then stopped, eyes widening. "Your da was a Syldoon?"

"No. I was giving an example. Explaining the term. Retainer."

Lloi looked puzzled. "So, not a Syldoon, but a soldier then. Your da was a soldier."

I tried hard to keep the frustration off my face. "No. Likely a merchant or a noble. Any man with some wealth or power can have a retainer. A retainer is like a servant, or someone in a man's service anyway."

"Well, why didn't you just say as much, then? Got to go confusing things with terms that don't mean nothing in particular."

I opted not to debate the point, and was nearly going to drop the topic altogether, when she rolled her hand in a circle. "Go on then. Tell me about your da's man who come calling. Only do it without confusing things no more."

I smiled despite myself. "Fair enough. I'm not sure how he found me. Maybe my father had known of me for some time, though if he had, I'm not sure why he waited so long to send a ret—... his man. Either way, the man was there at my father's behest to—"

Lloi's eyes started to narrow but I rode past any objections or queries. "My father sent him to offer my mother a bargain. For some coin, the man was going to take me away and set me up in a university. I didn't really understand what was happening at all. But my mother didn't exactly agonize over the decision, so it all moved very quickly. She accepted the terms and money, however much it was, made me gather my things, gave me one stiff hug, and sent me off with the man.

"I was confused. I thought maybe he was my father, but he explained in no uncertain terms that he wasn't. He loaded me and my meager belongings onto a cart and led me away from the Jackal."

"Your ma?"

I was about to clarify when I saw her gap-toothed grin. "You are for-given for thinking so. Yes, he led me off, telling me I was heading to a school. I didn't really know what that entailed, never having seen one, but hoped my father would be there, as that was the only thing that kept me from bawling the entire time. The thought that at least I would finally know who my father was."

She scrutinized my expression. "Guessing you didn't though, did you?"

"No. No, I didn't. Altunis—my father's servant, as I discovered, though that was about all I'd learn about the man. He wasn't exactly forthcoming. Altunis transported me to a university several days ride away. And after paying my tuition, deposited me there among strangers. My father paid for my schooling for the duration of my stay, but never visited me or the school that I knew of. I never met him. I don't know if he had other bastards, or put them up somewhere if he did. I might even have had brothers and sisters at the university and never known it. And I never saw Altunis again to ask.

"While my mother could be cold at times, cruel even, it was crueler still to allow me to be wrenched out of that life so abruptly, and to have any illusions about ever meeting my father completely shredded. I never forgave her for that."

I hadn't expected to provide that many details, but they seemed to be coming out of their own accord, and even over a tenyear later, the memo-ries they evoked were still a little jagged. "So, while I might not have suffered as you did, Lloi, I do know something about losing a family, real and imagined. And I know something about bitterness, too."

"Expecting you do. Only that's where the comparison ends real sudden like. I got no bitter to speak of."

I stared at her, incredulous. "How could you not? What happened to you was far worse than my fate." The words were out before I could stop them. But if she was stung at all, she didn't show it, and I tried to move past it quickly. "Why did your people do that, Lloi? That's what I don't really understand. You said 'on account of what you were.' What was that? Why would they treat you like that?"

Lloi cocked her head to the side and looked at me queerly. "Huh. I was thinking Captain Noose must have told you a fair bit more than he done told you."

She stood, having to stoop only a little. "Real nice chatting with you, bookmaster. Real nice. Excepting the part about your family. But I'm thinking we won't be doing much more of that before you round some things off with the captain there. Gets real particular about who says what without his say so. Anytime you want to share some seeds, though, you just say as much. Got near as many as you got questions."

Lloi stepped over my legs, nearly tripping on an ankle as I tried to pull them out of her path. She disentangled herself and looked down at me. "This wagon gets tiny right quick, don't it?"

Then she hunchwalked to the fore of the wagon, pulled the flap back, and shouted, "Coming through, Captain Noose."

Braylar jumped slightly just before the flap fell closed behind her. I heard him say, "I've told you before, don't shout in my ear, yes?"

"You said so, yeah. But I also know how you don't like being snuck up on much neither. Last time I snuck up on you, you got more raw than the last time I shouted coming through, so I figured I'd go with the shouting again."

"I take your point. But if you shout *or* sneak again, you'll be walking the rest of the way. Perhaps in the harness."

I suspected that wasn't as much of a jest as it should've been.

They fell silent and left me to wonder at this strange former savage turned whore turned, what, exactly, scout? Servant? Retainer? I nearly laughed, though the whole thing was infinitely more sad than funny. And yet she told her story—what she did tell of it, anyway—in such flat, emotionless terms, so at odds at the utter tragedy of the tale. It was all so exceptionally strange and perplexing.

We rode the road from Rivermost for some time, though it was mostly just a collection of ruts. After setting my pages to dry, and hearing no noteworthy conversations coming from the front of the wagon—Braylar and Lloi had lapsed into that silence only old comrades or complete strangers can sustain or tolerate—I moved to the rear. There were some travelers far in the distance, but their wagon must have been going just a bit slower than ours, as it incrementally grew smaller on the horizon until it was barely distinguishable as anything at all.

I fell asleep like that, head resting against a barrel. When I woke, we weren't on the road, the sun had slipped much lower in the sky, and my face probably looked like the wood. I climbed out of the wagon and looked around. The road was some distance off, and I would've missed it in the tall grass if it weren't for a single man leading an ox-drawn cart down it. I walked around to the front. Braylar had unharnessed the horses and led them off to graze. Braylar's own horses were still tethered on the side, and one looked up at me briefly before returning to its grassy meal. Neither Lloi nor her horse were in sight. Braylar was brushing the horses while they ate. I raised my arm and waved. The gesture wasn't returned.

I waited for some time as he led his horses back and fitted them to the harness again. I thought he'd ask for my assistance, but he didn't, which I thought just as well—my experience with horses was certainly of little value, and I was sure I would've only gotten in the way. Braylar pulled himself back up to the bench and acknowledged me for the first time when I said, "Lloi doesn't stay in one spot for very long. Where's she off to now?"

"I do believe you're infatuated. She's off scouting the area."

I looked around, seeing little besides rut and grass. "Is there that much to scout?"

"There are four basic elements to soldiering: training, logistics, strategy, and tactics. Of these, the first is the only one you can do—that is, with even moderate success—without the aid of intelligence. There's more than one way to gather intelligence, but scouting is surely the most fundamental and immediate. Particularly in a foreign land. So, while we're not a full company on a large-scale campaign, the principles remain the same. I have enemies, known and unknown, I'm not in friendly territory, and I wouldn't travel without intelligence of what is over the horizon, yes? Lloi rides the horizon." He cast a sideways glance at me and added, "Fear not. She'll find us. She's a creature of the steppe. We could be a thousand miles distant, but so long as we were still in the grass, I'm confident she would track us down. More importantly, she knows the route we intend to take."

Like so many things he said, this did nothing to clarify anything. I asked, foolishly perhaps, "Is Lloi your woman?" I would've said lady, but that clearly didn't apply.

Captain Killcoin laughed and punched me on the arm so hard I nearly fell off the bench. "That's the height of hilarity, Arki. Truly. Even if I could love one such as her—and that, if you failed to observe, is what I find so amusing—but even if that were possible, do you suspect I'd retain her on a dangerous journey such as this? Or order her to scout alone, and not rend the hair from my scalp in worry? No. A camp follower who cooks a good quail or sucks a good cock, you keep around. But someone who's ensnared your heart is someone you leave at home for peace of mind."

I started to ask something else but he cut me off, "Enough on that. When I determine the time is ripe, you shall know more of her... utility to me, and not a moment before. And if that only inflames your curiosity, I say to you, a writer without curiosity is a bird without feathers."

I expected he'd turn us about and return us to the road, but we continued rolling on over the tall grass, gusts of wind turning it about like choppy waves. I held my tongue, waiting, thinking perhaps he was simply anticipating a curve in road ahead, and that we were only crossing a relatively small stretch of steppe before stumbling across it again.

However, the time passed in silence and nothing was going as expected. As calmly as possible, I said, "We're not returning to the road."

"Very astute. And I'll preempt a few more observations to save you the trouble: the sky is still above us; the sun continues trekking west; our wagon is pulled by horses, not unicorns."

"But... I don't understand. Why did we take the road at all if you only intended to leave it?"

He replied, "Immediately riding off into the wilderness would have drawn undue attention. It's simply not done. But there are few eyes this far out, and I no longer wish to be part of traffic. And as to the why of it, that's for me to reveal, not for you to puzzle out. I hired you to archive, not navigate. When next you're hired to navigate, your counsel on such subjects shall be welcome and warranted, but not before."

I tried to quell the small bursts of panic in my chest. "But we'll... we'll get lost won't we?"

He laughed. "I don't intend to strike through the heart of the Green Sea. We only cut across one small bay. And though Lloi hasn't called this place home for some years, she still knows it well enough to guide us through. Fear not, Arki. I'll return us to civilization soon enough."

I could tell his patience with my line of questioning was growing thin, but I couldn't stop myself. "But... but the grass isn't safe, is it? There are Grass Dogs, and I've heard of a number of creatures that—"

"We will be safer there than on the road. Of that, you can be sure."

"But there are Hornmen on the road, to protect travelers. And—"

"And do you believe no one is accosted or robbed or killed on the road?"

Now I understood the point Mulldoos was arguing before leaving Rivermost. "I didn't say that. But surely it must be safer than going where there's no protection at—"

"Enough." He pulled his gloves tighter on his hands and glared at me. "You yammer like an old addled woman. Be silent or go back in the wagon."

So rebuffed, I opted to get off the bench and walk alongside the wagon for a few miles. As the sun neared the horizon, he signaled that we were halting for the day to make camp. Braylar leapt down and unharnessed the horses. I offered to help, hoping he'd decline, but he nodded. While I was hardly comfortable around them, I followed his lead, unbuckling the straps as he had. We didn't lead them out to graze, however. Braylar retrieved some hobbles from the wagon and fitted them to the horses' legs. Then he handed me a brush. Not being a groom, I wasn't sure about the best way to proceed and made the mistake of asking.

He replied, "You stick it as far up their asses as you can. When you're through, withdraw it and brush your hair. It will make your coat shine."

Opting not to follow those lovely directions, I did the best I could. Though I'm sure it was an inexpert and clumsy job, and I was probably too delicate, or too rough, the horses were benign enough, and the chestnut-colored one even bumped me with its snout in what I assumed was approval of sorts.

Braylar returned with a bucket of grain and fed them. I wondered aloud why we fed the horses grain when there was grass in every conceivable direction.

"A mixed diet is best. You're bookish in the extreme. Have you never encountered a horse before? Or were all of your previous patrons walkers?"

I ignored that and asked, "Do you need help preparing a fire?"

"We're still not so very far from the road you were so loath to leave, and a fire would serve as a beacon for any brigands. One fire means only a few people huddled around it. And that means easy prey, yes?"

Knowing that I was likely to only irritate more, I asked, "What about a lantern?"

"By all means," he said, "if you want to draw every raider in the territory down on us, light one. Light two! Did we bring two? If not, then one will have to suffice." He laughed. "I brought it in the event that I must use it. If that time comes, you'll know, because it will be lit. Not before. Record whatever you wish to record before the light fails, or wait until after dawn. Your choice. Were it mine, I would eat some of that goat and find a spot in the wagon before the whole world goes black. For one accustomed to the city, it can be disconcerting. So, sup and repose. Or starve and be fretful. The choice is yours."

The night was mostly undone by fretting. While I enjoyed seeing new cities and locales, I never really enjoyed the travel between, and that was even with companions on a short road, with fires, hot food, and a modicum of merriment. Not all at my expense. From the university in Highgrove to Rivermost, with all the small stops in between, more often than not I begged the kindness of strangers to allow me to travel with them, and given the dangers on the road, most travelers were more than happy to have one more among their number, even if I clearly looked incapable of defending anything or anyone. But those were well-trod byways patrolled by Hornmen, and the duration was never all that long.

Here... we'd clearly left behind traffic, and commerce, and community. All the things ordinary people clung to as they moved from place to place. There was nothing at all out here, except the unknown, and large quantities of it. Emptiness in all directions. Or the appearance of emptiness. Who knew what things crept or slithered among the grass, or buried beneath it.

And Braylar was correct about the dark—I'd never seen the stars look so sharp, and the crowned moon was in its full glory, both the moon itself and its single ring bleeding bright light everywhere. Sleeping in the wilderness didn't prove restful. The pots gently chimed against each other throughout the night. The wagon rocked on its springs, driven by the wind, and while the flaps were secured front and back, they billowed like the sails of a small ship as cold drafts found their way into the wagon and beneath my blankets.

I finally fell into a fitful slumber when I heard Lloi ride up. She unsaddled her horse, fed it, saying gentle things in her tongue, which must have been soothing, because I went back to sleep immediately. When I awoke at dawn, she was gone again. I rose and stretched, splashed some water on my face, and climbed out the front of the wagon. Braylar was finishing rolling up his sleeping mat.

After filling our bellies, we took care of the other tasks that needed tending: feeding the horses, harnessing them, checking all the straps and wheels and axle and tongue and anything else that moved for something in need of repair. Discovering nothing, we set off. I took my place alongside him on the bench and asked, "Would you like me to get the writing table? Is there anything you'd like to record or dictate?"

Without looking at me he said, "Record the grass."

Most of my previous patrons could hardly stop their mouths—they regaled me with mundane minutia and inane stories, most of which involved the glories of mercantile conquest. Hardly riveting, but it was why they hired me. Pollus the apothecary, old wheezy Winnozin the priest, Nullo the foul-mouthed (and foul-smelling) tanner, Lektin the pinched-faced banker. Dull and duller, the whole lot. Even the Lady Anzella, who inherited her husband's shipping business after the plague took him, and managed not only to keep it afloat, but to make it thrive... beyond the novelty that she was a woman entrepreneur, and a successful one at that, she was just as mannish in her ability to bore a person to tears.

They all shared one thing in common—they loved to talk about themselves, and it was my job to keep them prattling as long as possible, asking as many questions as I could think of to keep their narratives (and my employment) going. However, few jobs lasted more than a year; only one patron kept me on for near two. Being social-climbing burghers who'd generally made their own fortunes rather than inheriting them in noble fashion, they clutched those hard-earned coins tight, which ultimately always proved at odds with just how long-winded they were inclined to be. They would have talked forever if they hadn't had to pay for the recording.

But the captain seemed completely disinterested in talking to me at all, except when absolutely necessary, and rebuffed most attempts at conversation. So long as I was paid, I wasn't particularly bothered by this, but it was queer, and more than that, had the effect of stretching the hours out interminably.

Sitting inside the wagon, I often looked out the back. Except for the cloud of dust and absence of horses, it was identical to the front—an endless trail surrounded by an endless expanse of tall green grass, rustling as far as the eye could see. We couldn't have been more alone, and it felt as if we were truly the last travelers on Earth, doomed to travel these steppes together forever.

The next day passed exactly as the previous day had. The only real deviation in our journey was that Lloi was absent. She didn't return in the middle of the night. She didn't return at all.

⊕

The following day, after our usual morning rituals and preparations, Braylar summoned me to join him. When I took my seat, he glanced at me briefly. "You never look well-rested. I'm beginning to think that you don't have it in you."

I didn't bother countering that I slept just fine when I wasn't trapped on a wagon in the wilderness with the least loquacious man in the known world.

We sat in our customary silence for a time when Braylar finally said, "Have you grieved, Arki?"

I didn't answer right away, equally surprised he was asking me a question and uncertain what he expected as a response.

"No? I thought as much. You haven't lived until you've grieved. Death, life, together, the same. And if you've only experienced life you're only half-alive. Of course, there are many kinds of grief. When we're betrayed, when a lover leaves us in the middle of the night, when our fortunes overturn and dump us penniless in a ditch. Anywhere there's loss, there's a little grief. But they're minor, and quick to disappear. We can take a new lover, take revenge on our betrayer, take the fortune of someone else. The losses can be recouped, and this is what makes these griefs minor, fleeting, inconsequential.

"But when you lose something that can never be replaced, and more particularly, someone, then you'll know grief, true grief. The kind that tortures and warps and threatens to destroy, the kind that turns your insides to ash, that draws you toward madness or your own death. This grief will never leave you, ever. It will change shape, and if you survive its initial ravages, it will subdue, but it will never leave, periodically springing up again to catch you unaware with a new fierceness, like a plague that lies dormant for years only to return again with renewed ferocity. You'll never fully escape it. For your sake, I hope you experience this grief soon. You'll be that much closer to living a complete life."

After that happy outburst, he lapsed into silence again. I was about to return to the wagon when he pointed out a figure on the horizon. At first I was worried it might be a Grass Dog, but his smile told me it was only his Grass Dog. When Lloi finally reined in next to us, Braylar said, "Report. What have you seen?"

She jerked a thumb in the direction she came from. "More than seen. Found."

When she didn't immediately expound, Braylar sighed. "Yes?"

"Best see it for yourself. I could spend the time telling you about it, but without presupposing I know what you'll say or do, I know you'll be wanting to just see it yourself anyway. So, you want me to lead you there?"

"How far away is this find of yours—should we follow on horse?"

"Horse be quicker, sure as spit. But seeing as to what I saw, I wouldn't be leaving the wagon untended, Captain Noose, not if it were my wagon. Which it weren't, of course. Just saying."

Braylar seemed to be balancing between amusement and annoyance. "Very well, I'll heed your cryptic and garbled advice. Wagon it is."

Lloi's horse trotted ahead of us. Braylar snapped the reins and had the horses moving at a fairly brisk pace—we rumbled over the ground, rocking as we went. Still, Lloi's horse was quicker, even with its short legs, and she maintained enough distance between us that she was only a silhouette on the horizon, stopping on occasion to ensure the wagon didn't fall too far behind.

Finally, Lloi stopped and got down off her horse. Braylar looked at me and said, "Pay attention. I believe this might be something worth recording." Then he hopped off the wagon and it rocked gently on its springs.

I got caught on a nail getting down, nearly tearing my tunic, and by the time my feet were on the ground, Braylar was striding after Lloi.

I hurried to catch up, but there was no need—they stopped a short distance away before a large area where the grass had been trampled down. That's when I noticed the stench. Two odors intertwined, instantly recognizable to anyone who's paid a visit to the butcher—meat and death.

As I approached, I saw something past Lloi's shoulder, rising up above the grass. One of the largest creatures I'd ever seen was lying on its side before us. Easily as big as our wagon, perhaps bigger still.

It had short, squat legs, so that its belly must have swung very low to the ground, but now that belly was torn open, its thick, tangled, ropy innards strewn along with a great deal of dried blood across the flattened grass.

After a moment, Braylar and Lloi walked on, but never having seen anything like this before, I couldn't help circling and taking account. Most of its body was covered in bulbous scales of dark gray, almost charcoal, interspersed with strange tufts of stiff hair. It had a short tail, a shorter neck, and a wedge-shaped head. Its mouth was agape, huge purple tongue lolling over knobby teeth, eyes like small black stones still open under a broad, bony ridge. Large flies scattered from the open wound at its belly as I came close, buzzing their protest. Its hide, more of an armor, really, was marked with white scars or punctures, particularly around the neck and head.

I looked up, and when I didn't see my companions right away, there was a flash of panic before I noticed the tops of their heads twenty feet away. I walked over quickly and found another scene of carnage, much more dreadful than the first.

There was a chariot upended, comprised mostly of stiff grass. Harnessed to the front was a dead dog at least as big as Lloi's pony, its thick mottled fur caked in a wide splatter of blood. Its throat had been torn out. I imagined what kind of creature could kill a dog this big, and in such gruesome, efficient fashion, and I couldn't stymie a shiver.

Most of the harness straps disappeared underneath the dog, but it appeared there had been another dog pulling the chariot, though if it was in the vicinity, I didn't see it. I wondered if that's what Lloi and Braylar were inspecting and walked in their direction, suddenly wishing I'd stayed with the wagon.

Braylar and Lloi were squatting before a dead man, disemboweled from sternum to crotch, his bloated guts slung across his waist and pooling in the grass on either side.

I turned away, gagging, struggling to keep my last meal in my stomach. I tried to think on something else, anything else—beautiful flowers, a rolling brook, pen and ink—and the nausea nearly passed until I remembered I ate dried goat that morning, and then there was no stopping it—my stomach roiled and heaved. I took several steps back towards the chariot and vomited into the grass.

I dreaded Braylar's ridicule and didn't want to embarrass myself by spitting up bile, but I also didn't want to walk alone back to the wagon. Whatever assaulted the Grass Dogs was still out here somewhere. And so, once I was sure my knees had wobbled their last, I approached again, reluctantly.

Braylar had just finished asking a question.

She pointed. "Over there."

The two of them began walking without sparing me another look.

I glanced down at the man again, though I was careful not to linger on his innards. He shared Lloi's dark coloring, both in skin and hair. Feet, sandaled; legs, bound in strips of felt wrapped tight; chest (what I allowed myself to see), once housed in a breastplate of dark gray leather that had been slashed open; left arm, still clutching a long wooden shield that had been flung wide; his spear is a few feet away, just outside the dried blood that coated the grass in all directions. He had a gray helmet that bore a striking resemblance to a bowl and was obviously fashioned out of the hide of a beast like the one also dead nearby. His eyes stared up into the cloudless sky, mouth still open in an unfinished scream. A fly traipsed across his lips and I turned away to find Braylar and Lloi before my stomach betrayed me again, my feet heavy as I dreaded what else they might be investigating.

They were standing on either side of another dead body, though this one was thankfully face down in the grass. For a moment, I feared Braylar meant to turn him over with his foot, shuddered, and began to avert my eyes.

Braylar saw, smiled quick and small. "No matter. Dead is dead. So, Lloi, you have my attention in full. Tell me what happened here."

"Wasn't here. But I can hazard a guess or two."

"As could I. But I'm hopeful yours will contain more insight."

Lloi pointed back where we came from. "That beast back there, what my people call a rooter, it—"

Braylar interrupted. "No longer, Lloi." She looked confused until Braylar clarified. "They haven't been your people for some time." Surprisingly, this was said somewhat gently, less a reprimand than a reminder.

Lloi pulled her misshapen hat off her head. "Nah. They're still my people, even if I'm not theirs. Can't help who you are, Captain Noose. Can't help it none at all."

Braylar looked poised to argue, but conceded the point. "As you will, Lloi. Continue, then. What of the beast?"

"Called a rooter, on account of it eating not much more than roots. But mean as spit, for all that—can crush a man easier than I can crush a flower. Usually hunt them with a small party, like this, though I'm guessing they wished they'd a brought a bigger one right about now. But here, they got two chariots, probably four or five men, and—"

"Two? Where is the other, then, and those that rode on it?"

Lloi waved away a big fly. "I'm coming to that, short. Get there faster, you just let me." She set the hat on her head and adjusted it, but I couldn't fathom why—it was only a different kind of shapeless now. "Trails and ruts say two chariots, four, maybe five men. They hunt this rooter to ground, I'm thinking. Wasn't expecting them to be this close to the road, but I'm guessing they followed that old devil away from a herd, he led them on a chase outside where they meant to go. You notice the skin? Thick. Tough to kill a rooter with spears. But worth it, if you can manage. So they chased, finally made the kill back there."

We followed her back toward the chariot and dog. "Looks like they set to butchering when something took them unawares. Guessing the two we got dead here, they were carving the rooter. The other two or three, back over here with the chariots. Must have been when they heard it."

She didn't elaborate as she walked around the perimeter of the scene, her hand grazing the tops of the grass.

Braylar snapped, "What, pray tell, did they hear?"

"Ripper come on them. Looks like it attacked near the chariots first."

I said, "Ripper? Let me guess. On account of it eviscerating everything?"

"If that word means ripping, then yeah, on account of the ripping. Biggest killer on the plains. Vicious bird, taller than a man on horse, and faster too, least in short bursts. Quicker and meaner than anything you ever see. No wings to speak of, but rippers got arms with long claws. Hook their prey still when they shred it with that massive beak of theirs. Eat ferrets, groundhog, gazelle, pretty much whatever else it come across. Loves horse. They usually steer clear of men and dogs, though, least of all, when in number. Can't rightly say what it was doing here. Could be it had its eye on the old rooter, too, got territorial. Could be its stomach was just that empty. Guessing it came on them unawares. One wagon had time to cut loose. But those poor bastards, looks like one tried to run, the other tried to fight. Either way, dead is dead."

Braylar dropped his hand to the flail on his hip and scanned the horizon. "Thank you for advising me to don armor before leaving the wagon. Most kind."

"Wouldn't help you none, if the ripper come calling. Steel armor would've surprised it some, true enough—not much of that out this way—but just would've taken a chunk from somewhere that didn't taste so steely. You ever see a ripper up close, pretty much the last thing you ever see, no matter what you're wearing. Unless you're sitting in an iron box. But we got a real shortage of those around here too."

She looked off across the grassland. "Ripper didn't stay here long, guessing it took off after that other chariot. Guessing there's another scene played out just like this one, some miles away. Guessing the ripper's getting its fill right now, else it would've run back here already, before the scavengers come calling. That's what I'm guessing."

Braylar turned and began walking back towards the wagon, rather quickly. "Next time you're tempted to lead us to a ripper's trencher, think better of it, Lloi."

We got moving again. Though it could've been my imagination, Braylar seemed to be snapping the reins with more enthusiasm. He asked Lloi to sit alongside him on the bench and began shooting volleys of questions at her, all dealing with what she saw while scouting. Particular tracks or trails, the locations of rivers or dried river beds, outcrops, likely spots for ambush, other signs of the Grass Dogs, rooters, or rippers.

A small cluster of strange trees appeared off to our tight. The trunks were incredibly thick—wider than three stocky men standing shoulder to shoulder—but they were also very short, no taller than our wagon. The branches were stout, too, comprising a dense canopy of foliage with prickly looking leaves. I couldn't imagine many trees surviving the wind on these plains, but these appeared oddly suited to the task. It was only a small cluster, though, the trees huddled together, and they quickly disappeared.

We were now truly in the wild. If there was any doubt, Lloi leading us to the ripper's bloodbath confirmed it completely. We were deep in the wilderness, in the middle of the alien Green Sea, far from anything or anyone familiar, and I was as afraid as I'd ever been in my life. I should've heeded my mother's advice. Even if she was wrong about most everything else, she was absolutely point on when it came to avoiding the Syldoon.

⊕

Lloi and Braylar alternated watch during the night. I volunteered to help and was equally relieved and insulted when Braylar said they wouldn't trust their lives to my vigilance.

Lloi was gone with daybreak, if not before. I didn't see how she could spend half the night on watch and then a full day scouting ahead or behind us, but her endurance didn't seem to flag at all.

After we set off, the wind picked up considerably, turning into a roaring, howling thing. Braylar pulled his scarf up to his eyes to keep the grit out of his mouth and nose. I tried asking him a question, and he swore repeatedly and told me to be silent, as if I were in league with the wind.

When we finally halted for the day, the wind hadn't abated at all. We ate and I attempted to sleep. But between listening for Lloi's return or the ripper's approach, it was largely a restless night. Lloi didn't return. But at least the ripper didn't either.

The next day was much of the same. No reprieve from the wind. No sign of Lloi.

After feeding the rest of the horses, Braylar saddled Scorn. As he was getting ready to ride off, his crossbow and quiver on either side of the saddle, I asked him what I should do if the ripper showed up.

He either failed to hear me or failed to care and rode off without a word.

So abandoned, I sat inside, the wagon rocking back and forth, the canvas quivering against the wooden ribs, and the hand axe at the ready, though I knew I had little chance of fending a ripper off if those Grass Dogs fared so poorly.

Hours later, Braylar returned and dismounted. Alone. One glare killed any questions I might have had.

Another restless night. And another dawn without Lloi.

By mid-afternoon the following day, the wind finally ceased. The grass stopped churning, the horses lifted their heads once more, and we began to move at our normal pace.

After another quiet hour, I sat next to him. He said, "And you were worried this wouldn't be a pleasant journey."

Whatever mirth he was trying to summon disappeared when I asked, "Is Lloi… does she usually go this long? Is she—"

"I can't say," he replied. "You must have failed to notice, but I'm not with her, I'm with you. She's alive or she's dead. One of those is a certainty. Beyond that, it's pointless to question. I would have her rejoin us, but I can't will it—"

Braylar stopped mid-sentence and closed his eyes. The twitch returned on the edge of his lips, the scars lifting and falling. He cocked his head to the side as if he were straining to hear something far away, then stood and pulled the flail off his belt, the corners of his mouth beginning to twitch more rapidly. And his lips opened and closed slightly, as if he were trying to find the beginnings of words that refused to come out.

Suddenly, he raised the haft of the flail in the air, the two spiked Deserters swinging gently on their chains. Then he began spinning the heads, slowly at first, so they began a gentle arc, and then faster, until the chains were whistling through the air. With each pass, he mouthed the non-words more frantically.

He stood on the seat, spinning the flail, turning at the waist, this way and that, like some twisted, warlike weathervane moved by a wind only he could feel. I'd never had direct dealings with a man afflicted with madness, but I was sure those were likely signs.

Not knowing what else to do, I asked, "Captain Killcoin? Can I get you something? Some, uh, some wine perhaps?"

He cursed, told me to be silent, and continued turning.

All I could do was watch, until, like a storm that threatens but is blown past by the wind, the spinning slowed and then stopped, and he grabbed the chains with one hand to still them before placing the weapon back on his belt. And then, as suddenly as he stood and began the madness, he sat again, as if nothing occurred at all. Leaning forward, hands on his knees, he stared straight ahead, sweat on his brow.

I was trying to think of something to break the silence when he jumped off the wagon, moved a few feet off into the grass, pulled his trousers down, and emptied his bowels as loudly and grotesquely as I'd ever heard bowels emptied, a wet explosion as if all his insides murdered him and were trying to flee the scene of the crime at once.

Disgusted, I turned away.

A short time later, he walked back toward the wagon, face pale, hands shaking slightly. I couldn't begin to think of what to say, but he said, "I always have to shit before a fight. Now go into the wagon, Arki. Bring me the crossbow and bolts. The quiver should be propped up alongside it."

I didn't move right away and his head snapped in my direction. "Be quick about it."

Utterly confused, I did as he asked and returned a few moments later, laying them on the seat. "Not for me. For you. You're going to learn how to span a crossbow today."

At a loss, I asked, "Span?"

"Span it. Load it. Load the crossbow, yes? That's what I said, was it not?"

He unloaded the crossbow and handed it to me. "This bow is beyond the pale. With some, usually for hunting, you load with your muscle and a foot in a stirrup. With more powerful ones, you need tools—a belt hook, pulley, crannequin, or demon's tongs. Here, you have the tongs, but as you can see, they aren't a separate tool, but a built-in mechanism. This decreases the load time. Especially mounted. But you have it easy—you'll be in a wagon and not a saddle. Now pay attention."

He pushed the lever forward and slipped the short pair of curved hooks on the thick hempen bowstring—if that's what it's called on a crossbow, I didn't know and didn't want to deal with more derision by asking. There was another pair of slotted prongs, much longer and gently curved, that were fitted on a metal rod protruding from either side of the stock. With a quick pull of the lever, the long prongs slid along the rod as the short hooks drew the string back and fitted it to a nock. He maneuvered the lever forward again, releasing the hooks, and then folded the contraption flat against the top of the stock.

So prepared, he dropped a bolt—at least I knew enough not to call it an arrow—into the groove in front of the string. He preceded to unload and load it once more as an example, unloaded it a final time and handed the crossbow and bolt to me, asking me if I had any questions.

I had dozens but withheld them.

He commanded, "Now you."

I made an attempt, albeit clumsily. While the lever mechanism eliminated the need for brute force, the action wasn't nearly as easy as he made it appear—the short hooks slid off the thick string several times.

Braylar scowled. "Faster. You must go faster. You aren't loading this to shoot quail, you're loading it to kill a man who wants to kill you. Now faster."

I tried to speed up, and fumbled even more.

He leaned over me. "A man is going to kill you. He'll do this if you aren't quicker. Be quicker."

I reached for the trigger and he grabbed my hand. "No. No loosing without a bolt. Very bad for the weapon. We'll simply have to do with losing some bolts until you get the hang of it, yes?"

With shaking fingers, I dropped the bolt in place as he'd done, aimed it off into the grass, and squeezed the long trigger. The crossbow jerked, the string twanged, and the bolt disappeared almost faster than I could see. I repeated this a few more times and noticed that Braylar was scanning the horizon to the south.

I looked as well and saw nothing and he said, "Did I tell you to cease? Continue. Continue, continue, continue. You must be fluid, you must be fast. Or you'll die. Continue."

Not understanding any of this, I continued nonetheless.

Over and over, losing count, bolt after bolt into the deep grass, my fingers getting sore until they began to blister. The demon's tongs, as he called them, made the process much less strenuous than it would've been using the back and legs alone, but my hand was still starting to cramp. Finally, after what seemed an eternity of repetition, he said, "Still too slow. But we have no more time. Which is just as well—I don't have an endless supply of bolts." And then he looked at the horizon again. "Very soon a group of riders will approach us. I don't know who they are. But there will be a handful or more. They'll be armed. And they won't be friends."

Predictably, I said, "I don't understand. How do you know that?"

He looked at me, eyes narrow. "You do remember our night at the Three Casks, yes? Our little rude awakening?"

It took me a moment before I understood what he was getting at. He hadn't spun his flail like a madman, but he'd somehow known blood would be spilled. "I still don't—"

"It doesn't matter. It's enough that I know. Now give me the crossbow, hide in the wagon, and be ready with the quiver. And hand me a blanket."

I simply looked at him, sure I'd misunderstood the directions.

He raised an eyebrow. "Was that too complicated, Arki? I thought it fairly simple. You didn't think I wanted you to shoot it, did you?" And then he laughed, though I clearly didn't know why.

I had no interest in handling the thing, let alone shooting it—I'd never even threatened someone with violence, let alone carried it out—but I didn't appreciate being made sport of. "Why did you have me reload it until my fingers bled if you didn't want me to shoot it?"

"Because, if I hand it back to you it will be empty. And you'll need to span it. I thought that much had been clear. You practiced reloading because… you're going to reload it. One job. That's all. And if you do it half as poorly as you just practiced, there's a very good chance we'll both die. Do you understand me now?"

I nodded numbly.

He took the crossbow from my hands. "Good. Now get in the wagon and keep your mouth shut. And hand me a blanket."

I was reaching for a blanket when I saw him open a chest near the front of the wagon. A moment later, he slipped a cuirass of brass scales over his head and then pulled another larger tunic on over that, covering the armor completely.

He saw me staring. "I did mention a battle was forthcoming, didn't I? I thought that much was clear. Now hide yourself."

After handing him the blanket, I sat down in the wagon and set the quiver next to me. At that moment, I thought Lloi was lucky to be running around in the grass with a ripper.

⊕

I was considering that riding off into the wilderness with a stranger, no matter how much fame or money might be won, was perhaps the worst idea ever, when I heard something. Hoofbeats. Faint, so much so that I didn't recognize them as such at first. But real enough. As they got closer, I could tell they belonged to several horses.

Braylar whispered, "Six. Better than seven. Much worse than four." I wasn't sure if he was speaking to me, himself, or the flail.

I scooted against the wall of canvas, and noticed a worn spot, just thin enough that I could see out without anyone seeing in. There were six riders. One had a shirt of rusty and poorly-patched mail that barely stretched over his wide girth. He was much older than the other five, and I assumed he was the leader. He had straight gray hair hanging in a sweaty curtain beneath his iron helm, and a thick white mustache that obscured most of his mouth. In his hand, a round, wooden shield, and a sword in a scabbard at his side. On his other side, a cracked and weathered horn hanging from a baldric. That didn't bode well.

The other five riders wore dirty gambesons, similar to the quilted jerkins the city watch wore in Rivermost, though these were raw, undyed, and thicker. They had either short axes or long daggers at their hips, and carried spears and shields, each with a quiver of javelins alongside their saddles. These soldiers looked around as they approached and shifted in their saddles like they ached to be out of them. They look inexperienced, bored, and young. But they were definitely a handful of armed men. Just as Braylar predicted.

Our wagon rumbled and creaked along slowly, tack and harness jingling. The five young soldiers halted about thirty feet away, with the leader riding a bit closer, and Braylar stopped the wagon. And I began to sweat in earnest. Three of the soldiers moved out of my square of vision, still maintaining their distance, fanning out slightly, but I could still see Braylar's back, the leader, and two of the young men in quilted armor.

The man in mail spoke—he sounded congenial enough, and I hoped Braylar was wrong about their intentions. "Greetings. I'm Hornman Urlin. And you are…?"

"Very pleased to see you." Though I couldn't see his face, it sounded like he was smiling. Smiling was good. Unexpected, but good. "I am Thutro. Sometimes called Thutro the Prosperous, though few enough remember the second part now."

Hornman Urlin crossed his arms in front of his substantial lap and leaned forward. "Heading to the Great Fair, then?"

Braylar sounded nothing but affable, which must have taken heroic effort. "Yes, I am. I suppose you hear that quite a bit this time of year?"

Hornman Urlin nodded. "A good number of folks on the way to the Fair. A good number, true enough. But you picked a strange road to take, stranger. No road at all."

"I thought it looked suspiciously grassy as well."

"Why not take the trade roads, friend Thutro? Safer on the road, with fellow travelers."

"Fellow travelers, yes. But also brigands who prey on them. You and your men, you do a good job protecting travelers, I have no doubt. But you can't be everywhere, no? So, being undefended, I thought it safer to stay away from the roads."

The Hornman didn't take long mulling this over. "Maybe. Maybe safer. The Grass Dogs might have a thing or three to say about that, I'm thinking. But maybe it's not safety you're worried about at all. Maybe you're carrying something you wouldn't want inspected on the roads. Maybe your cargo, you don't want inspected at all. Could that be it?" He said this casually, jovially even, which seemed to be at cross-purposes with the intent.

"Possible? No. It's true. I don't want my goods inspected. But that's only because of their extreme paucity. It hasn't been a good year. A good stretch longer than that, truth be known. Ten years ago, I had five wagons, all outfitted with drivers and guards. Five years ago, three, outfitted with my reluctant brothers and their lazy sons. This year, as the last of my fortunes deserted me, my family did as well. So I'm left to shepherd myself and depend on the good fortune of meeting protectors in the wilderness, rather than brigands and nomads. So you're correct, I'm reluctant to show my small goods, but please, if you would shame a broken man further, inspect as you must. It won't take you long. You'll find nothing objectionable."

Braylar told these lies with complete ease and conviction. It was really quite impressive.

Hornman Urlin shaded his eyes against the setting sun and surveyed the wagon again. "And this pauperish cargo of yours of no objectionable nature, what is it then?"

No hesitation. "Quills. Parchment. Inks. A fine stylus or two."

Urlin laughed, monstrous mustache shaking like a tree bough overburdened with snow. "Quills, is it?"

"Clerics and lawyers are a pestilence on this world, but they do have their uses. A wise man would avoid their company altogether, it's true, but a man of commerce, a merchant with a strong stomach, he might find a way to work their company to his benefit."

Hornman Urlin continued to laugh. This seemed like a clever stratagem on Braylar's part—he claimed to possess goods unlikely to interest a Hornman and his crew, and even those Hornmen who could read and write enjoyed making sport of those who make it their professions. "Fleecing the fleecers? I salute you. But five wagons? That's what you said, wasn't it? Five? And guards? For quills?"

Braylar continued to lie as easily as he breathed. "Clerics and lawyers are notorious for clutching their coins with iron fingers, but they're also vain. And I carry nothing but the finest materials. Even in my depleted state, I refuse to sell unworthy merchandise. For quality, rare quality, the clerics and lawyers paid, and paid dearly. I did well enough to warrant the wagons as my reputation increased, and the guards were necessary to protect my wares. If a merchant loses his goods, he loses everything. But now, well… the plague claims men from all walks, but the last outbreak struck clerics and lawyers with particular ferocity. Perhaps the gods have a sense of humor after all, eh?

"But it's been years now, and their ranks have been slow to recover. I tell myself that it's only a matter of time, that more fleecers will be called to their duty soon enough. But until then, I load and unload my single wagon, dream of lost riches, and struggle on. I couldn't afford a crippled guard in my state. I can barely afford the food to carry me between Fairs. I—" Braylar lifted a hand. "Pray forgive me, good Hornman. I don't seek your pity. The life of a merchant is hard, and I'm reduced, it's true, but I carry great hope to the Great Fair. And again, I'm far luckier to have met a Hornman, rather than a nomad or brigand, so forgive me for prattling on. I'm sure even in this wilderness, you have pressing duties."

If Hornman Urlin's face was any indication, he didn't register this deference as feigned, and seemed to enjoy receiving it. "You do me great honor, merchant Thutro. But what I do is duty, duty alone. We see a wagon having wandered far from the road, we investigate. Sorry to hear of your troubles, but duty is duty."

"Yes, of course. I'm glad to hear that some still take their posts seriously. I thank fortune that I met you. I wish you well, and pray that you continue to protect the innocent, and punish those deserving of it."

"I pray likewise. But I'm thinking I'll still need to inspect those wares of yours, innocent though they might be. Man can't do half of a duty and be done, now can he?"

Braylar paused, and when he responded again, the deference was sliding free. "No, of course. Duty must be fulfilled in total, or not at all. But I'm curious about something, Hornman Urine."

This wasn't going to end well.

The Hornman straightened in the saddle, face coloring. "That's Urlin, merchant. Hornman Urlin."

Braylar didn't acknowledge the correction. "Your order is charged with protecting the weary travelers of the world on the well-worn tracks they trod, correct? That, and taxing them egregiously at toll stations, to pay for your noble efforts. But first and foremost, patrolling the road, yes?"

The Hornman nodded curtly. "You hit the mark, merchant. Though I'm misliking your tone. I suggest you rein it in some."

In Braylarian fashion, he did the opposite. "Therein lies the curiosity, you see. You correctly point out that I'm far from the road, but the same charge could be leveled at you. It strikes me as peculiar that Hornmen would be compelled to ride so far from it. Quite peculiar.

"The road is your lifeblood. In fact, it seems to me that there's only one reason you might have drifted from the road you're sworn to protect."

Hornman Urlin's patience was drying up. "Two ways of going about this, merchant. You step down off that rig, meekly, let us conduct our business, and we'll be on our way. Or you keep on crowing like you are, and my men haul you down, beat you bloody, and everything else happens exactly the same. Either way, you're coming down now. Only decision you need to make is how."

Braylar paid no heed at all. "It seems very likely, in fact, that the reason you slipped so far from your assigned stretch of highway and all the witnesses that travel on it is you seek to engage in something nefarious. In fact, I suspect you want to inspect my supplies not because you suspect them of being contraband, but because you're inclined to engage in some criminal activity yourself. Yes, it seems very likely you're thinking of lightening my load. And to that I say, I wouldn't hand over a wooden penny to a brigand, but I'd at least respect his honesty in the attempt. But you and yours… you're a perversion of your purpose."

The Hornman drew his sword slowly. "You got some mouth on you, merchant. You get down off that wagon, real quiet, maybe I let you live. Maybe even leave you a horse. But you keep flapping your tongue, I'm going to cut it out, cut you down, and do a little more cutting just for the sheer pleasure of it."

Braylar pulled the blanket off his lap and leveled the crossbow at the Hornman. "Granted, this isn't a siege bow spanned by a windlass, but it's powerful enough to get the job done. The question isn't whether the bolt will kill you, but which organ I plunk and how long you lay dying. At this range, I can pick and choose. Do you have a preference?"

We were doomed.

I grabbed the quiver of bolts.

The leader appraised the crossbow, then the owner, looking at Braylar as if seeing him for the first time. He tried to smile, but it was clearly forced. "It's one on six, merchant. You'll die."

Braylar nodded slowly. "That's likely true, but you'll beat me to the afterlife, Urine. You could ride off, and we both could live. But I'm guessing you won't do that."

The three soldiers I saw looked at the leader, shifting the grip on their spears, uncertainty on their faces. I couldn't see the rest, but I'm guessing they shared the same look. The leader licked his lower lip, overlarge mustache jiggling above the pink tip of his tongue, and he seemed to waiver a moment as well, and then, eyes still on Braylar, he jerked his head to the side. I heard horses moving as his men began to close in. The leader pointed his sword at Braylar. "You lower the bolter right now. Do it and—"

Braylar loosed his crossbow. The next instant, the leader fell into the grass and lay twitching there, fingers clutching the fletching on his chest. Braylar threw the crossbow through the flap—it slammed into my arm, knocking the quiver loose, bolts spilling in all directions. I looked up as I tried to reclaim them—two soldiers closed in on Braylar with spears raised overhead. And then he moved as fast as a snake. Faster. He reached beneath his seat and pulled out two smaller steel crossbows, one in each hand.

Both soldiers saw this and instinctively tried to turn their horses from their course. Braylar shot a bolt at each, hitting one soldier in the shoulder as he tried to wheel his horse around, missing the second entirely, though not by much. Both soldiers were riding away from him for the moment, neither a danger of throwing a spear in his direction.

Not so for the third soldier behind them—he came on, spear raised above his shoulder, standing in his stirrups, and all he saw before him was an unarmed man who was about to die.

Braylar tossed the crossbows into the grass on either side and then crouched there, still as stone, head tilted slightly to the left as if he were straining to hear something. Any other man would've jumped behind the bench for cover or leaped free of the wagon, or failing that, at least pulled the buckler off his belt. Braylar did nothing. It looked like his courage or rashness had finally deserted him now that he needed it most. I was sure he was a dead man.

And then several things happened in such quick succession, even now I'm uncertain if I perceived them accurately or the precise order in which they occurred. As the young solider cocked his arm back to throw the spear, Braylar flicked the haft of the flail off his thigh with his left hand and reached over and grabbed it in the air with the other. The soldier released the spear as Braylar pulled the flail off his belt and dodged to his right. The spear struck exactly where he'd been crouching, puncturing the bench, splinters flying. I thought he'd fall off the wagon then, but he'd reached back and grabbed the haft of the spear behind him as he moved, despite not being able to see it. This was truly impressive, the sort of thing you only see at fairs by knife throwers and acrobats who've rehearsed their movements their entire lives and learned them from their fathers and father's fathers. But as he was dodging, reaching, and grabbing with his left hand, his right came across his body with the flail, snapping it out towards the young soldier with more speed than I would've guessed possible. Though all of this was nearly a blur, and I was witnessing it through a worn patch of canvas, there was one detail I recall with perfect clarity. The boy's eyes. He clearly expected to pin Braylar to the bench, and when he didn't, and he saw the unarmed man suddenly armed, it still took his mind a moment to register the danger, and then his eyes began to widen, and continued to widen as he saw the spiked flail heads arcing out towards him. The soldier tried to duck behind his horse's neck for cover. I couldn't see the terminus of the attack, only the boy ducking and Braylar grabbing onto the spear behind him with one hand to steady himself as he reached as far to the right as he could, the two spiked heads whistling... but the rest was lost even as I pressed my face as close to the edge of the faded canvas as I could, practically pushing myself through it in an effort to see the result of this impossible act. But thankfully, I saw none of it, and the horse's hoofbeats combined with the blood pounding in my ears rendered that sense useless as well. I was left to guess if he'd struck or missed.

After lashing out, Braylar pulled himself back, jumped over the seat and into the wagon, knocking me backwards. He pulled the flap shut and I looked at his weapon, my stomach rolling as I saw the bright spots of blood and a small tuft of brown hair decorating one of the spiked heads. Then I saw the dark spatter of tiny drops on the side of the canvas, like ink that had been flung from the quill of a drunken poet.

I'd been so absorbed in watching I hadn't retrieved all of the bolts—most were still scattered on the wooden bed of the wagon. Braylar kicked the crossbow at me and hissed, "Load it, you shrunken cock."

Stunned by everything that was happening, I didn't respond immediately, but then saw in his eyes that the violence would turn on me in an instant if I failed. I worked the lever as quickly as I could. A moment later, a bolt was in the groove and I started to hand it back to him.

"No," he said, "you might need to loose it yet." He pointed at the rear of the wagon. "If you see anyone come through, pull the trigger. Don't jerk it—you'll shoot through the roof."

Horses were whinnying outside, ours and theirs. I heard a horseman ride past on our left. There was a shout, followed by another, but I couldn't make out what was said. It sounded like they were arguing.

Braylar pulled his helm on, the nasal and cheek guards obscuring much of his face, and snatched the buckler off his belt. It didn't look like there was room to swing his flail in the wagon, but I thought advising him on matters of bloodletting was probably a bad idea. He glanced at me and gestured towards the rear flap. "If a man comes through there without a bolt in his face, I'll toss you into the grass to fend for yourself. Do you understand?"

I tried to imagine what it would be like to pull the long trigger as he had, releasing death so quickly.

He shouted, "Attend me! Do you understand?"

I nodded quickly, but silently wondered if I could truly do the horrific thing that he ordered me to do.

I looked at the back flap and held my breath. Trying to distract myself from the possibility of shooting a man in the face, I asked a flurry of questions, my voice a frightened whisper: how had he known the Hornmen were coming? how had he managed to dodge the spear so miraculously? as well as several others I don't recall. He swore and told me to be silent. I glanced at him, long enough to see that his eyes were closed again. I turned my attention back to the rear and waited quietly as long as my patience could stand it. Unable to stop myself, I said, "Maybe they'll ride off now. The leader is down, and others wounded. Maybe—"

"Only one is dead. Now watch that back flap and—" He stopped and hissed "Silence!"

I heard another horse galloping past again, very close this time, and then a javelin tore through the canvas on my left and stuck in the side of the barrel behind me, quivering there. It was a little shorter than the spears they carried, but seemed no less deadly for it. It's amazing my bladder didn't set free. I stared at the javelin until Braylar yanked it from the barrel and stuck it point down in the floor near his place in the front of the wagon. He looked back at me. "Take those sacks of grain and push them against—"

Another javelin tore through the canvas from the other side and continued its path through the opposite panel, disappearing into the grass.

Then I heard the wagon's axle creak as the load changed. Someone else had climbed aboard. A moment later I felt Braylar shift and turned to see why. A soldier was pushing through the front flap with his shield and was stepping over the bench. Braylar snapped the flail forward, as if he were wielding a whip, the movement so exact and economical. The spiked heads flashed out and the soldier raised his shield to block the strike. He caught the haft of the flail on the rim but the chains and heads wrapped around and shot behind, striking his hand or arm. The soldier had been throwing his own blow at the same time, but Braylar caught the haft of the small axe with the edge of his buckler. Though the axe didn't have a spike on top, the soldier thrust it forward towards Braylar's face. It skidded off his temple as Braylar smashed the solider with his buckler. The soldier's mouth and nose exploded as if he'd been hit with a stone from a catapult. He opened the red ruin of his mouth, no doubt to scream, but Braylar slammed the edge of the buckler into the side of his head and he toppled backwards out through the flap without a sound.

I turned to the rear of the wagon and a spear tip flashed before my eyes. I thought for a moment it was another javelin and then realized the spear was held by a soldier entering the rear. It had been a wild thrust, and clanged off one of the pots hanging in front of me. Without thinking I squeezed the long metal trigger of the crossbow. The bolt was loosed, sailing high through the rear flap and into the grass beyond, a shot somehow even wilder than the spear thrust.

The young soldier drew back to thrust again and I tried to scoot back, bumping into the barrel behind me. The soldier lined up his second thrust better, and I was sure it would pierce me in the chest, but it struck the crossbow I was cradling in front of me. The soldier wrenched it free, nearly pulling the crossbow out of my hands with it, and I again tried unsuccessfully to scoot back through the barrel, my heels skidding on the wooden floor in front of me. The spearhead came forward again, but Braylar's buckler caught the tip and deflected it past my cheek.

And then he was moving past me. The soldier might have been overeager or frightened when he first entered the wagon, but he recovered quickly enough—he feinted a thrust at Braylar's face, no doubt hoping that Braylar would lift the buckler and temporarily blind himself, and then aimed his real thrust much lower, at Braylar's stomach. Braylar didn't fall for the feint or overcommit himself in the block—he brought the buckler back down quickly when he saw the true strike and knocked the spearhead off line to his left. The soldier was drawing the spear back but before he could thrust it again Braylar had closed the distance between them and snapped the flail out, the spiked heads flying forward in a blur. The soldier raised his shield and caught both heads on the surface, splinters of wood exploding as he did, but he lost sight of Braylar when he did. He thrust blindly, but Braylar was already past the spearhead. He snapped the flail heads forward again, his wrist and forearm doing the work rather than the wild swing of his arm I imagined was necessary to work the weapon. I thought the heads would simply smash into the shield again, but the soldier was lowering it to look over the edge—the shield caught one Deserter but the other whipped past the edge and into the soldier's helm, just above his eyes.

The soldier stumbled back, raising the shield as a reflex to protect himself even though the blow had already landed. He dropped his spear and fumbled for the dagger at his belt, but he was clearly dazed. His hand hadn't even come across the hilt when the flail heads snapped down and caught him on the outside of his knee. The soldier screamed and almost fell, his leg barely supporting his weight. Braylar redirected the flail heads, up and back around to the other side towards his opponent's head again, but even dazed and injured, the solider kept his wits about him and lifted the shield, catching the heads before they could do more damage. The soldier found his dagger as well, and stepped forward and thrust it towards Braylar's belly. Braylar brought the edge of his buckler down hard on the soldier's wrist. The soldier yelped like a scalded dog and dropped the dagger, his wrist clearly broken, and staggered backwards. But in doing so, he gave Braylar the room to use his flail again and he used it. The spiked heads landed on the soldier's exposed neck, rending the flesh easier than canvas on the wagon, and he fell to his knees. He dropped his shield and reached up with both hands as he bled from his wounds and struggled to breathe, eyes wild with panic. Braylar watched him struggle for a moment. The soldier made short, wet, gasping sounds, the blood trickling between his fingers and staining his gambeson, eyes darting around the wagon, and for a moment, I felt his panic as urgently as if it were my own. Even though this soldier had tried to stab me and nearly succeeded, he looked only like a terrified boy now and I felt nothing but horror and pity, and wished only that his suffering would end.

And then, suddenly, it did.

Braylar brought his flail up and whipped it forward again. Even with a shattered knee, a broken wrist, and a destroyed throat, the soldier lifted his good arm above his head to defend himself, not realizing that if he was successful he'd only prolong his terror and pain. But thank the Truth, his arm offered little in the way of protection—the chains wrapped over his forearm and the flail heads crashed into the top of his helm. Mercifully, the soldier collapsed to the floor. Only the smallest twitch betrayed that a moment before he'd been a terrified young soldier fighting for survival. Now he was only a broken and bloodied body that continued to stain the floorboards five feet from where I sat. But I'd seen enough sacrifices to know that even his bleeding was short-lived, and would stop right after his heart stopped beating.

Braylar looked down at me and at the crossbow, no doubt appraising both of us for any significant damage, and sneered. I saw then that blood ran down the side of his face from where the axe haft had scored a hit, but it seemed an insignificant amount, especially in light of the large puddle of blood surrounding the dead soldier at the rear. My stomach churned as I stared at the prone figure, and then Braylar hit my arm hard with the edge of the buckler. "Span that crossbow, you whoreson. And if I see you loose it again before you line up your target, I'll gut you myself." I loaded the crossbow again as quickly as I could, though my hands were shaky and I fumbled quite a bit. I just finished fitting a bolt to the slot when another javelin flew through the canvas—it slid off Braylar's shoulder and then through the canvas on the opposite side.

He spun, cursing, his buckler up, and I wondered why he wasn't bleeding badly before remembering the scale corselet he wore beneath his tunic. Braylar said, "Buckle the quiver around my waist. Quickly."

I didn't understand but knew better than to ask. I finished buckling and then he said, "Slip the crossbow strap around my neck."

I must have stared at him like a dullard, because he raised the buckler as if to strike me and yelled, each word louder than the last, "Now, now, now!"

I did as commanded, more confused and frightened than ever.

Then Braylar began to walk toward the front of the wagon, flail and buckler in front of him, crossbow hanging on his side. Realizing he was abandoning me, I scooted towards him, grabbed his torn tunic and asked him what he wanted me to do.

He looked at the dead soldier and the spear and dagger alongside him. "I see no shortage of weapons. And you don't need to load any of them. If anyone else enters, stab them in the face. Gut them. Kill them." He turned to go but I didn't let go of his tunic, not caring that I was surely a coward in his eyes. He looked at me fiercely and said, "Kill the soldiers or kill yourself, I don't care. Your life is your own." He pulled his arm free and moved toward the flap at the front.

I considered the spear for a moment, shuddering as I looked at the blood all over its haft, imagining how sticky and gummy it would feel in my hands. I looked at the hand axe and shovel, and both seemed clumsy to me, so I picked up the dagger instead, looking back and forth between the rear flap and the one Braylar was just about to leave from. But before I could ask him what he meant to do, he swung the flail out through the flap to the right—I saw it strike the canvas—and then he sent the flail heads to the left with the same effect. He pulled the flap aside and stepped over the bench, buckler out before him. His head swiveled left to right, and then he ducked and brought the buckler up quickly. A javelin skipped off the top of it and flew into the distance behind him. The flap fell shut and then, judging by the creak of the axle and shifting wagon, he jumped off. And I was alone, armed with a sack of grain and a dagger.

I wondered what madness had overtaken him that he thought he could outrun them on foot, but then remembered he had his own mount tethered to the side. A moment later I heard him ride off.

I felt utterly deserted and desperate. I thought another javelin would sail through and strike me at any instant, or another soldier would enter the wagon, and wondered absurdly whether it would be more painful to die being chopped by an axe, stabbed by a spear, or pierced by a javelin. I wondered if perhaps I could surrender, and then remembered that well-aimed or not, I had shot at one of the soldiers.

Then I heard the shouts from both sides of the wagon, followed by more horses galloping off after Braylar.

He'd drawn them off. It's possible—perhaps likely—that hadn't been his intention. Given how poorly I'd performed at the task he assigned, I'm sure I wasn't a primary concern for him just then. But intentional or not, I heard the horses ride away, their riders yelling with the youthful bloodlust of hunters who have sighted their prey.

I crept to the front of the wagon and, after listening for nearby sounds and confident that no one remained behind, pulled the flap open just far enough to see what happened. Braylar was ahead of the three riders, but the distance wasn't great and they had their javelins held above their shoulders. I noticed one of the riders had a dark splotch on the back of his padded jerkin, and assumed he was the one Braylar had struck as he'd ridden by in the initial attack.

Braylar was holding the crossbow with both hands, flail and buckler again on his belt. I'm sure the young soldiers assumed they'd won by putting him to flight, and it was only a matter of time before they captured or killed him or both.

That isn't what happened.

Braylar turned around as far as he could, controlling his horse with his knees, and then they saw he was still armed. I didn't see the bolt fly but I didn't need to. Three horsemen were suddenly two, and one riderless horse galloped off in a different direction.

The remaining two soldiers whipped their horses to close the distance. A javelin sailed through the air but fell a couple horse lengths short. That boy, the one with the stain on his jerkin, whom Braylar had previously injured, still managed to pull another from the long quiver at his side. The pursuit continued.

I thought Braylar would have no choice but to ride off now, hoping to disappear in the coming dark, and then his pursuers would eventually return here, whether they'd hunted their quarry down or not. And then no bag of grain was going to protect or conceal me.

I considered grabbing as many supplies as I could carry and taking a horse, but I had absolutely no idea where to go. That way also led to death, but took a less direct route. I considered then that my only option lay in hiding in the grass somewhere and hoping they simply didn't find me. I didn't know if Braylar would return for me, but thought if he lived, he'd eventually make his way back for his cargo, if nothing else.

But I didn't flee into the grass, as Braylar didn't flee the battle.

He was maneuvering in a wide circle, working the lever on his crossbow while guiding his horse with his legs, and a moment later turned in the saddle and shot again at his pursuers. The bolt didn't find its target, but the two soldiers suddenly seemed much less confident in their hunt, and slowed their pace. Still galloping, Braylar reloaded again with a speed and efficiency that was amazing. Then, seeing his pursuers falling behind, he slowed his horse to take better aim. The young Hornmen had seen enough. They rode off in the other direction. Fast.

Braylar halted his horse and stood tall in the stirrups, crossbow level as he took careful aim. I was sure he'd shoot again, and equally sure another horse would lose its rider, but then Braylar slowly lowered his weapon and sat back down in the saddle, shoulders slumped forward.

The soldiers fled in the direction they had originally come from.

I sat there in the wagon, heart thumping like a trapped animal. I'd never known such terror nor witnessed such carnage. I was split in twain, one half morbidly fascinated and disgusted by such violence and waste of life, the other half celebrating that I'd survived, and glad it was me sitting there in my sweat and stink, still breathing, and not lying in a heap at the back of the wagon like a bloody bundle of meat.

I climbed out of the wagon and saw Braylar in the distance, slowly riding in my direction, the crossbow hanging from the strap at his side. Then I heard a noise below me, and suddenly remembered the other soldier Braylar had bashed out of the wagon. He was in the grass, struggling to crawl out from beneath the horse and harness. I wasn't sure if I should slink back into the wagon or call for help. He tried to stand, wobbled and almost fell back to his knees. That's when he turned and saw me, the front of his gambeson covered in blood, face a ruin, eyes full of fear.

The soldier turned and stumbled as he tried to run. I waved to Braylar and realized I was still holding the dagger—the bloodied soldier must have assumed I was coming to finish him off.

Braylar saw me and pushed his horse to a trot, and then saw the fleeing soldier and spurred his horse forward, riding hard.

The soldier hadn't gone far when Braylar turned his horse before him, the crossbow aimed at his chest. The soldier stopped, realizing he couldn't outrun a bolt, and dropped to his knees, arms raised in the air, the left more awkwardly, as the gambeson was torn near the elbow and Braylar's earlier strike had clearly wounded him there as well.

While I'd been paralyzed by fear just a moment before, I now found myself scrambling off the bench and down into the grass, nearly falling face first as I did, shouting "no" as I ran up to the pair.

Braylar looked at me and made no effort to disguise his irritation. "Is there something you need?"

I stopped alongside the soldier. "Wait. Don't do this."

Braylar glanced at the dagger and back to me. "Do you wish to do it, then?"

"No. And I don't want you to either."

Braylar's horse pawed the grassy earth, equally as impatient as his master. "And what would you have me do? Take him prisoner?"

The question was asked in such a way that any answer other than "no" would only be worthy of ridicule. I replied, "And why not?"

"Perhaps you've forgotten, but we're headed back to civilization soon. Perhaps you've also forgotten, civilization is a place where they don't appreciate their militia—even their thieving bandit militia—being held captive after their entire outfit has been killed or driven from the field. Please tell me you've forgotten these facts, lest I think you a complete ass."

"You can't kill him," I replied.

"I can. In fact, it isn't altogether difficult." Braylar drummed his fingers along the outside of his crossbow. "A little pressure is all it takes. Now, step aside unless you want his blood on you."

The soldier moaned then, a mournful, honking sound through his battered nose. I pleaded, "Don't take him prisoner, then—release him."

"Simply let him wander into the wilderness, until he winds up getting torn to pieces by a hungry family of rippers or skinned alive by Grass Dogs? Is that your idea of mercy, then? It would be better to kill him quick now."

He leveled the crossbow at the soldier's chest, but I surprised all three of us by stepping in front of the soldier. "He's unarmed," I protested. "Badly injured. He's no danger to you."

Braylar didn't lower the crossbow, and for an instant I was sure I'd acted far too rashly, but he didn't shoot. "Injuries heal. And what's more, tongues wag. He's seen me. That's no large matter—the others who fled, they can identify me as well. But he's also seen you. This unarmed, badly injured boy who's so wholly won your heart, he's the only one who knows you exist."

I couldn't argue this point, and so didn't. "If his life or death don't affect you, only me, shouldn't I be the one deciding his fate?"

Braylar lowered the crossbow slightly and his horse snorted. "And you would have me let him go, even though he can identify you? You have your own fate to consider, so I recommend you consider it well."

I turned and looked down at the soldier, his arms still in the air. There was a large welt on the side of his head, his eyes were bloodshot, nose twisted in the wrong direction, lips swollen to obscene proportions, face crusted with dark blood. I knew what I was doing might be madness, or at least monstrous stupidity, but I'd seen enough bloodshed for one day. And so I said to the solider, "Do you swear that you won't speak of what happened here?"

He nodded quickly as spittle dribbled from the corners of his lips.

I couldn't hope to intimidate like Braylar might, so I mustered as much solemnity as possible. "You must swear it. On the life I'm giving you. Swear that you'll say nothing of this. If your commander or comrades ask what befell you, you must say you were struck in the head, which your injuries will bear out, and that you remember only falling from the wagon, crawling free when this man rode off, and then riding off yourself before he returned. If you speak of what occurred here, or of me, I won't do anything to save you again. In fact, this man will likely take his time killing you, and enjoy every moment. Do you understand?"

He nodded and said he did, although it was absurdly difficult to make out through his torn and puffy lips.

I asked, "And you swear to reveal nothing?"

He said, with a great deal of desperation, "Ah sweah."

Braylar laughed behind me, clearly mocking, but I didn't turn around. I believed the soldier meant his oath just then, but I wasn't certain he'd keep it. Still, there was no turning back. So I told him he could have his horse and whatever food and water he'd brought.

He looked past my shoulder, at Braylar, and back to me again, wondering if he was being toyed with.

I told him to go and I thought tears would roll down his cheeks. He said, "Thank oo" and tripped over his feet, barely righting himself as he ran off through the grass to claim his horse.

Even after he was in the saddle, he gave a final furtive look in our direction before digging his heels into his horse's flanks and galloping off.

Braylar ordered me to remove the body from the wagon. I balked, but he insisted, claiming I was lucky that was the full extent of my punishment, given my incompetence during the battle and foolishness after. There wasn't much I could say to that.

After steeling myself to the task, I unlatched the back gate of the wagon. The dead soldier was slumped in a pile, the floorboards stained a dark red all around, nearly black. I took hold of his belt and the one ankle I could reach, closed my eyes and tried unsuccessfully to pretend I was moving something other than a body, and pulled until I felt the weight slide free of the gate and fall in the grass. Forcing myself not to look at the body or its awful wounds, I quickly walked to the front. Braylar was standing next to the horses. He moved from one to the next, rubbing their necks, wiping them down with handfuls of grass, and though it was difficult to reconcile coming from a man who'd shot two men today and struck down two more, he was apologizing to the horses for having to endure such an ordeal.

I stood there, looking at the spear that was still lodged in the seat. My eyes traveled up to the canvas flap, and the small spray of blood, the handiwork of Braylar's buckler. Looking away, I noticed he was walking into the grass. His back was stiff, arms at his sides, feet heavy and halting as if his balance were off.

Wondering if he was hurt, I called after him, but he didn't respond. I started after him.

He eyes were closed, face pale in the fading light. He braced one arm on his knee and turned his back to me. His shoulders shook, and for a moment I thought he might be weeping, but then he suddenly turned to the side and vomited, doubled over. He wiped his mouth with his forearm, started to straighten, and then took several steps forward before heaving violently again, almost falling to his knees with the force of it.

Staring, I wondering at this oddity, when he compounded it further. Hands on his knees, he cursed and muttered something to himself. Although it was still little more than a rough whisper, I heard him say, "Are you not appeased? Have I not sacrificed enough? Leave me." And then he trailed off, repeating himself, "Leave me be."

I walked back to the wagon. Not long after, he returned. He grabbed the spear with both hands, pulled it free from the seat, and threw it in the covered section. "Get in."

I said, "You drove our attackers off. They're gone. We're safe."

"Safety is an illusion for imbeciles. Get in."

He waited a moment, and when I didn't reply, flicked the reins and the wagon creaked into motion. I stumbled alongside awkwardly, trying and failing to get a good handhold to pull myself up.

He stopped the horses, looked down, and said, "I tell you to load, you load, I tell you to get in, you get in, I tell you to shit, you shit. This is our arrangement. As you've seen already, our lives, mine and yours, may depend on you doing what I say when I say it. Do you understand? This is our arrangement."

I nodded and he allowed me to climb on. I didn't want to sit next to him and made my way inside the wagon again. The sight of the large bloodstain on the floor sent my stomach fluttering, so I sat down, leaned against the side panel, and positioned a barrel to block the view as much as possible. And recorded these events to the best of my abilities, which admittedly, was somewhat suspect, given that my hands were still shaking and mind racing from the battle and its aftermath. That said, it was the best that I could muster.

We traveled some miles from the site of the attack in the dark before making camp with only the dimmest of moonlight to light our work.

When I finally crawled back in the wagon and tried to sleep, careful to stay far from the stain at the rear, my mind kept revisiting moments of the battle, a chaotic jumble… the spearhead coming at me like a striking serpent, or that same soldier's body pumping his last lifeblood onto the wagon floor after Braylar had struck him repeatedly with the vicious flail; the Hornman captain gently stroking the fletching of the bolt that barely protruded from his chest, as if touching the wing of an injured bird; the soldier with the ruined mouth pleading for his life, bubbles of spit and blood dancing on his torn lips.

Sleep was elusive, to say the least.

I woke in the morning when the wagon lurched into motion. There was some jerky by my side, a hard heel of bread, and a flask of water. I hadn't heard him harness the horses, or move inside the wagon, but he'd obviously done them.

After eating what I could, I rejoined Braylar on the bench. We sat in silence. I wondered if this was a normal reaction among the soldiering kind—did they need time to put their violent deeds in order or to forget them? Was he filled with thoughts of guilt? Triumph? Regret? I couldn't say, and doubted my companion would if I asked, so I didn't.

Instead, I said, "You don't seem to have an especially good relationship with these Hornmen, do you?"

"I don't have a good relationship with anyone, Arki. I would've thought that much obvious by now."

"What were they doing out here in the Green Sea?"

He looked at me and shook his head, "I would've thought that obvious as well. Road tolls only go so far. Hornmen are opportunists like anyone else. Only with swords."

"Meaning?"

"Meaning, you quivering dullard, there's profit to be had in the grass. Smugglers, sly merchants attempting to slide past the toll stations, pilgrims, anyone else who can be bullied and—"

He broke off suddenly, closing his eyes. After a moment, his head snapped forward. He pulled the scarf loose and touched the back of his neck, and his hand came away bright with blood. He dabbed at his neck a few more times, looked at his hand again, swore quietly, and then casually wiped the blood on my pants. I jumped and attempted to move away, but it was too late.

I looked at his neck. "You're wounded?"

He nodded slowly, voice strangely flat, like he'd woken from a deep slumber and wasn't sure of his whereabouts. "A wound, yes."

"From the attack?" I asked.

"From the attack?" he said, suddenly far away. "You could say that. Yes."

"Do you need… that is, do you need any help? Assistance cleaning it maybe?"

He paused a long time before answering. "No need to clean it. I wouldn't trust you to do so if there were. But it will bleed no more. The wound has closed."

Having seen how much blood coated his hands, I didn't believe him. Realizing it was impudent and possibly dangerous but unable to restrain myself, I leaned over and looked at his neck. There was no wound at all. Only a scar. An old, white, long-healed scar.

He saw me inspecting and pulled the scarf up higher, covering his neck. "Begone, nurse-mother."

I looked at the blood he'd smeared on me and said, "But scars don't bleed."

"You're correct. The wound isn't mine." He mistook my confused silence for skepticism and added, "I'm many things, but charlatan isn't one of them. The wound isn't my own. It was inflicted on another, by my hand."

He closed his eyes and ignored my slew of questions. Receiving no answers, I relented and waited. Braylar rubbed his temple with the knuckle of his thumb, eyes still closed, scowling. Unsure if I wanted to truly know the answer, I asked if he was well.

He didn't respond, didn't even move.

I waited and waited, uncertain what to do, when he finally opened his eyes again and blinked several times, like a man coming out of a darkened room into bright sunlight. "No conversation. We're done. Go inside the wagon. Walk alongside. I don't care what you do, so long as you're silent."

I started to say something, but he said, "Don't make me tell you again. If I must silence you myself, I will."

That's all it took. I returned to the interior of the wagon. The bleeding scar would've been strange enough on its own, but Braylar's behavior only compounded it. Every time I started to think I'd seen the oddest thing on this journey, I was proven wrong.

I looked at the red smear on my leg and then glanced at the much larger bloody stain near the gate. So much blood. Front to rear, the wagon was marked with it.

I rolled a barrel over the stain, nearly covering it, but not quite. I pushed a box over the remainder, and resolved not to think on the things that happened in the wagon yesterday. It was a hollow resolution.

We traveled the rest of the day in silence. Like a hound that had been kicked but couldn't help itself, I kept one ear perked, waiting for Braylar to call me back to his side, but that never happened, and I was reluctant to approach.

He pinched his nose or knuckled his temple on more than one occasion, and if his face was any indication, he was sorely grieved by something.

I wondered if this was the result of the blow he received from the haft of the soldier's axe, but while I'm no expert in judging such things, the helm seemed to absorb the brunt of it, and he had only a mild abrasion on his scalp and no apparent swelling. Still, this was all exceedingly peculiar, even for him.

The second day after the attack began much as the previous day ended, with Braylar uninterested in anything, even mundane conversation. A few directives to be silent, some clipped orders, and a handful of threats, though lacking the usual venom or verve.

I was riding inside when he quietly announced, "The boy is dead. I felt it coming since yesterday, but... he's dead now."

I immediately moved to the front, sat next to him, and asked, "Who? What boy?"

He looked at me like I was the one behaving strangely. "The soldier boy. I struck him across the neck as he passed, do you recall? The back of the head. The neck. Do you see?" He locked eyes with me, waiting. I glanced at his neck and the dried blood on his scarf. He nodded. "There you go. Now you have it."

I was absolutely positive I didn't. And almost as sure I didn't want it.

"He lingered for a time," he said. "But now he's dead for a certainty."

With a shiver crossing my shoulders, I asked, whispering without meaning to, "How do you know?"

He pulled the flail off his hip again, and I reflexively scanned the horizon for approaching horses. Seeing nothing, I looked back to him. He held one of the Deserters on a level with his own, rubbing the edge of his thumb across a spike as he stared into the small contorted face.

"Bloodsounder." He twisted the head quickly and the chain jingled.

I was awash in confusion. "The boy's name was Bloodsounder?"

"No, you idiot. The flail." Eyes narrowing when I still didn't comprehend, he added, "You asked how I know, yes? His death? Well, I'm telling you. Bloodsounder. Bloodsounder; the flail. The flail; Bloodsounder. It isn't so very complicated."

Sure the question would come out wrong no matter how I phrased it, I asked, "How does Bloodsounder... tell you these things?"

His lip twitched, and the twin scars with it. "I wouldn't use that word. Tell. That implies voices, where there are none. Unless you mean in the sense of signs. Tracks in the earth can tell you what made them, how many travel, what direction they go, if you know how to read them. If that's your meaning, then yes, Bloodsounder tells me he's dead. In so many signs." He closed his eyes and said, "I now know several things about the man-child I struck down. Things I'd much sooner not know."

He inhaled deeply through his nose, nostrils flaring, and closed his eyes. "He loved pears. The smell of their blossoms in the spring, an invisible cloud. The texture of their skin, when perfectly ripe. But especially the taste. And the fact that he first bedded a lass in no bed at all, but underneath the pear tree on his farm. In their rutting, they rolled over the overripe pears that had fallen, soiled their clothes in the juice as the bees buzzed around them."

I watched his face, eyes still pressed shut, and he looked pained as he spoke. "That same girl whose purity he stole among the pears, he married. Under the very same tree. And they had some small life together, happy, as far as small lives go. But it didn't last long. He was recruited by the Hornmen and quartered in a castle, far from the farm, the pears, and his new ripe wife. His duties kept him on the road for most of the next year. When he was finally allowed to return, he discovered she'd been struck a mortal blow defending the farm from bandits. An arrow... " His forehead wrinkled. "No... not an arrow, a spear, a spear thrust. Spear or sword, but most likely spear—the wound was too large to be made by an arrow. But by the time our boy had returned a Hornman, it was too late. She was alive, but there was no forestalling the end, as the wound had festered.

"He sat by her side, three days, four, wiping her brow as the wound worked its greasy green magic, burrowing deeper into her flesh, filling her with a raging heat no damp cloth would absolve. It would've been awful enough if she'd been screaming. But she whimpered mostly, waiting for the end, which was somehow worse. Whimpered and mewed and called out nonsensical things while the fever burned the life out of her. But one thing she kept repeating wasn't gibberish. He prayed he heard wrong, but after the tenth repetition, he could no longer pretend he had. A name. His brother's name. His brother who had stayed behind while he trained as a Hornling.

"While I don't know if he murdered his brother, I do know he remained with his faithless wife in her last moments as she tossed and turned in the fester dream. I think he hated her, but still he stayed. I would have abandoned her to murder the brother, but he stayed. And would remember those last days and hours with horrible vividness. Her lying there, sweat-slicked hair plastered to the mattress, face blanched, all the color having gone to the wound and the sick, hot flesh around it. And the choking stench rising off her. Like a thousand rotting pears."

He opened his eyes, blinking quickly. "And now I remember it as well. As if I'd been standing in that very sickroom with the dying slattern and the heart-wounded soldier. This, Bloodsounder does. Bombards me with memories such as these. Random, horrible, stolen memories. And these signs, this telling? That's how I know the final thing. That young Hornman, who stood by his faithless wife and watched her die, and later rode out into the grass with his greedy fat captain... he's now dead himself. Because the stolen memories only come to me after a man I've struck with the flail dies."

He stared at the flail head with equal parts hate and disgust. After a long pause, he added, "The other I killed with this grotesque little monster and its twin, in the wagon, his stolen memories have been flooding into mine already. Yesterday. Last night. This morning. But the boy's have just begun." He dropped the flail head and it clinked off the other. "And if previous experience is any measure, they won't stop. At least, not until I'm cleansed."

"Cleansed? What... how—"

He turned and regarded me, "I will either be cleansed or I won't. If it happens, it will be explained, and if not... not."

I pressed on, "And if you can't be... cleansed?"

He rattled the chains. "Difficult to say. Each time is a little different. But one thing is the same—the onslaught of stolen memories will continue. They begin to blot out my own already. How much more, I can't say. I only killed two men with the flail. It could be worse. But even two...? It will be nothing good, I tell you that. Better to be tormented by ghosts, I think. That must be easier to endure. But these memories... the most heinous grave robbing imaginable. It's as if I'd killed someone I knew intimately. I learn things about the dead their closest comrades weren't privy to, secrets and fears and dreams that should've died with them and yet live in me. And it fills me with corrosive grief."

I sat in stunned silence, completely out of questions.

He let out a long sigh and leaned forward, his usual rigid posture broken. "I can see you're struggling with this. But struggle somewhere else just now."

I didn't move right away and he shouted, "I said enough! Leave me!"

When I finally started to rise, he grabbed my wrist and squeezed tighter than a shackle. "One last thing. I've revealed something to you few enough know. Reveal it to anyone else, and I won't need Bloodsounder to tell me you're dead. Your spattered brains will be proof enough. Do you understand?"

I nodded quickly and he released me. I climbed inside, sweat coming fast, mind drowning in too many thoughts to name. Stealing memories from the dead? The stuff of dark fairy tales. What else could it be but madness? And yet… what of the bleeding scar? His foreknowledge of the approach of the Hornmen? I saw those. Didn't I? If not madness, what was it? Was he hounded by demons? Spirits? Something else?

All I knew was, an inanimate object couldn't do these things.

Could it?

I began to wonder if the endless steppe sapped a man of his wits. Maybe it was me who was going mad. Perhaps we were losing our minds in tandem.

Nearly getting impaled by a spear had been the most frightening thing I'd ever experienced. And yet, his revelation filled me with a dread far more gripping. And far less temporary.

The wind picked up again, buffeting the wagon, and I sat and listened to it howl. I'd entered the wild with a haunted, cursed, or blighted man, and I prayed I'd find my way back out again.

The next days, Braylar retreated as far away as a person can who still sits right next to you, like a snake disappearing into a hole. His eyes, when open, took no real notice of the surroundings. He closed them for long stretches, apparently trusting the horse's judgment. He paid no attention to the huge flies plaguing us, even when they landed on him. One looked ready to crawl across his eye until he absently swatted at it.

As I passed through the flap at the front and looked out, I spotted something in the distance. It looked large, though it was difficult to judge such things on those flat plains. Out of habit, I asked Braylar what it was, and why we appeared to be heading towards it, but as might be expected, if he knew the answer to either he kept them a secret.

As we got closer, I saw it was some kind of structure built entirely of sod. While it was only one story tall, it was built on three very thick tiers of sod. I wondered if the building was some kind of meeting place, and that filled me with equal parts hope and anxiety.

While the construction was crude, the building otherwise had all of the regular features—walls, windows, an open doorway. The far corner had collapsed, revealing that the walls were several feet thick. The roof also was made of large slabs of sod, and in a choice surely more whimsical than practical, the builders left the grass on top of the roof, and the old, brittle, yellow blades rubbed against each other in the breeze, producing an endless chorus of tiny clicks and clacks like a thousand miniature wood chimes.

I craned my neck to see it as we traveled past. Part of me longed to jump off the wagon, run back to the earthen hall, and scream for him to halt, to turn around, but I was sure he'd simply leave me there, and possibly not even notice my absence.

And so I moved back inside the wagon and sat down near the rear. I watched the blighted structure recede into the distance as it lost distinction and form and eventually disappeared altogether. I thought it might be the last building I ever saw.

I closed the flap and tied it shut.

⊕

The wagon battle had occurred five days prior, and just when I didn't think it was possible, things took a turn for the worse. Near midday, I was walking alongside, expecting him to stop and care for the horses, but he didn't.

I asked him why we hadn't halted, but he ignored me entirely, maintaining his maddening half-lidded stare. While the last few days he'd performed all the necessary tasks like a man nearly asleep, at least he performed them. But he had degenerated from the taciturn, cantankerous patron who brought me into the grass into a husk. I told him the horses needed to rest, to eat, but there was no response; he only sat there, back rigid, eyes locked onto the patch of grass directly ahead of us.

I wasn't sure what to do, and was weighing the wisdom or folly in trying to wrest the reins from him, when he closed his eyes and toppled over, smacking his head on the bench.

The horses took that as their cue to finally stop. I ran over to him, climbed onto the wagon. He was completely unresponsive when I shook him.

I got a flask of water, dipped the hem of my tunic in it, and pressed the cloth against his forehead and stubbly cheek, but he didn't stir. Unsure whether to move him or not, I finally decided to try, which proved more difficult than I would've imagined, as his body was completely limp, like a drunkard's. I carried/dragged him into the wagon and lay him down, with a sleeping roll propped under his head. His chest rose and fell, small shallow breaths, but that was the only sign of life. I probably could've set fire to his shoes and he wouldn't have stirred.

I had no idea how to help the captain, so I went back outside to attend to the horses. After grooming one, I checked on him again, but nothing had changed. And nothing changed the rest of the afternoon.

Dusk came on, and he might as well have been a stone effigy. Though I argued with myself before doing it, I finally lit the lantern and hung it overhead. The light coming through the horn panels bathed the interior of the wagon in a buttery glow.

I secretly hoped this blatant violation of his orders would've roused him, but there was no movement.

He was still fully clothed, and while I didn't plan on stripping him down entirely, I unwrapped the scarf from around his neck and removed his leather shoes. Neither action prompted a reaction. Trying to think of what else might make him comfortable, I looked at his weapon belts, and then pulled the long dagger free and set it on a barrel.

I reached out twice to pull Bloodsounder off the hook, but fear stopped me short. I tried a third time, but as my hand wrapped around the handle, Braylar moaned in his deep slumber, a low tortured sound, and his body spasmed until I released my hold.

While I doubted the ugly weapon was the cause of his condition, I had to acknowledge that small possibility. And if that were true, I was left to wonder if Bloodsounder could afflict others the same way it had damaged him. I had no intention of striking anyone with it, but thought that merely holding it could be enough. And that convinced me to stay my hand. I felt foolish, but better foolish than bedeviled.

I loaded the crossbow, set it within easy reach, and sat there, trying to stay alert.

And failed.

I jolted awake when a hand shook me and almost shot a bolt through the roof. I thought Braylar had finally risen, but it took me a moment to realize he was still lying there. I started to spin with the crossbow to face whoever had woken me.

Lloi grabbed the weapon and whistled. "Easy there. I like the holes I got where I got them. No need for no new ones."

I looked at her and said, rather stupidly, "Lloi?"

She smiled her gap-toothed grin. "Bookmaster." Then she looked down at Braylar, and her smile disappeared.

I set the crossbow down, and tried to explain, "We were worried, well, at least I was, that a ripper had... that you weren't coming back. What happened to you? Where have you been?"

She hunkered down next to Braylar and slapped his cheek, not altogether gently. His head shifted position, but otherwise he didn't move or respond. She asked, "How many?"

I looked at her, wondering if I were still asleep.

"Killed. With that flail of his? How many?"

"Two," I replied, and then for reasons unknown, repeated it, "two."

"About four days back? Five?"

"Yes, five days. Well, one didn't die right away. At least, Braylar—that is, Captain Killcoin—he said he didn't. That he knew he hadn't. He thought he died a day or two after the attack."

She grunted and then lifted his tunic up, looking at his belly and chest. "How long has Captain Noose been laid low?"

"He fell yesterday. Driving the wagon." I moved closer and looked over her shoulder. "What's… what's wrong with him, Lloi?"

She responded not with an answer but with another question, after looking at the two-headed flail and then back to me. "You try to take it?"

I felt like a child caught stealing, though I knew I hadn't done anything wrong.

"I was going to try to make him more comfortable, so he could rest. But…"

"But he didn't like that none, did he? Tried it, too, first time he went down like this. Actually got it off his belt, and he started screaming like I was murdering him with something hot and sharp. And he's not like to give it up more if he's awake neither."

I glanced at Bloodsounder and then back to her. As was usually the case, I felt like there was more to what she was saying than what she was saying. "The weapon warns him sometimes. Of violence. That much I get. But the cost seems high. The nausea, the wounds that aren't his, now this. Why wouldn't he just be rid of it, Lloi?"

She arched her bushy eyebrows. "Thinking you would've puzzled that clear by now. More a matter of can't than won't."

"Can't?"

"On balance, you're on the mark—that wicked thing on his belt done more harm than good. He had any choice, he'd be rid of it already, I'm thinking."

"But he… can't be rid of it?"

"Thinking we established that, bookmaster."

I sighed. "So we did. What I mean is, why? Why can't he be rid of it?"

"Wasn't with him, but heard tell he tried burying it once, figuring that was where it come from. Back to the ground, like a body you don't want nobody else to find. Him and some Nooses with him. Dropped the last dirt on top, probably without a whole lot of eulogizing, and then rode off. Didn't get real far, though."

She stopped. I waited. When she didn't continue, I started to open my mouth and she said, "Guessing you'll want to know what happened after that, too, so I'll just tell you. Crippling pain brought him down. They thought he was dying. Like to have, until they knocked their heads together long enough to figure out what to do. Rushed back, got those shovels dirty again, and brought that vicious thing back out of the earth. Seemed it didn't much like being buried like that. Captain stopped screaming when it was back in his hands."

I was about to ask something else, but she held up her nubs. "Right now, the whyfores of getting rid of it got nothing to do with us. I just got to get him through this spell."

We both looked at Braylar for a long moment and then I asked, "So you'll be able to help him, then?"

"Won't be any kind of easy. I been here right after... But two killed, and five days? Done that many, but never that long. Memoridon could manage. Least, that's what's said. But none of their kind wandering out this way. So I'll do what I can do." She laid her palm on Braylar's forehead. Quietly, and directed to the prone man on the floor, she said, "I would've been here sooner if I was able. Fact was, I was trying to lead danger the opposite way, keep you out of another scrape. But you wouldn't have it. Ordered me away. I told you you ought not to, but..." She sighed. "Now you might not never wake to hear how right I was."

I understood little and less. "I have no idea what's happening here, Lloi."

"You ever seen a man bit by a snake? Got the poison coursing through him? Now, maybe it's a pit snake, just hurts the man bad, or maybe it's a brass viper, kills him dead. Either way, you catch it early, open the wound, draw it out, that man might get better. Might not. But wait too long? Real sick or real dead. This is that, only the flail the thing done the biting, and those dead memories are the poison. Can't say how bad Captain Noose is like to get—this is the worst I seen him. But I got to get that poison out, and I got to do it now, so you step on back and let me get to draining."

I stood up. "What can I do to help?"

"Make sure I drink plenty," she said. "Water, fine, wine, better. Do that, and keep your lips locked, that'll be the rightest kind of help you can give."

I found a flask and watched as Lloi knelt next to him, her good hand on his belly, and the nubby stump on his forehead. She lowered her head until it touched his sternum, then slowly raised it, rolling and turning it side to side slightly as she began to chant something I assumed was in her native tongue, until she tilted her head back as far as it would go, chin pointing at the canvas. She did this over and over, the only small changes coming in her humming or chanting.

I sat and watched, feeling equally mystified and obtrusive, as if I were witnessing some deviant act or sacred rite meant to be private. And yet what else was I supposed to do, go outside and sit in the dark?

And so I waited and held my tongue. After a time, my eyes began closing, but Lloi's chanting, while lilting, wasn't rhythmic or repetitive enough to allow me to fall asleep. Every time I was close, the pitch or delivery changed, or a new kind of alien syllable was introduced, and my eyes opened again.

I looked over after one such occurrence, and she paused her chanting, although the strange bobbing continued, and she looked over at me and opened her mouth. I remembered her request, and started to hand her the flask, but she shook her head. She paused mid-rise long enough for me to put the flask to her lips and tip it up. She took several swallows before pulling her lips away as wine dribbled down her chin and fell on Braylar's chest.

And then she continued her ritual, with a smear of wine on her forehead after she touched down again, and I immediately thought of the large blood stain I'd hidden in the rear of the wagon.

This went on the remainder of the night, with Lloi pausing briefly on occasion to take some wine, and the chanting undergoing subtle changes, and little other variation as the hours crept by. As dawn came on, I put out the lantern and chewed some goat that was especially stringy. I offered some to Lloi, but she only looked at the flask, which I gave her. By now, we'd worked out the transfer of liquid so nothing was spilled, but Lloi's hair was sticky and matted in front from our previous slips. I patted at her with a damp cloth as best I could and settled back against the side of the wagon.

I was nodding off again when Lloi finally stopped chanting. I looked at her as she fell back against a barrel, eyes shut, face pale. She pointed her toes away from her and then rolled her sandaled feet in circles, to either work out stiff muscles or keep them from seizing up.

I asked if she wanted food or drink but she declined both. I looked at Braylar, but besides the splotches of wine on his skin, he seemed unchanged. I whispered, "What happens next?"

She pulled her legs up to her chest and laid her head on her knees. She sounded absolutely exhausted and hoarse when she finally replied, "Can't say." Then she forced herself up, legs wobbly, holding the barrel for support. "Need some rest now. He wakes, you wake me. Otherwise, you leave me be."

She disappeared through the front flap and the wagon rocked as she jumped off. A few moments later, I heard her vomiting. Even after I was sure she'd emptied her stomach, she continued to make awful clenching, heaving, sputtering noises.

I wasn't sure which was the greater oddity—a Syldoon whose Deserter-inspired weapon allegedly stole memories from the dead, or a disfigured Grass Dog who presumably drew those memories out of him like poison. Or an archivist who believed either one.

And that was the last thought I had before falling into a depthless dreamless slumber.

I woke when the wagon began moving forward, feeling so tired I was unsure whether I'd slept for mere moments or a month. I sat up and the first thing I noticed was that a prone Braylar had been replaced by a seated Lloi, facing the rear of the wagon.

I stretched and sat up as well. When she heard me, she turned and offered me her small pouch of seeds in her nubby hand, which I declined. She popped a few more in her mouth, working them open with a dexterity rodents would have admired before spitting out the shells. "Captain

Noose figured he been drifting off course long enough. Time to get rolling right and center again. Didn't bother waking you, on account of you not sleeping last night. I already told him what befell while I was riding solo, but he cautioned me to be ready to retell it again, should you have questions. Which we both figured you might, as you can't seem to help yourself. So," she offered me the seed pouch again, which I accepted this time. "Ask what you got to ask."

I wasn't sure where to begin. My questions came in a flood, "What happened to you? Where did you disappear? Were you outrunning the ripper, or—"

She held up her hands, or hand-and-a-half anyway. "Whoa, easy there, bookmaster. Nah, wasn't no ripper delayed me none. That is, I seen the feathered bastard, and followed at a real respectful distance for a fair bit. But I knew he hadn't seen the wagon. They got a real taste for horse. He seen the horses, would've been too good a meal to pass up, wagon or no. That ripper moved off in the opposite direction, so he weren't a worry no more. No, the reason I didn't come back right quick was, there was a Grass Dog party, looking for those hunters that ripper gutted. Big one, armed to the teeth. They had some outriders, doing what I been doing, and they were heading for the tracks this wagon left in the earth. They found those, that party would've run you to ground, killed you deader than dirt, no question. So I gave them a different track to follow, led them back toward the ripper trail. Tried to, anyway. They turned before they caught it, headed back to the party for the night. So I spent the next couple of days and nights laying down track after track, staying just ahead of them."

I noticed how exhausted she looked earlier, but attributed that to what-ever it was she did last night—I never considered how little she might have slept in the days leading up to it.

She said, "Couple of times, I thought they was going to hit the ruts this big rig left, and they might have, too, except I finally got them to follow me to the chariot tracks. Not sure if they ever caught that ripper. Big party like that, they probably never even seen him. By the time I got clear of them and found your trail again, took me a good while to catch up to the carnage you left behind. Thought for a flash that war party found you, but if they had, no way you would've rolled off. So that was a real mystery."

I asked, "Did you find bodies?"

She spit some husks out. "Blood, yes, bodies, no. Wouldn't have been too mysterious a mystery if I'd come across a bunch of bodies. I saw tracks, and found a few weapons, which told me it wasn't any kind of Grass Dogs you tangled with, but that was it. So I got my pony moving fast as I could until I closed the distance. Found you last night, asleep with a crossbow in your lap. The rest you know. Or not. But can't say what I can tell you that'll clear it up any."

"So... what is it you do exactly? For him, to him?"

Judging by her expression and the way her top lip puffed out as she rolled her tongue behind it, I assume a husk got jammed in the space in her teeth. A second later, it went flying out the back emphatically. I'm not sure if she was more annoyed by my line of questioning or the trapped husk.

"Real hard to put it right," she said. "Partly, because I don't know for certain. They say a Memoridon could bore you to tears piling one explanation atop another. Never met one. Probably a good thing, that. But I'll tell you this much. Men think memories are like murals or statues or objects, all stored in a huge gallery, some kind of collection that captures the truth of whatever happened, never changes none. But that ain't so. They can capture the untruth of something, just as easy. They can change, especially as time leads to time."

I said, "That doesn't really sound... accurate to me, Lloi. What can we trust if not our memories?"

She leaned forward. "Hoping you'd ask. Happens I got an example in mind for you. Let's say you're in a town, walking down a busy thoroughfare. You see a woman in front of you, comely, mannered, real nice on the eyes. You're watching the way her hips tilt this way and that, when all of a sudden, a thug cuts the pouch off her belt and takes off running down the street. She screams 'thief!' but nobody stops the wretch in time. Escapes clean. So an hour later, the city watch is asking around, wanting to know if anybody got a solid look at the man. You step forward, you were right there behind when it happened. Three other people step forward, too. And separate, you all describe what you saw. Or think you saw. Thing of it is, the city watch is awful confused, because every single one of you got something different to say. You claim the man was middle height, had brown hair, wearing a green tunic. Somebody else there says he was a tall dusty fairhair with a bluish tunic, and black boots. Another thought he was on the shorter side of things, couldn't recall the hair, but thought he had a tuft of beard on his chin, brown boots.

"See what I'm getting at? All of you would've sworn you saw what you saw, but the cutpursing happened awful quick, and your eyes were fixed on those swaying hips just before, and each of you got a different kind of perspective for the thing. Tall witness might have thought the thug was short, when he might have just been short to him, but middling to you.

"Each account could be different, when each of you saw the single thing. So your memory of the thing would feel true enough to you, but that don't mean it reflects something real. Maybe one of you in this make believe got it right, maybe none of you did. Hard to say for certain.

"To each man himself, his memories seems as solid and factual as a stone mosaic, an urn he could turn around and heft, a flower he could sniff. But when I go inside another, I don't see it or feel it like that. Everything is shimmery, shifting, like it's bathed in mist and shadow, like... like walking down the foggiest street you can think of, with everything looking not like itself at all.

"I can move down those streets, through those dusky galleries, the man with the memories might never know I was there. Even if I move something around, tweak it some, take it like a cutpurse myself, I move unseen. Like a ghost, or time." She puffed out her cheeks and exhaled. "Like I said, real hard to put words to it and have it make any sort of sense. But with Captain Noose there, it's a different thing altogether. I go into his memories, I see the same thing I see in anybody's—shady, funny around the edges, echoes where there ought to be none, things shifting right as I look at them square. Now, I go in after he killed someone dead with that flail of his, and it's... different. Those stolen memories, they don't look like his own. Oh, they're murky, sure enough, and all the rest. But they... leak. Every one of them, puddling something that might as well be poison, which is why I said as much last night. They don't belong, and I don't go in and take them out, they continue that bitter leaking until they... well, I can't say for a surety what would happen. But I got my suspicions. Captain Noose might never wake up, Or if he does, might wake a hollowed-out man, no memories of his own. Maybe none at all. Can't say."

She said this with zeal and conviction, but I wasn't certain I understood. Or believed. "So… are you saying you, uh, retrieve these memories somehow?"

"Yep. That's right," she said. "I go in, find them, take them out of him and into me, and then I destroy them. Walking into another's memories, easy enough, though I don't always know what I'm seeing there. But taking them gets trickier, and trickier still when they burn to the touch."

"Was this why you were vomiting? Why he was vomiting?"

She replied, "You're right quick. Makes you queasy something fierce, having somebody else's memories inside you, no matter how you want to picture it. Weren't meant to be there. Torques your stomach five directions at once. I could show you, you like?"

I quickly shook my head.

"Thought not." She closed her pouch. "Got nothing else to add, just now. So—"

"Lloi," I interrupted. She looked at me, tired. I didn't want to press her, but my head was still swarming with questions. "You mentioned the Memoridon. I know little about them, other than the sorts of things everyone hears. They're memory mages of some kind, right? But—"

"Can't say I like this wagon none," she cast a meaningful glance towards the front where Braylar sat unseen, "but I need some more rest, and I won't be getting none in the saddle, so wagon it is. You grab yourself something to fill your belly, bookmaster, head up on front now. Expect Captain Noose is expecting you, and if ever a man liked to wait less than him, I never met him and hope never to."

She gave me another long look, and I nodded.

My stomach was indeed rumbling, despite the talk of vomit, so I filled it as quickly as I could and rejoined Braylar.

He said nothing at first, staring straight ahead. But finally, "You know more than you should already. Be oh so careful with that. Knowledge is a often a very dangerous thing."

I had no idea how to properly respond. Who would I tell? I wasn't even sure what had really happened, so I didn't know what I could tell even if there was someone tempting offering their ear. I would surely be thought a madman. Maybe the fact I was starting to believe all of this made me one already.

Braylar handed me the flask and said, "Oh, light the lantern again without my permission and Lloi won't be the only one missing pieces." I took the flask and nodded. He added, "But thank you for keeping watch over me. You could've taken a horse and left. That would've been sensible. Most would have. So… thank you for staying."

Even if it meant getting more exchanges with threats laced with strange praise, it was good to have Braylar back from wherever he'd disappeared to.

⊕

Several hours later Lloi emerged, looking not much better, but arguing that she was ready to scout some more. Braylar was reluctant to let her go. But she pointed out that we'd already encountered more in the grass than we wanted to. And so off she went.

However, she returned sooner than expected. Hearing her approach, I hopped over the bench as Lloi reined up. Braylar looked past her to the horizon, his hand on Bloodsounder. "Report."

She rolled her head around slowly on her neck, complying only just before he was about to dress her down. "Couple of wagons. Heading in this general kind of direction, though a little more on the northerly side. Easy enough to slip around them."

Braylar stopped scanning the horizon and turned his full attention to her. "Hostile? Or accompanied by rippers, dragons, wraiths, or anything else unsavory that you might neglect to tell us about?"

She shrugged. "Not that I seen. Watched them file past before doubling back this way. Small wagons, a handful of folk on foot. Walking staffs about the only weapon I could see."

He ran his hand through his hair. "Does all of the grassland get this much traffic, or did you just pick the most popular route?"

"Can't say what they're doing out this way. Besides inviting attack, that is. But I don't see them causing trouble for no one. Still, you wanted to know what's ahead to avoid what you could, so I'm telling you what's ahead. If you want to steer clear, just redirect a bit more to—"

He held up a hand. "How much smaller are the wagons?"

Lloi took her cap off her head, spun it around on her nubby hand.

"Can't say for a certainty. Didn't creep up and measure it. Both shorter than this rig, but while one was pulled by two horse, the other was hooked onto four, so while I can't speculate as to total length, couldn't have been too poor a comparison."

He lowered his hand and nodded slowly, as if consenting to his own plan. "Lead us to them."

Lloi stopped spinning her cap. "Captain Noose?"

"You heard me."

She stood in her stirrups. "It won't be no problem to skirt around them. Won't even lose much in the way of time. We—"

"We go, Lloi. Now."

Lloi filled her cheeks with air and then exhaled long and slow. "You're the captain, captain."

"Sometimes I wonder." He pointed at the horizon. "Lead on."

She did. A few hours later, with dusk not far out, I saw a pair of wagons. Closer still, I made out people walking in front and behind, some riding on mules. All told, there appeared to be a half dozen or so. When we closed the distance enough to make out these details, the procession stopped where they were, directly in our path some distance ahead.

I'd seen many caravans in many cities, particularly Rivermost, and if this was a caravan, it was the shabbiest and most poorly protected in the known world. They also didn't comport themselves like soldiers of any kind, just as Lloi had indicated.

All those in the wagons were adults, almost evenly split male to female. They were a variety of ages, and disparate in dress. Two had simple tunics and robes, made from rough and patched linens. The others had belts and fine pouches. There was no silk or velvet or telltale signs of nobility, but it was clear servants and yeomen walked among merchants.

Braylar said "Pilgrims" under his breath with the same amount of disdain he might have used for lepers or cockroaches.

When we were about thirty feet away, Braylar pulled the reins and we came to a stop. Some of the pilgrims exchanged whispers and glances, and then a woman approached us. She was short and stout and had three chins that I counted, and her grooved face was shaded in a ridiculously wide-brimmed floppy hat. She had garters on her hose, buttons on her dress, and a lovely bag hanging from her belt. While not wealthy, she was no peasant. Probably the lady of a small household somewhere, and the others her retainers.

Lloi was riding alongside us. She pushed her shapeless hat around on her head. "Just like I said. Nobody more dangerous than a mole rat."

The woman carried herself with confidence as she approached us, a huge smile on her face. I wondered how she managed such abundant friendliness considering the grim visage of the man she was about to address, but the smile seemed genuine, if a bit oversized.

She raised an arm and waved, looked at the three of us, eyes pausing momentarily on Lloi, and then she said, "Greetings, travelers! Well met. I'm Jebaneeza, sometimes called Jebaneeza Wrong Hand." I realized then that she'd waved with her left hand. "I don't mind this address—in fact, I rather like it—so you may call me as such. If it pleases you, of course." I didn't imagine it was possible, but her smile seemed to grow as she said this, and the wrinkles deepened around her eyes.

She seemed pleasant, especially after sharing mile after silent mile with my patron; it occurred to me that under different circumstances I'm sure I would have grown to like her.

Jebaneeza waited for us to introduce ourselves. I looked at Braylar, and he was looking at everything before him—the wagon, the people standing around it, their clothing—critically, measuring, in that cold and distant way of his. I began to feel uneasy.

He looked at her. "Wrong Hand, eh? It's a shame that bynames are so often filled with malice or cruelty, yes? It's good you've come to terms with yours. How is it you find yourself traveling among the grasses?"

Her smile shrank a size or two, and her eyes didn't seem quite as merry as they had, but she kept on as if she were speaking to a long-time friend. "We're on a pilgrimage. My companions and I, that is. There's a shrine in the center of the Green Sea, devoted to—"

"This shrine of yours," Braylar leaned forward, "it's made of grass and sod, yes?"

Jebaneeza shook her head. "Oh it isn't mine. No, no. It belongs to anyone who would visit. And as for the grass, I've never seen it before, but one of my companions has, although I don't recall him commenting on the construction. Hmm. Sod. Seems a shame to construct a shrine out of sod, but I suppose there aren't many alternatives in the Green Sea, are there?"

Braylar lost none of his grimness. "There are no alternatives. And it's not the center."

She tilted her head back to get a better look at him, and I noticed her eyes were of the skyiest blue. She said, "I'm sorry, I don't quite follow you. The center?"

"Of the Green Sea. The shrine isn't in the center. We passed it only a few days back."

It took me a moment to realize what he was referring to; I hadn't considered that the ramshackle building might be a shrine, and I was surprised he'd been cognizant at all during that time.

Jebaneeza's smile returned to its unnatural size once more. "Delightful! Oh, when you asked about the sod, I assumed you hadn't seen it either. You've seen it, then? Of course you have, you just told me as much. And is it glorious then?"

Braylar smiled, neither pleasant nor attractive. "If you consider sod glorious, it is most glorious."

There was a silence that seemed to comfort none of us save Braylar, and she broke it to say, "Well. It's close then? Good. That is good. I imagined we had quite a distance yet to go." This was followed by more silence.

I thought I might retrieve her smile by saying, "It's surprisingly well put together. Considering the material. It's simple, but elegant, if a bit in disrepair."

Jebaneeza lit up again. "Lovely, just lovely. I can't wait to see it. I've meant to for many years. I've visited nearly every shrine in this area, you know. But the shrine of Cuthlan—the one in the Green Sea, I'm not sure if you knew that, but it's the shrine of Cuthlan. That's his name. Cuthlan the Lame. Ah, yes," she addressed Braylar again, "I see what you mean about nicknames. Or what was it you called it? Bynames? Bynames. Yes, they do seem mean-spirited, don't they? Or at least not very complimentary. I'd never really considered it before. But even religious figures don't seem to be spa—"

Braylar interrupted. "Have you been in the Green Sea before, Wrong Hand?"

She corrected him, "Jebaneeza Wrong Hand. Or just Jebaneeza, if it please you. 'Wrong Hand' seems, well, as I said, mean-spirited. Especially alone, like that, 'Wrong Hand.' But—"

"You've never traveled on it, yes?"

I imagine she was regretting approaching our wagon just then. "Yes. I mean no. No, I haven't traveled on it. But my companion, as I believe I mentioned earlier, my companion has. And my family hails—"

"Your companion is a fool to lead you here. Unless you have a battalion hidden in that wagon."

"Battalion? Soldiers, do you mean? No, of course not. Don't be ridiculous."

"And no weapons? Are none among you armed, or able to defend yourselves?"

"No. Why should we be? We're on a pilgrimage, as I told you."

Braylar shook his head. "The Green Sea is a dangerous place to travel. Or did your companion forget to tell you that?"

"No," she said, then amended, "that is, he mentioned that it wasn't entirely safe, of course. But he said we could travel unmolested, being on a pilgrimage. And I believe him. Our gods will protect us."

Braylar laughed his ugly laugh and said, "Then you're a bigger fool than he is, Wrong Hand."

And then he pulled his crossbow from beneath the seat and pointed it at her.

She gasped and took a step back. She looked back and forth between the crossbow and Braylar, very quickly, before blurting, "What? How dare you?"

Braylar gestured at the wagon with the crossbow before letting it drift back to her chest. "Now tell your companions to unload the wagon in the front."

"But we're pilgrims! We have nothing of value!"

"Listen to me carefully, pilgrim. I'm stealing nothing. You will unload your wagon and we will unload ours. You'll ride off in our wagon, we'll ride off in yours. You'll keep your goods, we'll keep ours. Simple, yes? Now do it."

She put her hands on her substantial hips and said, "Switch wagons? What madness is this? I'll do no such thing."

Braylar sighed. "You might have noticed, I have a crossbow pointed at your chest. Perhaps you've never seen one work before. Let me explain: If I press this trigger, it will send a bolt right through your lungs, possibly even out the other side. You'll fall in the grass, gasping. A great deal of blood will pour out of the hole. And you'll stop breathing. This, too, is very simple. Now, your fellow pilgrims might cooperate more readily if I shoot you dead, given over to terror or panic, but then again, they might not. Panic does queer things to people, and righteous wrath, worse still. Rather than cooperate, they'd probably object. And if they did, I'd probably have to shoot, bludgeon, or stab them too. Now, I have no interest in killing anyone today. But if you press the issue, I have no qualms about it either."

She sputtered, "You would… you wouldn't dare!"

I was appalled this was happening, and didn't understand why it was happening, but I had no idea how to stop it from happening either. It occurred to me, albeit briefly, that I could try to wrest the crossbow away from Braylar, but I knew that would only end with me killed in one of several ways. And so I did the only thing I could: I attempted to make this happen as bloodlessly as possible.

I told Jebaneeza, "Unfortunately, he would. He's a godless pagan, who shows no respect for anything that walks or crawls. And I doubt his short retainer on the pony is likely to take your side of things. I suggest you do as he says."

She looked at me, aghast, and said, "You seemed so polite, so mannerly. How can you be a part of this? How can you allow this, this…" she searched for the right word, "this brigand to do this?"

I didn't have a ready-made response. "He's the one with the crossbow, m'lady. Now please, do as he says. If you do, I guarantee no one will be hurt."

Of course, I had no power to guarantee anything, but she wasn't mollified anyway. "You're no better then! Not a whit! In fact—"

But Braylar didn't let her finish. "Enough. Do as I say, and you'll live to see your silly shrine. Contest me, and you won't live at all. And your people will likely follow. And maybe out of spite, I'll go back and burn that shrine to the ground and piss on it besides. So make up your mind. Now."

There was a moment when I was sure she'd attempt to stand her ground, and Braylar would have little choice but to shoot her down or leave off the peculiar idea of swapping wagons, but I suspected that no Syldoon would back down in such a situation, and especially not this one. Jebaneeza looked back and forth between Lloi and Braylar, and finally pragmatism and self-preservation won out. She shook her head, turned on her heel and walked back to her wagon.

This all seemed like a sudden fantastic dream. I had a hundred questions, but when Jebaneeza got out of earshot, I looked at Braylar and asked the most pressing one, "Would you have shot her?"

He didn't look at me, but kept the crossbow pointed at her as she began speaking to her companions in very animated fashion. "I would take no joy in it." That was the depth and breadth.

I turned to Lloi. "And you?"

She shrugged her shoulders. "Told you already. I do what needs doing. That's what I do."

Dazed before, I became angry then, saying to Braylar, "What purpose does any of this serve?"

"Perhaps you forget. We were involved in an incident several days back. Some Hornmen were killed. I imagine this knowledge has been posted at border forts across the land by now. They'll be looking for this wagon. Torn, blue canvas, spattered with blood. A spear hole in the seat. A huge bloodstain in the inside. Is it coming back to you now?" I didn't respond. "Good. So we must be rid of this rig, yes? Now is better than later."

"But this is no better than what the Hornman did to you. It's extortion, or robbery, or—"

"It is neither. They'll still have a wagon. And in fact, unless I grossly misjudge, ours is the newer of the two, and worth quite a bit more. Though, admittedly, it could use a little work."

"But the authorities are looking for this one. If they find them in—"

"Start unloading our supplies, Arki. Now. Lloi will assist you." She nodded and dismounted.

Before considering the weight of the words I said, "I want no part of this."

He laughed but his eyes didn't stray from the pilgrims. "You should have mentioned that during our first interview. Now, there are several witnesses that will happily identify you as a fellow brigand. At the very least you would lose a hand if caught. And what's more, if we don't do this thing, and the authorities, as you call them, do find us, you'll be hung. Remember why we're trying to offload this."

I objected without thinking, "But the soldiers didn't see me. They—"

"All but one. You are very forgetful. But even if he keeps his swollen lips closed, do you really believe that will save your neck? If so, you're a bigger fool than the pilgrims."

I stood up, and filled with some newfound courage, said, "I can go with them. The pilgrims. Right now. I can leave."

Lloi looked at me, her expression mostly curious.

Braylar said, "And you'd find a bolt in your back before you got halfway there. I would rather not shoot you. Truly. But that's exactly what will happen, just the same. You're the third. What more is a fourth?"

"Third?" I asked stupidly, and then compounded with, "Fourth?"

"The first archivist was killed by an arrow no doubt aimed for me. The second I killed myself. For disobedience that bore a striking resemblance to yours just now. If I must hire a fourth, I must hire a fourth. I prefer not to—it's a time-consuming process, and tedious in the extreme—but that's entirely up to you."

This chilled me, and I sat back down, lightheaded. But I didn't have long to consider the implications before he ordered me to go in the wagon and begin unloading the supplies out the back. Lloi had already walked around to the rear and pulled the gate down.

Numb and uncertain, I did as commanded.

Lloi and I worked side by side, and though she was lacking digits and was smaller and a woman besides, she moved with economy and speed and seemed to move two containers to my one. I tried not to look at her much, sure I would only say something to slink lower in her estimation. But she called me over to help her with a barrel, and as we rolled it toward the gate, she said, "Never seen Captain Noose do nothing without calculating real hard on it. This here won't be no exception." She jumped down and said, "Met the last bookmaster, in case you wondered. Traveled with him a fair bit, same as I done with you. And I got to say, it didn't split my heart none to see what happened to him. He earned what Captain Noose gave him, and more besides. Got off easy, you ask me." After I helped her hoist the barrel into the grass, she added, "You mind that tongue of yours, though. Not a one of us some priceless treasure, you understand. Hate to see you with a bolt in your ribs. Really hate to see that flail crack your skull. Just one more thing for me to clean up." She smiled and punched me in the shoulder, and then jumped back in the wagon.

Sometime later, dirty and drenched in sweat, I thought we'd finished the last of it and was leaning against the side when Lloi said, "Nuh-uh. Nearly there. One more thing yet."

I looked over my shoulder, and seeing nothing inside, said, "I'm no master of sums, but I can count to one and I don't seen a single thing in there."

She smiled again and climbed back in. "Reason for that."

I stayed on the ground, waiting for her to realize the wagon was in fact very empty, when she knelt down and began pulling at one of floorboards. I was about to remind her that Braylar ordered us only to unload the wagon, not dismantle it, when I saw her lift a panel up off the floor of the wagon. I climbed back in then and looked over her shoulder. There was a compartment hidden in the floor, and there was a long narrow box inside.

Lloi said, "Give me a hand here, bookmaster."

I helped her lift the box out of the compartment, though it was surprisingly heavy. While she was sliding the panel back in place, I said, "What is this? And why was it stowed in such secrecy?"

"You didn't think Captain Noose chose to ride clear of the roads because he got an appreciation for tall grass and butterflies, did you?"

"What's inside?"

She winked. "Told you he got his reasons, didn't I? When he sees fit to share them, I'm guessing you don't get yourself shot you'll be the next to know."

I was about to ask another question when I heard Jebaneeza. Lloi and I walked around to the front of the wagon.

She was standing before Braylar. "The wagon is empty. And now what will you do with us, you, you... brigand? That is what you are, you know? A cowardly thief, to attack defenseless pilgrims like this."

Braylar laid the crossbow across his lap. "I suggest you defend yourself on your next pilgrimage. As I said, you'll soon be on your way. Tell one of your men over there to assist my fellow brigands in loading our goods in your wagon. We'll swap horses as well. Then we'll be on our way. You'll have your two wagons, we'll have one, and we'll all happily move off in the opposite direction. Is this clear?"

Jebaneeza's eyes narrowed, and she pointed a fat finger at Braylar. "I'll report you. I hope you know that. I'll report you to the first border patrol the very first chance I get. We won't be going to the shrine, we'll be going straight to the authorities now."

"Shame about your shrine. Such a fine day for zealotry. But before you go running off to vent your outrage and cry for justice, you should know that Hornmen are already looking for this very wagon. Apparently they're under the impression that the owners are responsible for the deaths of one or two of their agents. Possibly more, I don't know. It might be a dangerous thing indeed to ride this wagon into any populated area, particularly one populated by border soldiers. In fact, were I riding in such a wagon, I'd rid myself of it as soon as possible, and by any means necessary. Such a wagon can bring nothing but ill luck. Still, it's yours now, and you can do with it what you will."

She opened her mouth to speak, closed it, shook her finger again, and then blurted, "If this is true, then you... you're a murderer and a brigand!"

He shifted the crossbow on his lap, lazily almost, so that the bolt was pointing in Jebaneeza's direction again, and said, "Now, order one of your men—and one man only—to take our supplies and load up the other wagon. My companions will assist. You can load your supplies into this one as soon as we've gone. Do you understand? Or do I perhaps need to draw a diagram in the dirt?"

Her face grew very flushed, and though her anger was neither frightening or intimidating, it was certainly bold. "You're a bully, and a thief, and a self-professed murderer! And—"

"I profess nothing."

"And when you're captured, I hope they, I hope they..." she paused, not as if she were searching for the words, but as if she knew them and were trying to hold them back. "I hope they string you up by your neck and hang you until dead! I do! Dead, dead, dead!"

Braylar raised his eyebrows. "So uncharitable, Lady Pious. Very unbecoming. Truly." He pointed the crossbow directly at her this time so there was no mistaking his intention. "Now load, before we add pilgrim slayer to the list, yes?"

She seemed more incensed than ever—I doubt righteous outrage could manifest itself more clearly than it did just then—but she was done protesting. She stomped back to her wagons, hips shaking thunderously, the folds of her skirts gathered up in one hand. If she had a tail it would've been twitching like a wet cat's.

A few minutes later one of the other pilgrims came over to begin hauling our supplies to the other wagon. He was young, and judging by his shabby clothes, a servant of some sort. When I tried to hand him a crate, he flinched as if my hand were a poker from a fire.

Lloi and I did our best to avoid him as we all loaded the other wagon, and he returned the favor, though we stumbled across each other awkwardly more than once.

The boy only had a few trips left to make, and so I returned to sit next to Braylar. After a time, he said, "Don't look so distraught, Arki. We're doing only what we have to do. Nothing more."

That was little enough consolation.

After everything was stowed to Braylar's satisfaction, we switched the team of horses, tethered the other mounts to the new wagon, and started off, leaving a very confused and angry group of pilgrims in our wake.

While the shorter pilgrim wagon had a wooden cover, the one we'd taken wasn't too dissimilar from the bloodied one we left behind. Aside from being slightly smaller, as Lloi had predicted, and badly in need of a new coat of paint, it had the same kind of canvas top, wooden ribs, a seat in front. The chief difference was this wagon didn't come equipped with a covert compartment in the floor, so the long box Braylar had secreted away earlier was now sitting among the rest of the supplies, albeit covered by a blanket. I was torn between wondering what it could contain that should have caused this criminally-inclined journey, and angry with myself for caring at all.

We traveled as far as we could before daylight gave out, and then a little further besides. I assumed Braylar wanted to put as much distance between us and the scene of his latest encounter as possible, though I didn't ask. When we finally made camp, I moved the horses off and tended to them far from his gaze, not trusting myself to hold my tongue. I slept inside, though there was less room to recline now, and Braylar and Lloi remained outside. Few words were spoken by the pair, and none by me.

The next morning, the wind picked up appreciably, and some gusts were almost violent. I dozed for a while until I felt the wagon lurch. I looked out the back flap and was startled to see we'd turned onto a road. I couldn't believe it at first. I was beginning to think I'd never see one again. But one look out the back confirmed it.

Not long after, he ordered Lloi to ride ahead, and while she argued with him, Braylar was unmoved. "As you can see, we're no longer in the grass. I hardly think we're going to get lost."

"Oh, I figure you can find your way well enough now. But that might be more cause for me to stay close. If you take my meaning."

"It's unlikely I'll be killing anyone else before we reach our destination. And if it somehow proves necessary, I'll be sure to dispatch the villains with blade or bolt, never fear."

She didn't respond, and I imagined her twisting, rolling, or otherwise contorting her silly cap again.

Braylar said, "As much as your tender worrying warms me through and through, the rest of the company is likely beginning to fret as well, given our tardiness. So I need you to advise them we'll be there shortly. Ride to the inn. Now. Without objection, interjection, or renunciation of any kind. Are we clear, Lloi?"

"No need to whip me with big words, Captain Noose. I'm riding out, I'm riding out." And so she did.

I wondered what would happen if I simply ran. Maybe Braylar wouldn't hunt me. Though I doubt he'd allow his third archivist to wander the land with such damning information on parchment. Now that I thought about it, it was surprising he hadn't killed more archivists.

Braylar called out to me, "Arki, please join me."

He sounded in good spirits indeed. What a curative, robbing and threatening pilgrims in the wilderness! I planned to suggest as much next time he fell into his invisible abyss, if Lloi didn't prove handy.

I took a seat next to him.

"I'm guessing you're guessing about our destination again, yes?"

I didn't respond right away.

"Ah, I've offended you. I'm not sure who is more to blame—you for having such delicate sensibilities or me for tearing them asunder so frequently with my indelicate action and speech."

That must be what passed for an apology among barbarians or Syldoon. Perhaps both.

"Well, we're nearing civilization once more, and you can be sure, I do my uttermost to be civil in such places. So put aside your sullen looks and bruised emotions. Or don't. As ever, the choice is your own."

✛

A quiet uneventful day and a half passed before a rider approached, and from her stiff carriage and small pony, it was obvious from some distance that it was Lloi.

She reined up in front of us, and Braylar scowled. "I believe I ordered you to wait for us with the others, did I not?"

"Others don't much like me waiting around with them, Captain Noose. Least, one in particular. Best for everyone if I waited on the road."

Braylar asked, "So, have you been there at all, then? Or did you simply decide to disobey me completely?"

"Oh, I been there." Lloi waved a fly away. "Never disobeyed you in the entirety. Not once. I let them know you was coming. Mulldoos about spit out his ale when he found out I rode ahead with you still behind. I told him I wasn't doing nothing but following orders, and even then, only reluctant-like. He asked what held you up, and when I told him what happened out here in the grass, he scalded me something fierce. Being derelict in duty, he said. I told him again, you ordered, so there I went, and if that were dereliction of some sort, then he was a cockless wet nurse. Hewspear hadn't been there, Mulldoos and me, we might have tussled a bit just then, but he was, Hewspear that is, so we didn't. But Mulldoos ordered me out of his sight, told me to tell you they'll be just behind me. So I rode back out here. And for that, I get accused of shirking this way or that too. Which, I have to say, after the abuse I suffered from that pale whoreson lieutenant of yours, ain't no kind of balm at all."

Braylar rolled his eyes. "If by some miracle visited upon me by a jestful spirit, I come to understand the half-reasoning and action of women, you'll still be a murky mystery to me, Lloi of Redsoil."

Lloi looked at me and said, "And if you can ever figure out a way of divining whether Captain Noose is paying compliment or insult, you tell me straight away, because most times, he's talking about a foot above my head."

"Lloi, you are an insufferable—" He stopped, and I feared he felt violence approaching again, and was somewhat shocked to discover I no longer doubted the flail's curse at all. I didn't understand it, but I didn't disbelieve either. But he must've only heard the horses galloping towards us an instant before I did.

Lloi pulled her hat off her head. "Didn't waste no time, did they?"

Mulldoos and Hewspear reined up first, with Vendurro and Glesswik just behind. While Mulldoos was glaring at Lloi, Vendurro whistled and said, "Never seen anybody go through wagons faster than you, Cap. Three in the last tenday? Some kind of record, that."

Glesswik patted his horse's neck. "Four."

Vendurro looked over at him. "What's that?"

"Four wagons, you dumb whoreson. Four."

Vendurro looked ready to argue, stopped himself, and then went right ahead. "The one in Rivermost, the one we outfitted with the smuggler floor, and this one here. Who's the dumb whoreson now?"

"Still you. Guessing Cap will be wanting to get rid of this one right quick. Be needing a fourth straight away. Ain't that right, Cap?"

Vendurro sighed. "You can't count wagons that don't exist or ain't been swapped yet. That's foolishness. Might as well call it ten, then, or twenty, or—"

Braylar said, "We'll be needing a fourth when we reach Alespell. That is a fact. But so long as we're counting, I count you all dumb bastards for disobeying a direct order."

Mulldoos rode alongside us, looking smug. "I'm a big enough man to admit when I'm wrong. And I got to say, couldn't have been more wrong. You didn't need us out there in the grass at all. No, not one bit. By the gods, an extra detail would've only slowed things down for no good plaguing reason. No danger at all out there in the grass. Can't say what I was thinking there."

Braylar smiled, if a little. "Very good, lieutenant, very good. Your point is well taken."

"Not quite sure what that means. But it sure can't be you'll pay more heed next time every one of your men objects to a course of action. Can't mean that, because—"

The amusement was gone. "Enough, Mulldoos." Mulldoos seemed no less smug, but he let it go as Braylar looked at his small company. "You're here now. That's all that matters. Tend to your horses. We hold for the night. Then to Alespell."

The Syldoon dismounted, all save Lloi, who decided to ride off back down the road. She never got enough of scouting or had already had too much of Mulldoos. Both seemed equally possible. Everyone launched into activities they'd clearly done thousands of times before—saddles and bridles were unfastened and dropped on the ground, helms and greaves, lamellar shirts and bazubands or bracers placed in bags to protect them from elements, horses seen to.

I helped Braylar with our normal routine, undoing the harnesses, feeding and watering the horses (we switched to flaked maize, as we were finally running low on oats, and some parsnips in strips), hobbling the horses near the wagon when we were through, brushing them, and rubbing them down with herbs that kept the worst of the biting insects at bay. When that was complete, he told me the harness leather looked dry, so my job for the remainder of the evening was to break the harness down and rub it thoroughly with neat's-foot oil.

Vendurro offered me his saddle to lean against while I worked. I thanked him, asking why he wouldn't need it.

He rolled up his sleeves and gave his toothy grin. "Worse jobs than oiling harness." Then he disappeared into the wagon and returned holding a shovel, a smaller spade, and a large sack, full of something. Vendurro tried handing the spade and sack to Glesswik, who argued that he should have the shovel and no sack instead. The pair moved off several feet into the short grass, bickering.

I leaned back against Vendurro's saddle and dipped a rag into the oil and began working it into the leather.

Hewspear was leaning against his saddle, carving away at a flute. Mulldoos was working his falchion across a whetstone in deliberate strokes, oiling as he went. Braylar was replacing some scales on his cuirass that had been damaged during the wagon attack in the Green Sea. He worked a large needle and sinew through the brass scales, connecting them to the other scales in the row and also to the leather backing.

While Glesswik and Vendurro didn't seem to know how to do anything without running commentary about how big an ass the other was, the other Syldoon went about their tasks in relative silence, with only Hewspear humming quietly. Figuring this was as good a time as any to try to get some more information, I said, "You might've guessed by now, but I'm not Anjurian. So I've never had direct dealings with your kind before, and—"

"What kind is that?" Mulldoos asked, swiping his thick blade across the whetstone. "Can't wait to hear this."

I rubbed the oil into the leather a little harder. "The Syldoon, I mean. I don't know much about you. I've only heard stories really."

"About how we eat virgins? And babies?" Mulldoos laughed, clearly enjoying my discomfort.

Vendurro stopped bickering long enough to hear the exchange and added, "Or at least our mothers. Heard that a time or two." He jammed his shovel into the ground and pushed it in deeper with his heel.

I tried again, "Well, I know you're slave soldiers, but—"

"Then you know horseshit, scribbler." Mulldoos shook his head, the blade running along the stone again with an unnerving "skiiiiit."

"I thought—"

"We all been freed," Glesswik called over, his smaller spade plunging into the earth. "Rite of manumission. Every Syldoon goes through it."

"They make it that far, they do." Mulldoos said.

Braylar added, "Agreed. It's a rough tenyear indeed."

I looked at the wrinkled leather straps, wondering if they would ever be properly saturated. "So, how does it work exactly? You were taken as slaves, and then what? What happened during the tenyear?"

Mulldoos pressed a thumb against one side of his nose and blew snot out the other. It didn't miss me by much. "Weren't taken. Given." I raised an eyebrow and he continued, "Our people gave us to them, when we were children. Been a couple of centuries since the Syldoon needed to raid for slaves."

I asked, "Why would your people do that? And what people were those exactly?"

Hewspear held his flute up to his eye and looked down its length. He shook his head, not satisfied with his work. "The hinterlands, my young friend. We all hailed from lands far from the center of the empire."

Mulldoos laughed. "Oh gods. You wanted a history lesson, scribbler, you got the right windmill for the job. This ought to be good."

Hewspear set the flute in his lap and ran his hand through his black and gray beard. "Before the Syldoon were the Syldoon, there was a king, hundreds of years ago, named Hulsinn, who ruled over lands far to the west of here, a country called Oliad. Oliad was surrounded by hostile, barbaric people. On all sides, sporadic warfare and trembling borders. But Hulsinn was clever—he knew attrition wouldn't favor Oliad—every time he turned his attention to one border, another one was overrun. So, being a far-thinker, he devised a far-reaching plan. He began raiding the camps of his enemies, stealing their children in the middle of the night, and—"

"Didn't eat any, though." Vendurro kept digging.

"—enslaving them. But he didn't waste them in the fields or in construction of gaudy monuments, as is often the case with slaves. No. He trained them. A decade of intense military instruction, a tenyear of constant propaganda. Brought in as boys from barbarian tribes—prideful, ill-mannered, already proficient in weapons and familiar with warfare, they were transformed into disciplined, merciless men who knew how to kill even more efficiently as part of a unit. And they were taught to hate their homeland. Each year Hulsinn enslaved more. And a decade later, when he deemed the first group battle-ready, he set them loose against his enemies, against their old families, their old people. Their enemies now. Hulsinn led them into battle himself. They fought like mad dogs. And his borders trembled no more."

"Riveting." Skiiiiiiiiiiit.

I considered everything Hewspear said, and then asked, "But Mulldoos said you were given as slaves. Raiding wasn't necessary any more. I still don't understand why parents would give up their children to their overlords so willingly."

"Like I said," skiiiiiiiiiit, "you know horseshit. Where you from, boy? By the coloring, I'd say Vulmyria. Maybe Urvace, am I right?"

I had no idea what my father looked like, but I'd clearly inherited the fair skin and hair from my mother anyway, which did little enough to disguise blushes of any kind. "I was born in a road inn, if you must know, but it was on the border of Vulmyria, yes."

He stopped sharpening and laughed. "Bastard boy, I'm guessing." I colored up worse as he continued. "Got nothing against bastards—no worse or better than most, on the whole—but uppity provincial bastards who think they know something when they know shit all... well, that's altogether different, ain't it? So I'm curious, where do you get off telling us what we're about when you got no experience on the subject?"

Braylar pricked his finger and sucked at the blood before saying, "In fairness, Lieutenant, our good scholar was asking questions, not making proclamations." He turned to me. "To a parent in the hinterlands, plagued by constant warfare with other tribes or clans, often scraping and scrapping to simply survive another day, this was an opportunity that would never occur otherwise. They hoped their sons and daughters would become rich or powerful after they were freed. And as time passed, they began to see it as an honor if their children were chosen when the recruiters made their annual visit, and from this uneasy understanding, established the tradition of holding Choosings.

"Make no mistake, the children still enter slavery of a sort—they'll have no choices for the next ten years, and their days will be spent in obedience. But they're also not slaves in the typical sense of the word. In many parts of this world, a slave is a creature who is choiceless, but futureless as well. They tend a field, or mine the earth, or pull the galley oar, and that is what they'll die doing. Even the best-off of them, they clean their master's teeth and ears, wash the dirt and shit from their smallclothes, perhaps serve as objects of pleasure, and they'll die doing that as well. There's no movement for a slave. They begin and end their lives in the exact same spot.

"But Syldoon slaves are different creatures. For the ten years after they're chosen, they have neither voice nor choice, but they don't do the same thing endlessly. Oh, they do their fair share of physical labor, mucking stables, scrubbing pots, butchering hogs, carrying wood and stone—"

"Cleaning latrines, shining officer's boot, digging holes, always digging more holes..." Vendurro offered as he leveraged a large chunk of earth out of the ground and moved it to the side.

"But they're also trained," Braylar continued, "and trained and trained. They drill with every weapon imaginable. They sit in classes, learning to read and write, and later, learning new languages, military history, and tactics. Figures and sums as well, the names of the constellations, the sciences of the masters, the proper way to bandage a wound and the poultice to apply to keep it from festering. How to groom a horse and compose a sonnet. The language of blazonry and the art of sculpting and painting. In short, their education is broad, and wildly diverse."

"But a shovel ain't never too far away," Glesswik added, grunting as he worked a chunk of sod out as well, making the hole larger.

"True enough," Braylar said, needle moving again. "But several years later, after they've been exposed to every field of study, their teachers and instructors evaluate them and decide the direction their lives will take for the remainder of their days as Syldoon slaves. Those who show promise with mathematics will be trained as military engineers, and tacticians. Those who display a knack for riding and an affinity for horses will train as cavalry. Those with languages and a good memory for nomenclature, to diplomacy. And so on, each slave being tracked into those avenues they show the most aptitude for. Regardless of what track they take, all of them will continue with their military drilling, as all of them are ultimately soldiers, serving the soldiering class.

"Still no choices. They are well-trained and well-groomed slaves, to be sure, but slaves nonetheless. It's only at the end of their training, a decade later, that they'll have their first moment of autonomy. They're freed in a grand ceremony, and upon the day of their manumission, also free to decide whether they wish to stay or go. It's a choice that can never be undone. Whether they walk or stay, they pledge their lives to that movement forever.

"If the newly freed Syldoon stay, they're a part of their household until they die, and swear loyalty to it above all other things. They're bound to their household, and will serve it and no other until the end of their days. If that household flourishes, they flourish with it. Should it wilt, or be destroyed by another, their fate will be the same."

"So," Hewspear said, his small knife working again on the flute, "the tribes give up some of their children, because if they're chosen by a powerful Syldoon Tower, they might very well grow to be rich and powerful. And while the Syldoon are forbidden from returning to their homelands, their generosity isn't. Very often, some of that good fortune finds its way back to the tribe."

Vendurro was breathing heavier as jabbed his blade into the ground. "You didn't mention the Memoridon, Cap. Kind of important, that. That ceremony—"

Braylar said, "I believe we've regaled our archivist with enough of our history for now.

"Are you fine diggers nearly through? Our archivist has been pining for a fire for many days."

Glesswik pulled up another large swath of earth. While the grass was shorter than in the Green Sea, the roots seemed just as dense; the chunks of sod were coming up in large squares and rectangles. He upended the sack he'd taken from the wagon, and dumped a number of roughly oval-shaped things onto the grass next to the hole. "Wasn't much in the way of wood around these parts, Cap, but Lloi thought these might come in handy. Left them before riding out. You'll have to pardon the stink though." He began breaking open the ovals and stuffing them with tufts of dry grass.

It took me a minute to recognize Lloi's gift for what it was. Rooter dung.

Mulldoos must have reached that conclusion at the same time and finally stopped sharpening. "By the gods, she's an awful whore, she is. Plagues me even when she's not plaguing here."

Ven was taking the strips of earth they'd dug up and lining them around the perimeter of the hole, with the dirt and roots facing where the fire would be. He said, "Told you there's worse things than working some leather over." Then he laughed and tipped his head in Glesswik's direction.

Gless was bent over, stuffing more of the rooter dung with grass, but he caught the gesture. "Don't think I'm doing this alone, you skinny whore-son. Plenty of shit to go around."

Braylar turned to me. "You shall have a bit of warmth at last, Arki. Though it's actually a blessing no one's had time to hunt anything. Cooking over a shitfire is several kinds of unpleasant."

I sighed and kept after the harness, supposing that shitfire was better than no fire at all. As it turned out, that might have been a specious proposition.

We continued the last leg to Alespell in the morning, and the remainder of the journey passed without incident. We overtook a pair of men on foot that moved far off the road and into the grass to get out of our path and avoid our dust as much as possible. A short time later, we encountered a deserted village, separated from the road by some fields that once had presumably been tilled but now had grown practically wild again. Only a mossy stone wall gave some indication of its boundary. There were a few beaten and ramshackle windmills along the perimeter, one that couldn't possibly lean any further without falling over completely. While several communities have recovered from the last plague, this obviously wasn't one of them.

But after that, the villages were prosperous, and busy, and the closer we got to Alespell, the more crowded the road got, with traffic increasing every time we passed another small community.

Besides being more populated, I noticed the countryside was changing in other ways as well. Shorter, scrubby blades replaced the tall, thin grass, and there were more clusters of trees, too, and not all of them short and squat. The land began to roll, gently at first, and with every mile closer to Alespell, becoming hillier and hillier. Nothing too rugged, but compared to the flat vastness of the steppe, it felt like we rolled over mountains.

As we crested such a hill, I suddenly saw Alespell laid out before me, and it was surely something to widen the eyes. Rivermost was fairly large—a walled city with a teeming population, a castle, a university— and originally hailing from a hamlet, and bouncing between small cities after university, I experienced some amazement when I first arrived there. But Alespell made Rivermost seem like a tiny, provincial trading outpost by comparison.

The bulk of the city was situated along the eastern bank of the broad River Debt, with a wet moat or canal around the entire perimeter, but there was another section I assumed was added later as the city prospered, on its western bank, and again a canal had been dug around the circumference and served as a very wide moat.

Both sections had crenellated curtain walls built out of snowstone that were the hugest I'd ever seen, at least forty feet tall, and strengthened by too many semi-circular bastions and flanking towers to count. On the far eastern side of the city, an impressive castle rose up above everything else on a massive granite outcrop.

We headed towards the western gate. Before we reached it, we passed buildings on both sides of the road. To the right, a small walled compound. Braylar anticipated my inquiry. "A Hornmen stronghold. And a hospital."

Vendurro said, "You want to stop and hoist a mug or three there, Cap? Seems you and them get on real well."

Braylar ignored him and snapped the reins. On our left, on a small hill above the river, there was another large walled enclosure, with several copper domes visible above. Braylar said, "The Plum Temple." I expected more, but he left it at that.

I said, "That seems to be impressive fortification for a temple."

He raised one eyebrow as he appraised the temple and then me. "Some priests need more protection than others. If Lloi were here riding alongside, I'm sure she would be spitting in its general direction just now."

Glesswik added, "Or barking curses in Dog."

I looked up at the domes again, the metal a mottled green, then back to Braylar. "Why would—?"

But he'd anticipated my question. "I believe Lloi informed you that she and I met in a whorehouse, yes?"

I nodded and he said, "Well, she belonged to a silk station. One we frequented regularly, as it was en route to another barony we were operating in. While they had whores for a variety of tastes, and mine ran to the refined—"

"Leastwise, not the disfigured," Mulldoos offered.

"You couldn't help but notice everyone in the silk station, one time or another. Coarse or smooth, fingered or fingerless. So I'd seen Lloi, and between her demeanor, her mouth, and her other oddities, she certainly stood out. One particular occasion, I noticed an underpriest of Truth leaving her quarters. This struck me as odd."

"That a priest would have… appetites?"

"No, priests are only men, no matter what they say. But this one was well dressed and composed, and could've afforded any girl there. I was curious why he chose Lloi. After he departed, I asked the whoremaster. He was reluctant at first, but plied with coin, he admitted that the underpriest had interviewed her, nothing more. I asked for more details, which called for more coin. As it turned out, the underpriest wasn't there for himself at all."

Hewspear had ridden close enough to hear the conversation and said, "It seemed High Priest Henlester had been acting most unpriestly."

Braylar tilted his head. "Or exceedingly priestly, depending on what sort of clerics you consort with. The underpriest was there to broker broken flesh for his master, Henlester. Though Lloi wasn't quite down to his standards."

I wasn't sure what that meant and asked for clarification, which Mulldoos provided, unfortunately. "Missing fingers only got him salivating. Seems Henlester liked his whores good and mutilated. One eye plucked out, good; both, better. Lopped off limbs, burnt faces, those got him really stiffpricked. Lloi just wasn't damaged enough. Good thing, for him anyway. She probably would've bit his prick clean off."

I tried to remove that image from my mind as quickly as possible as I said to Braylar, "But I'm still confused as to how she came to be in your company."

He replied, "After I learned of her interview with the underpriest, I wanted to speak with her myself. The whoremaster wasn't keen on this idea, but—" He patted Bloodsounder, "I can be quite persuasive."

Mulldoos said, "Coin only goes so far."

"So, having gained an audience with said stumpy, nubby whore, I began to press for her for more details about her conversation with the underpriest."

I asked, "Why?" Braylar raised an eyebrow at the interruption and threw a scowl my way. "That is, why were you interested, if you don't mind my asking?"

"I do," Braylar replied as we rolled past the Plum Temple. "I will tell you only this—the debaucherous High Priest was someone we were already interested in, for reasons that need not concern you just now. So, I spoke with her, and learned that she'd been close to another whore who'd recently been procured from the silk station by the underpriest. According to Lloi, the prostitutes Henlester took an interest in didn't meet a happy end. Satisfied with the information I had, I rose to leave. But I didn't make it to the door."

I asked the obvious question. "Why not?"

Mulldoos interjected before Braylar could respond. "Cap forgot to mention something on the important side. He was light in the company just then. And he'd done some bloody persuading a few days prior."

It took me a moment before piecing it together. "So, you used Blood-sounder and had no one who could… tend to you?"

Mulldoos whistled, "Came by that all on your lonesome, did you?"

"That's correct," Braylar said. "The effects were becoming worse. I stumbled and barely made it to the bed, my head bursting with bright lights, my stomach tearing in two. Lloi knelt next to me. I ordered her to fetch the whoremaster, but she ignored me. She looked me up and down, in that very disconcerting way she has. I'd had minor episodes before, but this was something far worse. I was paralyzed with pain, and blacked out. I don't know how long I was out, but when I was fully aware again, the pain was gone, and Lloi was slumped in the corner, vomit on her chin. I wasn't sure what she'd done, or how she'd done it, but I knew she had to come with me."

"So," I said, "You bought her. Freed her from the station."

"I did. Immediately."

Mulldoos must have seen the disappointment on my face. "You think-ing he did it out of the sunny goodness in his heart, were you?" He laughed, shaking his head. "No whetstone in the world'll fix that for you." He flicked his reins and rode further ahead. Traveling with the Syldoon would surely scour away any naïve or romantic notions I might have once possessed.

As we approached the first gate tower, we slowed down, and then stopped repeatedly, as all of the traffic on our side of the river funneled through two entryways, one narrow to accommodate those on foot, horse, or don-key, and another wide, for those with carts and wagons. It was midday, so there appeared to be an equal number of people leaving and entering the city, shouldering past each other, swearing about being swindled, chatter-ing with excitement about seeing things and people from far-flung lands.

A group of musicians passed us on foot heading away from Alespell, one with two small drums on a belt at his waist, another bearing a lute on his back, one with a fiddle, and another with a long bone pipe. One member didn't have any instruments, but the arms of Baron Brune were embroidered on his tabard, three white swans on a purple field.

I'd seen a fair crier before, but never a whole musical ensemble. I said as much, and Glesswik echoed the sentiment, though more crudely. "Scribe's got it right there. Dirty rustics don't give a rat's shithole about a bunch of pretty troubadours. They come to the fair on account of three things: cheap wine, cheaper whores, and the chance to be layabouts instead of tilling some field. Nothing more, nothing less."

Vendurro replied, "You forgot dice, weird beasts in cages, and maybe a hung thief or three, for entertainment."

"Still don't need songs for any of that. That's all I'm getting at. Baron would've been better served with some signs tacked up with a picture of a whore's cunt and an arrow pointing this way."

Perhaps being raised by a loose mother with a mercenary bent made me more sensitive to the topic than most. Or it could be that soldiers were so fixated on the subject and discussed it with such vulgarity that anyone not of their ilk was offended. Either way, I wished I'd held my tongue.

We entered the first gate and crossed a wooden bridge that led over the slow-moving water. A drawbridge was down on the other side, and we entered a larger barbican in the middle of the canal. Across an open enclosure in the barbican, and onto a covered stone bridge, horseshoes and iron-rimmed wagon wheels rang loudly. While there are some small square windows in the walls, it might as well have been a cave for all the light it really afforded, and traffic nearly stopped as everyone's eyes adjusted and people bumped and jostled.

Finally, after another gatehouse, we emerged into the western suburb of Alespell, which was itself bigger than most cities. The majority of the buildings were timber or wattle and daub, but there were a fair num-ber constructed of snowstone as well, and these were almost universally roofed in tiles a dusky wine color. I assumed those were the homes of the wealthier burghers in the city. Mosaics appeared on the walls of wood or stone, some depicting animals, people, or recognizable objects, others more abstract patterns. But on practically every surface, there was either a single bar made of enameled squares, or two running parallel. When one bar, it was a color that seemed to alternate depending on what sector of the city you were in, and where there were two, the higher one was always purple.

Braylar said, "The single or lower bar designates districts. As to the other, you'll quickly notice that some wild drunkard designed the layout of Alespell, which might account for the name. Streets run in every direction, crisscrossing at strange angles at every pass. The purple bar, if you happen to luck into finding it, tells you that you're headed towards either the castle or a gate."

Hewspear and Mulldoos had fallen back alongside us and Hewspear said, "And if you look up, you'll note another clue that you're on your way to meet the good baron."

I glanced up and saw that on this street, in addition to the parallel enamel bars, there were also chains strung between the buildings on either side, and hanging from these, large copper pots filled with broad-petaled purple flowers.

Mulldoos said, "Got a real stiffprick for the purples, don't he?"

"Bet it comes in handy though," Vendurro added, "when you're stumbling around drunk-blind, trying to find something to guide you."

"That's what we got you for."

The western suburb seemed to be mostly residential buildings, with the occasional small temple breaking them up. Like any city, some of the construction was more in need of repair, but I noticed a walled section off another street heading south that seemed particularly blighted and crumbling. It hadn't been whitewashed in ages, maybe ever; the snowstone had turned an ugly yellow.

I asked Braylar, "Who lives in that quarter?"

"Grass Dogs who have been... domesticated. Those are the kennels. You'll find them in some cities on the shore of the Green Sea, but especially the larger ones like Alespell. Home to a mixture, really. Refugees from clan warfare. Families of the Dogs who smelled a finer life outside of the Sea, and entered the kingdom's service as auxiliary soldiers."

"It doesn't look like the Grass Dogs are very welcome in Alespell."

"You're correct," he said. "They aren't entirely trusted. Or wanted. Which is why they're housed in these walled alienages even lepers would find insulting. The baronies might make use of Dogs on occasion, or tolerate their presence, but they don't encourage it."

Hewspear, riding alongside, added, "And those that leave the Sea can never return. They're equally reviled by their former clans and the baronial folk they live amongst. So whether here by choice or cruel necessity, it's a most unpleasant place to be. If Lloi were among us now, you'd hear a long, clumsy diatribe about the kennels."

We came to another gate flanked by two massive machiolated drum towers. There was another lengthy delay and it took me a moment to understand why. A pair of guards collected a fair tax from everyone approaching the gate.

Braylar handed his coins to a sweat-stained guard and then we were finally through. Passing underneath the gate, we found ourselves on another wide bridge, this time crossing the slow-moving River Debt. There were huge statues of armored men on either side of the bridge, rising high above us and looking decidedly stern, each holding a tall staff with a standard fixed on top, snapping in the breeze. Every major fiefdom in the kingdom seemed to be represented.

I overheard Hewspear and Mulldoos arguing and leaned forward to make out the conversation. "No place is impregnable," Mulldoos said, "that's all I'm saying. It could be done."

"Very little is impossible, it's true. But I've yet to hear how you would accomplish this impressive feat of siegecraft. Please, do explain."

"Like I said, no direct assault. Too costly."

"Agreed. And you would have no luck mining, the river is too deep."

"True enough. Maybe not the canal, though, round the other side."

"Perhaps not—I haven't measured it," Hewspear said. "But I suspect the architect took that into account. Let's assume it's sufficiently deep to prohibit tunneling. What does that leave you? Certainly not starvation. No besieging force could hope to outlast the stores here, or provisions brought up river, or—"

Mulldoos shook his head. "What dumb horsecunt of a besieger is going to let a flatboat of grain glide in unmolested? Not me."

"Surely not. You're as clever a horsecunt as they come. But you've also seen the silos and warehouses here—do you suspect they're merely for show?"

"Listen, you wrinkled goat, I'm telling you…"

They rode ahead, and I noticed the numerous stalls on either side of the bridge, situated between the statues. Some were larger than others, but most were wooden-framed with canvas sides and tops. At every one, a merchants called out his wares… hairpins of ivory, brooches of brass, and badges of the finest pewter; plaque belts both simple and wildly adorned by precious stones and metals; pattens made from a variety of wood;

aromatic fruit, both common and alien; charred meats, boiled eggs, and ruddy-looking cheeses; dice allegedly carved from the tusks of creatures so rare they haven't even appeared in bestiaries yet; hoods of every color managed by dye; brass braziers and tooled chests; leather bottles, costrels, and tankards; weak ale and watery wine to fill them, despite the threat of wandering guildmasters and inspectors who would confiscate such swill.

Guards were stationed at several spots along the bridge to keep traffic moving and discourage theft. I suspected they were having trouble with both. When we finally left the Bridge of Heroes, it was a relief, though Alespell proper was no less crowded.

We approached an open plaza, and it was obvious people from every station and kingdom milled about, as the myriad of languages and dress was overwhelming. Peasants in undyed homespun walked next to Hornmen and fieflords with rich coats and long tunics trimmed with ermine, marten, fox, and squirrel, all mingling casually in the one place that it was natural for forty days a year. On foot, on horse, on donkey, here to sell a hen, buy a fabulous bolt of silk, cajole, bargain, gamble, accuse, drink, and gawk.

While there were a staggering number of stalls around the perimeter of the plaza, most larger than those on the bridge, there were also a few permanent structures. The moneychangers' hall was on the opposite side, bustling as expected, and the spice halls were there as well, the merchants who occupied them guarded by their own private contingents of armed men. Everywhere you looked, smelled, or listened, there was a chaotic jumble of sensations. A man chasing a runaway goose nearly got run over by our wagon. A boy with a dead gull tied to a string ran between horses' hooves, two scrawny cats hot on his heels. Men and women carried bawling children on their shoulders to keep them out of the press of humanity, and there was the pervasive stench of sweat and closeness, as many of the fairgoers had obviously not visited the renowned Alespell baths. Sheep bleated in apparent protest as they were driven around a gurgling fountain in the center of the plaza. Gulls wheeled overheard, looking to dive should any food hit the ground that wasn't immediately swallowed up by the dogs skulking between stalls. Hot pie carts were ubiquitous, and the smells of meat and crumbly crust were nearly as powerful as the vendors' cries.

Left to my own devices, I would have wandered the plazas and market-places for days on end, observing my fill, but we turned down a smaller street before I had a chance to even begin to take it all in. I was disappointed, but there were still a dozen days left of the fair, so I was sure I'd get my opportunity soon enough.

With three- and four-story buildings everywhere, crowded so close they practically blocked out the sky, and the streets turning every direction, it really was a warren. I doubted the enamel bars would do much good in guiding me if I was on my own and lost.

It was nearly dusk when we stopped in front of a three-story inn. A large hanging sign had been newly painted, no doubt for the Great Fair: a pair of legs, with a dog laying across the boots with its head down.

Braylar said, "The Grieving Dog. Granted, it doesn't have the cantankerous innkeep, bashful wench, or horrible ale of the Three Casks, but it will have to do."

We headed down a small alley, and when we rounded a corner I saw a stable yard much like the Three Casks', though bigger, patrolled by a number of grooms and stable boys. As Braylar jumped down and the others dismounted, there was a swarm of activity—coins passing hands, grooms taking reins, quick questions exchanged, boys running to the wagon to begin unloading supplies.

Finally, real civilization again.

After I gathered my case, supplies, and meager belongings and climbed off the wagon, Braylar told Glesswik and Vendurro, "See to it that the package makes its way to my room. Then tell the rest of the men I've returned. We'll be back in action shortly."

Vendurro started to salute but Glesswik hit him in the arm and they disappeared behind the wagon, cursing each other.

Thunder rumbled close, as if a giant hopped across the rooftops, and I instinctively began to cover my writing case and supplies. A moment later, the first tentative drops of rain began to fall. Hewspear pointed to an entrance to the Grieving Dog. "Shelter, sweet shelter."

Inside, the layout was similar to a thousand other inns across the land, though all of the furniture and trappings were of finer quality. There was a large tapestry hanging above the bar that depicted women in various states of undress stomping grapes in a huge basin.

There was a woman behind the bar as well as above it, though she didn't look the type to cavort among grapes. Braylar leaned in close and said, "There are many who curse the plague, but women who survived aren't among them. There are far more jobs than men can do."

She was on the pillowy side, but still comely, even in her middle years. I wondered if it was a father or husband who died and left her the inn. As we approached, she recognized Braylar. "Welcome back, my lord. Your suite is the same as you left it. Minus that tray of bones. I took care to have those removed." This came out as a warm rebuke, as from a slightly exasperated but bemused mother.

"You ought to take more care with your patron's possessions, Gremete. Who's to say I didn't have a particular fondness for those bones? Perhaps I'd even been pining for them."

"You can do almost anything you like under my roof, so long as you don't attract vermin."

Mulldoos said, "You should have thought of that before you let us in the door."

She inspected the rim of a mug. "So long as you don't multiply." Then she looked up. "Your men have the keys. I've ordered some hot water for baths I'm awful hopeful you'll take. And someone will be by to see you get something with new bones in it." There was a brief smile and she returned to work.

I followed the group up some stairs. At the top, we headed down a hall and Braylar knocked on a door. A moment later, the lock was undone and we entered a fairly large common room that had four doors in it, leading to separate sleeping quarters. Vendurro shut the door behind us and handed Braylar some keys.

Braylar pointed me towards a door. "That room is yours. Lloi has been here already, so there should be a tub in there waiting for you, as Gremete said. Food will follow. After that you, Hew, and I have a visit with... an old friend."

He didn't volunteer any more information, and I resisted the urge to ask, knowing it would only lead to frustration. I entered my room, and there was a wooden tub as promised, water still steaming, next to a bed and table.

Setting my supplies down, I heard some laughter outside and walked over to the window. My room overlooked a large courtyard that shared a wall with the stable yard, and it was filled with dozens of oak trees, under which were a multitude of long tables, many still occupied by carousers largely protected from the rain.

There was more laughter and some singing. It wouldn't be the quietest room, but after our long trek through the empty steppe, it felt good to be in a crowded city again.

After a long soak, I headed towards the common quarters. The smell of food hit me even before I opened my door. The Syldoon were sitting around the table, plates laden with roast grouse, thick cheese, dark bread, and pitchers of ale.

I took a seat on a bench between Vendurro and Glesswik. Hewspear, Vendurro, and Mulldoos were arguing about who made the finest helmets, Glesswik had so much food in his mouth he couldn't have spoken to anyone, and Braylar was silent.

The grouse smelled so good my fingers were shaking as I filled my plate. It seemed like months ago that I'd last eaten a proper meal.

After sampling some of everything, and washing it down with ale four times as good as what the Canker served in Rivermost, I waited until there was a good break in the conversation before asking Braylar about something that I'd been wondering about for some time. My chances of being bludgeoned to death were likely smaller since returning from the grassland. "At the Three Casks, when that Hornman tried to run you through, you dodged it without seeing what was coming. I thought at the time you must have heard the sword clear the scabbard, or maybe caught a glimpse of something, or maybe even just been lucky, But that wasn't it, was it? You felt something then, too, didn't you? Just like you did before the Hornmen appeared in the steppe."

Vendurro hit me in the arm with the back of his hand. "Told you there was something unnatural-like going on with that wicked flail, didn't I?

Well, I didn't really, because Mulldoos was near enough to cutting my throat for even hinting at it. Couldn't say much at all. But now you see what I meant, don't you? I been riding with the Cap for some time before anyone thought to share anything about it with me. Lot longer than you. Count yourself lucky. Or unlucky. Depending on how you count. But don't look to me for help on that score. I can't even count wagons, can I Gless?" He laughed, and I found myself doing the same. And it felt good. Surprisingly good.

Hewspear nodded his approval as he pulled some blackened skin off his grouse. "You picked a sharp one, Captain."

Braylar only gave the briefest of twitch-smiles, but that was confirmation enough.

I continued, "You obviously got a warning of sorts in the grass, before those other Hornmen came to rob us. You knew how many there would be, and that they meant us harm. But I'm still confused about something. Back at the Casks, you woke me, and said you knew something was coming. Violence. You knew violence was coming. And assumed it would involve you. But it didn't. Could you, or someone," I looked at the other Syldoon, "please explain that?"

No one else jumped into the fray so Braylar finally drank and cleared his throat. "The warnings… they're like dreams, sometimes only slivers of dreams. A fleeting image, a half-felt feeling. My stomach will suddenly churn, my skin will grow hot. Sometimes I'll taste blood in my mouth where there is none, or hear a scream when no sound has been uttered. Sometimes I'll smell the shit that soils a man's hosen as he dies, or feel the rush of an arrow past my cheek when none was shot. Phantom images, sensations. Such was the case at the Casks. I saw a pool of blood on that very table, though who it belonged to, I couldn't say.

"Other times, more rarely, everything coalesces—image, sound, all the senses, and it becomes clear what I'm seeing is a memory, before it's made, a memory from someone immersed in this violence. Me, someone else, someone who dies, someone who lives. And if this… advance memory is sharp enough, it sometimes serves as a warning. These flashes of violence I see before they occur, they've saved my life several times, and on occasion, my entire company as well."

Hewspear raised a mug of ale in toast. "Truer words never spoken."

"But they can be suspect too," Braylar added. "There have been times I felt sure something was going to play out a certain way, and was proven wrong, almost to my ruin. But if you consult your notes rather than your memory, you'll find that that night at the Three Casks, I didn't say we were the targets, or that we were involved at all. I feared as much. Wide difference. But even when I believe I know what will happen for certes, I'll rarely say as much. Because the warnings deceive. Just as they deceived me that night."

I thought about that as I nibbled at some cheese—it was crumbly, with red veins that hinted at some obscure spice, and actually much better than I would've expected. Washing it down, I asked Braylar, "When the soldier rode past and threw the spear at you. You stayed on the bench, didn't move or dodge, until it was almost too late. It was amazing, really. Was that another instance Bloodsounder gave you warning?"

Braylar's mouth curved ever so slightly. "Do you find it so hard to believe that I possess some modicum of unassisted martial prowess?"

The Syldoon laughed, and I said, "But that isn't really an answer."

Vendurro wiped some grease off his chin with the back of his hand. "Like to be the only kind you get. Best get used to it."

Braylar's smile grew a touch, though was no less enigmatic, as he chose not to elaborate. I tried a different tack, "I've been thinking about something else that came up at the Casks. Mulldoos said your emperor insisted you have a chronicler. And in the grass, Captain Killcoin told me that I wasn't the first."

Mulldoos tore off some meat and laughed. "Waited until you had him in the middle of nowhere for the big reveal, eh, Cap? You're a cruel and clever bastard, you are."

I ignored him. "Why exactly was it mandated? Make no mistake, I'm grateful to have the work, but I'm wondering why your company needs an official account."

No one responded right away. Everyone looked at Braylar for a cue or permission. He nodded at Hewspear who said, "The empire is made up of countless factions, large and small. And we are always conspiring against each other. So every emperor knows that it's not a question of if a coup will happen, but when."

Mulldoos burped. "Jumpy as cats, our emperors.'"

Hewspear continued, "So Emperor Cynead decided to institute the policy that there must be a record of each company's activities. Especially those so far from home." He indicated the room with a wave of his hand.

"And let me guess. Your faction—your Tower—they're not huge supporters of Emperor Cynead."

Hewspear tapped the side of his nose with a long finger. "Our Tower supported the previous emperor, Thumarr. Now deposed these five years. It wouldn't be a stretch to say we bear more scrutiny than most."

I weighed all that for a moment and then said, "So he orders an accounting, but he trusts men he doesn't trust at all to keep a faithful account? I could record whatever Captain Killcoin told me to record. Who's to say it's accurate at all? Again, I'm glad to have a patron, and payment, but why wouldn't the emperor appoint his own chronicler to ensure the auditing was faithful?"

Mulldoos shook his head as he threw a bone on his plate. "There's that dull edge again."

I didn't understand.

Rooting around in his ear with a greasy finger, Glesswik volunteered, "He did."

I still didn't understand.

Hewspear added, "The first chronicler was appointed, Arki."

At last things fell into place, like tumblers in a lock, but that just brought up more questions. The kind that made my stomach twist. "The first one, the appointed one—"

Mulldoos drew a finger across his throat and laughed like it was the funniest gesture in the world, and I continued, fumbling the words, "If you head home, if you're recalled, and me with you, won't the emperor, that is, he'll know your chronicler... he'll know I wasn't the one he assigned, won't he?"

Mulldoos shrugged. "Wasn't all that hard finding two stringy scribblers that looked alike. Three was a bit tougher—you're a touch shorter than the rest, with a bigger nose—but..." He shrugged his shoulders.

My position seemed even more precarious than it had even a few moments ago, and seeing that expression on my face, Hewspear said, "It was a clerk who did the actual appointing. Several years ago now. Clerks change. Records get lost. Time passes. And—"

"And," Braylar interrupted, "we haven't been recalled in any event. We still have much to accomplish in this region. Do your job. Do it well. The rest will take care of itself. We start now." He rose and said, "You and Hewspear accompany me. The rest of you can do what you like with your hours. Drink, dice, what have you. Only don't tussle with the city watch, don't draw attention to yourself, and don't spill any blood."

Vendurro shook his head, "So, lock ourselves in our rooms is what you're saying?"

"The next few days are critical to our success here. Best remember that." He and Hewspear started towards the door and I stuffed some bread in my mouth, took a final swallow of beer, and hurried to follow. We headed down the stairs and made our way through the crowd on the lower floor of the Grieving Dog. Lloi, as usual, was off doing something at the behest of Braylar.

We stepped out into the rain. If we were anywhere but Alespell during the Great Fair, it would've convinced most travelers to stay indoors, as it was coming down as hard and fast as nails. But the main thoroughfare was almost as crowded as the inn, and would probably become even more congested until curfew was finally called throughout the fortified city.

Braylar pulled his scarf tighter around his neck and, looking up at the sky, said, "Bad night for crossbows."

"Bad night for crossbows," Hewspear agreed, pulling his hood up.

I pulled my hands into my sleeves and said, "Bad night for almost anything, except sitting in front of a fire with some mulled wine. Why aren't we doing that?" The pair ignored me as they pressed through the people in front of us.

The baron's castle was vaguely visible against the night sky, but lanterns and a few lit windows along its towers and walls created fuzzy halos of light as it sat high on the hill above the city, like some great hunching beast or god.

Though none of Braylar's retinue had said anything explicitly that led me to believe we were up to evil deeds this night, I couldn't shake the feeling that there was a great deal left unsaid that would confirm my suspicions. I asked, not for the first time, "Why do you need me for this, exactly?"

Braylar replied, "Because I ordered you, exactly. You have done little enough to really earn your keep thus far. You really begin tonight. Observe. And when we are through, record."

Several times I was very nearly swallowed up by the multitudes as we walked along, but Hewspear stopped Braylar and allowed me to catch up, which must have irked him to no end, but Braylar never stopped long enough to scold me or pierce me with one of his looks.

We turned down several narrower streets as we wound our way through the city, and it was such an incredible maze that if I had to find my way back to the inn, no amount of enameled bars would help.

Every street was filled with the requisite jugglers, charlatans, and doomsayers, but the crowds thinned as we got farther from Wide Street, if only a little. After an infinity of turns, we stopped briefly in front of a building. There were several scrawny boys and girls hawking fruit near the doors, which were presently shut, and a large group waiting to enter. I was about to ask Hewspear what we were doing there when I saw the sign hanging from a broken hinge between two torches: three lion heads in dire need of new paint. A playhouse, then. In some ways, this wasn't overly surprising—of low repute among the nobility and high repute among the lower denizens of any city, this seemed as likely a destination as any for my companions, though I was still in the dark about what their purpose might be.

Braylar guided us around the side of the building and down an alley that led to the rear. It was so narrow I could've touched the walls on either side without stretching, and it took several moments for my eyes to adjust as we stumbled over unseen debris.

We stopped in front of a small door, and Braylar knocked four times. It swung out quickly, and Braylar had to step back to avoid being hit. A short man in garish clothes peered out at us, likely having even more trouble seeing than we did. He addressed Hewspear, "Took you long enough. I was near to locking it." He glanced at Braylar and me, and then back to Braylar. "This your master, then?"

Braylar took a step forward. "Indeed. And you must be the player my man spoke so highly of."

The player didn't look like a man spoken of highly very often, but he seemed immune to the praise as he cast a glance down the alley and then spoke to Hewspear, "You said nothing about three. Just your master.

Didn't even know if you were coming back, but even so, that makes two. Nothing said about three."

Braylar held out a small pouch filled with coins. "I hope that doesn't trouble you overmuch. While I'm sure this playhouse is above suspicion, a man can't be too careful. I am, after all, entering in rather unorthodox fashion. I wish only to remain safe."

The player reached out to take the pouch before Braylar considered withdrawing it. "Makes me nervous is all."

Braylar smiled. "You'll find it a bit sweeter than expected, for your trouble and nerves."

The man gave the pouch a quick toss before slipping it in his tunic. "Trouble and nerves is right. Anyone finds out it was me that let you in, anyone at—"

"As I said, sweeter than agreed upon. Lead us in out of the rain, please." Though this was phrased as a request, the tone made it clear it was an order and one to be delayed at peril.

The player let us through the door without another word. He closed it behind us and snapped a large rusty lock shut, mumbling as he did, "Big risk, big risk. Ought not to be doing this at all, but—"

As he was turning to face us he nearly touched noses with Braylar who had moved next to him. "Are you balking at our agreement, player?"

The short man took a step back into the locked door and looked at Hewspear and me, as if we might rescue him, and seeing no help there, replied, "No, no, course not. You paid. Extra, you say. No need to even count it. If I was filled with a little reluctance, I might, you see, but I didn't. None at all. No need. But, it's just…"

He trailed off as Braylar took a small step forward. "Yes?"

"If the baron were to find out it were me that let you in, it—"

"Concern yourself only with your lines, my friend. The baron will be overjoyed at the surprise, you can be sure. Now then…" He clapped the actor on the shoulder and moved out of his way.

The player stepped past him quickly. "As you say, as you say…" and led us down a hallway, vaguely lit by a horn lantern hanging at the end.

We followed the actor to a set of stairs and down into the bowels of the theatre, the lantern now bobbing from his hand. At the bottom, he guided us through a few more passageways, and we followed him to another door.

The sound of the key in the lock was obscenely loud in the silence, and the lantern jiggled in his other hand as he struggled to fit the key and work the mechanism. Finally, the gearworks turned and he pushed the door open on rusty hinges.

The player hung the lantern on a hook on the wall. We were in a small supply room filled with dusty props and cabinets of all sizes. On the opposite side was another door, the paint of ages mostly peeled and gone.

Still clearly uneasy, the player pointed at the other door. "Close of curtain, we'll be in there. The baron likes to see us in our masks and finery and such, so he comes down right away, just as I said. A real man of the arts, he is. We wouldn't even be here, if it weren't for his charity."

Braylar smiled, and it appeared to be genuine and warm. But I suspected the player had no idea what skilled company he was in just then. "I, too, wish to offer my patronage, and you'll find me only slightly less generous. I have no baronage, it's true, but the fair has been most kind to me this year, and your company will be rewarded, as promised."

The man nodded. "Sure then you don't want to watch with the rest? Good show tonight, good show. Or you can come in now, meet some of the other players if—"

"I'll have a seat tomorrow. Tonight, I want only to be reunited with my good friend. It's been too long. And I do so want to see his face when I step out to greet him."

The player said, "Well then, through that door, close of curtain, as I said."

"As you said. Good show, my friend."

The man nodded a final time and stepped through the opposite door, closing it behind him.

Braylar walked over to the door we entered through, tested it and found it still unlocked. "How far do you trust this man, Hewspear?"

Hewspear laughed as he tested the other door, also finding it unlocked, and replied, "As far as you can trust a man who takes a small pouch of coin to do something unscrupulous."

Braylar looked around the small room. "And do you suspect the player will play us?" He asked this as if it were an exercise in rhetoric rather than a query with our lives staked on the wager.

Hewspear opened a cabinet door or two, investigating the age-old props stored inside. "I suspect he's a man of low cunning, most likely happy to have stumbled into some extra coin to spend on women and wine. I'm not sure what his play would be, even if he was inclined to make one. If he reported our presence to the company master now, he'd likely lose his wages for a month for failing to do so earlier."

"Unless he's already done it," I volunteered.

Both men looked at me in surprise, as if they'd forgotten I was in the room with them.

Braylar tilted his head. "Continue."

I shrugged my shoulders. "He could've reported it to the company master just after Hewspear first contacted him."

Braylar nodded. "And?"

"And this could be a ruse on his part, playing the role of, well, a player. While the exit is blocked off. Guards could be assembling now."

Braylar countered, "A playhouse doesn't have guards, lord scribbler."

I pressed on, "But the baron does. I assume. Don't most of them?"

Hewspear laughed then, coins jingling in his beard. "The player would have soiled himself if he tried to approach the baron. And then he would have been whipped for wasting baronial time, and then lost a month's wages for being a fool."

"Maybe. But the company master might not. If the player reported this, that is. He might have some standing with the baron. Or the Player's Guild. That is, if the player were truly worried you were up to something."

Braylar steepled his fingers together and smiled, and without a twitch to be seen. "Very good."

Despite the meager praise, my former fears came rushing back. I asked, "What are we up to? Why are we here?"

Hewspear interrupted this discussion, addressing the captain, "Do you think the player plays us, then?"

Braylar sat down on an old trunk and leaned against the wall. "I can't say. It's certainly possible. And I mislike having so few exits to consider. But we are here, are we not? We're here to play this out tonight, regardless of what other players might be up to, and that is what we do."

I asked again, "Why are we at a theatre with no intention of seeing a play? I don't believe you're an old comrade of this baron, even if you fooled the player."

Braylar said, "And I don't particularly care what you believe. You're here to do one thing, and one thing only. Our intentions aren't your concern."

I began to protest, but Braylar silenced me with a glare, the part of generous noble altogether gone now. "Observe now. Record later. That is all."

And so I sat down as well, waiting to observe something, becoming increasingly worried about what that might be.

⊕

My suspicions doubled and trebled. Was Braylar here to threaten the baron? Bribe him? Abduct him? Do him bodily harm? While the baron might consider himself a great patron of the arts and enjoy commingling with his lessers, he certainly wouldn't come into the playhouse depths without guards. Two men, Syldoon or not, wouldn't be a match for the baron's household guards. Unless they hoped to surprise him, ambush him here.

The audience rumbled in the playhouse above us, stomping their feet in appreciation of the show. Braylar's eyes were closed and he might have been sleeping. Hewspear was sitting on a stool, whittling his flute, the shavings collecting in the dust around him. I wondered if that was what assassins looked like before committing a heinous deed. Peaceful, serene?

I couldn't believe that was what they were here for. It was too awful to really consider. But if it were true, what options did I have? Flee down the tunnel or into the players' chambers? Shout a warning to the baron when he was on the other side of the panel? Record the crime in all its gory details, as I'd been detained to do? Each way was ruin.

Braylar mentioned that today was a shortened program, with only a small playlet preceding the longer play. The performance would be over shortly. And the players would file into the chamber, awaiting the arrival of their benefactor, and we were waiting to do... something. Something that could very likely result in our imprisonments or deaths.

I wondered if the gods would be sympathetic if I stayed to bear witness to an assassination. If I somehow survived my association with this man, I silently swore I'd escape to a cave and begin a life of hermitage. With zeal. And gratitude.

There was a thunderous roar above us. Must have been a fine performance. I wondered what part the short garish player had.

It wouldn't be long now. My tunic was sticking to my sweaty sides.

Hewspear said, "Good man to open the playhouses up again. It's said, and not in a stage whisper, that he did it as much to needle the nobles as please the common man, who crave diversion from the harshness of life. The nobles consider them dens of indecency, a gathering hole for whores and cutpurses and all manner of nefarious characters. Which they are, in truth. But whatever the baron's reasons, I applaud him for it. If you'll pardon the expression. Always did enjoy a good play, myself." He smiled before blowing some shavings off the flute.

Braylar didn't open his eyes, but replied just the same, "Did you happen to see *Bright as Blood*? Before we campaigned in Muljuria?"

Hewspear set to carving again. "No, I didn't have the pleasure. I heard it was good, though."

"Gripping tale of betrayal and lust."

"I prefer the comedies, myself. Gripping tales of mistaken identity and lust. Or misjudgment and lust. Or fallacy and lust. I do like my lust, though. The lustier the better. So I probably would've enjoyed it, gore or no."

It was unnerving that they could banter so easily before doing something that was, at best, dangerous, and worst, blackly criminal.

I cleared my throat and said, "Someone, please tell me why we're in the moldy belly of a playhouse. What is our purpose here?"

After a long pause, Braylar surprised me. "You writerly folk are often guilty of a thing, I don't know the jargon you would use to describe it, so I'll put in it my own terms. On first inspection, the words you scribble, they're terrain language. They exist on the surface for all to see, representing one thing or another. But there's often another layer beneath, sometimes several, yes? This represents something else entirely, this subterranean language, and it takes a keen ear to puzzle out what is represented here. Playwrights are particularly prone to doing this, in my experience. That's their gift. In any event, what transpires in the world of the playhouse above us just now, that's terrainean, and evident to all. We're subterranean. The meaning that lurks beneath."

Braylar chuckled, as if he'd just uncorked the secret to some fantastic riddle. If Hewspear understood or shared the joke, he gave no indication, returning to his careful whittling after Braylar finished speaking. Then we heard voices. Coming closer, on the other side of the panel. Laughter.

What might have been hooting. The players returning.

Hewspear stood and stretched, hands locked behind his back as he raised his arms up. Braylar stirred as well, standing and frowning at the dust and puddles. "All the baron's patronage and not a broom to be found. Pity."

He stepped back to the door we came in, retrieved his small knife and pulled the door open a crack, peering into the dark hallway. "If this is indeed an ambush, they're doing a fine job of disguising it."

Braylar looked at me and jerked a thumb towards the opposite door. "We'll leave you in a moment. Stay just inside this door—I'll leave it slightly ajar. Bear witness. Whatever happens."

I found it hard to imagine that two words strung together could be imbued with such ominous overtones. Knowing I wouldn't get an answer, certainly not one to my liking or free of ridicule, I moved to the spot he indicated, wondering a final time if "whatever happens" was something I'd deeply regret doing nothing to halt or delay. But I'd served under this man long enough now to know he didn't look kindly upon interference to his plans, whatever they entailed. So I moved and continued doing what I was hired to do.

Braylar and Hewspear positioned themselves close to the sliding panel, listening to the pleased voices that couldn't be too far on the other side. The Syldoon waited, time seeming to play tricks, as what couldn't have been long felt like a nerve-tweaking eternity.

Finally, we heard the general murmuring and laughter die down as one voice rose above the others, no doubt announcing the arrival of the baron (and, though the voice could have no way of knowing it, "whatever happens"). I wondered if it was the company master speaking, and where the garish player was just then. Did he truly believe Braylar's story? Would I have? I supposed so. For a taciturn man so gifted in bloodletting, he had the ability to be remarkably glib and charming. At least in short bursts.

Braylar and Hewspear exchanged a glance as they listened. I heard another voice. Though it seemed to be coming from the far side of the players' chamber, and the words were indistinct, it had a richness to it, an assurance, that could only belong to one of high nobility.

I sat on the stool, straining forward, and listened as the baron slowly made his way through the room, congratulating this man and that, doling out his praise as if it were gold itself, and at each instance, rewarded by hearing purring gratitude.

It sounded like he was just on the other side of the panel. My heart was beating like a rabbit's as I watched Braylar pull the panel open quickly. The only thing that kept me from crying out immediately was the fact that they didn't draw their weapons first.

The Syldoon stepped through, and true to his word, Braylar left the panel slightly ajar. There were a few straw mannequins in various states of dress just in front, and it was clear from their positioning that this storage area was rarely used (and certainly not thought to be occupied). Just beyond the cluster of mannequins, the baron was touching a man on the shoulder and smiling.

The players were so enamored with their patron, and the patron with his benevolent patronage, that neither party noticed the arrival of the Syldoon. However, as I imagined, the baron didn't come into the chamber alone or trusting his safety solely to gratitude. Four men in mail and baronial surcoats were standing just behind him, and though they were obviously not expecting any sudden arrivals from behind mannequins, they reacted fairly quickly just the same, moving forward to place their bodies between the baron and the Syldoon.

Baron Brune was a man of middle years, with eyes and hair the color of tarnished pewter, and though his face was deeply lined, there was a wryness there, the ease of someone who hadn't taken his setbacks or failures as seriously as perhaps he ought to have. He took stock of the Syldoon. "What's this? More theatre lovers among us?"

One of the guards stepped forward, hand on the hilt of his sword. "I'll be taking those weapons now, boys."

Braylar replied, "I'm afraid I can't allow that. Assassinations are so very difficult as it is—unarmed, almost impossible."

It took everyone a moment to react to these words, but when they did, it was chaos. My heart nearly exploded in my chest. Several players sprang out of their stools and backed away, stumbling over each other. The guards all drew their swords. The baron, surprisingly, reacted the least of all of us as his guards began moving forward, ready to cut down the Syldoon, even though they still hadn't drawn weapons.

Braylar added, though only loud enough for the guards and baron to hear, "At least, that's what High Priest Henlester believes we're doing here tonight. Instead, I'd like to offer a proposition, if you would be so kind as to hear me out, my lord."

The leader of the guards with a grayshot beard placed his sword point on Braylar's chest. "Unbuckle those sidearms, slow as the sun, or we take them off your corpses."

Three other guards stepped alongside him while the fifth ordered the players out of the room. The company master objected, albeit briefly, but the guard's sword convinced him to be pliant.

Baron Brune stepped forward, his hand nowhere near his own sword, his voice still absolutely level. "I do so enjoy propositions. Almost as much as theatre. Who would've expected that I'd find both here tonight. But I imagine that my captain will honor his pledge to mow you down. That's why I pay him so handsomely, after all. So, in the name of entertaining propositions delivered in unusual places, I beg you, please disarm yourselves. Or I'll be left to wonder what two unusual dead men had meant to discuss that they'd go to such lengths to obtain my audience."

I expected Braylar to do as bid, but as always, that was my repeated mistake. "Your captain of guards is a man of little nonsense and great violence, which I utterly respect. But if we had wanted to do you harm, we could've done so already."

The captain let his sword drift underneath Braylar's chin. "Had you tried I'd need to clean your blood off my new boots."

Braylar replied, with exceptional calm, given the circumstances, "And do you suppose the room behind us fits only two? I imagine you'd know had you checked thoroughly. Which you clearly didn't. You do know that most assassinations are done by the mob than lone individuals, yes? We could've fit a mob and a half in the bowels of this place, all waiting on the other side of that door. If we'd wished your lord harm, we would've visited it upon him already." He turned back to the baron. "Regardless, I, Captain Braylar Killcoin, disarm for no man, save my Tower commander or emperor, and then, with great misgiving. I'm afraid I decline."

The baron said, "Ahh, emperor, is it? We so rarely see Syldoon in this barony. Or this kingdom for that matter. Truly interesting. Captain Gurdinn, rehome your sword if you'd be so kind. This encounter grows more entertaining by the moment."

Beyond a brief hesitation, Gurdinn didn't betray any disobedience, but he seemed to dislike this order a great deal. The other guards followed his lead, though they seem confused and perhaps a little disheartened at not having the opportunity to cut would-be assassins to pieces.

The baron sat down on one of the stools vacated by a player and pointed to two others. His guards flanked him as the Syldoon sat opposite. "So, you allege that a trusted member of my council, a holy man no less, has promised what I'm hoping was considerable coin to snuff out my life at the Three Lions. An amazing tale. I would hear more details of this. I'm also interested in how two Syldoon find themselves in my province, soliciting such unsavory offers. Please. Continue."

Braylar sat. "You can be sure, lord baron, that the Syldoon Empire receives many an unsavory offer, and so has little need to solicit any. My man," he gestured towards Hewspear, "was approached a week ago. Someone wished to know if the Syldoon were interested in pursuing a venture of extreme... unsavoriness."

The baron raised a finger. "I must interrupt. How, do you suspect, this... representative, knew that you were Syldoon, and how did you come to believe he represented a priest, let alone High Priest Henlester?"

Braylar looked at Hewspear who picked the story up. "There are actually a small number of us in Alespell just now. Most staying at the Grieving Dog. We haven't announced our presence with trumpets or jugglers, my lord, but a Syldoon with a loose tongue and whore on his lap might have spilled the secret with his seed, if you take my meaning."

The baron smiled and Hewspear continued, "Whores have looser tongues than drunken soldiers, and rumors have legs, as they say. I expect that the priests had just as good a chance of discovering us here as any, my lord. As to how I knew this was a servant of the priests, I surely didn't. He could've been representing the glassblowers guild for all I knew. After hearing him out, I agreed to meet with him the next day with my answer. He set up the meet through a courier. But I had him followed. This man wasn't a complete novice to subterfuge—he checked several times to see if he'd grown a tail, and led my man on a merry chase—but lead he did, and eventually to the temple on a hill on the west side of the city."

It was impossible to tell if the baron was sitting in full belief, but he nodded again. "The Plum Temple. Hmmm. Yes. I'd like to hear the particulars of this offer, if you would."

Hewspear said, "I was in the ale garden, at the rear of the Grieving Dog. I'm not sure if you've had cause to visit there, my lord, but the garden is something to behold. Several large trees that I suspect aren't native to this land, no doubt brought here at great cost simply to provide shade.

"A man approached, asked if he could speak to me a moment in private. Curious, I agreed. He then asked if I was a Syldonian soldier. I was taken aback somewhat, but wanted to see where this led, so admitted that I was. He moved into the meat of his proposal without more preamble, apparently worried we would be joined by more ears. He claimed to represent someone who bore you no love at all, and wondered if the sentiment was shared. I replied without commitment one way or the other, hoping to hear him out in his entirety. He continued, saying that love of the kingdom was no love at all if it was words and no action. I pressed him to unpack that statement, which he did, saying this barony could no longer abide by its baron, who was threatening the nature of things. That's what he said. 'Threatening the nature of things.'

"I asked then what he intended to do about it, and that's when he stated that it was too dangerous to move with local men, as allegiances were suspect, but that outsiders such as ourselves, particularly those who bore you no love at all, might be bought to carry out a dark deed that would benefit the barony and kingdom greatly. To play this out in full, I told him I cared less about baronies than my light purse, and he promised the benefit there would be equally good."

For a man listening to a dialogue about his impending death, the baron seemed remarkably undistressed, either disbelieving the tale, or disbelieving it could be carried out. "I'm hoping this man offered a great deal as enticement for such a venture fraught with grave risk."

Hewspear replied, "He said if you were removed, the man who seceded you would bring order to the region. He mentioned that you were as a plague to the king, and that a good many men with much to gain would be exceptionally grateful. I, of course, wanted a number fixed to this gratitude. He replied that he was prepared to offer ten thousand in silver."

"It's good to be valued so highly," the baron said. "And so, why report this to me in these strange circumstances then? Why not carry the action out? As you noted so keenly, I'm often rash and sacrifice personal safety in order to mingle with the lowborn. There are probably several locations I could've made a tempting target, and you exposed this as one of them." Gurdinn's face grew purple at this, though he said nothing as the baron continued, "So why not assassinate me? Why would the mighty Syldoon Empire care what befalls a minor baron so far from their borders?"

Braylar replied, "You do yourself a disservice. There's no such thing as a minor baron, particularly in this kingdom where the barons have nearly as much sway over the running of the kingdom as the king himself. More, it could be argued. But you're correct, our interests are hardly selfless. They are, not surprisingly, quite mercenary in fact. It's widely known you patronize the merchants and guilds, and do whatever you can to sponsor their growth. This has surely upset your nobles and holy men. But putting that aside, we hope that a man who recognizes the importance of all things mercantile would be persuaded to advocate for increased trade between our kingdoms. Your Great Fair, while clearly living up to its reputation, would increase profits immeasurably if Syldonian goods also found stalls here."

The baron laughed. "You seem well-informed for would-be assassins. But then you must know that I'm currently not in the king's favor. In fact, some would say that I'm squarely in the middle of his disfavor. Why not eliminate me, or at least allow the priests to hire someone else to do so if you wanted to keep your hands clean, in the hopes that my successor proved less an irritant to our very young monarch?"

"You're a powerful man with powerful friends, despite what you say. We would do what we can to improve your status at court."

"We?"

Braylar uncapped a leather container and pulled out a scroll. "This document permits me to speak on behalf of the emperor himself in this matter. We would have trade routes reopened between our kingdoms, my lord. And your young king, if you'll forgive me for saying so, has been misled greatly in this matter. Men like yourself could lay strong argument before the king. That's our purpose in your province, and why there are other Syldoon in other baronies unrolling similar documents before similar barons. Though I suspect not in the moldy basement of a crumbling theatre. But the priest's proposition forced us to act a little sooner than we intended. Your assassination would surely upset our plans."

After reading the document, the baron said, "There's still the matter of me being greatly out of favor. I suspect my young liege mislikes my rubbing elbows with guildmasters as much as my own fieflords here."

"As I said, my lord, some work still needs to be done to smooth the way. A Syldonian diplomat is on his way to visit your king now, to assist in… healing the divisions in your kingdom. There are a good number of barons no longer enjoying his good graces—you're hardly alone. Just as there has been violence along our borders for decades. We would have our peoples deal with each other peaceably. To that end, we'll do what we can to see that the young king maintains his throne and the respect of his people during this difficult period of ascension, and that advisors don't poison his good reason. We'll do our best to convince the king to shorten the shadow of his disfavor. Once you've been welcomed back to court and his beneficent graces, and you and the other barons assume your rightful place in the assembly, we're hoping you could make the argument for a more open and mutually beneficial relationship between our peoples.

"Which is why we're here with you tonight. Your positions are widely known. Your potential successor? Who can say. We would sooner deal with the known than unknown."

The baron sat back in his chair. "So, then, Voice of the Syldoon, you're here to save my life and help restore my place in Kingdom Assembly. All to possibly create trade agreements between our kingdoms?"

Braylar leaned forward. "The stability of your kingdom is of the utmost importance to us, Baron Brune, and civil war in your barony would assuredly not be in our best interests. Tends to dampen foreign trade quite a bit when all of your resources are funneled into killing each other."

"Most kind."

"Not speaking on behalf of anyone save myself, I can tell you plainly that the welfare of your subjects interests me only so far as it affects the traffic of goods and ideas between us. I'm here to preserve that. To do that, I must preserve you."

The baron turned to Gurdinn. "A play, political intrigue, and assassinations and civil war averted. Who knew we had so much excitement in store for us when we left the castle today?" Back to Braylar. "And what is it you would have me do, Captain Killcoin?"

"Ten or twelve players have no doubt fled into the night, spreading word that two assassins confronted you in the underbelly of the theatre. If you were seen leaving here, half-carried perhaps, returning directly to your castle in such haste that your carriage nearly ran down some revelers in the street…"

He left the thought unfinished for the baron, who picked it up, "I'm to be an amateur player, appearing the corpse then, am I?"

Hewspear said, "You could bathe yourself in buckets of fake gore if you really want to play the part. This is a playhouse, after all, I'm sure there's some here in one cabinet or other. But the spectacle of your flight coupled with the rumors in the streets will be enough to sell the illusion, I've no doubt."

Baron Brune drummed his fingers on his knees. "This would cause panic in the barony. Perhaps celebration in some corners, but surely panic in others. All during the height of the Great Fair? And to what end?"

Braylar replied, "It would take several days for the rumors to take on the strength of truth, assuming you stayed secluded in your castle and didn't venture forth to dispel them. But we agreed to meet with those who would see you dead to accept payment two days from now. You can send a few men to accompany us, to the ruined temple in the crook of the river Debt. We can capture the man there and turn him over to you for interrogation. You'll learn the identity of the man or men who move against you. I suspect he doesn't act independently."

"And this charade you propose, this spectacle—"

"Ends the moment you've learned the identity and captured or killed all parties responsible. But in order for this plan to succeed, it's vital it appears you're dead or dying. I also suspect that the man or men who hired me have spies in your circle. The contact alerted us you'd be here tonight, and vulnerable to attack. Only someone well placed could've known that, yes? So, announce nothing publicly, and allow the rumors to grow as you stay secluded in your chamber and reveal these plans to no one else. Once you've destroyed your enemies and rooted out any spies, you emerge to put the rumors to rest, claiming you were merely ill. Certainly your town guards can prevent any civil unrest for a few days while this small playlet runs its course. Obviously, their numbers are swelling just now with the fair on."

The baron pursed his lips. "You put me in an awkward position, Captain. You'll forgive me if I'm skeptical, but I haven't verified these documents of yours to a certainty, haven't met with my council, or even had time to consider this fully alone. I'm prone to acting impulsively, it's no secret, and enjoy spectacle more than most men, but this... you ask a great deal. This is an awkward position. Precarious, even. Even if I believed you in full, something of such import must be weighed and measured against possible ramifications. And if I'm struck by suspicion as to your claims, why shouldn't I detain you in order to confirm your version of these events? Or better still, why not aggressively pursue the validity of claims on my own? I pride myself on maintaining a stable of truly gifted interrogators. I've no doubt they could unearth the truth, no matter how deeply buried."

Now it was Braylar's turn to seem relatively unfazed, despite the fact that his life hung in the balance. "As to the first or second, that would be a prudent course of action, I must admit. But in doing so, you'll assuredly lose any chance of capturing the man who hired me to kill you. We swore you would die this night. I'm confident that if he has eyes inside your castle, it would be no difficult feat to mark you entering the playhouse here tonight, and marking the nature of your departure as well. If you leave to consult with your council, you'll either alert his eyes in the streets or his spies in your house. You might as well send a courier to your enemies promising time to vacate their grounds and form a new plan. And as to me, if not detained, I would be forced to flee with my men. I have no idea how large the contingent that moves against you, but even with your small lapse in security tonight, you're fairly well guarded. My force has no built-in protection. And if detained, well, I would simply be an unwilling guest while you waited for correspondence, and hence, verification, to travel, during which you lose a grand opportunity of uprooting the cabal formed against you. It could be the High Priest, as I suspect. It could be another member of their order. It's also possible that the man who hired us is only loosely affiliated with the Plum Temple. He mentioned 'great men' behind this, so who is to say?

"And as to the third option, you strike me as a man who judges well the capabilities of those in his service. Interrogating me is your baronial prerogative, of course. But while I'm but a humble tool to the Syldoon Empire, we're a notoriously protective fraternity, and generally choose to torture or kill our own, looking unfavorably at outsiders who avail themselves to do the same. I can't say for certain, but I strongly suspect that the Syldoon would not only lose interest in assisting you reclaim your rightful place in the assembly, but they might even take an assault on me as an assault on the Empire itself. Again, this has less to do with me overvaluing myself than it does the prickly nature of the Syldonian heart."

Braylar maintained the placidity of someone describing how springs and bolts move in a lock, adding, "Your decision is of course your own, Baron Brune. I can't hope to counsel you further. I have outlined one way to proceed. However, should you choose to pursue this course of action, I advise you to do so shortly."

The baron tapped his chin twice with a long forefinger. "Precarious, at best."

Gurdinn stepped next to the baron and kneeled. "I've held my tongue this entire time, my lord, but I hope that you aren't seriously considering doing as this man says. He's a Black Noose. He can't be trusted."

The baron waved a hand for Gurdinn to rise. "You've ever been a loyal servant, Captain Gurdinn, as your father was to mine. What would you advise?"

"Whatever you will, my lord. So long as it isn't putting faith in this horsetwat. Release him, arrest him, kill him now, doesn't matter to me, so long as you don't trust this lying—"

Braylar interrupted, "Lord Lackyouth, I've no doubt you've provided your baron sound counsel in the past, but it does seem as if you're letting passion obscure your reason just now. I believe we've just met, and yet you hook me arm in arm with all the devils who walk the sordid earth."

Gurdinn ignored him, still speaking to the baron. "I would sooner soak my cock in honey and ask a bear not to bite than trust a Black Noose, my lord."

Braylar clapped and said, "I wouldn't have suspected you of such color-ful wit, Captain Honeycock. You're a man of surprising gifts."

Gurdinn wheeled on him, hand on his sword. "Shut your mouth, right quick."

"Enough, the both of you." The baron stood and slowly paced the length of the chamber. He made several passes as everyone waited in silence for his answer, and then, speaking mostly to himself, he said, "It's true that if the Syldoon had meant me harm, they could've done as much already."

Gurdinn began to object but the baron cut him off, "It's no rebuke, captain. You have often times remarked I ought to go more heavily guarded, and you've never been fond of my visits here. The lapse in security is as much my doing as yours, rest easy. But it's a fact that I was vulnerable, and if these Syldoon had meant harm, they had their opportunity."

He continued pacing. "I'm not in the habit of immediately trusting strangers in my own barony, let alone those from an Empire counted enemy not long ago." Finally, he turned and regarded Gurdinn again. "But I don't see the harm in playing this out as the Syldoon captain suggests. We leave here tonight in a rush, you and your men ushering me to the castle with all speed. I'm not convinced there are spies in my circle, but having already made one mistake in coming here so lightly guarded, I'm not prepared to possibly make another. So I'll stay closed in my chamber, and only my lady wife and the men in this room shall know the reason."

Gurdinn persisted, "My lord, even if there's a parcel of truth to what the Black Noose says, if you do this, you'll create undue rumors, panic even, as you said yourself. You threaten your own Great Fair with what you consider."

"The Fair is always profitable, but grown dull of late. This will remedy that. Say no more—I no longer consider, Captain Gurdinn, I've decided. Rumors will fester, true, but I can't risk undue deliberation. If the Syldoon are correct, we have a means here of trapping the conspirators and learning the identity of traitors in our midst. If the allegations prove substantial as air, I can dispel any rumors shortly enough. The Great Fair would continue unabated, even if I burst into flames for all the world to see, I have no doubt.

"So, while I sit on my deathbed, you'll accompany the captain to the meeting in two day's time. Seeing how peaceable you two are, I'm loath to send you, Captain, but I'm even more troubled by the thought of sending another in your stead to guard my interests there."

The baron faced Braylar. "You'll be in command of this venture, Captain Killcoin. But only this venture."

Gurdinn began to object again, but the baron raised a hand. "I've heard your mind, and I don't need to hear it again. You're to obey the Syldoon explicitly in this enterprise, Captain Gurdinn, so long as the events play out as predicted. If you suspect subterfuge, or this man betrays us in any way, you may act accordingly, but otherwise you'll hold your biases to your heart as a closeted secret that will ruin you if revealed. Do you understand me?"

Gurdinn's face was obscured, but I imagined it attaining several new shades of red as he nodded his assent with a great deal of stiffness.

Braylar stood and made a small bow. "You act wisely in this matter, lord baron."

The baron smiled. "That remains to be seen. If nothing else, I've benefited from your lesson in scouting out my path for the day, particularly in leisure. There's simply no telling who you might encounter and where." He turned to leave and stopped. "As my men carry my ambushed body from the premises, what will you do? If eyes do indeed look out for me, they must look out for you as well."

"I believe we'll leave the way we came in, like rats through the alley."

"Very good. And how shall Captain Gurdinn call on you? I assume you don't want him sharing a drink with you in the common room of the, Grieving Dog, was it?"

Braylar nodded. "It was, and you assume correctly." To Gurdinn, "Meet us three miles from the North Gate. Two days hence, when we are to meet with the priest, just after dawn, on the side of the road to Redvale. A small group of your men, only, and if you require armor, make sure it's blackened or covered. We will lead you to the priests and their promised payment for illicit deeds, but only if you don't give our position away by clunking about or flashing in the sun."

Gurdinn didn't respond and Braylar said, "I'll take your hateful stare as agreeable acquiescence, Captain Honeycock, but I do hope you're less reticent once on the road. I would hate to jeopardize your lord's safety because of failed communication."

Gurdinn glared long and hard, and the baron led his men towards the stairwell they came down. The stairs squeaked with their weight as Braylar and Hewspear rejoined me.

Braylar looked immensely pleased with himself. "We go. Curfew is but a short time off, and I've no wish to tussle with the city watch. I don't imagine they'd readily accept this tale as an excuse."

⊕

The pair in front of me was silent as we walked back to the Grieving Dog, and the rain had subsided to a drizzle barely more substantial than mist. Looking around and seeing no one nearby, I started asking a question, but Braylar stopped me with, "I might need a scribe, but no one said I needed one with a tongue."

When we arrived, Mulldoos was in one corner, dicing with what looked like city guards, although they didn't appear to be guarding anything except their ale just now. Hewspear walked over to their table and got his attention while Braylar led me to our suite.

As we entered, I asked him if he was willing to discuss what happened now that we were in a secure location.

He replied, "There's no such thing. And I'll tell you more when it becomes necessary. You would do well to leave it to me to determine when that is."

Hewspear and Mulldoos joined us just after and Braylar locked the door. Then Braylar turned to me. "Retire for the night. Don't fear—all will be divulged soon enough. And when it is, you can ask as many questions as you like. Well, at least as many as I like."

He led his lieutenants into his room, no doubt to discuss all those things I wanted desperately to be privy to.

I laid in bed for a long time, listening to the revelers in the courtyard below descend into deeper drunkenness, wondering if anyone had been killed in the inn (it seemed likely, given the name), and considering whether these Syldoon were all that they appeared.

The next day, I was essentially held captive, not allowed to even go down the stairs to the common room or ale garden. Two Syldoon I hadn't seen before alternated shifts guarding the antechamber. Each time I tried to pass, they informed me that the captain's orders were explicit. I wasn't to leave. I considered climbing out the window and down a tree, but I suspected disaster for me if I did, so I contented myself with waiting in my room.

I was asleep on my bed in the afternoon when my door opened. Braylar sat down opposite me, and when I didn't respond, he said, "Your breathing has changed—you fool no one."

I sat up and asked why he wouldn't allow me to even leave our suite and he replied, "We have come too far to risk our plan being undermined by a loose tongue or disloyal scribe. Tomorrow, you travel with us, but for the remainder of today, you'll stay here. Don't fear—you shall have your opportunity to explore the fair in due time, but not just yet. I have no need for your trust, only your obedience. So. Tomorrow we move."

The next morning, one of the new Syldoon—Tomner, he said his name was—woke me before dawn. I dressed and entered the antechamber, finding Braylar, Mulldoos, Hewspear, Lloi, and Tomner waiting. I'd seen a few other Syldoon come and go while sequestered, but it appeared they were remaining behind in Alespell. I assumed Vendurro and Glesswik were already ahead. Mulldoos was pulling a tunic on over his head, swearing as it caught on the lamellar plates of his armor. The others had covered their armor already.

We headed to the stables and the grooms had everyone's mount prepared. Braylar had chosen a brown mare with a wild splash of white down its middle for me. I wondered if it would bite, or kick, or buck, sure he would've chosen an ill-tempered beast, but it seemed disinterested enough. I would've preferred a wagon, even one with a massive bloodstain inside.

We rode through Alespell in the predawn dark, encountering no one, the clopping of our horse's hooves obscenely loud with no other noise for competition. When we reached the North Gate, I expected the guards to detain us, but Gurdinn must have already alerted them to our departure, as the portcullis was up and the drawbridge down, despite the fact that curfew hadn't been called. After exchanging some words with Braylar, the guards let us through.

We put some miles behind us, still seeing no one, before coming across Gurdinn and four soldiers on the side of the road. True to Braylar's instructions, they had long tunics over their hauberks, but nothing that marked them as Brunesmen. They could easily have been caravan guards, bandits, or itinerant mercenaries.

When we reined up, Braylar said, "So very good of you to join us, Captain Honeycock."

Gurdinn looked us over, and if he thought it strange that a Grass Dog and an unarmed, unpenned scribe were in the company, he hid it well enough. "Lead on, Black Noose."

Braylar ordered Tomner to ride ahead of the party. Whatever else might be said about the man, he didn't take scouting lightly.

We traveled on the road throughout the morning, seeing only the odd small clumps of travelers at first, and then thickening traffic heading to Alespell, though we were the only group going in the opposite direction at that hour.

Unaccustomed as I was to riding, it wasn't long before my legs and lower back ached abominably. Few words were exchanged by anyone, even when we stopped briefly to allow the horses to rest and eat. Late morning, we left the road for good, and I experienced the usual misgivings—even a bandit-plagued road still offered the illusion of safety. But I doubted anyone was interested in my opinion, so withheld it.

Lloi fell back and rode alongside me. There was some distance between us and the nearest Syldoon, but I was still surprised when she leaned over a bit, and quietly said, "Always seem to make them right uneasy. Guessing I set even old Hewspear's nerves to jangling, and he's the most tolerant of the bunch. What's your excuse for being stuck at the back?" She gave her customary gap-toothed smile.

"I imagine they aren't keen on either of our kind us in their company. Scribes and… what is it you do, again?"

She shook her head and laughed quietly. "Besides slink around in Captain Noose's skull, you mean? You do make a body smile, bookmaster. That you do."

I'd been waiting for an opportunity to bring a topic up again, and this seemed as good a time as any. "Lloi, back in the grass," I kept my voice at nearly whisper level, "you mentioned Memoridons. But I sensed you didn't want to say anything with Captain Killcoin nearby. Why was that?"

She glanced at the captain at the front of our column. "Like I said, never met one. But I heard the Syldoon talk about them from time to time, mostly when they thought I wasn't nearby or listening none. Syldoon as hard as they come, afraid of little and less. But the way they talk about them memory witches, they got a real healthy respect for them, about two paces shy of fear."

"But from the stories, I always got the impression the Syldoon controlled the Memoridon."

She shrugged. "You can put a collar on a ripper and drop it in a cage, but unless you chop off the beak and rip out the claws, you still best step lightly, unless you like the idea of being real dead real fast."

"Dead?" I said, loud enough that one of Baron Brune's soldiers heard and glanced over his shoulder. I carefully lowered my voice again. "Don't they do what you do, or something like it? I don't understand—why they are so dangerous?"

She waited until she was sure no one was listening. "They can creep through a man's memories, same as me, sure enough. Said they can track a man by his memories, too. Though I couldn't hazard a guess as to how. So the Syldoon use them as spies, doing recon and the like. But it's also said they can strike a man down, just by looking at him. Cripple, maim, kill, drop him to the dirt like a stone."

"Why... why can't you do that?" I asked, suddenly very glad she couldn't.

"No clue how. I barely know how to do what I do now. Mostly taught myself, stumbling in the dark. The Memoridon, they recruit their own, same as the Syldoon, real young. They find someone who got the gift of it, they snatch them right up, train them the same way you train a man to swing a sword or scribble on that parchment like you. Talent with no teachers barely talents at all, and rough ones as that."

I looked at Lloi, never considering before that she might have had other latent abilities that could have been harnessed if she'd come under Syldoon care earlier in her life. Either way, she would have had few enough choices, and been a tool regardless. Albeit a more deadly one, had she become a Memoridon. But she wouldn't have been mutilated, or whored out, and she would be powerful, if what she said was accurate and not merely unfounded rumor. I wondered what that version of Lloi would have been like. It was difficult to imagine.

"When the captain discovered what you could do, why didn't he bring you back to the empire, or wherever it is Memoridon are trained? Wouldn't you have been more, uh, useful to him if you had some tutelage or mentorship?"

Lloi looked up the line again to be sure none of Braylar's retinue were in earshot, which would have been difficult, since I could barely hear her over the clomping of hooves. Satisfied, she said, "Got the real solid impression the Syldoon give the memory witches as wide a berth as they're able. Seems to be most times, you attracted their attention, you attracted nothing of any kind you wanted. Things go sour right quick when the witches and the soldiers mix it up.

"That, and Captain Noose got a sister who's one."

That was exceptionally unexpected. "A Memoridon? His sister?"

"Yup. And from what I gather, the only blood they got betwixt them is poison bad."

I was about to ask more when a Syldoon soldier rejoined the group and spoke briefly with Braylar. I expected that meant we were nearing our destination. We rode up a steep wooded hill, winding our way through bent and bowed trees that must have been ancient. Braylar told us all to dismount before we reached the top, and we walked our horses the rest of the way.

At the top of the hill, I saw the temple ruins laid out below us, nestled in the crook of a sludgy brown river. While the temple had probably been quite a sight a thousand years ago, it was now mostly a shell. The roof and whatever domes or tiles or spires it had once possessed were completely gone, dragged off to serve other buildings when the temple had been abandoned. There were sections of the wall still intact, though few enough, and arches here and there, some even freestanding, but much of that had been picked clean as well. I wondered why it had been abandoned, but the answer was clear when I looked at the meadows and river behind the ruins.

The Godveil.

The air shimmered slightly, like hot air rising off an arid plain that warps whatever appears beyond. The only difference was, this shimmering continued much higher into the sky, bending even the bottoms of the dense clouds, and it wasn't isolated to one particular spot, but crossed the entire shallow valley floor, over the river, and up into the woods beyond, continuing until it disappeared behind the ridge. And once my eye had caught it, the senses picked up two other things as well—the tiniest noise, so remote it was barely audible, like the last note played by a harp, hanging in the air just before it disappeared entirely, only this note never quite got that far. It simply hung there, thrumming so low you would be hard pressed to notice it at all if you hadn't already seen the warping air. There was also a whiff of a mildly unpleasant odor, a combination of singed hair and vinegar, so faint and unobtrusive, you might have thought you imagined it if the other signals weren't there to tell you the Godveil was in the vicinity. I'd seen it once, when I was very young, but it had been from very far away, and for only a short time.

I'd run away from home—though I can't recall why now. Some tiff with my mother, no doubt. Most children threaten as much, and never journey too far from the front door, but I promised myself I was going to run as far as I could, never to return. I even packed some food and clothes, and slipped off through the woods. I didn't know where I was headed, only that I was going to keep going. And I might have. I put several miles behind me when suddenly the woods got quiet. There were no more bird calls. No more scurrying squirrels. Just empty, still woods. And then I saw it, through the trees... the Godveil. My mother had warned me it was out there, somewhere, and that it was the deadliest thing in the world that no living thing could abide. And looking around the deserted woods, I could see she was right. No one lived near the Godveil, or trafficked in the vicinity if they could help it. To do so was to invite death. So I ran back home as fast as my feet could carry me. My mother whipped me double hard when she learned where I'd gone, and made me swear I'd never do anything half so stupid again. And I hadn't. Until accompanying the Syldoon.

It's said the Godveil wraps around the entire world, stretching over mountains, deserts, and every other empty, desolate locale. I hoped never to travel widely enough to confirm or deny that claim, but there was no mistaking that however long or short it was, some part of the Godveil ran its ethereal course behind the ruins before us. There was a good reason no one lived close to the Veil, or built near it either—there were no active settlements, outposts, or communities anywhere along its entire length, if reports were to be believed.

The only structures remotely close were utterly deserted. All I could imagine was that this temple had predated the Veil.

Lloi made some strange fluttery sign over her chest and face and looked shaken. When she saw me staring at her she let out a deep breath. "Like I told you, when my people figured what I could do, they gave me a choice. Leave off some finger bits, or part the Veil. Weren't much of a choice, really." And then she shivered, which made me shiver as well, despite the warm, heavy air.

That was obviously an expression, "part the Veil," and ironic at that. You could walk towards it, but no could walk through it. The Veil didn't part for anyone. But trying, approaching it too closely, that meant the end, just as surely as walking off a cliff.

I glanced around. The Brunesmen looked uncomfortable being this close as well, and one mumbled a near-silent prayer. Another behind me spoke quietly, with a kind of awe, "Back in Threespire, they got lodges. Call them dream stations. Built right close to the Veil. Never been there, but I hear you pay some coin, you get tethered to the lodge, to a post anyways, so you can walk just close enough. Said the world opens behind your eyes when you do, you see things that never been seen before."

Another Brunesman replied, "Same where I'm from. Call them something different though. Must be something to it, I reckon. You reckon?"

Mulldoos looked at the pair. "I reckon you two are just about the dumbest bastards in the wide world. Only dumber being some fools willing to pay for a tethering. Veil's the same as any other natural thing that can kill you. Fire, lightning. Nothing more mystical than that. Only thing that opens up if you get real close is the back of your skull." He looked up at the broiling clouds. "You don't run around with your sword in the air when it's thundering, you don't go walking towards the Veil. Unless you figure being dead sounds mighty fine. Simple as that."

Hewspear replied, "Is it? Fires run their course and eventually burn out, and lightning flashes once and is gone. But our grandfather's grandfathers have seen the Godveil, and their grandfather's grandfathers besides. A thousand years, maybe more, shifting, but never changing. Calling to any who would travel close, drawing them closer. A beautiful seductress who kills. You don't find that strange?"

Mulldoos laughed. "I find superstitious old goats strange."

After a pause, a Brunesman suggested, "It's said you can see the Deserters, you get close enough. Moving like shadows on the other side. Catch a glimpse of them from time to time. Maybe that's why they build the dream stations."

Even now, long, long after those old gods abandoned humanity, they were still mentioned with a kind of reverence.

By most anyway. Voice wrought with scorn, Mulldoos said, "Called Deserters for a reason. They good and left us clean, back when your grandfathers' grandfathers got grandfathers with grandfathers, ain't that right, Hew? They abandoned our sorry asses. You think they're sitting pretty on the other side, posing for a painting? Dumb horsecunts, the lot of you. Deserters ain't never coming back, ain't never going to be seen again. Maybe they died on the other side. I hope they did. If we deserved deserting, they deserve something worse. But either way, they're gone forever and more, and there's no sense talking about it. So quit your cunty yapping before I take your purses and throw you into the Veil myself."

That put an end to the discussion. But while Mulldoos had ridiculed and threatened everyone into silence, it didn't change the tension still hanging in the air. There was that barely perceptible pull from the Veil, even from this distance. More than a simple desire to see how many bones might lay strewn along its course. This wasn't curiosity, wasn't even just fascination. It was a horrible compulsion to step closer, to approach the Veil, despite the surety that to do so could only end in doom. Mulldoos was wrong on that count—there wasn't anything natural about it.

But the tension wasn't only about the Veil itself, but the Deserters who'd created it. Ages had come and gone since they stranded us on this half of the world, but even though their temples had been torn down by decree, their names forbidden and lost, nothing could wash away the malaise they left behind. People rarely thought or spoke of them, but when they did, it was impossible not to acknowledge... they abandoned us because we had failed. There were different accounts in different lands, but they ultimately amounted to the same thing—we were too weak, too passionate, too ignorant. We'd disappointed the oldest gods in such a profound and egregious way they decided we were hopeless. And so they left. They abdicated, left the throne vacant. New gods had sprung up in their absence, lesser gods to fill the void, but the Deserter's judgment and condemnation still hung over all of us. Their desertion was unconscionable, but the reasons for it were inescapably damning. To think of the Deserters was to meditate on our own awful foibles.

But while everyone else was fixated on the Godveil and regarding it with quiet awe, fear, or in the case of Mulldoos, real or feigned contempt, and perhaps contemplating our failings as a race, just like I was, I noticed that Braylar was staring at something at the front of the ruined temple, rapt as rapt could be.

Stone stairs led to a single archway in what remained of a wall, with a large pedestal on either side. While one pedestal was empty, the one to the right of the arch supported a massive bust as tall as a man. This wasn't all that unusual—temples new and old often housed sculptures of gods, heroes, martyrs, and mystics. However, looking more closely, I saw what arrested Braylar's attention.

The giant head was roughly human in proportion and shape from the cheekbones down, albeit thick-lipped and foreboding, but the similarities ended abruptly at eye level. Or what would have been eye level. Where a man should have had eyes, this statue had two large horns protruding out and up, as well as a ring of somewhat smaller horns circling its head the entire way around. It also had two rows of short horns, spikes really, extending from front to back. The familiarity was obvious. The heads on Braylar's flail were more stylized than the giant bust, and screaming in rage or pain while this head was utterly stoic and solemn, but it was clear both sculptures were inspired by the same source. This had been a temple for the Deserter Gods, back when they had names and widespread worshipers. Before the Deserters erected the Veil to cover their escape from us.

Braylar's left hand had dropped down to Bloodsounder, and he was staring down at the Veil beyond the ruins.

I stepped closer to him and whispered, "Is something wrong, Captain?"

His left hand flicked the chains and his eyes didn't leave the Veil. "You feel the draw, yes? The subtle but powerful urge to approach, to unravel its mysteries, or your own?"

I nodded, and he did as well, but then said, "I do not."

I looked at him closely. There was no twitching around the lips, no sweat on the brow, no angry scowl. In fact, he looked as calm as I'd ever seen him. Quietly, he said, "The first time I saw the Veil was many years before. And as it happened, I was far closer than we are now. So I felt the pull, bone deep. Our division was trying to evade a much larger force on our heels, and the terrain pushed us much closer to the Veil than our commanders would have liked. It was incredibly difficult to resist the pull. We actually lost several soldiers—warnings mean nothing when you come that close, you simply ride or walk to the Veil until your mind is blasted and you fall down dead in its shadow. And several years after that, I had cause to travel near it again. And while the pull wasn't quite as potent, it was still there. So I remember it well."

He turned his head and looked at me. "But now, I feel nothing at all. No tug, no draw, no impulse to approach it. Nothing. It's as if... as if the Veil weren't there at all."

He said this last in amazement. And for good reason. I'd never heard anyone utter this before. Everyone knew someone or had heard of someone drawn to the Veil, slaughtered by it. It was ubiquitous. But to say he felt nothing at all... it was like saying he stuck his hand in the fire and felt no heat.

I glanced down at his flail, and then back to the bust at the temple, looked at the images of the Deserters. "Did you, before, did you have—"

"No. The first two times I'd encountered the Veil were before I'd unearthed Bloodsounder." He looked back down the hill.

"What does it mean?'

He shook his head and for once seemed truly at a loss. "I don't know," he admitted. "It is... significant. But what is signified... I don't know."

Others had gathered nearby, so the conversation was over. But I was mystified.

We'd gotten as close to the temple as we dared without leaving the heavy cover of the trees on the hill. Further down, bush and bramble gave way to a large tract of wildflowers and meadow that led to the ruins. It was as secluded a spot as could be hoped for, and must have been ideal and idyllic for whatever priests made this place their home in another age. Now, it served as the perfect spot for a secret meeting, well away from the traffic of the trade road ten miles to the west, and in little danger of being accidentally stumbled upon, as even the closest farmstead was in the next valley, far from the Veil and its dangers and ramifications. It occurred to me that a location so well chosen for a clandestine meeting was also the perfect spot for an ambush or treachery.

I looked back at our party when I heard Braylar grilling Vendurro and Glesswik, who had stepped out of the trees to join us.

"You saw no movement then? Nothing to indicate a hostile presence?"

Vendurro replied, "No, Cap. Gless and me, Xen too, we've been here since dawn yesterday, exactly as ordered. Circled as close as we could without giving away our positions or getting too near the Veil, and as far as I can tell, we're the only hostile presence in these parts. We split watches, so there's been an eye open the entire time. No one in the temple grounds, and so far, no movement along the perimeter neither."

Braylar pressed him. "As far as you can tell? Are you confident that the woods are clear, or is that merely a guess?"

Vendurro's cheeks colored and his jaw tightened, but before he could fashion a response, Glesswik said, "Three sets of eyes are better than one, Cap, but they ain't as good as ten, if you take my meaning. We ate cold rations, moved as cautious as we could, and circled close. Shifting watch the entire time, like Ven told you. No ambush in the bush that we seen. I don't know that I'd stake my life on it, but—"

"You stake yours and ours as well. Make no mistake."

"Well, then, two days of scouting and screening says it looks like a safe field. That's as much as I can say, Cap."

Braylar nodded at both. "Very well, then. As always, much will be risked on appearances. Assuming he isn't already hiding among the wildflowers, High Priest Turncloak should arrive shortly. Is Xen still in position near the goat track?"

Glesswik said, "He is, Captain."

"Very good. Vendurro, take a position close enough to Xen to hear his signal, no closer. Glesswik, return to the track and alert me the minute you see anything more threatening than a grouse."

Glesswik and Vendurro both saluted and moved off in different directions through the woods.

We all looked to Braylar for the next order while Gurdinn and his men waited several paces away. Braylar stared at the ruins below us and took a deep breath. His eyes were closed, his fingers absently running up and down the flail chains.

Mulldoos moved close and lowered his voice. "You look like you just found a bloody finger in your soup. I had to guess, Cap, I'd have to say you're disappointed there's no trap."

Braylar sighed, eyes still closed. "Oh, there's a trap, Mulldoos. I just haven't figured out the mechanism yet."

"The trap's ours. We're the trap."

Braylar didn't reply, or look convinced. Mulldoos looked at Hewspear and stepped away again, shaking his head slightly.

Gurdinn approached. "What did your scouts report, Syldoon?"

Braylar said nothing, turning slightly left and right. Gurdinn cleared his throat, but Braylar ignored him, shaking the chains slightly, as if to wake the weapon.

"Your scouts, Syldoon? Do we proceed, or is there cause for concern?"

Braylar opened his eyes and faced Gurdinn. "You'll address me as captain, or 'sir', or 'my lord', as is your fashion."

Gurdinn rolled his lower jaw around like a cow chewing cud, and seemed to be measuring several uncivil and potentially dangerous responses.

Braylar smiled. "I shouldn't need to remind you, although I will because I enjoy your black looks so, but your baron saw fit to place me in command of this mission, and therefore, in command of you and your men. If you fail again to address me as my rank affords, then I have grave doubts as to whether you'll obey my orders once the time comes to spill blood. It would pain me greatly to report to Baron Brune that this mission was jeopardized, and subsequently, his life left in danger, due to insubordination on the part of his representative, but that's exactly what I'll do if I'm not certain of your obedience."

Gurdinn had evil in his eyes, and all of the men looked on anxiously to see how this contest would be resolved, but he finally replied, "Very well. Can I assume then that we're proceeding as planned? Captain."

The last was offered very grudgingly, but Braylar let the point go as he released the chains. "We will proceed, yes."

"You must forgive me... Captain, but it sounds like you have reservations."

Braylar kept his voice level as he replied, "My scouts are exceptional, and I trust their judgment above all others. I've risked my life countless times on their intelligence, and I have no reason to believe they missed any signs in the last two days. However, High Priest Turncloak agreed to this location, so I'm immediately suspicious. Not that he'll attempt still more treachery, because that's a foregone inevitability, but I'm gravely surprised that my scouts didn't encounter anything to confirm that suspicion."

"He believes the deed is done," Gurdinn said. "It's possible he arrives intending only to pay you."

Braylar laughed. "It's possible I'll bed a thousand virgins tonight, and about as likely. He arranged to have his natural lord assassinated. Do you believe he's suddenly overcome by a desire to honor his agreements with the alleged assassins? No, he'll do anything to ensure anyone with knowledge of his complicity lives as short a time as possible."

"Perhaps he won't show. Have you considered that?"

"I consider everything. But Henlester or an underpriest will show, and he'll attempt to kill us. Outside his inner circle, we're the only direct link to his complicity. He'll need to kill us and wash his hands of all blood as quickly as possible. Whatever else he planned or is planning, he'll be here today."

Gurdinn smiled, though it was thin as the edge of a blade. "Sounds like you have a good deal of experience covering up evidence. Captain."

Braylar nodded. "More than you know, Brunesman. I'm complicit in a good many unsavory things."

"If it's to happen at all, maybe the ambush will take place on the road back to the city."

"Perhaps."

The sky was the color of ingot iron, and the air was warm and heavy with moisture. It was a miracle we weren't already drenched in rain. Far off beyond the hills, heat lightning flashed briefly, but there was no thunder to be heard.

We waited. And waited. And waited some more. Finally, Braylar had enough. He turned and faced Hewspear. "Is the pennon in place?"

Hewspear lifted his long slashing spear, the priest's signal pennon attached to the blade. "It is, Captain."

Mulldoos pulled his falchion out of the scabbard a few inches and slid it back in, then checked that his buckler slid free of the belt easily as well. He pulled his helmet on as Hewspear did the same. "About time."

Braylar rolled his shoulders, his left hand never straying far from Bloodsounder. "If the timorous priests won't show themselves, we'll have to present ourselves and demonstrate our good intentions." He faced everyone else. "We're going down. The underpriest and his underlings should step out of the trees shortly. They—"

Gurdinn broke in. "How do you know they're here? Your men have reported no arrivals."

"I assure you, the underpriest is here, and will reveal himself shortly." Braylar turned to Lloi. "If Vendurro reports sight of anyone besides the underpriest's party, blow your horn and we withdraw with speed."

Gurdinn laughed at that and Braylar turned his gaze back to him. "If all goes as planned, Brunesman, then lead your men out the moment you see the sign that our little ruse is over. Tomner, you as well."

Gurdinn said, "Oh, most certainly, my lord. Should the elusive traitors suddenly materialize, my men will be ready." He didn't bother to disguise his disdain for the smaller man in front of him. "And what will the sign be?"

"One of the priest's men will be lying in his blood, gurgling his last breath. I should hope that will be clear enough for you, yes? If for some reason you're still confused, consult Lloi—she'll be more than happy to explain the particulars again."

With that, Braylar mounted his horse, as did Hewspear and Mulldoos. They rode out of the tree line and down the hill toward the ruins, leaning far back in the saddle to compensate for the incline. They made a good show of looking around for the underpriest and his men, as if they'd just arrived. Hewspear kept his spear with the pennon straight and high for all to see as the ground slowly flattened out and they neared the first broken wall and dismounted. They tethered their horses to a scraggly bush and waited.

The heat lightning continued to flash, closer now. As the moments dragged on, I began to suspect we were truly alone in this broken and forbidding place that men and gods saw fit to abandon. But then the underpriest and three men stepped out of the woods on the far side of the temple, leading their horses on foot, reins in hand.

I looked over at Lloi and the soldiers. Lloi remained impassive, and Gurdinn squinted his eyes to see more clearly, but his men all shared the same excitement now that their quarry was finally close at hand. The other two Syldoon appeared calm.

"That's an underpriest of Truth," Gurdinn said. "The bastard was right. But that doesn't make the priest a traitor."

Lloi's eyes followed Braylar. "Proof is coming right quick, don't you worry none."

Below, Hewspear gestured with his free hand and Braylar and Mulldoos looked in the direction he indicated. Mulldoos strapped a round shield to his left forearm and then the three of them stepped over a low spot in the shattered wall and approached the center of the ruins.

The underpriest and his three men left their horses at the outer wall on the opposite side of the temple and made their way towards the center as well. The underpriest was wearing a long green tunic of his order, but he also had the plum-colored small cape and hood that marked him as something more than an initiate, and the hood was pulled back, revealing a mostly bald head. Besides the leather satchel on his side, he didn't appear to be carrying anything. The other three men were clearly guards, and were wearing long green surcoats that, judging from the sheen and movement, appeared to be silk. Two of them were wearing nasal helms and carried halberds, but the third had on a greathelm that completely obscured his face, and he had a large shield strapped to his back, and a sword and dagger on his waist.

The two groups wound their way around collapsed columns and through several arches and the remains of walls, making their way through the debris slowly towards the open square at the middle, as apparently arranged. The wall closest to the river was largely intact, and clearly rose high enough to indicate that the temple had once had at least three stories. The walls with the arched doorways didn't rise near as high, but they too were largely intact on the ground floor, so that both groups disappeared and reappeared as they closed in on the selected area.

The groups stopped about twenty paces apart.

I looked around again, wondering if everyone's bellies were churning as much as mine. Gurdinn's men were hardened and hand-chosen, but I assumed they were accustomed to patrolling the palace and keeping crowds at bay, not warfare. Still, there were only four men in the center of the temple who might draw blade against them, so perhaps the odds emboldened them or heated their blood. I didn't ask and couldn't say.

Turning back to the temple, I saw the underpriest pointing at the pennon, obviously realizing it was a poor disguise for a spear. Even from this distance, the shrug of Hewspear's shoulders was clear and he casually indicated the underpriest's guards with a wave of his hand.

The underpriest appeared to be quite angry. Hewspear shrugged again and waited him out. I glanced in the direction of the woods the other Syldoon were still hiding in, dreading one of them suddenly appearing to warn us more hostile troops had been sighted. But aside from the delicate sound of another pine cone dropping to the needled ground, and the breathing of the men around men, there was only stillness.

Whatever debate the two groups in the ruins had been having seemed to have concluded as they stepped closer, stopping six or seven paces apart now. A few more words were exchanged between Hewspear and the underpriest, the pennon rippling in the wind above them.

At last, both the underpriest and Hewspear stepped forward and the underpriest pulled the strap of the satchel over his head and threw it on the ground between them. It seemed he'd planned no trap at all, and was honoring his part of the dark bargain he'd made.

Hewspear laid the haft of the spear on his shoulder, took another step, and began to lean down as if to take up the satchel. But then he straightened immediately, his spear flying forward in two hands, thrusting into the guard to the right of the underpriest.

Hewspear had moved so quickly and abruptly, the guard hadn't had time to dodge and the pennoned point of his spear struck him square in the belly. He doubled over and reached for the spear, but I didn't see the expected splash of blood. Hewspear pulled his spear back and chopped down at the man's shoulder. Even from this distance, I heard bone snap, but while the surcoat was torn open, there was still no blood—the torn surcoat revealed the mail hidden on the inside. Bloodied or not, the man dropped to the ground, the severed pennon fluttering and falling alongside him.

Mulldoos turned his round shield so the edge faced another halberdier, and I saw a blur of movement. The halberdier stumbled backwards, a bolt protruding from his chest, and fell to the stones. I didn't understand what had happened until I saw Mulldoos discarding his shield—there was crossbow attached to the inside, which made for a one-shot surprise attack.

Odds suddenly reversed, the other two guards pulled the priest backwards and the three of them were retreating towards their horses, the guard with the greathelm now armed with sword and shield. Mulldoos and Braylar had their weapons and bucklers in hand now, and they stepped up alongside Hewspear, the three of them advancing forward.

Lloi shouted, "Now, Horntoad, send your men now! Tomner, go!"

I wondered at the urgency, as Braylar and his retinue had the advantage, but then I saw what she'd seen. Two lines of men were emerging from the ground closest to the towering, complete wall on the far side of the temple. I was sure my eyes deceived me—it seemed as if they materialized out of the very ground. And then I realized they had—they'd been waiting in two crypts covered in brush and grass mats, and now they were formed up, dirty and no doubt stiff, but a fighting force of twelve men, advancing at a trot, two hundred paces off. This was the trap Braylar had sensed but not seen.

The captain of the guards pushed the underpriest back with the edge of his shield and yelled something at him. The underpriest hesitated, head turning towards the river, no doubt looking for the arrival of his rescuers.

Braylar, Mulldoos, and Hewspear advanced and the captain shouted at the priest again, pushing him behind him as he kept walking backwards, the other guard at his side. The three Syldoon fanned out, but then Mulldoos glanced to his left and saw two guards scrambling over a low wall, followed by several more, moving quickly now they'd sighted the underpriest and his attackers.

Mulldoos must have called out a warning, as Braylar and Hewspear both looked there as well. Braylar took another step towards the underpriest but Mulldoos tried to move in front of him, shouting as he did. Braylar glanced at the approaching guards, back to the underpriest, gauging the distance and the little time he had, and then he began to move backwards towards the archway they'd entered from. With twelve men advancing on them and the rest of his reinforcements halfway up the hill, the three Syldoon couldn't possibly hold out—they turned and ran for the archway.

The underpriest stepped towards the satchel lying between puddles, but the captain of guards slid his sword back in the scabbard and grabbed him by the shoulder, pointing towards their horses. The underpriest rounded on him and screamed in unpriestly fashion, but the captain gestured towards the Brunesmen and Syldoon coming down the hill as fast as they were able. The underpriest still seemed reluctant to leave, probably confident in their numbers, but even if he might not have moved as quickly as his protector liked, he began slowly walking in the direction of the horses. That must have been good enough for his captain, who didn't touch or coerce him again.

It seemed they were sure to reach the horses and mount up, but then Vendurro came crashing out of the woods, riding hard for the three tethered horses on the perimeter of the temple. The halberdier and his captain ran forward, sword again in the captain's hand, the underpriest jogging behind them. Vendurro reached the horses first and ripped their reins free from the branches.

The guard and captain were fifteen paces away, and the underpriest just behind him, when Vendurro lifted his crossbow and leveled it at the trio. They stopped and the captain raised his shield. Suddenly seeing the danger, the underpriest jumped behind the men in armor.

Standing next to me, Lloi said, just loud enough for me to hear, "The halberd. Shoot the halberd. Do it."

Vendurro shouted something, but whatever it was, the guards took no notice as neither of them moved or seemed to respond. Vendurro pulled his right hand away from the long trigger and pointed, presumably at the priest, and then shouted again.

Lloi whispered, "Do it, quick now."

As if he'd finally heard her, Vendurro loosed, although he failed to heed her choice of targets—the bolt blasted through the raised shield and skidded off the top of the captain's helm. He stumbled back into the underpriest, falling to his knees. The halberdier charged forward. Vendurro kicked his heels into his horse, and the stolen horses followed. I thought he was going to trample the halberdier, but he turned the horses so they came between himself and the guard. Having no opportunity to strike, the halberdier did the wise thing and got out of the way as fast as he could. Vendurro led the horses at a canter back up the hill and into the woods.

The guard ran back to the captain and helped him to his feet. He rose unsteadily, but he clearly wasn't dead or mortally injured.

I looked back towards the middle of the temple. The three Syldoon ran out of a second archway, but then Braylar stopped. Mulldoos and Hewspear both took a few more steps and then turned to look back at Braylar. He gestured at the hill with his buckler, at Gurdinn and the other men nearing the bottom, and then he pointed back towards their three horses. Mulldoos clearly didn't like whatever Braylar was proposing, but Braylar shouted something else, gestured one last time, and then ran back towards some of the more complete pillars in the chamber.

Mulldoos started after him, but then Hewspear shouted something. Mulldoos looked at him and shook his head, liking whatever Hewspear said no better, but Hewspear grabbed him by the shoulder and pulled him away. With a last look at Braylar, who was now hidden from view behind a pillar, Mulldoos turned and the pair ran towards the archway. Just as they reached it, Hewspear stopped and looked back at the chamber they had just left. Several of the guards raced in pursuit, but they appeared to have split up. It took me a moment to find them. They were circling the outskirts of the temple, making their way towards the three tethered Syldonian horses.

Those pursuing Hewspear and Mulldoos ran through the chamber, oblivious to Braylar, and raced for the far archway. I asked Lloi, "Why did Braylar break off from the others like that?"

"He come for the priest. Won't be leaving without him, I'm thinking."

I looked back to the temple, certain that several men were going to die today.

Mulldoos was standing a few paces inside the archway, waiting for his pursuers, while Hewspear was pressed against the wall, slashing spear held tight.

The archway was only wide enough for one man to come through at a time. The first guard entered, his large shield held before him, and Mulldoos slashed at his head. The guard blocked the blow and took another step, just clearing the archway, when Hewspear drove his spear into the guard's exposed side. The long blade punched into the man's ribs, and Hewspear pushed him hard against the stone archway as Mulldoos slashed again, this time taking him across the face, just below the nasal of his helm.

The guard collapsed, and Hewspear pulled his weapon free—this time the spearhead was bloody. The next guard attempted to step over the body, but Hewspear slashed at his thigh. The spear blade didn't shear the mail beneath the surcoat, but the man was clearly hurt, as he pulled back.

Another guard attempted to breach the archway. As he stepped forward Hewspear feinted a thrust at his head. The guard began to raise his shield but he saw the real thrust aimed for his leg in time, bringing his shield down quickly to knock the spearpoint aside. As he did, Mulldoos slashed at the guard's sword arm. The guard stepped into the attack, deflecting it with his sword, and tried to move forward so more of his comrades could fight their way in. But he slipped in the dead guard's blood. Hewspear's next thrust caught him in the neck, just above the surcoated mail coat. He spasmed and fell alongside the other body, struggling weakly as he died.

The four remaining guards didn't seem to be in a hurry to attempt the archway after that, especially since it was partially blocked by two bodies. While they were debating what to do, Braylar moved between the large pillars to their rear and slipped through the opposite archway unseen.

He ran back towards the center of the temple. Reaching it, he glanced around, and seeing no one, kept moving, darting between pillars, heading roughly in the direction of the underpriest.

There was a noise behind us. Lloi and I both spun around, her with a crossbow balanced on her stumpy hand. Vendurro stepped between the trees. "Whoa, girl. Easy. Same side." He grinned at me as if lives weren't hanging in the balance below. "What's happening?"

Lloi pointed to the Syldonian horses and the priest's guards who were now surrounding them. "Six there. Three or four still in the middle, Mull-doos and Hewspear holding them off. Gurdinn and the rest are making for the horses."

Vendurro surveyed the rest of the temple. "Cap?"

Lloi pointed to the other end. "Making a grab for the priest." She looked at Vendurro and said, "You should have shot the halberd. No shield." There was no mistaking the accusing tone.

Vendurro avoided her stare. "The other guard looked more important."

"They're both alive. That's important. Next time, don't fuss about rank. Kill who you can kill." The anger in her voice told me she wasn't certain there would be a next time.

"I'll remember that, General Lloi. Now, let's get down there."

Lloi shook her head. "Captain Noose ordered us to guard them horses, and that's exactly what I figure to do. You might want to be going on back to the other side and doing the same. Don't call them orders for nothing."

"They need our help."

"Need us to do what they ordered us to do."

Vendurro took a step towards her. "Listen, girl, they—"

I told them both to look. Braylar had made his way behind a pillar near the two guards and the underpriest, who was sitting on a broken column, mopping at his bald brow with a cloth. The halberdier was pacing, and when Braylar heard him near the pillar, he stepped out and struck. Blood-sounder slammed into the side of the guard's helmet and he dropped like a sack of grain.

Braylar moved around the body and towards the underpriest, but the captain of the guards stepped between. As Braylar and the captain began to slowly circle each other, the underpriest decided he'd seen enough and ran in the other direction.

I heard the dull thwack of weapons striking wood and the sharp clang of weapons meeting each other or bits of armor and scanned the rest of the temple. Gurdinn and his men were fighting the underpriest's guards near the horses, and there seemed to be little order to the conflict—it was a mad melee, where men fought without formation or discipline and simply tried to survive. I glanced quickly at the middle of the temple. The standoff between Mulldoos and Hewspear and the guards hadn't changed, but only two guards were near the archway. The other two had made it to the edge of the temple, near the high drop-off. Both had their shields on their back and swords sheathed as they climbed up some the stones near the edge and tried to clamber over the wall.

I heard a cry and turned to see one of Gurdinn's men cut down by a pair of priest guards. He tried to retreat up the steps leading to the temple, but exposed his lower legs in doing so. One guard struck him in the shin, the other in the opposite knee, and then he was down on his back. Both guards leaped up the stairs and hacked at him until he stopped jerking. Then they started back down the steps to help their companions.

Vendurro stood between Lloi and the temple to be sure he had her attention. "Stay until you grow more fingers if you like, but I'm going down." He left the cover of the trees and Lloi ran deeper into the woods. I thought for a moment she'd fled, which made me want to run as well, but she returned leading two horses by the reins.

She mounted as soon as she was clear of the overhanging branches, and whistled for Vendurro. He turned and looked back up at her.

Lloi said, "We ride or not at all. Never make it otherwise."

Vendurro shook his head. "They'll break their legs." But disregarding his own warning, he mounted his horse as well. Without another word, they sat as far back in their saddles as they could and plummeted down the side of the hill. I was sure Vendurro was right, but whatever gods favor foolish rescues opted to grant them clemency as they stayed in the saddle and the horses didn't fall.

Despite the number of men trying to kill each other on the end of the temple closest to me, I couldn't stop myself from watching what unfolded on the other end between Braylar and the captain of the guards. Braylar was moving around to the captain's shield side, Bloodsounder behind the buckler, when he stepped forward and snapped the flail heads at the captain's helm. The captain moved out of range and Braylar shuffled forward, feet barely leaving the ground as he allowed the flail heads to continue their arc before lashing out at the captain's knee. The captain didn't attempt to avoid the blow this time, but blocked the flail with the bottom of his shield, stepping in as he did, his sword a blur.

Braylar punched out with his buckler and deflected the blade and then it was his turn to clear range as the two continued moving around each other, looking for an opening, testing each other's defenses. Braylar moved to his left and threw a shot over his buckler and toward the captain's helm. The captain blocked it, but Braylar changed direction and passed to the other side with his quick shuffle, and as the heads struck the shield and ricocheted off, Braylar spun them around. They were aimed at the captain's hip, and while the captain got his shield around in time to catch the chains, the heads disappeared, and judging from the way the captain jumped, they struck something behind his shield.

They continued like this, Braylar circling, attacking from the extreme edge of his range, using his peculiar angles to keep the captain's shield on the move, bits of wood exploding whenever the flail heads struck the shield itself. I didn't see him land any more shots, but the captain seemed less mobile, and while he threw some blows of his own, Braylar always stepped away, avoiding them or turning them with his buckler.

Braylar was content to orbit and wear the larger man down, when suddenly the captain charged in. Braylar stepped back and to the side, attempting to retreat at an angle, but the captain moved with him as he threw a combination of blows. Braylar dodged the first, blocked the second and third with his buckler before throwing a shot of his own. The flail heads were aimed at the captain's sword arm, but the shield blocked the chains. They got stuck for an instant on the edge of the shield on a spot that Braylar had torn away, and as Braylar struggled to free his flail, the captain stepped in close and thrust at his chest. Braylar deflected the thrust just enough with his buckler—it sliced through his tunic and slid along the outside of his scale shirt, but then the captain smashed Braylar in the side of the helm with the edge of his shield.

Braylar flew back and the flail ripped free of the shield. The blow must have stunned him, because he looked ready to fall to the ground. At the last moment, he stuck his buckler out and used it on the stone floor to maintain his balance, his wrist bending awkwardly as he did, and I thought he was going to break it. But somehow, he kept his feet as he stumbled forward in an awkward shamble to keep from falling on his face. Then he slid into a colossal section of toppled pillar, slamming into it with his shoulder. The captain was right behind him, sword coming down. Braylar must have sensed the attack—he dodged to his left and the blade scraped along the pillar, scarring the old stone.

Braylar spun around as the captain pressed forward again, deflecting the next blow with his buckler as he lashed out himself. The flail arced out low, parallel with the ground. One or both of the spiked heads struck the captain in the left knee, just below the mail surcoat. The captain took another step towards Braylar, but his leg buckled and he almost fell as Braylar used the brief respite to retreat several steps.

The captain came after Braylar again, but now it was with a pronounced limp, and I could see the blood trickling down his leg. Braylar was obviously aware of this as well, because he moved away from the pillar, again controlling the range of the engagement. Braylar snapped his wrist forward, and the flail heads flew towards the captain's great helm. The captain brought his shield up in time, the spikes again tearing into the wood, splinters flying. But Braylar used that shot merely to set up his second, around the captain's shield, striking the captain in the left hip.

The captain spun to keep Braylar in front of him, slashing with his sword, but he hit only air as Braylar had stepped back out again. It occurred to me then the captain had missed his best opportunity for killing Braylar. His left leg and hip were both wounded now, and while I couldn't possibly judge the extent of those injuries, the captain was clearly hobbled.

This captain must have realized this as well, because he came on hard before Braylar could attack again. But while Braylar had attempted to sidestep away from the captain before, he now met the attack head on. The captain threw a blow aimed towards Braylar's head that Braylar punchblocked with his buckler, throwing a shot of his own. The flail heads smashed into the side of the captain's helm and ricocheted away. The captain lowered his head and tried to blindly bull Braylar with his shield. But Braylar had moved to his right, whipping the flail heads around with him. They cleared the top of the shield and struck the captain in the back of the helm as he passed.

The captain took another step, and then his left leg gave out. He used a pillar to brace himself, but the flail struck his elbow and the sword clattered to the stone floor. The captain drove Braylar back with his shield, and it worked for a moment, as Braylar stepped out of its path, but then he was back in, hooking the edge of the shield with his buckler and ripping it aside. The flail heads smashed into the captain's chest and he staggered back into the pillar. Again, Bloodsounder snapped straight forward, hitting the great helm just beneath the eye slot. The captain brought his shield around and struck Braylar in the side, but there wasn't nearly enough strength in the blow to do serious damage. The flail heads flew out and struck the captain in the ribs.

The captain slid down the pillar as his legs gave out completely, shield now useless at his side, and Braylar raised his flail above his head to finish him off. But the recovered halberdier was rushing forward, the long point at the top of his polearm aimed for Braylar's back. Braylar spun around, knocking the halberd point aside with his buckler, but the guard slammed his body into Braylar's. The pair went flying past the captain and tripped over some stones.

Braylar dropped his flail and buckler when he hit the ground and the guard landed on top of him, still holding onto the haft of the polearm and pressing it onto Braylar's chest. Braylar planted his helm on the ground and arched his back, trying to roll the guard off, but the guard had anticipated the move and placed his legs on the outside of Braylar's, clamping them together. He pushed the haft towards Braylar's neck, arms outstretched, and Braylar grabbed it with both hands to keep it away. But the guard was larger and apparently stronger, and he was in the better position. As Braylar struggled to keep from choking, I saw the captain of the guards slowly roll onto his hands and knees, greathelm bobbing.

Braylar let go of the halberd haft briefly and punched the guard in the side, but whatever padding was under the mail and the surcoat nullified the blow, as the guard didn't react at all and instead pushed the haft forward until it was beneath Braylar's chin.

I looked back towards the other end of the temple, but the Syldoon and Brunesmen were locked in their own combat with the rest of the guards, with Lloi and Vendurro now in the mix, and Mulldoos and Hewspear were still holding off the other guards. No one was coming. I looked back to Braylar, saw him still struggling, and it was like standing on shore watching a drowning man far out to sea. Even if I'd been the most competent soldier in the world, I couldn't have possibly reached him in time.

I wanted to shut my eyes or walk away, but I couldn't. I knew if Braylar were to die, I had to see it. Not because I wanted to. I didn't bear the man any love, but I didn't have any desire to see his life end either. No, I had to see it because there was no one else to bear witness; it would fall on me to watch it in its entirety and maintain the record, complete what I'd begun.

But then I realized while I couldn't possibly reach Braylar in time, I had something that could. There was a moment of indecision—I was sure if I left, Braylar would die in the brief time I wasn't watching—but there was a small chance I could change his fate. I turned and ran into the woods, grabbing a loaded crossbow off the saddle of one of the Syldoon horses, and returned as quickly as I could.

The guard was still trying to squeeze the life out of Braylar. I raised the crossbow, sighted down its length, and tried to steady my hands. I didn't trust myself to try to hit the guard—at that distance, even an accurate marksman had just about as much chance of hitting Braylar as the man choking him, and I was no accurate marksman. So I aimed for a column near the pair, high and to the right.

Waiting to exhale, I squeezed the long trigger. The bolt flew free and I tracked it as best I could. It sailed straight for the majority of its path, only beginning to arc slightly at the end. But that slight drop from where I'd aimed was almost enough to end the fight one way or the other—it struck the column in a small puff of dust just above the guard's shoulder.

The guard's head jerked and turned left and right like a bird's, but he must've released some of the pressure on Braylar as he did. Braylar groped for his long dagger, twisting his body as much as he could to grab the hilt. The guard's head snapped back down as he felt Braylar shift and he seemed to redouble his efforts to crush his windpipe. But my distraction had been enough. Braylar brought the dagger up fast into the guard's side. The dagger didn't penetrate the mail, or at least not much, but unlike Braylar's fist, the guard seemed to feel this blow and Braylar jabbed again in the same spot. The guard let go of the haft with his left hand and punched Braylar in the face. Braylar stabbed at his side again, and the guard flinched once more, but when he raised his arm to deliver another blow, Braylar thrust the dagger up—the blade struck the guard in the throat, just above the mail coat and beneath the jaw. Blood sprayed onto Braylar's arm and face. The guard rolled off, pulling the bloody dagger free. He pressed his hand against the wound and tried to stop the flow of blood that seemed impossibly bright in the sunlight.

Braylar got to his hands and knees, holding his own throat, head down as he coughed. But when he looked up, he saw the guard sitting near him and crawled forward. The guard tried to flee as best he could, crabbing away backwards, heels digging into the ground, right arm supporting him as he wobbled from side to side, still holding his wound. It was like two badly wounded insects fighting to the death. Braylar threw himself forward, ramming his elbow into the guard's hand and throat, almost toppling over as he did. The guard fell onto his back and then tried to slowly rise. Braylar smashed his elbow into his throat twice more until the guard finally stopped moving.

Head down, Braylar knelt next to him, the sleeve of his tunic spattered with blood from elbow to cuff, his left hand on his own throat again. He crawled over to the dagger, wiping the blade on the dead guard before slipping it back into the sheath at his side.

He got to his feet, teetering as if drunk, and then turned and looked at the column that had been chipped by the crossbow bolt, and then up into the woods in my direction. Suddenly, for reasons I couldn't understand, it seemed very important he knew who'd shot the crossbow. Braylar was bending down to retrieve his flail as I stepped out from behind the trunk of the tree to reveal myself, but then I saw him suddenly look to his right after he straightened.

The captain of the guards was struggling to regain his feet, leaning on the column for support, sword hanging limply from his mangled right arm. While Braylar could've advanced and finished him off right then, he stood there, waiting, hand on his throat.

The captain turned around, still using the column, and tried to hoist his shield into the air, nearly dropping it before finally getting a firm grip. His great helm swiveled slowly before it fixed on Braylar. He took a halting step, and pulled his near-useless left leg behind him, his shoulders crooked as he favored his bruised or broken ribs, the sword laid across the top of his battered shield, as he didn't have the strength to hold it up with his injured arm alone.

Braylar rubbed the back of his arm across his face to mop up the sweat and blood coming out of his nose, and then he beckoned the captain on once.

The captain lurched forward, bent and broken, but undefeated just the same. There was something about this physical act of defiance that was moving, heroic even. He could've waited until he was alone and safe, or upon realizing that Braylar was still there, could've lowered his weapon and surrendered. Instead, he chose a path that would surely lead to his death. Perhaps he felt the wounds he'd sustained were severe enough that he was unlikely to survive, or perhaps he was too dazed to know just how badly he was hurt. But it seemed to me that he was cognizant and made his choice, resigning himself to death but not defeat.

Braylar had never whirled the flail heads around in dramatic circles before delivering a blow, preferring instead to send them in motion only during the actual attack. But he did so now, spinning the twin heads above him as he gripped the haft with both hands.

When the captain was five paces away, he pushed himself forward with whatever last reservoir of strength he had. Braylar let him come on and then stepped to his left as the captain dropped the sword off the shield and thrust it forward. The thrust missed wide and Braylar torqued his whole body into the final, twisting, vicious blow. The flail heads crashed into the side of the captain's greathelm, caving it in as he fell forward. The blow was a tremendous one, and I was very glad the helm didn't come free, because I didn't want to see what kind of damage had been done.

The captain was surely dead before he hit the ground, but even so, his fingers didn't release the sword even after he struck stone. This seemed to be his final defiant gesture, as blood began to pool around his helm.

Braylar squatted down beside his foe, the flail heads and the chains spooling on the ground as he touched the captain's back with the tips of his fingers. He lowered his head for a moment before rising quickly. He retrieved his buckler, took one last, longing look in the direction the underpriest had fled in, then ran towards the sound of combat coming from the opposite side of the ruins.

Mulldoos and Hewspear had retreated from the first complete wall and archway and run towards the sound of combat, with their pursuers hesitating briefly and then following. The other underpriest's guards, Syldoon, and Brunesmen had all moved to the same general spot near the front of the temple. Braylar was running towards the combat as well, and I saw another figure arrive—it took me a moment to realize it was Glesswik.

With everyone converging, it seemed that the Syldoon and the Brunesmen stood a decent chance of surviving the melee, but the outcome was far from certain. Two of the underpriest's guards advanced on a Brunesman, who blocked the first three blows. He couldn't block, parry, or avoid the next: a sword slashed him across his calf. He lost his balance, never to regain it again. The two guards closed in and threw a flurry of blows from two sides, battering him backwards into the steps—several blows didn't compromise his mail, but still inflicted damage to flesh and bone beneath, and other blows struck him across the wrist and unarmored legs. Having dropped his sword, he tried to curl under his shield, but one of the guards kicked it aside and they both stabbed and slashed repeatedly. One guard thrust a final time in the thigh, and when he didn't jerk or flinch, they both ran back down the stairs into the fray.

It occurred to me that if the Syldoon and Brunesmen were all cut down, I'd need to flee and try to find the remaining Syldoon back on the road. I looked away from the battle and was turning to check on the horses in the woods behind me when I saw something on the opposite end of the temple.

I feared more of the underpriest's guards had arrived, but if it had been guards, surely they'd have been joining the battle. So I thought I must've seen some animal moving, or perhaps nothing at all, but then, at the base of the temple along the high stone platform, I saw it again. Something or someone was trying to look around the corner. I stepped closer, hiding behind the tree in front of me as best I could, and then saw the underpriest peer around again, trying to gauge if there were any threats nearby. Seeing nothing, he began to run towards the woods where Vendurro had originally ridden away with his horses. Then, perhaps remembering Vendurro, he stopped, likely realizing that if anyone were there, they'd already be riding out to apprehend him. He looked over his shoulder a final time and then began climbing the hill as quickly as he could.

I looked back to the other end of the temple. The wild, broken melee was total chaos now, the victors still in grave doubt. Even if the Syldoon prevailed, no one could see the other side of the temple—they'd never know the underpriest was there to pursue him.

Even while I was running back to the horses, I cursed myself for a fool—the battle could easily turn against Braylar and his retinue, and if they were defeated, the only thing I would accomplish by wildly chasing down the underpriest would be to expose myself to the victorious party, who would be all too pleased to punish a prisoner for the losses they'd sustained. Still, I felt I had to try. Though I didn't understand the impulse, there was some small part of me that wanted to impress men like Braylar and Gurdinn, and I cursed myself for allowing that minority to rule the majority of common sense.

Rather than waste more time trying to span the crossbow I held, I dropped it on the forested floor and ran back to a Syldoon horse, pulled a crossbow out of the leather case on its side and checked to make sure it was loaded. Seeing that it was, I ran around to my own horse and climbed the saddle as quickly as possible, which is to say, not exceptionally fast, given that I was trying to do so without accidentally shooting my horse in the back of the head. Kicking my heels into the horse's flanks, we bolted down the small track Vendurro had emerged from earlier. Even on flat, even ground, I'm a suspect rider, but hurtling through the woods, up and down inclines, I was terrified, and it was all I could do not to fall from the saddle or get hung up on a branch. I felt them grabbing at me from all sides, and laid myself low behind the horse's neck, and closed my eyes so they wouldn't get scratched out. I had no idea how I might find the priest in the dense foliage, or what I would do even if I did, but I had begun the chase, and I would be thrice-cursed if I didn't at least complete the attempt.

We emerged in a small glade, and I looked everywhere, wondering where I was or what direction to go, but the horse had no such problems, or didn't trust its rider to make a decision, good or no. We trotted through some tall grass and up a small embankment. I saw no break in the woods above us, but I told myself the horse probably knew what it was doing, so urged it forward and ducked my head down again as he approached the brush and trees. The horse was breathing heavily with the effort, but it seemed strong and willing.

We trotted through a small space between two trees, winding between the twisted trunks and into thicker foliage, and then found what passed for a path. It was overgrown, and we couldn't move with much speed at first, but the brush thinned slightly, and seeing the space open up, I again prompted the horse forward. It seemed glad to run once more, even if it was only an exaggerated canter.

I get lost in city streets even with beggars trading directions for small coin, so I had little sense of how far we'd come, or where we might be in relation to the temple or our original hiding place. We began moving downhill again, and the horse picked up speed, branches flying by in brown blur.

The spaces between trees grew, and as the ground leveled, I pulled on the reins. Unused to its awkward rider, it took several tugs before the horse obeyed, but we finally came to a stop. I looked everywhere and tried to listen, although my own heavy breathing distorted everything I might have heard. Trees and more trees, and I was about to urge the horse forward again, sure I'd accomplished nothing except getting lost in the woods. But then, perhaps one hundred paces away, there was a brief flash of color. Plum. The underpriest's small cape. It disappeared as quickly as I'd seen it, but I kicked my heels into the horse's flanks and we were off again, hooves crunching pine cones.

As we closed the gap and dodged between trees, I saw the underpriest in flight ahead of us. I clicked as loudly as possible, and when that had no noticeable effect, I put my heels to my horse again, and nearly dropped the crossbow as we suddenly picked up more speed. The horse navigated as best it could, but it wasn't concerned about the branches that flew above its head, and one low-hanging pine branch struck me so hard in the face and chest I was sure I would be pulled from the saddle or discharge my weapon. There was sap on my forehead and no doubt twenty scratches, but otherwise I was unharmed.

I looked around, my face as close to the back of my horse's neck as possible, wondering if I'd overridden the mark and passed the underpriest hiding in the brush, but the purple gave him away again as he darted from behind a tree when he heard my approach.

I yelled at him to stop, but he hiked up his tunic with both arms and ran as fast as he could. I gave chase, eyes so fixed on my fleeing quarry that I didn't notice we were approaching the edge of the woods again. I burst through some bushes and found myself at the top of a hill. Shading my eyes with one hand and blinking, I saw the figure of the priest further down. He was trying to make his way without losing his footing, but once he glanced over his shoulder and spotted me, he hurtled down as quickly as he could.

My horse charged forward without any extra encouragement, no doubt happy to have left the labyrinth of trees and bushes behind us. The hill wasn't as steep on this side of the valley, but I'd never ridden down a hill before, so it might as well have been a sheer cliff. The underpriest tripped and fell, rolling over and over, tunic flapping wildly about his legs and arms.

Somehow, we stayed upright and came to a stop at the bottom near the dizzy and bruised underpriest. He lay on his side in some tall grass, panting, eyes closed, knees tucked up halfway to his chest. I tugged at the reins and spun around to face him, the crossbow nearly slipping out of my right hand until I let go of the reins and steadied it with my left. While the underpriest surely knew I was there, he didn't open his eyes to look at me. I glanced around. We were alone.

I tried to get my breathing under control, but my lungs seemed determined to betray my fear and exhilaration. I didn't trust myself to speak, but even if I had, now that I actually had the underpriest prone and defenseless in front of me, I realized I had no idea what to do. If I said too much, I was sure to reveal that I wasn't a soldier or even a common tavern brawler. And if that happened, I didn't know how the underpriest would respond. He was unarmed, and I had a crossbow pointed down at him, so that was in my favor, but once he opened his eyes and steadied himself, if he sensed that I wasn't a bloodspiller by trade, he could easily run again, or possibly even try to overwhelm or disarm me. And I wasn't sure I could squeeze the long trigger if he did. When I'd done so in the wagon with Braylar, that was facing an armed soldier with the intent to dismember me, and even there, I'd missed badly from five feet away.

I knew I'd need to bluff the underpriest into believing I was a man of action with little remorse, and the only way I could do that was to try to imagine what Braylar would say. I was considering which words to begin with when the underpriest opened his eyes and fixed them on me. They were wet and red-rimmed, as if he'd been sitting too close to a smoky fire or had been long weeping, but I suspected that was either his natural condition, or perhaps a reaction to some plant or flower in the vicinity. His eyes stayed on me as he sat up, and they were filled with malevolence. It seemed his balance hadn't quite returned from his many spins down the hill, as he slowly made his way to his feet.

I tried to approximate Braylar's tone. "I don't want to shoot you. I really don't. But I will if you run again."

The underpriest stood where he was, swatting some of the mud and dirt off his clothes, and stopped to pick some twigs out of his hair before looking at me again. I was debating what to say next when the underpriest said, "Do you have any idea who you're dealing with, boy?"

I forced the next string of words out more slowly than the first. "Yes. My prisoner. Now, you'll walk in front of me as—"

"Not me, you fool. The high priest. I'm the high priest's man. If you assault me, you assault the high priest, and—"

It was my turn to interrupt. "You're my prisoner. That's all I need to know." I tried to instill Braylarian steel into those words, and probably failed miserably.

The underpriest replied as if he hadn't heard me. "You'll suffer greatly for this. All of this. The high priest will flail you alive when he discovers—"

"No." I looked in the direction of the temple and then back to the underpriest. "The man back there with the flail will be doing all the flailing. Now, walk in that direction. Ten paces ahead of me. No more. No less. And be quiet please, or I'll be forced to shoot you."

The underpriest started up at me defiantly, and I tried to resist the awful urge to wipe at the syrupy stain on my forehead that was beginning to itch abominably. I didn't think the underpriest would rush me—that seemed beyond him—but if he turned and ran, I didn't think I could really shoot him either. He'd never stop again, and I might as well have brought his horse with and handed it back to him, wishing him safe journey.

His red-rimmed stare didn't falter, and it seemed that he was considering the seriousness of my threat, weighed against what might be won if he chose the correct words to cow me into letting him go.

I was almost panicked into saying something else, even though I knew the more I said the greater my chances of being seen through, when the underpriest began to slowly walk back towards the temple. I kept the crossbow trained on him as he went past and waited until he could no longer see me before dropping one hand to the reins and tugging the horse around, sure if he noticed I couldn't lead my horse with my legs alone he'd see through my poorly purchased disguise as well.

He moved at an unhurried pace, and the truth was, I wasn't in a hurry to hurry him—I had no idea what awaited us back at the temple. If the Syldoon and Brunesmen were defeated, I was doing nothing but delivering myself into the hands of my enemy. Or their enemy, who by association, made them my enemy. There was possibly still time to release the underpriest and ride towards freedom, and a voice inside cursed me for chasing him down and leaving a perfectly good hiding place. I looked into the woods on the hill above me, certain that any moment another group of the high priest's guards would come down the hill towards us. But, possessed by a foolish impulse, I'd captured the underpriest, so there was nothing left but to see it through to the end. So, we continued with the underpriest walking silently in front of me until we finally made our way back to the ruins. His sense of direction was more sound than mine. Had I been left alone, it might have taken me the rest of the day.

As we came out of the woods and began skirting the perimeter of the ruins, I heard the gurgle of the river and the sound of the wind. The sounds of battle—steel ringing, grunts and cries, screams as men died—were no more. I could only guess who'd won, and didn't want to.

The Godveil was still some ways off, but I caught glances of it through the ruined walls. Its pull was much greater now. I slowed and then nearly stopped as I looked at it wavering in the distance over the river, the thrumming last-note of some unseen instrument louder, the smell of singe and vinegar more powerful. Still knowing it was death to do so, I wanted to turn my horse and ride closer. I pinched the skin on my wrist and kept moving. If the Syldoon had managed to defeat the priest guards, it must only have been because they'd spent two days secreted away in the vault, cramped in the dark with their shit and piss, but worst of all, fighting off the overwhelming urge to come out and walk towards the Veil.

When we rounded the corner of the temple and closed in on the steps where the bulk of the fighting took place, I heard the low moans of the wounded and the sound of men talking heatedly, punctuated now and then by a shout. Several people were talking at once, but I only made out the odd angry word.

The bodies of two of the underpriest's guards were lying across each other at the foot of the stairs, like a belated sacrifice to the Deserters. Someone stepped out from behind a pillar, shouting something in my direction, and I instinctively aimed my crossbow at him, almost pulling the trigger before recognizing he was a Brunesmen. He sheathed his sword and called out over his shoulder, "Your man lives. And he isn't alone."

Suddenly there were several men approaching between a row of pillars, Gurdinn and Braylar among them. A Brunesmen was pushing a prisoner forward, one of the underpriest's guards, a bandage across his bare chest and shoulder, arms tied behind him.

Braylar opened his mouth to speak to me, but stopped as he saw the underpriest. Two things crossed his face—shock, though fleeting, which was perhaps understandable, and then what might have been anger, which lasted longer, and truly confused me. Gratitude was nowhere to be seen. He stopped in front of the underpriest and said, "Welcome back, your holiness. We were worried you'd lost your way in the wild."

Braylar's voice was raspy and thin, testament to nearly being choked to death. He spoke to those behind him, his eyes never leaving the underpriest. "Someone bind this man's hands so he doesn't lose his way again."

The underpriest looked at his injured guard. "I'm a man of Truth, and you'll release the both of us this instant." He pointed at Braylar. "If you turn that man over to us, I'll forget that anyone else was involved in this treachery."

Braylar stepped forward and struck the underpriest across the face with the back of his hand. "Treachery? You would speak to us of treachery, worm? Bind him and gag him."

The underpriest would have been taken off his feet by the blow if he hadn't stumbled into my horse, which snorted at the impact. He straightened himself and addressed Gurdinn, "He has assaulted an underpriest of Truth, and in doing so, assaulted the high priest himself. He can't be saved. But you have the power to save yourself. You—"

Given the animosity Gurdinn bore Braylar, I expected him to hear the underpriest out, but he surprised me. "I don't yet know the full depths of your involvement in this treason, but I soon will. Today, I only know that your men assaulted agents of the baron, and in doing so, assaulted the baron himself." He turned to the soldier who'd first spotted us. "Do as the Syldoon commanded—bind and gag him immediately."

Braylar gave Gurdinn a small nod and then addressed what remained of the company. "We depart this forsaken place. Now."

Gurdinn was in the middle of saying something to one of his soldiers, but hearing Braylar's announcement, turned to him. "Two of the underpriest's guards escaped. We've wasted enough time already. Let's hunt them down, and then we can gather our dead and wounded and return home."

This had clearly been the source of the argument I heard riding up to the ruins. Mulldoos answered him, "He told you already, we got no time at all. None. And we got less time to argue about it."

Gurdinn glanced at Mulldoos for a moment and then looked at Braylar again. "Your man said the surrounding area was clear. The guards—"

Braylar was as grim as I've ever seen him. "My man's name was Glesswik, and he's dead. And we'll be his rearguard in the afterlife if we delay here another moment. We mount up. Now."

It was only then I realized that Glesswik wasn't among the group of survivors. Gurdinn said, "We've both lost men here today. I only pray it was worth it. But the underpriest has no reinforcements nearby. The two guards are on foot, or were when they escaped, so if we track them down, we can capture them. But only if we head after them now."

Braylar's patience, rarely bountiful, was now completely depleted. "This underpriest had men planted for an ambush at least two days in advance, and planned it for some time before that. Do you really believe he'd have reinforcements so far from the engagement? I'll answer for you, he wouldn't. And if he doesn't, then we have no assurance that's where his men are heading. In all likelihood, they're running straight towards a grove or cave a few miles from here. My best tracker is dead. We couldn't possibly hope to catch those two guards in the wildlands in time. So, we return to the city as quickly as possible. Thanks to my man," he gestured at me, "we have what we came here for. Put the dead on the free horses.

We ride hard. We ride now. That is all."

Gurdinn replied, "There's time—"

"This discussion is over. Mount up. That's an order." Braylar pointed at the Brunesman who just finished tying the underpriest's hands together. "Get those two on the spare horses. And tie their legs together underneath. We wouldn't want to lose them along the way." He regarded the underpriest. "I advise you and your man to keep your legs clamped tight, holy man. Should you fall, it will prove a most uncomfortable ride to the city."

Gurdinn turned and walked over to the men, most of whom were already in their saddles. Braylar looked at Gurdinn, practically daring him to dispute his rule in this matter again, and when no protests were forthcoming, he climbed onto his horse and led the way back up the hill. I climbed onto my own horse and moved alongside Lloi as we headed up. Glesswik was laid across his horse like a sack of grain, just like the other Syldoon next to him—Tomner—and the two Brunesmen behind. Tomner had been struck across the back deep enough to sever his spine if not decapitate him completely. With every movement his horse made, his head wobbled.

I gagged and turned in my saddle, stomach heaving, though nothing came out of my mouth except some residue of bile. My shoulders rocked forward again, and I looked around, glad I was in the rear and seen by nobody save Lloi. I wiped my mouth with the back of my sleeve, wondering if the vomit was truly going to come then, willing it out of my body so I could be done with it. But all I could manage was some heinous bitter spit.

Finally confident the spell was over, I sat back up. Lloi handed me a leather flask. I pulled the stopper and took a small swallow. It was old tart wine that spoke of abandoned orchards and dried-up vines, but it was an improvement over the bile, so I took another grateful swallow.

I handed the flask back to her with shaky hands, thanking her. She nodded and took a swallow herself. "Glesswik hated wine. Said he hated it, that is. But he drank more than most any two men." She lifted the flask to her lips again, swallowed enough that some drained down her chin, and handed it back to me. I took another small swallow before returning it.

Lloi seemed about ready to tip the flask up again for another swig but then decided against it. She held the flask back out to me a final time, but

I couldn't stomach another and worried that I was in danger of keeping what I'd drunk in my stomach, so declined.

More than halfway up the hill, I was looking over my shoulder at the temple retreating behind us, half expecting more of the underpriest's guards to suddenly emerge from the ruins or surrounding woods. There were bright splashes of blood at the entrance, most obviously on the steps leading to the arch, but also spattered here and there among the outer columns. Before meeting Braylar, I never imagined I'd witness such a scene of carnage, let alone somehow be a part of it. I wasn't really a scholar anymore, having walked off that path now forever. Regardless what else occurred, I knew I'd never return to that life the same—though what I'd become or was becoming, I didn't know.

Lloi said, "You did well. Back there." I didn't respond right away, and she pointed ahead. "Capturing the priest. All this, for nothing, less than spit, we return without him. Captain Noose might say it—probably not, most like—but capturing that priest, could be you saved some lives, whether you fought or no."

I leaned forward as the incline became more pronounced. "What do you mean?"

She lowered her voice so the closest Brunesmen couldn't hear. "Returning to their baron, no priest in tow? Well, might not have sat too well with him, is all. All loss, no gain? Bad trade, bookmaster. Nobles like gain, like it fierce. All they live for, most of them. And those that rob them of it tend to not be living long at all. So, you and me, different as we are, we're two..." She hunted for the right word, and grinned when she found it, "retainer who got something in common. We might not be Syldoon, but we might not be anything else now, neither."

That gave me a shiver, and I didn't know how to respond, so I only nodded. Braylar and Gurdinn led our small column through the woods, our passage muffled by the thick carpet of needles on the forest floor. I began to say something else to Lloi, but before I had three words out, she reached over and grabbed my arm.

I glanced up the column and saw that the riders, both dead and alive, rode through the forest in total silence. Only the closest Brunesmen had heard me speak and had turned around, no doubt to tell me to shut my mouth before seeing that Lloi had been quicker. I looked away from him and waited until he was facing forwards in the saddle again before looking up, my cheeks again flush.

I cursed myself, silently, of course. It was possible that I truly was one of the Syldoon now, by proxy if nothing else, but I wondered if I'd ever learn to conduct myself in a way that was more… military. I always seemed to be doing something or other to elicit either scorn or chastisement. It was easy to see how Braylar's other archivists hadn't survived long with his company.

The trek back to the road seemed to take less time than it had to get to the temple. Suddenly, the trees gave way again to tall yellow grass, and our group was moving with more speed as we made our way to the road. I looked back at the trees behind us. We were alone.

Braylar wheeled his horse around and held up a hand, and we all came to a stop. Voice still hoarse, he ordered Hewspear to remain behind as a rearguard while we continued ahead. Hewspear saluted and rode off to the trees on the opposite side of the road to take up a hidden position. He sat stiff in the saddle, and I wondered what injuries he'd sustained.

Braylar looked up and down our small column, then fixed on Vendurro, his horse alongside the body of Glesswik. "Ride until you sight Xen. Tell him we're on the move and he's to scout the road ahead. Report back when finished."

Vendurro didn't respond immediately and Braylar shouted as much as his bruised throat would allow, "Syldoon! I gave you an order. Ride to Xen. Now."

Vendurro looked down at Glesswik once before kicking his heels into his horse and galloping off.

Braylar addressed the rest of us, "We sleep in Alespell tonight. But not if you blow a horse. Ride hard, but not too hard." He spun around and led us down the road.

I looked for Hewspear, but he was already hidden, and then for Vendurro, but he was disappearing around the bend of trees ahead, the sound of his horse's hooves disappearing with him. What remained of our company, bandaged and bent, was a pitiful group indeed. I considered our prospects of surviving any kind of attack minute, and utterly bleak if we were outnumbered, which seemed the most likely possibility. And so I tried to force myself to look straight ahead, at the Brunesman's horse in front of me.

Before long, Braylar called back for Lloi and myself, demanding we join him. I looked at Lloi, she shrugged her shoulders, and we rode up the column. The underpriest turned and stared at me with all the violence a bound and gagged man could muster, and the Brunesmen largely ignored us. We took our place alongside Braylar and Mulldoos.

Mulldoos looked at me, his face even more pale than usual, lips tight, as if each small movement in the saddle were an agony that he was unwilling to let show, and I realized he must have been injured as well, though I couldn't tell where.

Braylar, too, didn't seem to be faring well, though his physical injuries seemed to be the least of it. Lloi rode as close as she could and whispered, "Captain Noose?"

Braylar nodded, eyes closed, and if our brief history together told me anything, he was battling things unseen to the rest of us. I still found this difficult to believe, never having encountered anything like it before, but I'd seen enough to convince me he was no madman. Well, not wholly.

He licked his lips. "I'm well, Lloi." His voice was still like tangled underbrush. "Well enough." He straightened his back and rolled his posture back up to the rigid position it was so commonly in, though this seemed to take a great effort. Then he looked at me. "You shot the crossbow, yes?"

The question surprised me. "Yes. It was me."

He asked, "And were you trying to hit me or him?"

When we'd first met, I might have been reluctant to answer, turning his words over carefully, like overturning stones with the knowledge that a snake was coiled under one of them. But I was too tired. "I was trying to distract the guard."

"Well then, it was a fine shot. A fine shot, truly."

Unaccustomed to his praise, I was silent, waiting briefly for a barb or nasty qualifier. None came, and so I mumbled my thanks.

That was the extent of our exchange on the subject, as he turned to Lloi and said, "When we return, I'll have need of you."

"You got need of me now. Might be there is no later."

"There's a later if I will it so, and I do." He rubbed his bruised throat and closed his eyes.

Mulldoos chuckled and said, "Cap here is a master of will, he is. More willful than the gods with half as much regret. Doubt that at your peril."

I expected Braylar to send me back to the rear again but he didn't. And he didn't speak to anyone else again. There are some men who are silent in a way that indicates they're wrestling with their thoughts or drawn into a waking dreamworld, in both cases, withdrawing from those around them. Braylar was the opposite—his silence seemed to radiate outwards with an almost physical force. It was heavy and oppressive, either driving those around him away or deep into their own reveries, or demanding something be said to break the uncomfortable quiet. There were times his scorn was preferable to his silence. I was tempted to speak, either to him or one of his two remaining retinue, but held my tongue. And so we rode along, silent from the front of the column to rear. Heat lightning stole closer, but still no thunder.

A few miles later, Vendurro came back down the road to meet us. When he reined up, Braylar asked, "What of the road?"

Vendurro's voice was flat. "Road's clear, Cap. Least, it was last I looked. Not looking now."

"Very good. Rejoin the column."

Vendurro saluted and started to turn his horse, but Braylar reached over and grabbed his shoulder, squeezing once. Vendurro licked his lips but didn't look at Braylar, and the captain released him. Vendurro rode back beside Glesswik's horse and body.

The hours dragged by, each more unnerving than the last. The procession was full of funeral quality, in mood if not in finery. We rode along, mute as the miles came and went, stopping once to briefly water the horses. We passed small hills harboring fugitive clumps of trees among the small pastures and homesteads, accessed by smaller paths leading off the road. We saw several fields of sheep, and now and then a man mending a hedge. Even then, with the wild abandoned temple many miles behind us and Alespell and the baron's protection drawing closer, the silence didn't lift.

Then we saw a figure galloping down the road towards us. Xen was alone, but we all knew there was only one reason for him to be galloping. He reined up, horse spewing foam out of the corners of its mouth, sweat pouring down his face. He looked over his shoulder briefly, but one shout from Mulldoos and he spun back around and gathered himself. "More of the priest's men. Riding hard. Coming down the road."

Braylar asked, "How many?"

"Hard to say, Cap. Didn't stop to introduce myself. More than ten. Less than twenty. Riding in a column."

"How far back?"

Xen started to glance over his shoulder again but stopped himself. "A mile? Two? No, less than two. But more than a mile, I say."

Braylar looked at Gurdinn, who'd ridden up to hear the report. Gurdinn assessed our small company with a scowl. "We don't have the numbers to engage them. Not directly. We should find a defensible position." He pointed behind us. "That copse of trees looks to be on a small hill. I say, we ride there, take cover in the trees. Hope they ride by. It's the closest cover. I see no other choice." If he believed this plan might actually work, it didn't carry through to his voice, which was less than inspiring.

Braylar was still facing up the road, eyes closed. "They won't."

Gurdinn looked confused. "Won't what?"

Braylar let out a deep breath and opened his eyes. "They won't ride by."

"Might not. They might not. We don't know."

Braylar had a flail head in one hand as he replied, almost sadly, "I know."

Gurdinn puffed his cheeks out and swore. "You don't. But even if you're somehow right, we should still take the high ground. Force the bastards to come to us. They'll be lancers. We should dismount in the trees, make them engage us on foot. So, to the copse then? We don't have much time."

All of us were looking at the two commanders, our futures fixed in the center of their debate. Gurdinn said, "We hide, then fight if need be. We have no other choice. And no time."

Braylar acknowledged Gurdinn slowly, almost as if seeing him for the first time. "Yes. The copse. Get your men moving now."

Gurdinn grunted, indignant that Braylar had taken too long to arrive at such an obvious decision. But as he took up the reins of his horse he stopped and looked at Braylar. "Wait. My men? What of yours?"

Braylar ignored him and turned to Mulldoos and Vendurro. Glancing up at the clouds, not yet letting loose their rain, he said, "A good day for crossbows, yet. Do you whoresons still remember how to ride?"

Mulldoos whooped and punched the air, suddenly fifteen years younger. "About damn time."

He and Vendurro pulled their crossbows from the leather cases at their sides and spanned them, working the levers with expert ease.

Gurdinn looked at the three Syldoon as if they had sprouted blue feathers from their heads. "Ride where? You just agreed we head to the copse."

Braylar loaded his own crossbow. "I agreed you needed to head to the copse. Take your men and the injured. Lloi, Xen, and Arki will accompany you. Hewspear has no doubt noted that we stopped, and will likely join you as well. Ride to the copse at once. Leave the dead."

Gurdinn shook his head, face turning crimson. "We stand no chance at all if we split our forces. None."

Braylar ignored him. "Lloi, fetch Glesswik's crossbow, Tomner's as well. Be quick about it. Go."

Gurdinn eyed the crossbows and the Syldoon holding them as Lloi ran back to the horses bearing the dead. "The three of you will be slaughtered. And us to follow. Our one chance is to stay together, engage them on ground of our choosing."

Braylar lifted the crossbow and looked down its length to the road beyond, as if willing a target to appear. "We ride. With the dead. You should go."

"The dead? What—"

A column of underpriest's lancers rode into view just then, perhaps a mile ahead of us. Braylar lowered the crossbow and faced Gurdinn. "Your plan has merit. We'll take out as many as we can. Then we'll lead them to the copse. You'll be waiting, with several crossbows still. Shoot as many as you can. If the survivors still approach, kill the underpriest and engage them on foot. It might not come to that, though."

Lloi handed Braylar Glesswik's crossbow and gave Tomner's to Mulldoos before climbing back in the saddle and pulling her own out of its case. Xen drew and spanned his as well.

Gurdinn laughed, a loud, raucous thing heavy with mockery. "Might not come to that? You might kill one or two, and then you'll be run down. Are you such a feast that their bloodlust will be slated after the consumption? Do you think they'll simply trample your corpses and ride off? You're an even bigger fool than I imagined. If you're determined to charge, then we all charge. Our forces are small enough, we aren't splitting them."

Braylar spun his horse around. "And you're exactly the size fool I took you for." He looked at Lloi and Xen. "If the good Brunesman chooses to ignore his own sound advice and doesn't ride to that copse, shoot him for disobeying a direct order."

I imagined this was some horrible joke, but Lloi already had her crossbow up and trained on Gurdinn.

Braylar looked at me. "You should have a crossbow in hand now as well. Priestmen, Brunesmen, you'll need to shoot someone."

Then he addressed Gurdinn again, "I don't have time to debate military tactics with you. Stay out of my way and go to the copse. Don't force my companions to shoot you. They're overwrought with conscience, and it would grieve them sorely."

The three Syldoon rode ahead, ignoring the Brunesmen who gaped at them. Braylar spoke to Mulldoos and Vendurro briefly and they untethered the horses bearing the dead from the line and began trotting down the road with them as they approached the column of lancers. I grabbed a crossbow, holding it in unsteady hands.

Gurdinn glared at Lloi and Xen; they each had a crossbow aimed at his chest. "He dooms us all."

Lloi shrugged. "Hadn't done it yet."

Gurdinn began to ride toward the copse with Lloi and Xen alongside, keeping pace. I allowed the other Brunesmen to ride past, crossbow angled toward the ground but clearly visible as a threat, though I was sure if any of them attacked, I would be less than useless. Each of them seemed to give me a darker glare than the last, and once they all passed, including the underpriest and his guard, I flicked the reins and started after them.

We reached the copse quickly enough, the ground rising underneath our horses' hooves as we climbed the small hill. We stopped short of entering the trees. I rode up near Lloi and Gurdinn. They dismounted, but I stayed in the saddle as I turned my stubborn horse around and watched the three Syldoon below who seemed so determined to throw their lives away. Gurdinn seemed right about that—splitting our numbers was the height of foolishness. Even someone untrained in tactics and strategies of warfare could see that. However, just as I couldn't turn away when I thought the underpriest's guard was going to crush Braylar's throat, I found myself wanting to see this event unfold as clearly as possible. If this was truly the day Braylar was to die, I wouldn't shrink from witnessing it.

I knew there was no chance of me doing anything to intervene this time.

The approaching column saw the Syldoon riding to intercept them and fanned out, breaking into a single line. If they slowed down to perform this maneuver, it was imperceptible to me, and it was clear that whether or not the riders were experts on the battlefield, they were certainly expert horsemen. The lancers, true to the name, were bearing lances and long shields, and they kept the lances perfectly upright as they galloped to meet their foes.

The Syldoon were still riding, though at a slower pace, two on one side of the horses bearing the dead, who were tethered together in a small line themselves, and one on the other, to keep the essentially riderless horses grouped together.

The Syldoon and lancers were roughly three hundred paces apart when the Syldoon lifted their crossbows. A moment later three bolts flew through the air. Only one of them struck anything, one of the lancer's shields.

I heard Gurdinn say, "Coward's weapons."

"Be glad the cowards thought to bring a few," Xen replied. "Probably save your life this day."

Gurdinn laughed, which, upon further reflection, seemed an odd reaction—he should have welcomed that possibility, but it seemed he truly believed we'd cast our lives away.

I watched the field below and silently conceded if that was Braylar's notion of evening the odds, it was a very poor strategy indeed. But then all three Syldoon reached forward as they continued riding, spanning the crossbows just as Braylar had done after the wagon attack in the Green Sea, more deftly and quickly than I would have believed possible while on large, moving animals. But sure enough, the crossbows were loaded and they were taking aim once again at the lancers, who had closed the distance almost in half.

At this range, all three of the bolts struck true. Two of the lancers fell from their saddles, badly wounded or dead, and a third held on bravely, despite having a bolt sticking out of his shoulder, though he slowed and fell behind the others.

The remaining riders lowered their lances, while the Syldoon reloaded their crossbows again. However, this time, all three dropped back and moved behind the horses bearing the dead. Though they were hardly harnessed together, the horses didn't try to flee in separate directions as I anticipated, and kept the same spacing and grouping.

The remaining lancers were almost upon them when the Syldoon loosed their third volley. Another lancer fell from his saddle, raising huge chunks of grass and sod as he hit the ground and rolled to a stop. Another had been struck in the thigh not protected by a shield, though how much his armor did to negate the injury I couldn't tell, as he rode on. The Syldoon had slowed just enough to let the riderless horses pass them, then fell in behind. Most of the lancers saw that the horses in the middle were bearing only dead men and were roped together and veered away at the last instant to avoid them. One of the lancers either failed to see the ropes or thought perhaps he could charge through them unaccosted. He was wrong. As he rode between two of the horses to spear the Syldoon, his horse attempted to jump the rope. But it caught its front legs and both horse and rider were pulled down as if by an unseen giant's hand. The two horses bearing the dead were nearly pulled down as well, and the other horses around them tried in vain to race off in a different directions, pulling the ropes tight and slowing the entire group down. One of them reared up and the dead body slung across its saddle toppled backwards, landing in the grass. Then the horses started forward, and it took me a moment to understand why. It had one of the lancer's spears stuck in its chest and was tossing its head side to side in panic and pain before trying to gallop off, drawing the other uninjured horses behind it.

The Syldoon slowed their mounts just enough to avoid being pulled into the tangle as the remaining lancers swept past on either side, then rode out from behind the chaotic jumble of horses and dead men.

Even from this distance, we could hear the lancer's horse scream as it attempted to rise, having broken one if not both of its front legs. It fell back to the ground. I'd never heard a horse in so much agony before, and it was truly an awful sound, almost human.

The Syldoon spanned their crossbows again as they rode on. The lancer who'd been shot in the shoulder and fallen behind the charge tried to spear Braylar's horse, but Braylar got clear and the lancer flew past.

Most of the lancers were turning their mounts and preparing to give chase, but one of them raised his long spear above his head and shouted something. Having gotten the attention of the other riders, he pointed once toward the three Syldoon, and then swept the spear in our direction. Three of the lancers wheeled around and galloped back to join their wounded companion. The other six kept riding for our copse. Everyone around me was leading their horses into the fragile shelter of the trees, but I stayed where I was, transfixed. The Syldoon reloaded their crossbows on the run and were turning to face their pursuers.

The wounded lancer was closest and I saw Mulldoos shoot a bolt into his horse's neck. The animal collapsed, crashing to the earth. The lancer didn't roll free and was crushed in the fall as the horse toppled forward in a tangle of limbs.

The other three lancers closed in, and Mulldoos galloped off while Braylar and Vendurro raised their crossbows and loosed again. One of their bolts struck another lancer in the helm. The bolt didn't penetrate, but it struck solidly before ricocheting into the grass. Vendurro and Braylar split off. The two remaining lancers began to pursue Vendurro, but they realized that in doing so they were exposing their backs to two Syldoon who were quickly reloading their crossbows and they turned and began riding towards us as well.

I jumped and nearly loosed my own crossbow as Hewspear grabbed my arm and told me to get off my horse and retreat into the trees. I hadn't even heard him ride up. The copse wasn't nearly as wooded as it had appeared from the lower ground—the trees were only loosely crowded together. The lancers coming for us wouldn't be able to mount a charge so long as we stayed behind the thin trunks, but they also wouldn't need to dismount in order to attack. Still, it was the only ground that offered anything in the way of a defensive position, so it was as good a place to mount a stand as any, even if it appeared to be a last stand.

I watched the riders coming up the hill and glanced around quickly. One of the Brunesmen was tying the horses bearing the underpriest and his guard to each other, and then the end of the rope around the closest tree trunk. Lloi and Hewspear were holding their crossbows, though not aiming them yet, and Hewspear had his long slashing spear and another loaded crossbow leaning against a tree alongside him. His face was pale, and he seemed to be in great pain.

Gurdinn was at the front and turned to face us. "Turn your horses sideways at the edge. Keep them there as long as you can. Those bastards ran from rope, they sure as sun will turn from a wall of horse. Make them ride around to get to us. Without speed and flat ground, they're just bigger targets." His men laughed, albeit nervously, but I noted Lloi, Xen, and Hewspear didn't. "Use your shields, use the trees, and stay together."

He turned and his men maneuvered their horses forward as I heard the lancers pounding towards us. It seemed impossible only six horses could make such a drumming, and I thanked Truth they weren't riding us down on level, unimpeded ground. If this was the kind of fear a handful of horses could instill in a man on the ground, I didn't see how even the most stalwart infantry managed to stand firm against a full cavalry charge.

I moved my own horse forward as best I could, fighting the urge to apologize to the beast for using it so callously. Lloi laid her crossbow down and did the same, whispering to it quietly, but Hewspear remained where he was, leaning forward with a hand on one knee, breathing slowly.

One of the Brunesmen yelled something down at the lancers as they started up the hill, and then another one took it up, and finally Gurdinn did as well. Their chant or warcry was a mystery to me. I wanted to yell something in defiance as well, but nothing sprang to mind. The lancers were three hundred paces away, perhaps less, and I wiped one of my hands on my tunic and raised my crossbow, taking aim.

Hewspear said, "Let them come closer. And take a step back from your horse. If it gets jittery and ruins your first shot, you might not get another."

I looked over at him, and while he was forcing himself to stand perfectly upright, his face was drained of color, and blue veins shone underneath a sheath of sweat, almost glowing.

"After we both loose, hand me the other crossbow, quick as you can, then load yours, quicker still. Can you do that? Did Captain Killcoin show you how to span one?"

I nodded.

"Excellent," he said. "An excellent skill, that. And as it happens, much more useful than brewing or playing a lute just now. Though I'm partial to a well-played lute. More so a well-brewed brew." He shocked me with a wink.

I gaped at him, but then he looked down the hill. "Take aim and loose on my word, not before."

I did as he commanded, wondering how he could be so steady. The lancers were halfway up the hill. I was looking down the length of my bolt at the man and horse a hundred paces away, watching the target grow and grow, shifting the crossbow slightly to track the movement, when I heard Hewspear finally say, "Shoot."

Lloi and Hewspear's crossbows released on either side of me and I squeezed the long trigger of mine. As much as I wanted to see if my bolt struck true, I knew Hewspear was waiting for me, and so I dropped my crossbow and handed another to him as fast as I could. I heard his crossbow discharge as I picked my crossbow back up and started to fit the claws of the lever on the hempen cord. The lancers were very close now, nearly on top of us, and I saw Hewspear's crossbow hit the ground as he stepped away to retrieve his spear. I was drawing the lever back when the lancers rode around the "wall of horse." Cord in place, I moved the lever forward just enough to release the hooks, laid it flat on the stock, and set a new bolt into the groove.

When I looked up, I saw four lancers turning their horses around in our small thicket, spears held overhead as they navigated through the trees and sought targets. One of them rode towards a Brunesman and stabbed down. The Brunesman dodged to the other side of a tree and slashed wildly at the rider. The lancer picked up the clumsy blow on the edge of his shield as he spun his snorting horse around and stabbed again.

I didn't wait to see what happened as Gurdinn rushed forward to aid his companion, looking instead for a closer target. There were a few trees between us, and I was loath to loose unless I had a clear shot and didn't risk hitting a tree, or worse, one of my companions. I was about to move off towards them when I saw movement to my right, much closer. Lloi dodged behind a tree, armed with her curved sword, and a lancer circled after her. The spearhead struck the tree just above her head and chunks of bark flew free as the lancer continued to circle, stabbing again.

His back was to me, and I knew the opportunity would disappear if I hesitated, so I stepped around a tree to get a better shot, took quick aim, and loosed. The bolt missed wide, striking the inside of his shield just beyond his shoulder.

The lancer spun his horse around, saw me, and kicked his heels into his mount. I took a few steps back instinctively, wanting to flee, but I knew there was nowhere to run except down the hill, where I'd be ridden down immediately. I froze, watching in terror as the lancer rode me down, arm cocked back to drive the spear through me.

Then another spear slashed the lancer across the chest. It didn't cleave the mail, but the lancer forgot about me and turned his horse to face the new threat. Hewspear thrust and the lancer deflected it with his shield, but Hewspear hooked the lugs of his spear behind the edge of the shield and pulled back hard, creating an opening for an instant.

Lloi was there then, darting forward and slashing at the rider's exposed thigh. Her sword struck, but it was impossible to see if she wounded him, and then he bashed Lloi with the bottom of his shield, catching her in the shoulder and driving her back a few steps. The lancer's horse reared up and struck Lloi in the chest with its front hooves—she dropped her sword as she flew into a tree. The lancer advanced and his horse snapped its jaws down, tearing a huge chunk of flesh off Lloi's cheek, exposing the bone beneath.

She collapsed, screaming as she rolled in the leaves and dirt, one hand on her face, and Hewspear drove his spear into the small of the lancer's back. The lancer tried to spin his horse around, but Hewspear spun with them, thrusting again, howling in pain or rage as he did.

The second thrust pierced the links of mail and the gambeson beneath, coming away bloody, and the lancer arched his back, dropping his spear. The third thrust took him out of the saddle and the horse continued to spin, spitting foam from its lips as it lashed its hooves out to smash the attacker. Hewspear dodged behind a tree and slashed at the animal, but with its rider in the dirt near Lloi, it turned and ran off through the trees.

I was still rooted to the spot as Hewspear fell on the lancer as he struggled to get back to his feet, striking him between the neck and shoulder with a vicious blow. The lancer fell back to the ground, unmoving. Hewspear drove his spear into his back again to be sure.

Lloi still flailed where she lay, although her movements were less spastic and furious. That finally broke my paralysis and I dropped my crossbow and rushed towards her, calling out her name. She struggled with renewed vigor as I took her in my arms, and I nearly vomited as I saw the flap of flesh hanging above her exposed cheekbone. Her eyes were unfocused and her screams had subsided to a small squeal, and whatever energy she'd rediscovered fled quickly as I held her tightly, saying her name again and again. Then I felt a shaky hand on my shoulder and looked up.

Hewspear ordered me to release her, telling me her ribs or sternum were damaged, and my embrace did more harm than good. I slowly lowered Lloi to the ground and Hewspear knelt next to her, his ear above her mouth.

He looked at me and said, "She lives yet. But her breath is labored. I fear for her lungs more than her face. She is… bad."

I asked him what we needed to do to save her. Hewspear said nothing and I filled with despair. Then he moved over to the lancer's body, withdrew a dagger and tore some strips off the dead man's cloak, grunting with the effort. He handed me the strips of cloth. "Staunch the bleeding and bind her face as best you can. Pressure, but not too much. Do you have the stomach?"

I nodded, wondering if I really did, but if he saw the hesitation in my eyes, he said nothing. Hewspear rose, grunting with pain, and retrieved his spear from the grass. "Still fighting left. Once you're done with Lloi, best grab that bolter and follow me. Not much use binding the wounded if we all get killed."

Hewspear ran off towards the combat. I couldn't be sure, but it sounded like fewer blows were being exchanged. I knelt next to Lloi, patted her hand stupidly, and lied, telling her everything would be fine as I looked at the ruins of her face. With quivering fingers, I tried to put the flap of flesh back where it should have been, lifted her head, and wrapped the makeshift bandages around her cheek and jaw, leaving space for her mouth and nose. The cloth was soaked in blood immediately. Her breath came haphazardly, like a babe that had exhausted itself in crying.

My clumsy attempt at medicine finished, I tried to think of some pretext for staying—perhaps I needed to check the crude bandaging again, or monitor her wheezy breathing, or… But Hewspear was right—if we didn't drive off or defeat the lancers, we were all doomed.

I slid Lloi's sword into my belt and grabbed the crossbow, spanned it as quickly as possible, fumbling horribly, the devil's claw slipping a few times before I secured it. When the bolt was finally in place I picked up a quiver and ran off after Hewspear, eyes darting in all directions, expecting death to arrive from everywhere.

I heard shouting and saw movement between some trees—Gurdinn and another Brunesman were attempting to flank a lancer, his spear abandoned and replaced by a mace. He swung down at Gurdinn, horse stepping sideways, and Gurdinn turned the blow with his shield but didn't have the chance to attack himself as the horse spun to face him. Clearly Gurdinn knew a horse could be just as dangerous as the rider.

I looked for Hewspear but didn't see him. My first loyalty, such as it was, was to Braylar and his retinue, and I contemplated leaving the Brunesmen to their fight and seeking Hewspear out, but I also knew our best chance lay in unity, so I took a few steps closer and raised the crossbow, sighting down its length and hoping for a clear shot. The Brunesmen continued trying to position themselves on either side of the lancer, so the lancer himself made a very difficult target as he led his horse between trees to avoid being flanked.

I moved closer, crossbow at the ready. The lancer turned and advanced on the Brunesman, who retreated a few steps until he backed into a tree and stumbled. The lancer closed in, raining blows down, the Brunesman doing all he could to avoid them or block them as he tried to escape from between the tree and his adversary. But the horse slammed into him with his muscular shoulder and the Brunesman tripped and fell. He held his shield up as the horse advanced, hooves smashing down.

I couldn't see if the Brunesman had survived the initial flurry of hooves, but I knew he couldn't for long, so I ran forward, and was about to squeeze the long trigger when Gurdinn appeared again directly between us. The lancer pivoted in the saddle, catching Gurdinn's sword on the edge of his shield, and he spurred his horse forward before receiving a second, and moved off into the trees.

Gurdinn didn't pursue, stopping to take stock of his soldier. The Brunesman was alive, though he nearly fell to the dirt again as he tried to put weight on his leg. Gurdinn was offering his arm in support as I ran up to the pair. He heard me approach and faced me, sword raised, lowering it only slightly as he recognized me as one of Braylar's companions.

Gurdinn said, "The priest? Where is the underpriest?"

I told him I didn't know—when last I saw him, he was in the company of Brunesmen. He scowled and turned away, leading his companion through the thicket in stumbling pursuit of the horseman. I joined their side, scanning the copse for Hewspear or lancers.

We heard horses to our left and moved in that direction. As we cleared the last of the trees and looked down the small hill, we saw five of the lancers who had been engaged with Braylar coming up the hill, their gallop slowed only slightly by the ascent. Braylar, Mulldoos, and Vendurro fast behind them.

Gurdinn and his man moved back into the relative cover of the trees, an action that, though it might have only been delaying our inevitable destruction, seemed to be the only prudent course. Which is why what I did next, I can only attribute to battle madness.

I stepped forward to be sure I was clear of the overhanging branches, and took careful aim at the lancer in the lead. He saw me and ducked as low as he could behind his horse's neck as he kicked his heels in and urged his mount into more speed. He presented a small target, and his companions had followed his lead, making themselves smaller as well, but having seen the damage the horses were able to mete out, I lowered my aim slightly and squeezed the trigger.

The bolt struck a horse in the chest, a few hands below the neck. I stood there stupidly watching, expecting to see the horse fall to the earth in a cloud of dust or spray of blood, but it only turned its head and slowed long enough for the other lancers to pass it before the rider's spurs goaded it on. I realized I'd struck the horse's barding—whatever damage I caused was nowhere near enough.

I was about to turn and flee when I saw another rider slump forward, a bolt sticking up from between his shoulder blades. The lancer fell from the saddle, rolling twice before coming to a stop as his horse ran off.

Two of the lancers who saw their comrade fall hailed the others, and they all slowed down briefly and then changed direction, galloping away from both the copse and the Syldoon who were trailing them.

I thought Braylar might pursue, but the Syldoon slowed their horses and continued up the hill. Mulldoos stopped above the fallen lancer and loosed another bolt into the body. Ordinarily, this might have shocked me, but I felt only numb, and the crossbow in my hands suddenly seemed heavier than stone.

The Syldoon dismounted in front of me, tying off the horses to the closest tree. The horses' chests were swelling like bellows, and the three men were breathing heavily as well. Braylar looked down the hill—the lancers hadn't ridden off completely, but stopped in a small group on the outside of reasonable crossbow range.

Braylar looked at Vendurro and rasped, "They decide they're not done being shot at, report at once." He swung back to me then and looked at the crossbow. "You are unfanged."

There was a small lapse before I took his meaning and started spanning again. He stopped me with a hand on the shoulder. "What of the priest? Hewspear? The others?"

I told him that Gurdinn and his injured man had withdrawn, and I couldn't account for the others, save one. He waited while I swallowed and took a deep breath before telling him that Lloi was injured, perhaps mortally.

I expected Braylar to rage or profane the air, but he only coughed briefly and then reached up to massage his injured throat, his expression unchanging. A moment later, he said in a rough whisper, "The others then."

I wanted to ask his permission to check on Lloi but he'd already started off. Mulldoos fell in alongside me while Vendurro stayed to keep watch on the distant lancers. We navigated the trees, Mulldoos calling out, "Hewspear. Hewspear, you horsecock, answer."

We heard voices, one very loud, and followed them to the source. Gurdinn was standing over one of his soldiers, hands balled into fists, screaming down at him. Hewspear was leaning against a tree, holding onto his grounded spear with both hands, eyes closed. The Brunesman who had nearly been trampled to death was standing over the captured guard, though clearly favoring one leg. I didn't see the underpriest anywhere.

We approached and Braylar said something, made unintelligible by his damaged throat and the shouting Gurdinn continued to do. Braylar grabbed Gurdinn and swung him around. "The priest? Where is the underpriest?"

Gurdinn shook Braylar's hand away. "Our prize is dead." Then he pointed off into some dense thicket. "Beyond there."

Braylar again remained surprisingly impassive. "And what happened to the cleric, that he should find himself so newly dead?"

"After you ran off, we had to fend for ourselves here. When things looked grim," he turned and kicked the prone Brunesman, "this man struck him down. That account for the deadness enough for you, Black Noose?"

I thought Braylar might attack the Brunesman himself, or even Gurdinn, but after a small pause he replied, "Better a dead traitor than a free traitor. There are still four lancers out there. In the middle of our cowardly flight we killed the rest. But there might be more still we haven't met yet. I don't imagine we'll survive another encounter. We head to the city. Now."

Judging by the tenor of their conversation, I expected it to end in blows. But Gurdinn turned around quickly before saying anything more and began walking towards the Brunesman and the captive. He'd only taken two steps when Braylar added, "You really ought to address me as captain, Honeycock. It reminds everyone present who is issuing orders and who is following them. And you should be careful about fleeing a conversation before being dismissed, as I'm like to imagine that you're deserting, and might be tempted to strike you down."

I was certain their exchange would only end with one man dead. Gurdinn spun back around to face Braylar, who hadn't moved, but he somehow found it in himself to rein in his temper. "I'll see to my remaining men. Captain. And our horses. Captain. If you see to you and yours. Captain. Is there anything else, then? Captain?"

Braylar smiled wryly. "Excused, Captain Honeycock."

Gurdinn moved towards the prisoner and the Brunesman he'd viciously kicked got up and joined them as well.

After looking Hewspear over, Braylar turned to Mulldoos. "You'll need to collect Lloi and meet us at the other side of the copse, where the other horses are tethered. Arki can lead you. If those four lancers make another run at us, we can break them, but if there are more out there..."

Though Mulldoos obviously had no affection for me or Lloi, he didn't voice a complaint. To me, he said, "Take me to the cripple."

I led him to Lloi's body, still slumped against a tree.

Mulldoos squatted down in front of her and wiped his hands on his pants. He touched one of the strips of cloth on her face, and she moaned. "She wasn't the captain's pet, I'd smother her out of her misery right now. Gods be cruel."

I pointed out that the horse also probably broke some of her ribs or her sternum, and then added that she sustained these injuries saving

Hewspear's life (leaving out my own, as that would dilute the point I was making).

Mulldoos spit on the ground and glared at me. "Where're your broken bones, then? Your tattered flesh? Hewspear, the witch, both half dead. What of you?"

I said nothing, which proved to be a poor choice (though, in my meager defense, I doubt there was a good choice). Mulldoos rose and stood in front of me, face close, voice guttural. "I met plenty of sacks of shit in my life, and some of them were at least good in a scrap. But not you. No. Worthless. You're a worthless sack of slimy shit, you hear me?"

I wanted to protest that I might not have acted quickly, but I did act, and though I didn't prevent their injuries, I might have prevented them from being worse, but I knew that would only prompt more abuse, and so I kept my mouth shut and tried not to flinch as his spittle sprayed on my face.

He grabbed the crossbow out of my hands and started to walk away. I called after him, asking what he intended to do with Lloi. I thought he'd round on me in a fury, but he only said over his shoulder, "You got two arms. Only thing that makes you better than her. Carry her, you dumb horsecunt." Then he kept walking.

I slowly knelt next to her and looked at the poor girl's face, or what was visible at least. Her eyes moved behind the lids, and I thought they might flutter open any second, and she'd scream, but she barely stirred at all as I slid my arms beneath her.

As gently as I could, I lifted her off the ground, and then she twisted in my arms, and I whispered to her, tried to soothe her, though I doubt it did any good. She thrashed briefly and went limp again, falling against my chest like an exhausted child. Like an exhausted one-handed child, half-eaten and kicked to death by a horse. The colossal unfairness of the thing washed over me, and I felt more tired than I imagined possible as I carried her back to what remained of our party.

To avoid the clinging brambles and scrub, I circled around the trees towards the tethered horses. It didn't take us long to complete our circuit, and from the outside, the copse seemed much smaller than when we'd been in the middle, dodging behind tree trunks for our lives. Everyone else was saddled up already or just about to, and the final captive was on a horse, his ankles ties together beneath him, his hands tied firmly in front. Although, given the mass of bruises on his face, and the treatment the underpriest had received, I didn't think he'd be trying to flee anytime soon.

No one looked at me as I made my way to my horse. I looked for Braylar, but he'd already ridden down the small hill. Mulldoos and Hewspear were alongside him, Hewspear bent over, hunchbacked.

I considered asking one of the Brunesmen to help me, but the rest of the riders began making their way towards the Syldoon, and they ignored Lloi and me as if we were trees. I tried to convince myself Braylar would come back for me. Of all of us, he knew Lloi the best, and beyond that, depended on her the most, for things no one else could possibly understand. But he was only interested in leading us back to the city. I'd nearly forgotten about the lancers, and the underpriest's men that might still be roaming the wild, closing in on us.

I tried to climb into the saddle with Lloi in my arms, and nearly fell. I shifted her slightly and she cried out again. I told her we were heading home, and finally made it into the saddle on the third try.

I adjusted Lloi as best I could, but there was no way to make her comfortable. I tried not to jostle her as I flicked the reins and clicked at my horse, who slowly carried me down the hill. Lloi groaned and whimpered with each step the horse took, and I rode up alongside the Syldoon, my arms already beginning to burn from cradling her.

Hewspear looked over at me, face ashen, ribs clearly paining him. He nodded once, as if trying to stiffen my resolve or steel me for what was going to be an agonizing ride for her, and an exhausting one for me.

Braylar started off first, Hewspear and Vendurro on either side, and then Mulldoos, Xen, and I followed, with the Brunesmen and prisoner behind us as we set off towards Alespell once more. The roiling clouds had promised a heavy rain, but when it finally came, some miles later, it was just a drizzle. A full-on rain would have washed away some of the blood, sweat, mud, and gore that marked all of us. But the thin rain did little more than spread the filth around and lower spirits even further. The only redeeming feature was that Lloi seemed to go slack again, her whimpering subsiding.

I tried to think of anything except my shaking arms and aching back. I remembered an artist at Rivermost, a talented muralist who, like me, earned his coin by appealing to the vanity of major merchants and minor nobility. I couldn't remember his name, but I recalled one mural he did, on a cracked wall just outside a tavern he used to frequent. While nearly everything he painted for his patrons was full of color and crowded with lively characters, the wall outside the tavern was a scene of the aftermath of a war. Soldiers were leaving a battlefield strewn with corpses. Most of the soldiers were sitting in wagons, while a few rode, but they weren't celebrating the spoils of victory, laden with booty. They didn't even look grateful their lives had been spared among so many who hadn't. Almost to the man, their heads were hung, even the horses' heads were low, and they were the most dejected company I'd ever seen depicted, bandaged and battered, but still riding. Everything about the mural—colors, expressions, posture, mood—was muted, slack, sad.

While I was impressed with the atmosphere the muralist had manufactured, I couldn't understand how the victors of a battle could look so utterly lost or dejected. I thought he must have erred, never having witnessed real combat or is effects before. But looking around at our small, bloodied band, I realized that the artist's only failing had been in not truly capturing all the horrible details. He had bandages, but didn't show the gaping wounds. He showed grim faces, but not the jaw set so tight teeth might shatter as broken bones shifted with the ride. He showed corpses on the battlefield, but couldn't illustrate how it feels to survive when comrades and friends have fallen.

I promised myself if I ever made it back to Rivermost, I'd find that muralist and commission him to paint the brightest, most cheerful tavern scene imaginable, filled with impossibly beautiful serving girls and ruddy-cheeked carousers, and a hundred mugs clinking in happy toast.

And then I began to pray. Not to Truth, because of course Truth isn't interested in prayers. But to Countenance, to ease Lloi's suffering, if only a little, prayed as earnestly as I ever prayed for anything before. It kept the wet miles rolling by as I came up with elaborate vows for what I would do in return if my prayers were answered. Quit Braylar's "service" immediately. Chronicle only for those men and women who had nothing whatsoever to do with war. Join a reclusive temple so I could copy and recopy only old tomes and fantastic bestiaries. Leave chronicling behind altogether, and dedicate my life to service at a leper colony. I vowed that if Lloi recovered, I would carry her off from her fickle patron who left her behind for an archivist to save. I prayed because I fervently wanted to see Lloi recover, and because it distracted me from my own growing pains and weakness.

Lloi shook and twisted again, moaned, and continued moaning, and I looked around for help, and Hewspear was there then riding right next to me, his hand on Lloi's arm as she cried out, again and again, each time more sharp. And then she was silent once more, her head rolling forward onto her chest.

She was dead.

I realized, dumbly, that I hadn't understood how close she'd been. I'd expected her to wake again. I imagined her awful face would make people forget about her stumpy hand, and wondered if she might never again be herself, but I expected her to wake. I had had the opportunity to talk to her, console her, hum to her, make her some small gesture to possibly make her last moments more pleasant, and instead I chose to do whatever I could to distract myself from my own ordeal. Selfish. Only selfishness.

She hadn't caused my heart to swoon. She wasn't my childhood friend. I'd only known her a short time, and she'd shown herself to be as rough-hewn and indelicate as any lady who stalked the earth. But she was also honest and loyal, so very loyal, and of Braylar's retinue, I knew her best of all. She'd deserved better than this. Whatever gods ruled sediment and firmament were cruel to visit so much pain and hostility on her. She'd deserved so much better.

I realized I was crying as I held her tight to my chest, half hoping I'd been mistaken, that there was some spark of life I hadn't seen or felt. But Lloi was no more.

I heard two of the Brunesmen behind me talking quietly. The first said, "Mercy she's gone. She would've been good for only one thing, and then only after a dozen drinks."

The other replied, "All any of them are good for. At least the next whore I take will have a face and both hands."

I spun my horse around, as angry as I'd ever been in my life. At the merciless gods, vicious horses, my own incompetence and selfishness, the stupid soldiers, everything. I wasn't sure what I planned to do or say, but before doing anything, I lost my grip on Lloi and she slipped out of my arms and fell to the muddy ground.

One of the soldiers laughed and then I was drawing Lloi's sword from my belt, holding it in both hands, lifting it above my head to strike him down, to split him open as Lloi had been split. The soldier's eyes went wide, and he didn't have a chance to defend himself, and I knew I would smite him.

But a strong hand grabbed my wrist just before I began the downward stroke. Mulldoos had me. I looked at him, and would have struck him as well if I'd been strong enough to wrestle free. But he held firm. "Back in the belt, scribbler. Put it back in the belt."

I was shaking my head, but by now the soldier had reacted and moved his horse away. Even if Mulldoos had let go, the moment was gone, and my rage with it. I was only numb. As he unhanded me, I almost dropped the sword, my arms were so tired. I looked down at Lloi, her body in a heap, leggings and tunic filthy in the mud, and felt shame wash over me from a hundred directions. I started to dismount but Mulldoos said, "Front of the column. Now."

I thought he was going to leave her there, and though I knew I couldn't possibly overcome him, I wasn't about to compound all of my failures by abandoning her. But before I could do anything else, Mulldoos dismounted.

The soldier who I nearly attacked forced a laugh and said to Mulldoos, "You were almost a man lighter, Black Noose. You keep that whelp of yours on a shorter rope, you hear?"

Mulldoos turned and gave the soldier a stare that stole his smile. "I were you, Bruneboy, I'd shut my mouth tight as a priest's ass. Open it again and I'll let the whelp gut you. And he manages to screw that up, I got nothing against killing one more today. Nothing at all. You hear?"

And then he lifted Lloi's body out of the mud as easily as if he were picking up a sleeping babe or straw doll. He laid her in front of his saddle and mounted his horse. It pained me to see her slung like that, but he'd done it gently enough, and I couldn't really fault him. She was dead.

I rode alongside, passing the soldier who gave me a murderous look but wisely held his tongue, and followed Mulldoos to his place alongside Braylar. I was tempted to ask why he spared me the burden, or why he hadn't draped her over her own horse, as had been done with the other dead before Braylar had conscripted them in our defense earlier. But I said nothing. In the end, it didn't matter.

Others acknowledged us as we passed, if only with a sullen glance. When we reached the front of our party, Hewspear turned and looked at Lloi for a long time. He took a deep breath, grimaced, and whispered, "She saved my life and more with one hand. She might have saved the whole company with two." Then he gave a small smile, through pained and mostly for my benefit.

I looked at Braylar, tried to gauge him for some reaction, any reaction at all, but he was inscrutable. We rode along, and now that I wasn't charged with carrying Lloi and struggling to stay in the saddle, I hazarded a look behind us, but saw nothing beneath the gathering storm clouds besides Syldoon and Brunesmen.

Time continued to pass in that immeasurable way it does when you're exhausted but have no chance to sleep, and the drizzle slowly gave way to real rain, cold and stinging. Even though we hadn't reached the fortified city and safety from our enemies and the elements, hope began to stir the closer we got. If a little.

I fought the urge to look behind us, partly afraid I would see a column of lancers closing in, and partly because even if there were, there was absolutely nothing I could do about it. I stared ahead with the rest of the men. The rain picked up, so it was difficult to see very far ahead. I wondered if this was what it was like to be a ghost, alone, wandering through the gray nothingness. And as we crested a small hill, I finally made out the silhouette of Alespell ahead, its spires and towers shadowy smudges, but there was no mistaking it was there.

We sped up, not wanting to blow our horses so close to sanctuary, but it was impossible to resist. I still half expected an ambush to come down on us, even after we entered the North Gate. Every corner and cross street seemed a place for potential ambush. But we were unmolested. Gurdinn led his men and prisoner off without another word, and we made our way through the districts until we were at the stables of the Grieving Dog.

The horrible irony of our residence wasn't lost on me.

⊕

The next day, I woke from such a deep slumber I couldn't tell what time of day it was, or even what day it was. I vaguely remembered washing when we returned, flicking food around a plate, an eventually collapsing into bed. I'd never been more tired in my life. As I slowly roused and splashed water on my face, the previous day's events came back to me with all of the suddenness of falling through ice.

I dressed slowly, thinking how I'd barely escaped death, and how others hadn't been as fortunate. I wondered why I hadn't been summoned, but it was clear I was very much a secondary or tertiary consideration to the Syldoon at this point. Maybe even a non-consideration. I grabbed my writing supplies and record everything that had happened while it was still painfully fresh.

Finished, I stepped out into the antechamber that served as a common hub for Braylar's room. And what would've been Lloi's, though I suspected her body wasn't occupying it. Again, a dunk in the ice water, awash with guilt and sadness. Vendurro was sitting stiff-backed on a stool near the door leading to the hallway. He barely acknowledged me, which reminded me that he'd lost someone more dear to him than anyone to me. Which made me feel worse still for pitying myself.

I switched my writing case from arm to arm, and not knowing what to say or how to say it, I coughed gently.

He looked up, though still not alertly, and said, "Food's there, if you've got the stomach."

There was a plate of fruit and bread on the small table next to him. I didn't feel like eating, but my stomach rumbled, reminding me that I'd only taken a few mouthfuls of bread the previous night. I nodded my thanks and grabbed some cheese and washed it down with some ale that was only a touch better than water. I expected the food to taste like ash or bark or at least stale food, but it was wonderful.

Perhaps soldiers experienced and handled grief differently than common folk, or maybe they didn't deal with it at all. Maybe that was the key. I felt obligated to say something to Vendurro, but I knew whatever words I summoned would be inadequate, regardless of what he was in fact experiencing.

Still, the obligation overran any qualms, and so I cleared my throat, and then again, until he looked up at me, and said the simplest thing I could think of. "Glesswik seemed like a good man."

Vendurro nodded slowly, three times. "Bad husband, lousy father, but a good soldier and friend. None better."

Feeling more uncomfortable than I'd imagined, I told him I was sorry.

Vendurro nearly smiled, the corners of his lips turning ever so slightly before giving up. "Can't say I totally understand why we need a scribe so awful bad, but you're less of a lesion than the last one, or the one before that, when it comes to it."

I wasn't sure if that was deserving of proper thanks or not, but it was my turn to nod, and then I asked if he'd seen Captain Killcoin.

Vendurro cocked his head towards a door. "Asked me to send you in, after you filled your belly. Best not to keep him waiting. Real black mood."

I thanked him and moved across the chamber. I knocked, and when no one replied, knocked again. I looked back to Vendurro, but he was vacantly starting at the wall again. I opened the door and stepped inside. Braylar was sitting at a table, elbows on the edge, shoulders hunched, a tall flagon of ale and a mug in front of him, eyes red and watery. His hair, normally oiled and slicked back, was now in disarray. Bloodsounder was sitting on the table, the two chains splayed apart, and he regarded the heads as they regarded him. The horn shutters were shut behind him, and the room was bathed in a dull orange glow from the sun that shone through them. The bed didn't appear slept in.

I apologized for disturbing him and he laughed, took another swig from his flagon and said, with the crisp, over-enunciated words of a drunkard much-skilled in his craft, "You couldn't possibly disturb me any more than I am. Sit. Write. You were conscripted to script, yes? Your scriptorium is where you find it. Script."

I sat and unfolded the writing case and began scribbling some notes. He rotated his fingers in the air lazily and took another drink. And belched. And continued drinking.

I sat there, feeling ill at ease. Wondering how keenly he was feeling the absence of Lloi and her ministrations, and if he was going to sink completely within himself again, or if there was now something worse in store.

Braylar finished his mug, reached to refill it from the pottery flagon, and finding that empty as well, hurled it against the opposite wall. He began to shout Vendurro's name, but his throat pained him, and massaging it, he ordered, "Call him. Loudly. Immediately."

I yelled and received no response and Braylar slapped the table. "Scream it, you bastard, get him in here!"

I did, and a moment later, Vendurro stepped inside. "Cap?"

Braylar rubbed his throat for a moment before pointing at the remains of the flagon in the corner. "It seems I have need of another. Preferably one that doesn't shatter quite so readily. And holds more ale. Yes, bigger."

After a long pause, Vendurro replied, "As you say, Cap."

Before Vendurro could make his exit, Braylar called out, "You aren't turning mutinous over an order for ale, I hope?"

Vendurro shook his head. "No, Cap. Not doing any such thing."

"You hesitated, Vendurro. You aren't a hesitator. It's not in your nature. In fact, you could benefit from a little more reflection. But not just now." He tipped the mug over as if to make sure it was in fact empty and not just withholding out of spite. "Explain yourself."

Vendurro looked at me and it was my turn to shrug my shoulders.

Braylar said, "Speak freely, soldier."

"Begging your pardon, Cap. For the hesitating and all. Just wondering if maybe you'd like me to bar the door, while you get some rest."

"Wondering, or suggesting? I ask, Syldoon, because wondering is something a soldier is permitted, though advised against. Will the line withstand another assault? Is this the best ground to defend? Are the superior's orders truly sound? Such thoughts naturally occur, and none but a Memoridon prevents you from pursuing them. And, clearly, I'm no Memoridon. But unsolicited suggestions to said superior—those are not only discouraged, but could considerably shorten a soldiering career. So, I ask again, do you wonder or suggest? It sounded suspiciously like a suggestion."

"Begging your pardon again, Cap, but I wouldn't have said nothing at all, so it would have stood at wondering, but you prompted me, so I'm thinking it's a solicited suggestion. As it stands now, Cap."

The scars around his mouth twitched with a too-brief smile. "Deftly done, soldier. But need I remind you—I didn't solicit ale, I ordered it. I suggest you follow that order immediately."

After Vendurro pulled the door shut behind him with no hesitation this time, Braylar lifted both hands and massaged his temples with the tips of his fingers. He began to reach for the mug again before stopping himself. "I should've suggested he bring two pitchers."

Braylar moved one hand back and forth over a flail head, as if testing to see if it was too warm or too cold, before laying two fingertips on one of the horns and closing his eyes. After he said nothing else for some time, I feared he was already beginning to succumb to whatever had plagued him on the plains. Then he said, "You wonder—though silently, which I appreciate more than you know—what happens now, yes? Now, I drink. You are welcome to join me."

The door opened, and Mulldoos and Hewspear entered, Mulldoos with a pronounced limp, Hewspear, noticeably stiff and careful in his movements.

Mulldoos said, "You summoned us, Cap?"

"I did. Indeed, I did. Come, sit. Be at ease. More ale is on the way."

If they were surprised by seeing their captain drunk so early in the day, they disguised it well. Mulldoos spun a wooden chair around and crossed his arms on the back as he leaned forward.

Hewspear said, "Forgive me, Captain, but I'll stay standing."

Braylar turned to me. "It seems even my most loyal lieutenants are disinclined to follow my lead today." He examined Hewspear more closely, and then clicked his tongue in his mouth. "Ahh, your injuries. I'm negligent, yes? It's you who must do the forgiving. How do you fare, Hewspear? Truly?"

Hewspear, wheezing above a whisper, but only just, replied, "I'm alive. That's an unexpected turn of events. As to the rest, I'm bandaged."

Mulldoos snorted. "Until one of those ribs pricks your lungs and you start gurgling blood. Bandages do you a fat lot of good for that turn of events, huh?"

Braylar asked, "And you, Mother Mulldoos, how is your leg?"

"Nothing a little ale won't fix."

Hewspear started to laugh and then pulled up short. "Don't be deceived, Captain—he hobbles like a crippled beggar woman, and complains twice as much."

"Can't help but wonder," Mulldoos said, "when you rip open your lungs, will you choke on your blood or suffocate first? I'm hoping choke."

There was a quiet knock on the door, and then a serving boy entered with two tall pitchers of ale and more mugs. He kept his eye on the floor the entire time as he set them on the table, careful not to spill. He shuffled towards the broken flagon and pulled a stained rag out of his belt, but Braylar said, "That will do. Another time."

The boy looked at Braylar, then back down quickly. Braylar rasped, "Are you deaf and mute, boy? Get out of here before I have you whipped. In fact, I might have you whipped anyway. Get out while I think on it."

The boy turned and practically ran out of the room, almost slamming the door shut in his haste. "Insurrection and idiocy, from all sides. Will anyone who enters this room obey me today?"

Mulldoos filled the mugs. He was about to fill mine when I shook my head. "Suit yourself, scribbler."

Braylar raised his mug. "To the fallen."

The other two men did the same. "The fallen."

They all drank silently, when Braylar suddenly said, "I command men to fight. Command men to die. That's what I do. That's what they do. We're soldiers. We do what must be done. That's our sole consolation, our brief balm. What must be done. For a cause larger than ourselves. We engage our numerous enemies, on the battlements, in frozen fields, in alleys reeking of piss, in the bellies of mildewed theaters, in the weeds and dust of forsaken temples. We're the glorious ghostmakers. Or when it suits our master's purpose, manipulate our enemies instead, twist circumstance to our advantage, twist the long knife when we have to, assassinate. March on them in colorful columns, thunder down at them on the plains, unleash doom from afar or so close you can watch their hearts' last push as the bleeding stops. We ensnare them in plots and schemes beyond our reckoning, because we've been ordered to. We've broken the seals and deciphered the codes and made sense of imperial commands, though we can't fathom the greater agenda that underpins them, and we loot and steal and befriend and betray, breathing death in and out like heavy pollen on the wind. We are soldiers. We kill. We fall. Again. And again." He lifted head and stared at the beamed ceiling. Very quietly, "And again…"

Hewspear took a step towards Braylar and whisper-wheezed, "Captain?"

Braylar raised his mug, creaky voice creakier. "To the fallen." He gulped his ale, and after exchanging a look, Mulldoos and Hewspear did as well.

Braylar drained the entire mug and set it down, tapping the rim with a forefinger. As Mulldoos slowly refilled it, Braylar closed his eyes. "Ensure that the families receive their share of the widowcoin. That the estates are in order, fiefs or farms transferred without incident. And the bodies, of course. Take care of the bodies. Those we have still. Send their bones home, at least. We can do that much. We owe them that much, yes?"

Hewspear replied, "I'll see to it, Captain. Everything will be accounted for."

"Good. That's good."

Hewspear slowly swished the ale around in his cup, looking into it as if he might divine something useful. The silence stretched on for a bit, and he finally looked up. "And what of Lloi, Captain?"

Braylar hunched over even further. Quietly, he said, "What of her?"

Hewspear looked at Mulldoos, who simply raised his delicate eyebrows. "What shall we do with her? She isn't a Syldoon, and no one in the Citadel has much interest in her bones." He cast a quick glance in my direction before continuing, "What shall we do with her remains, Captain?"

"Dispose of her as you will." When no one responded immediately, he looked up and glanced from face to face, no doubt registering the accusation and pain on mine, the sadness on Hewspear's, and what might have been anger on Mulldoos', though that struck me as curious. "Do you think me a callous beast, that I don't spare more thought for her? Should I have thrown myself across her body in grief, and railed at the tragedy of it, while my own men looked on, spiteful that I'd done no such thing for the fallen Syldoon? Should I have stripped off my shirt and lashed myself for failing to protect her, to see her to a better end?" His voice was overtaxed and broke. "No. She's gone. Dead. But unlike the others, she has nowhere to go now. No one waits for her, hopes for her return, pines. No children. No husband. No one. And now she's no one." He closed his eyes and sighed. "A body. Only a body. Dispose of her as you will. I'll think no more on it."

Hewspear's face grew red and he leaned against the table, grunting with the effort. "Captain, she saved my life. And she did more than that for you—"

Mulldoos interjected, "It was no secret I never had any love for her or her kind. Witches and warlocks, the whole lot. Memoridon, rogue witch, same as spit to me. At least with your trained Memoridon, you know you're dealing with a professional. Cold and inhuman, maybe, but professional, to the last. But her, and her kind? Rogues got no one to show them what to do with themselves, how to manage what they can do." He tapped a thick finger against his temple. "You thought she crept among your bogs and sucked out your poisons. But no telling what damage she done in there, mucking around, unskilled. Might as well have been blind. Far as I know, her effort stirred up worse things hidden in the muck, damaged you more. I never wanted her among us, start to finish.

"What's more, she had nothing else to put the thing in balance. She was a crippled, disobedient Grass Dog whore when we took her, and I never saw much to suggest she ever became other than that. But the thing of it is, Cap, no matter how much I misliked her, and I misliked her plenty, she was loyal to you like no other. She'd have thrown her life away for you ten times over ten, and again just to prove a point. And while she was a monstrous boil on my ass, there's no denying she had grit." He leaned forward, lifting his mug for emphasis. "What I'm getting at, Cap, is… Hew's got the right of it. She deserves better than what you're giving her."

Braylar's eyes lit with anger, and he took a long drink, but they were still hot when he lowered his mug. "I always considered you a competent battlefield butcher, but it seems you missed your calling. You should have been an orator, a priest, a courtier. Mayhap a poet like our scribbler here. Truly, some spirited and compelling rhetoric. I don't believe I've ever heard you put that many words together before."

Mulldoos looked like he had an angry rebuttal, but called it back before unleashing it. "Mock all you want, but you know I'm right. Devils take you if you don't."

"I admit to no such thing, but even if I did, I ask again: What would you have me do with her? I welcome suggestions. Tie her to a horse and prop her up with a stick? Pass her on to the silk house that treated her with such kindness when she was among them? Give her bones to a battalion of drummers to follow us around, marking our passage in macabre rhythms? How do you suppose I honor our dead, crippled whore, who made you so nervous and still somehow stealthily earned your respect while you looked away? Eh? What is it you recommend?"

Mulldoos replied, without much enthusiasm or conviction, "Give her to the beetle masters, bring her bones back with us."

"To what end? It was difficult enough to deal with her alive. Do you suspect I want to cart around her bones as well?"

I offered, "Why not send her to the grass?"

Everyone looked and me, and Braylar replied, "I suggest you consult your notes again—her own family sold her to the least reputable slaver they happened to meet. After lopping off her fingers. No, there's no one for her there."

Hewspear said, "I think Arki has a point."

Braylar raised a single eyebrow. "Do you? Startling. Please, enlighten."

"We don't send her to anyone. But we could take her to the edge of Green Sea. Bury her there. Even leave her to feed the dogs, or whatever other creatures haunt the plains. She would've found some grisly justice in that. But the grass was the only thing she thought of as home, even if she was an exile. The grass rejects no one."

Braylar's eyes widened. "I never suspected I was surrounded by such insipid sentimentalists. With honeyed tongues, no less. Truly, a revelation." He stood, a bit unsteady, but placed one hand on the tabletop and righted himself, then flicked one of the flail heads. "To the grass, then? And will you two rapacious romantics take her—you, your ribs grinding to dust, and you, with your leg buckling underneath you? Is that the plan?"

Mulldoos looked towards me before answering. "I hauled her a long stretch yesterday. Not taking her a step farther, even with two good legs. But somebody will. Coin buys good couriers. Merchants leaving the Fair, pilgrims, hells, even a greedy Hornman or two. Turn any corner, you'll run into one of them. Somebody will take her there, we fill their pouches. Pains me to say it, but Brokespear over there has the right of it—Lloi would've liked that. She deserved that much, if nothing else. Send her to the grass and be done with it."

Braylar walked across the room, slowly but with surprising steadiness, considering how much he'd imbibed. His back to us, he said, "So be it. To the grass, then. Let the dogs welcome home one of their own."

He casually lifted a horn panel of the blinds and looked out. While it was still cloudy outside, they were thin clouds, and the brightness forced Braylar to take a step back. He dropped the panel and took another step, as if retreating from a foe, and then turned quickly, walked to the corner of the room, and vomited mostly in the chamber pot, hands on his knees.

The smell reached me almost immediately, harsh and sour and caustic, and I turned away, noticing that Hewspear and Mulldoos shared a quick look.

Braylar returned to the table, glaring at the flail heads as he did, as if the strength of his hatred might somehow cow them into submission. Wiping his mouth with the back of his hand, he filled his cup again. "Hard to maintain a stupor, when the stuff won't stay in your belly. And with Lloi gone, stupor is all that can help me."

Hewspear took a deep breath and held his side, then said, "I know you've heard this suggestion before, Captain, but given present circumstances, perhaps—"

"Perhaps nothing, Hew. We can't willingly invite a Memoridon among us. It's impossible. For reasons you're familiar with, so I won't waste my breath reiterating them."

Hewpsear didn't relent. "With Lloi gone—"

"We must find another rogue. And soon. That's my only recourse."

Mulldoos filled his cheeks with air before blowing it out. "It was freak luck we came across her, Cap. I don't know how you figure we'll find another. Maybe the old goat here is—"

"You're going to coordinate the hunt for another one, Mulldoos. So I suggest you devise a plan, and do so immediately. We'll be here for some time, so begin your efforts in Alespell." He looked down at Bloodsounder. "That is all."

Braylar coughed and took another drink, looking carefully at the three of us. Several moments passed, all awkwardly. Finally, he said, "Out with it, you two bastards. What niggles you now?"

Hewspear continued slowly sipping his drink and so it fell to Mulldoos. "Don't know that I'd call it any kind of niggling, Cap. Only that… that is, you know the men and me, even this old horsecunt, we'd follow you through feast or fire. Always have, always will."

"Dispense with the pretty qualifiers, lieutenant. They only make me nervous."

"Fair enough." Mulldoos laid his palms flat on the table, stared at the backs of his hands for a moment, an abundance of fine hair barely visible in the shafts of light. Then he looked up. "This whole Alespell business here… it's a huge heaping of shit stew, Cap."

"We're soldiers—we don't often have the luxury of choosing our meals. But explain, what is it that's so offended your palette?"

Mulldoos replied, "Well, we've been skulking about here for near two years now, laying plans, biding time, twiddling our cocks, all the men anxious for a little action, and we finally put something in motion just now, coddle the baron, spring the trap on the underpriest, spill some blood. All good, only it hadn't exactly worked out like we thought. Seems the trap got sprung on us—the underpriest dead, good men lost, your dog, too, and not much to show for it, except that guard." It sounded as if he intended to say more, his last word hanging, waiting for the next, but nothing else came as Braylar looked at him. Finally, after staring at Hewspear, then me, he said, "Shit stew. That guard—"

"Knows nothing. A pawn. Surely, he can't reveal anything to confirm the drama we played out for the good baron. Is that your worry?"

Mulldoos didn't respond immediately, picked up his mug as if needing something to do with his hands. "Guard's a guard. Even the captain of the guard probably didn't know much more than when and where the high priest shat, but that one we captured, no, he knows horseshit and less."

Braylar nodded and smiled. "Yes. Exactly."

Mulldoos turned to Hewspear. "Cap's grinning. Can't for the life of me unspool that one. You unspool that one? Because I'm thinking a dead underpriest and a guard that knows less than a cunt hair won't be helping our cause none." He looked back to Braylar. "Must be I'm looking at this thing sideways, though. Must be. Cap, you help me see it straight?"

Braylar said, "Not so much sideways, lieutenant, but you're looking at only a piece of the thing, rather than the whole. The guard won't reveal anything to confirm our version of events, it's true, but it's equally unlikely he can reveal anything to dispel our story. He doesn't know anything, as you pointed out, so he can't reveal anything. A neutral play. Had we actually delivered the underpriest into their hands," he pivoted on me, "something that was nearly accomplished, thanks to the exceptional bravery of our little scribbler here—he very well might have introduced information that would have raised doubts, doubts we could ill afford. So, despite what it cost us—and it did cost us—it's actually fortuitous we had only an ignorant guard as our bounty."

Clarity not coming on its own, I asked, "What do you mean by 'version'? Why did you go to the temple if you didn't intend to apprehend the priest?"

Before Braylar responded, Hewspear gave me a look brimming with pity. "You really haven't told him much, have you?"

"I told him what he needed to know, as he needed to know it. No more, no less. But now it's begun playing out and he has been entrenched with us, his tent is in the middle of our camp, there's nothing further served by being cryptic. He's embedded now." Braylar addressed me, "I'd hoped to see the underpriest dead. When the opportunity didn't avail itself to me, I thought at least he escaped. Until you came down the hill, leading him by the nose. That brought me no joy, I can tell you. But then a Brunesman took care of things in the copse, and it couldn't have played out better. Alive, he was dangerous to us, because he might have known or suspected some of Henlester's shady dealings."

"Forgive my saying so, but isn't assassination more serious than shady?"

Braylar replied, "The high priest had no plans to assassinate the baron. Or if he did, this is the first I've heard of it."

Once again, I found the ground shifting beneath my feet. I should've been used to it, sharing this man's company, but I never seemed to learn. Mulldoos said something, and Hewspear responded, but I was too stunned to pay much attention.

Braylar said, "The alleged assassination attempt, that was something conjured solely for the baron's benefit."

I floundered. "I don't understand. The underpriest requested the meeting. He showed up with payment. Didn't he?"

"True. He bore a satchel with gold," Braylar replied. "Very incriminating, yes? But the underpriest wasn't there to pay us for doing anything. Quite the opposite. It was a blackmail payoff. At least, he was there with the pretense of paying us. Until the earth belched out guards, and our traps were simultaneously sprung. Then, all illusion was dispelled."

"What was he allegedly paying you to keep secret, if not assassination dealings? His treatment of prostitutes?"

Braylar replied "While his depraved taste for disfigured whores alone might have been worthy of blackmail, we decided to keep digging. And so we waited until one of our own had penetrated the inner sanctum of his temple and discovered that, as suspected, his transgressions didn't end there."

Hewspear jumped in, "He's been engaged in some very creative book-keeping."

I waited for clarification and Mulldoos added, "Hadn't been paying his liege what he ought."

"And when we sent word we would expose him unless he paid dearly, he laid his trap while we laid ours. Blackmail was the ruse to draw out an agent of the high priest. Assassination was the ruse to draw out agents of the baron."

Mulldoos filled his mug again. "Still, it was a close thing, Cap. That Gurdinn, if he'd come down to the temple with us, he—"

"Couldn't," Braylar corrected. "He couldn't accompany us. Not so long as there was a chance we were telling the truth. Much as it galled him, he had to wait and watch, see how events transpired in the ruins. And while he suspects us of being capable of telling naught but lies—rightly, as it turns out—what he saw confirmed our tale. So you see, Mulldoos, while Captain Gurdinn will likely report grave misgivings about how things transpired or orders I gave, he can't say with any truth—and whatever else his faults, I suspect he's freighted with an abundance of cold honesty—he can't say that he witnessed anything to confirm suspicions that we were deceiving them at all. In fact, things could hardly have conspired better to give substance to our story.

"While I severely underestimated Henlester, the fact the underpriest came with a satchel of coins and planted an ambush of his own goes some distance to proving that the high priest was exceptionally guilty of something, and we have already supplied a likely enough reason. And as Brune demonstrated at the Three Casks, the baron sees treachery everywhere, and is willing to alienate his fieflords and even Hornmen to root it out. That, coupled with the fact that the one man at the temple who might have stood a chance of dispelling our little illusion was struck down in the brush…" Braylar raised his mug. "We sustained losses, but circumstances also worked to our favor. Now—"

Vendurro swung the door open, and called in. "Bruneboy come by." He walked over and handed the captain a scroll. "Got a summons, Cap."

Braylar sighed and ran a hand through his hair. He pulled Bloodsounder off the table with an awful scraping and clinking and secured it to his belt, then rose slowly. "Well. That was earlier than expected. Still... I can't very well refuse an opportunity for a social call, can I?"

Mulldoos stood and said, "We'll be coming with, Cap."

Hewspear added, "It would be a shame to pass up baronial hospitality. Rude even."

Braylar looked at his two lieutenants long and hard. "Perhaps you should stay. There's a chance this won't turn out well."

Mulldoos shrugged. "Things always turn to shit, sooner or later. We're coming."

"Very good." Braylar turned to me. I expected he would offer me the same reprieve, and given what I just learned, I would've been sorely tempted to accept, but he didn't. "To the baron's castle then."

We passed Vendurro in the common room, and Braylar ordered him to remain at the inn. As we left the Grieving Dog, the streets were already bustling with fairgoers. Between the mud from the previous day's rain and the horse and dog feces, it was impossible to keep my shoes clean, so I gave up trying. I fell in behind the Syldoon, and with Mulldoos at the point cursing and glaring, the throng parted for the most part, with him only occasionally shouldering someone to the side. We moved away from the plazas and main thoroughfare as quickly as possible, and the crowds thinned as we took side streets toward the castle. Up on its hill, it was impossible to miss, even if it disappeared behind a building for a moment.

The route was circuitous, as no two streets ran parallel for very long, and few among them were truly straight, but we finally cleared the last residences and found ourselves at the hill's base. Now, that close and with no obstructions, the hill seemed much higher than it had from the other side of Alespell.

We approached the first gate, which was flanked by two large towers on each side. I looked up and guards in purple and gray livery looked down. While the tall wooden doors of the gate were flung open, there were guards milling at the entrance, and one with bloodshot eyes walked over. After a drawn-out yawn, he said, "State your business."

Braylar handed over the scroll. "Late festivities?"

The guard ignored him, unrolled the scroll, scanned it and handed it back. "On your way then."

We passed through and began the slow ascent around the perimeter of the hill. The road was narrow, and it wound its way up, slowly spiraling. There were three more gates, each identical to the first with their flanking towers, and the scroll got us through them without incident. The muscles in my legs began to burn. I craned my neck and looked up at the walls and towers of the castle above as we walked. Wood hoardings jutted out, and with all the shutters and arrow loops, it was a gallery that could easily rain death down. I couldn't make out guards, but I'm sure they were up there, looking down on our small group as we sweated our way up the hill. Probably joking about what they would like to drop on our heads.

Mulldoos saw me and nearly read my mind, saying, "The bastard who built this place knew his business. Tough enough to clear the city walls, but anybody assaulting the castle would be in for a heap load of hurt. Arrows, stones, boiling piss. Real bad day, assaulting this place." He looked at Hewspear, who was struggling to breathe. "You going to make it, old goat?"

Face pale, Hew nodded and kept plodding up the hill. Mulldoos said, "Good, 'cause I ain't carrying you. A bone pops your lung, you're just going to have to sit and wheeze to death." He limped after.

We finally reached the castle's outer curtain wall. Where most of Alespell was constructed of snowstone that fairly glowed with the slightest hint of sun, the baron's castle was built of a charcoal gray stone that seemed to absorb light. I wiped my brow, tried to regulate my breathing, and looked over my shoulder at the city laid out far below us. Even the green copper domes seemed far away. All those people milling in the plazas and marketplaces, caught in the flow of commerce, haggling, laughing, dizzy with the oddities and entertainments of the Great Fair, absorbed in wonder and drunk on cheap wine and ale. For one day at least, their troubles and pains forgotten. And all of them oblivious to the halls of power above them. A life could be snuffed out on this hill and they'd never know, probably never care. My breathing didn't slow down, and not just because of the exertion of the climb.

Braylar grabbed my elbow and gave a squeeze, somewhere between gentle and forceful. "Easy, Arki. Only visiting a dear friend. Nothing more." For once, his lies didn't seem all that convincing.

The drawbridge was down over a deep dry moat carved into the rock, and our scroll got us entry through into the gatehouse. The portcullis was up. As we walked underneath, I couldn't help but notice the numerous murder holes in the ceiling above. A second gate flanked by guards, and we passed onto another section of floor. More murder holes above, but the odd thing was the floor was wood, and it almost felt like we were tramping across another drawbridge.

I looked over at Mulldoos and he was smiling. "Yup. Fiendish bastard built this." He stomped once on the floorboards. "Trap door. Anybody who somehow made it to the gatehouse probably not making it out real easy. Spikes below, I'm guessing. Big ones."

He seemed to really appreciate the craftsmanship. I nearly threw up.

At last we passed into the lower courtyard and back into the weak sunlight. As expected, there was noise and activity everywhere. Grooms hurrying to the stables; a man leading an ox out of the granary, his cart laden with heavy sacks; a hammer ringing in a smithy; a courier sprinting from one of the administrative buildings; several pigeons bursting out of the cylindrical dovecote alongside the kitchens, flying off in a tight group. The only person or thing not on the move was a guard assigned to protect the covered well on the other end of the courtyard. I looked up to the right and saw a covered allure and tall sanitary tower connected to the massive circular keep that rose several stories into the sky.

Braylar said, "I expect Lord Brune isn't counting kernels of corn or iron ingots. Come."

He led us underneath the allure and towards the keep that dominated the courtyard, rising high above everything else. There were large standards on top, but the air was heavy, moist, and instead of flapping or snapping, they hung limp on their poles. We approached the entrance stairs and more guards examined our scroll, but they didn't let us pass right away. An older guard missing an ear pulled a gambesoned guard aside, spoke to him quietly, and sent him running into the keep with the scroll.

A few awkward moments of silence passed and then Braylar said, "This keep is quite impressive. The plinth, the height, the machiolations. Yes, most impressive."

The earless guard looked at Braylar, blinked a few times, and then shrugged.

Braylar tried a different tack. "I've heard rumors the last few days that our baron is unwell. Is he on the mend, then?"

Earless shrugged again. "Guessing you'll be knowing soon enough."

That put an end to that. I worried Braylar was going to press the point, as that was his typical response when rebuffed, but he held his tongue. We waited there until the young guard returned. He ran down the stairs, handed Braylar the scroll, and told us we were clear to go. When we climbed and passed through the arched doorway into a long corbelled hallway, we were met by Gurdinn and a handful of surcoated guards. He didn't seem especially pleased to be our escort.

I felt rather than saw Hewspear and Mulldoos stiffen. Braylar said, "Ah, Captain Honeycock! So good to see you again. We really shouldn't allow so much time to pass between encounters like this. Criminal, really."

If we'd been anywhere else but his lord's keep, Gurdinn probably would have spit on the floor. As it was, he said, "The baron's waiting." He turned on his heel without waiting for a response.

The guards fell in behind us as we followed Gurdinn down the hall. Bas-reliefs of coats of arms broke up the walls on either side, occasionally interrupted by an unshuttered window or torch sconce. The torches weren't lit, and even with the shutters thrown open, the squares of light on the floor were weak at best. Bright light wouldn't have dispelled the foreboding, but it might have helped.

At the end of the hall, there was a set of stairs leading up and another spiraling down. Gurdinn waited next the stairwell going down.

Braylar stopped and looked at the stairs. "I know our friend baron is an independent thinker, but I would've expected him to maintain his solar and wardrobe above, in keeping with the fashion. A bit more light and air, such as it is."

Gurdinn's eyes narrowed. "And you'd be right. Though he's no friend to a Black Noose. Let's go." He started down the stairs.

Braylar's pursed his lips and he drummed his fingers along the surface of his buckler, but after a moment, he followed as commanded, and us behind him, with the Brunesmen bringing up the rear. The stairs wound down to the right, and here, with no windows or loopholes to offer even gloomy light, the torches were lit.

We passed several floors, the undercroft, other storage facilities, I'm not sure what else, and the air grew smokier. Our footfalls echoed off the stones, torchlight cast wild shadows as our passing caused the flames to dance ever so slightly, and the hairs on my body prickled, though whether from the drop in temperature or the direction we were heading, I couldn't say. Going down the stairs seemed hard on Hewspear and Mulldoos, and little better on Braylar's throat. I imagined climbing back up was going to be far worse. Assuming we did come back up.

My heart was hammering and my bladder full to bursting when we finally stopped at a small landing. The stairs kept going down, but we'd apparently reached our destination. Or at least the level it was on. Gurdinn unlocked a large door and pushed it in. As he led us down a hallway, the first thing I noticed was the overpowering smell of vinegar. There were wooden bowls of it along the floor on both sides. The stinging smell was incredible, enough to make the eyes water and nose burn. As we walked down the hall, passing doors, I couldn't begin to imagine why anyone would line the floor with bowls of vinegar. But then the reason suddenly became clear.

The vinegar was there to mask other smells. Worse smells. Blood. Urine. Feces. Burnt flesh. Death.

Even with a number of armed and armored guards behind me, and no weapon of my own, panic welled up and I nearly turned and ran. Braylar must have anticipated this, because he'd dropped back next to me, and his hand was on my arm, just above the elbow again, though this time as tight as a shackle. My head snapped in his direction and I probably would've shouted something if I'd been looking into any other set of eyes. But his had turned back into mossy stones, cold, hard, unrelenting. Had they been sympathetic or kind, I might have howled or cried out, but his glare stopped everything in my throat. He shook his head slowly and pushed my arm forward, and the rest of me followed, reluctantly.

That's when I heard the first scream.

Gurdinn stopped in front of a door at the end of the hall and unlocked it.

Braylar squeezed tighter, just in case I tried to flee, and I wanted to tell

him we needed to fight our way out or we were dead men, even as part of
me knew we couldn't possibly fight free of a keep, a castle, and a city. It
was madness. But so was staying there.

Gurdinn stood to the side of the door as another scream came out and
said, "In you go." To his credit, this was his moment to gloat, and he
didn't.

I tried convincing myself that if violence was coming, Braylar would
have felt it. But the screaming said violence was already there, and he
admitted that Bloodsounder sometimes deceived.

I'd never had such difficulty walking though a door before. Braylar's
steadying hand, half-guiding, half-supporting, was all that got me through
the portal. Gurdinn pulled the door shut behind us. It was a small room.
The baron was sitting in the chair closest to the door, one leg crossed over
the other, leaning back as if he were watching snow fall or listening to a
gurgling brook instead of witnessing a man being tortured. He had a long
black coat on, festooned with brass buttons down the front and on the
cuffs.

There were two other people in the room. A man in a long tunic who
was obviously the interrogator, a birthmark the color of eggplant covering
half his face that caused Mulldoos to lean close to Hew and whisper,
"Plague me—even likes his henchmen purple." And another figure, naked,
strapped down to a heavy table that was stained with every bodily fluid
imaginable. It took me a moment to realize this was the priest guard—his
face was contorted and unrecognizable. There was a strap with a sharp-
looking hook inserted in each corner of his mouth, blood trickling down
and pooling on the table. There was also a strapped hook in each nostril,
pulling his nose up. Thick leather straps crossed his forehead, neck, and
limbs, and he was completely immobile. The interrogator slowly turned a
handle on the side of the table and the priest guard screamed again, eyes
wide, tongue sticking out, spittle spraying, as Brune took a sip from his
goblet.

Then the baron looked over at us and smiled. There was nothing cruel
about it—just a warm, welcoming smile. It was horrible. "Ahh, very good
of you to join me. Thank you so much for coming on short notice. I must
say, Captain Killcoin, you and your companion looked in much better
health the other night. And who's this you've brought with you?"

Braylar gestured at Mulldoos with one hand and rasped, "This is one of my trusted lieutenants, Mulldoos." He gestured at me with the other. I expected a lie, but he told the truth. Mostly. "And this is my chronicler, Arkamondos. I admit, as a humble servant of the empire, I wouldn't retain one myself, but our emperor insisted. And Arkamondos didn't want to miss an opportunity for an audience with the baron, so here we are. Your powers of recovery are amazing, my lord."

Brune chuckled. "Gurdinn advised against inviting you here, of course, but our exchanges are so very lively, it seemed a shame not to have another one." He sat up in his chair and indicated the tortured man with a small tilt of his head. "I believe you're already acquainted with Henlester's guard here, so no need for introductions. I would say 'traitor's guard,' but we haven't determined that definitively, have we, Untovik?"

The interrogator laid his hand on the handle again and leaned in close over the prisoner, who choked on his spit as he said, or tried to say "no" repeatedly without tearing his face further.

Brune raised a finger. "Ahh, my apologies. My chief interrogator, Untovik. Untovik, these are the men responsible for Henlester's guard joining us." If Untovik listened or cared, he gave no sign. The baron turned to Braylar. "It's a pity you weren't able to deliver the underpriest, though. I do fear the guard here won't be especially… enlightening. Though that won't stop us from trying. No, we work with what we have, don't we, Untovik."

The interrogator replied by turning the handle a little more. Though they hadn't ripped his flesh deeply yet, the hooks did their work, nose and lips stretching and tearing just a little more, red rivulets running onto the table. The prisoner gurgled another wet and distorted scream.

"Yes," the baron said, "Too bad about losing the underpriest."

Stomach flipping, I quickly looked away from the tortured guard as Braylar replied, "You're correct, Baron Brune. We went through a great many pains to obtain him, and our losses were not light, I assure you. I was equally as disappointed he didn't live to see Alespell again."

I wondered if he'd lay the blame at Gurdinn's feet, but if he was tempted to, he resisted.

The baron lifted the goblet to his nose and inhaled deeply. "Do any of you fancy mead? We have some beekeepers in this barony who might be the most talented in the kingdom. I'm biased, of course."

He might not have expected anyone to take him up on his offer, but Hewspear replied, "Thank you, my lord. I'd like to sample some—I've heard it's quite good."

The baron handed Hewspear a goblet and filled it from a pitcher on a small table alongside him. "Anyone else?"

Mulldoos shook his head. "Too sweet for my tongue." As he watched the interrogator move around the table, his hand had drifted down to the pommel on his falchion, like a fierce hound with its hackles up.

Braylar accepted a goblet. The baron offered me one as well, and while I was terrified of not keeping it down, I hoped it would help me focus on something besides the awful scene in front of me, and so I nodded and mumbled a thank you.

I lifted it to my lips, hand shaking violently, and took a sip. It was pungent and mellow at first swallow, but then burned a golden trail down my throat. Strong, very strong. That was good.

Brune raised his goblet. "There's much more to good mead than the quality of honey, of course. The brewmasters here have their closely guarded secrets. Generations of perfecting their craft, and revealed only to guildmasters. Apprentices are kept in the dark for years. Isn't that something?" He sniffed the liquid. "So powerful and peculiar, secrets. Some are a professional matter. The brewmasters, as an example. Others are personal, closeted on account of shame or fear. I detest them on the whole. Nothing I hate more, really. Because in my experience, where there are secrets, there are usually traitors harboring them." He called over to his interrogator, "Would you be able to convince the brewmasters to reveal their methods, do you think?"

Untovik's reply came in the form of his prisoner screaming some more. I took another large swallow.

"Yes. I expect you could." Brune took another sip. "But you didn't come down here to hear me prattle on about bees and honey, did you? To business then. Gurdinn had a fair number of unflattering things to report about how you conducted yourself at the temple, and on the road back here. While he accepted responsibility for his man killing the underpriest, he also pointed out they wouldn't have found themselves in that position if you'd made better decisions. Claimed you jeopardized everyone's lives, and nearly undermined this little ruse you'd done so much to orchestrate. I'd be very interested to hear your version, if you don't mind, Captain Killcoin."

Braylar swirled his mead around in the goblet. "Your captain is staunchly loyal, and stalwart as well. Inspiring bravery, truly. But he's also something of a tremendous fool, my lord. Had we done anything differently, the odds are good you never would've received a report of any kind. Not unless Henlester left our corpses for you to find. And that would have been a murky report at best."

The baron smiled. "A difference of interpretation then? Not surprising, really. After all, Gurdinn clearly doesn't trust you or bear you any love. If he had his way, in fact, it would be all of you strapped down to tables just now." He refilled his goblet slowly. "So, you still believe High Priest Henlester is responsible for hiring you as assassins?"

"I saw nothing at the temple to indicate otherwise, my lord. The underpriest was there with payment for the deed. Which I'm sure Gurdinn delivered." Brune tilted his head in thanks, and Braylar continued, "They arranged an ambush, wanting to wipe out their co-conspirators. I don't know for a fact that Henlester ordered all of this, but all signs point in that direction."

"Such a shame we don't have the underpriest." The prisoner was trying to speak. Brune nodded at Untovik, who turned the wooden handle with a squeak. The prisoner gurgle-screamed again as the hooks bit deeper, knuckles white in his balled fists, feet twitching. "He might have been able to confirm some of this. But then again, perhaps not."

Brune stood and walked over to the table. The prisoner's eyes were rolling white, the cords in his neck bulging, blood trickling out his nose and his mouth, flowing more freely now.

Braylar said, "I don't presume to tell you your business, my lord, but have you sought out Henlester? I expect he would provide some interesting answers to any line of questioning you and your savvy interrogator here might pose."

Brune nodded to Untovik again. I closed my eyes tight and wished I could do the same with my ears, but this time the cranking of the handle wasn't accompanied by screaming. I looked—the interrogator was turning the handle back the other way, loosening the straps on the prisoner's head.

When they were finally slack, the baron pulled the hooks clear of the nose and mouth, dropped them on the table, and then wiped his hands on a rag. "As it happens, I sent a battalion to the High Priest's compound just after Gurdinn gave his report. But it seems Henlester had urgent business elsewhere just now. He disappeared in the night, taking his underpriests with him, leaving behind only a handful of servants and staff. I've spoken to a few already, but as you might expect, they have limited knowledge about the comings and goings of their master. Not terribly useful. Still, extracting secrets isn't half as challenging as detecting who has them in the first place, is it?"

I wasn't sure who he directed the question to, or if it was rhetorical, but no one responded. Brune wiped a rag across the prisoner's face, clearing off most of the bloody spit and snot.

The prisoner, finally able to turn his head, tried to talk, though his injured mouth muddied the words, "You never asked me anything, my lord! Ask me! Ask me whatever you want! Please! I'll tell you anything you want to know, my lord! Please... just please. Ask. Ask, my lord. Whatever you want."

Baron Brune looked down at him, smiling. "The truth. Not what you think I want to hear. Only the truth. Nothing more, nothing less. Can you do that, lad?"

The prisoner nodded vigorously, tears coming. "I can! I swear I can! Whatever you want!"

The baron patted the prisoner's wet cheek, and said, almost sadly, "Off to a poor start." He looked directly at Braylar. "You may go. Though not far, I hope. I do so appreciate your assistance. I could well have need of you again."

Braylar forced a smile, remarkably without twitches. "And miss another chance for a lively exchange? Never, my lord. Though perhaps next time it will be above ground."

Hewspear drained his goblet and put it on the platter. "Thank you for the mead, my lord. It was a complex flavor. Several unexpected spices." The baron didn't respond, his attention back on his prisoner.

I tipped my goblet up, nearly choking on the final gulp, and then we walked over to the door and filed out. There was only one guard outside, and he pulled the door shut after me and locked it without saying a word or looking at us. We began the long climb up the stairs. The only sound besides our heavy breathing was the occasional pop of a torch. Hewspear and Mulldoos were both struggling with their injuries.

When we got back to the main hall, Hewspear's breath was ragged and Mulldoos had to lean against the wall. Braylar didn't wait. He started towards the stairs leading out of the keep and called out, "All downhill from here. Let's go."

Braylar paused at the bottom of the stairs long enough for us to join him, than headed across the courtyard. I fell in alongside him, lightheaded and heavy-stomached. It felt good to be in the open air again, but I couldn't get the image of the prisoner out of my head. Seeing no one close, I said to Braylar, "You're letting them torture an innocent man."

He replied, "You give innocence a bad name, Arki. That guard protected a man who claimed to be a conduit to Truth, all the while abusing and murdering whores and cheating his liege lord. Admittedly, it's possible he was unaware of his master's true dealings. But we're all of us pawns, and many in games far beyond our understanding. I have no liking for torturers—even the best of them rarely unearth anything truly useful. I'm not glad for the man's suffering, but it ultimately serves our purpose, and that's an end to it."

I continued to protest, "And Henlester's steward or servants or whoever else he left behind? Are they just useful pawns too?"

Anger was flaming into fullness behind Braylar's gaze. "Perhaps the baron will use them more gently. Perhaps not. Either way, it was not my choice to abandon them to the cruel world. Their lives are beyond my reach, and therefore, beyond my caring."

I started to object, my voice rising, but he pushed me against a stone wall, hissing, "Still your tongue, archivist! That is not beyond my reach." He slowly released me and led us through the gatehouse and down the hill.

Mulldoos cleared his throat. "You want me to round up the boys, Cap?"

"Round them up?"

Mulldoos looked at Hewspear for some kind of confirmation. "Seems we played this thing out as far as we're able. Expect we'll be heading out."

Braylar led us through another gatehouse. Once we were out of earshot of the guards, he said, "And you, Hewspear? Are you as equally timorous?"

Mulldoos looked ready to object but Hewspear replied, "Our orders were to sow discord in this region, Captain. They gave us quite a bit of latitude in determining the how of it. We've planted the idea that one of Brune's trusted advisors betrayed him, sought his blood. It will be known that many guards are dead, the underpriest as well, and Henlester fled. Our whisperers will spread word in the streets, no matter what the baron does to contain it, or even if he believes it. Once burghers, priests, and fieflords learn of it, chaos might not ensue, but it could. And that's what we were tasked with. Lieutenant Mulldoos is stubborn and hard, but I say he's right. We've accomplished what the Citadel required of us, and as you noted, it's been costly already."

Braylar looked around to be sure no one could overhear us. "Stay, and we comply with our orders, we do our part to keep the Boy King in check, as commanded. And we're afforded a rare opportunity to truly wreak havoc in this barony. But we follow on Henlester's heels, flee Alespell, we not only cast doubt on Henlester's thirst for assassination, but we incriminate ourselves and give credence to any accusations Gurdinn lays against us. Flee, and we undermine all that we've accomplished here, and the deaths of our comrades are meaningless. Is that what you two want?"

No one responded right away, but finally Mulldoos shook his head and said to Hewspear, "Was I the only one down there in the dark? Wasn't just me was it? 'Cause right now, it sure feels like it. Seemed to me it was real clear the baron's just looking for an excuse to turn us over to old Mapface there." He looked at Braylar again. "We got no chance to do more than we done here, Cap. None. You think Brune's going to invite us to his inner sanctum for candied eels and sweet wine, open his coffers, hand out some titles? We're not winning that horsecunt over, not now, not ever. Stay, and only thing we got to look forward to is a trip back down to the baron's playroom."

Braylar said, "You hit upon it, Mulldoos, though I suspect you missed it in the same breath. The baron lives for plays and spectacle. He could have received us anywhere in the keep, but chose to have his audience there for obvious reasons. He wants to provoke us to act rashly, to reveal any secrets we have. Which is exactly what you propose."

Mulldoos rolled a tongue over his lower lip. "Seemed to me he was delivering a message. And I got it real clear. We stay, we end up on the torture table. Tomorrow, maybe the day after, as soon as he can prove we're double-dealing. That table's the only kind of future we got in Alespell. So let's tell our own we done what we came to and put this place behind us. Better yet, kick up dust on the road west and then send the report once we hit—"

Braylar stopped and turned on Mulldoos, their noses nearly touching. "I've heard enough! We don't flee. Do you understand, Mulldoos? Not now. Not ever."

Perhaps unwisely, judging by his captain's present fervor, Mulldoos replied, "Wide difference between a rout and a retreat. Never said flee, said leave. We done what the Citadel charged us with. Now—"

I thought Braylar might strike him, but instead, he said, through gritted teeth. "We. Stay." Then he started walking again. "Hewspear—see if any of our men can pick up Henlester's trail. I would very much like to find him before the baron does. Mulldoos—get me that rogue. I don't have much time."

Mulldoos rolled his jaw around. "And what's for you, then? Draining pitchers until Alespell runs dry?"

Braylar didn't respond until we cleared one of the gates and the guards. Quietly, he replied, "I'll be composing letters to grieving widows and harlots. But before I do, I'll tell you one thing, and tell it once. You and I have endured a great deal together over the years. You've saved my life. I've saved yours. None are more trusted or valued. But if our familiarity causes you to forget who your commanding officer is again, I'll ribbon the ground with your flesh. Are we clear?"

Mulldoos bit back a reply I'm sure would have earned him that whipping. Hewspear gave the smallest shake of his head as Mulldoos said, "Oh, we're plenty clear, Captain Killcoin. Plenty." He saluted, not caring who might see, and then stomped ahead, doing his best not to let the limp show. Hewspear kept pace with us as and was silent until we made it through the next gate and the road began to level off. Finally, having considered his words, he said, "I only have the vaguest idea what you are going through. And I'm glad of it. Without Lloi... I'm sure you suffer. Greatly. And of all men, I know some of the losses you've endured. I was there at the beginning, lad. So I know you're cold because you have to be. But Bray..." He waited, and when Braylar didn't respond, finished, "Mulldoos was wrong—Lloi's loyalty was nothing compared to his own.

But you test it, Captain. Sorely."

Braylar sighed, long and deep, but offered nothing in the way of rebuttal. When we made it back to flat ground, Hewspear shook his head and headed off down a sidestreet. Braylar kept walking in the general direction of our inn. I stayed next to him, saying nothing. He finally looked over at me, and blinked twice, quickly, as if he'd forgotten I was still there. "Shadowing me, yes? How very dutiful."

He closed his eyes and rubbed the bridge of his nose. I looked for the signs I'd seen out in the grassland, and asked if he needed anything. He laughed, though there was an undeniable edge to it. "Your tender worrying is very touching, but just because Lloi is dead, don't think I'm in need of another dull-witted shepherd."

I noticed some blood drops on the side of his scalp. Braylar reached up and touched a new wound that hadn't been there an hour ago, then looked at the red smear on his fingertips. "That is..." He closed his eyes, wiped his fingers on his tunic. "Leave me, Arki."

I looked around, unsure if I'd heard correctly. "Where... where shall I go?"

His eyes flickered open at my question. "You're in a city hosting one of the finest fairs in the land. Full of wonder. Delight. Go. Explore it. I have no more need of you today. You won't run. You're with us now, Arki. Irrevocably. Your fate, knotted with ours beyond untangling. You won't run. And even if you should forget that for a flicker of time, I'm sure you'll remember what befalls those who flee. So... to the stalls and the sights. Back to your room. Go where you will. Just leave me."

I didn't obey right away, until I saw his eyes narrow. Then I nodded, though still didn't move, unsure where I would head. His eyes were nearly slits, so I took a few directionless steps, figuring I would determine the destination en route. Behind me, Braylar asked, so quietly I barely heard the words, "You were fond of her, yes?"

I half-turned to answer, but didn't trust myself to keep my voice from quivering, and so stopped and only nodded quickly.

"Good." He sighed deeply. "Then you're that much closer to living a complete life—you finally know something of grief at last."

I faced him, but he was already striding away, which made me both angrier and suddenly bold. "If I'm such a vital member of the company now, then maybe you can finally tell me what's in that mysterious crate we've carted over half of creation."

He spun and advanced on me quickly, and I immediately wished I'd held my tongue. You would think I'd have mastered that by now.

His nose nearly touching mine, the captain said, "Your ability to record won't be hindered in the slightest if I rip out your tongue and nail it to a post, which is precisely what I mean to do if you spill our secrets in the street again. Do you understand me, scribe?"

Though I was still angry, I was more terrified, and so I nodded.

"Very good." He took a single step back. I expected him to spin on his heel and leave again. But he paused, as if considering something. Then, unexpectedly and quietly, he said, "It is full of the coronation clothes of the boy king. Or what he would have worn if we hadn't stolen them."

I was as stunned by the revelation itself as by the fact that he chose to reveal anything at all. "But… why? Why did you steal them? Wasn't he crowned some time ago?"

"The young monarch's ancestors have worn the royal robes, collar, and smock for every ceremony going back for time immemorial. He has not. We managed to steal them before the coronation, though it did take us some time to smuggle them out of the capital."

Suddenly things, some things anyway, began to make sense. "That's where you went after you hired me, wasn't it? When you took to the road after the interview. But I still don't understand why? Why go to such lengths? Do the Anjurians place that much stock in simple vestments?"

Braylar smiled, though with a predatory curve. "They place more stock in ceremony than any people alive or dead. There are a fair number who were dubious of their new monarch or his regent as it was. They pledged only the weakest of support. When word got out that the coronation trappings had disappeared, well, to them, it is simply one more indication that his reign is destined to be a short or disastrous one. Absence can be as powerful a sign as spectacle."

The Anjurians were a strange lot. What he said did make sense of a sort, at least from their perspective. "And what will you do with them?"

His scarred lip twitched. "You are finally beginning to think like a Syldoon. An excellent question, and you can be sure, when I have an excellent answer, you will be the fifth to know." He heard someone approaching, and without another word, turned and headed back in the direction of the inn.

My legs carried me forward, leaden and slow. I wound my way through the narrow streets, following the sound of the crowd, eager for any kind of distraction to keep my mind off birthmarked torturers, bedeviled captains, dead crippled nomad mystics, and Syldonian conspiracies and power plays.

After a dead-end and some backtracking, I finally made my way out of the warrens and into the plaza they called the Belly Bazaar. The smells reached me before I turned the final corner, and they were so rich and varied they even managed to overpower the human stench. Food carts and tables were scattered everywhere, and the sheer number of people was staggering. Thick slices of fresh baked bread—wheat, rye, barley, oat—abounded, sometimes adorned only with honey butter, other times serving as a plate or makeshift trencher for roasted bacon, pork, or carp (or at least the grease, for those who couldn't afford the meat proper). There were wooden bowls of pottage, thickened with everything imaginable—peas and grains, leeks and spinach, bits of cod or eel, eggs and yams. I saw small baked hens stuffed with grape leaves, meatballs dredged in flower and fried in olive oil, mutton on wooden skewers, and countless tarts, large and small. Baskets of fruit, local and exotic, drew the eye, and there were so many different kinds of nuts on hand I couldn't keep track. It was a dizzying assortment of food from all over the land, and an equally diverse group of people enjoying it.

My stomach churned, and I realized I was really hungry. After walking among the stalls, I settled on a mug of strong ale and a hunk of dark rye with several juicy-looking butter-and-garlic scallops on top. It seemed as good a place to start as any, though I was sure I'd be sampling something else after. And something after that.

I leaned against a barrel, eating my food, completely stunned that I was actually alone. It seemed like ages had come and gone since I had become entangled in the Syldonian intrigue and all the death and fear and betrayal and plotting that went with it. I was at one of the world's greatest fairs, finally out of my room and left to my own devices, and had some small coin in my pocket—I was going to do by best to enjoy it, if even for a day.

As I chewed a plump scallop, I was thinking about what I might like to see or do. Peruse all the goods in the marketplace? Perhaps head to the docks to watch the flat-bottomed ships sail past in the broad canal? Just find a place to watch the people go by? I was considering the merits of each, and actually warming to the idea of exploring, unimpeded, uninterrupted, just caught along in the current of the Great Fair. To be one of those tiny people I'd both envied and disparaged from the castle on the hill.

And then I felt the sensation of being watched. My first thought was that Braylar was testing me—he'd sent someone to make sure I didn't run, either out of Alespell or back to the baron. I scanned the crowds, wondering if I was simply imagining things, but then I saw it, across the plaza. Only it wasn't a Syldoon. The face was a sunset over war-torn lands, shiny purple and yellow, with a nose that had been brutally broken, and flesh that was still badly swollen. We locked eyes, to be sure we were seeing who we were seeing. While the odds weren't completely against us both being at the Fair—it was the largest attraction in the barony—we both seemed equally shocked at the recognition.

And then the boy spun and disappeared into the crowd, as if he'd never been there at all. He wasn't wearing a gambeson, and didn't appear to be armed, but there was no mistaking the young Hornman I'd spared in the grass.

I nearly choked on my scallop, tried to wash it down with ale, and then bent over sputtering and coughing.

I obviously just wasn't meant to enjoy the Great Fair. The moment of peace and contentment disappeared as if it hadn't existed at all. The Captain was right, my fate did seem to be irrevocably knotted to his.

I desperately hoped I might've been mistaken, but it was folly. I had seen the boy and he had seen me. Suddenly, my mercy didn't seem quite as noble as it had on the Green Sea. I tried to weigh my options, but the possibilities were colliding too quickly. I could do nothing, simply pretend I hadn't seen him. But if he reported me to a senior Hornman? I could rush back to the inn, but I knew what Braylar's reaction would be, and dreaded being on the receiving end of it. I could try to catch up to the boy, speak to him, but I'd already dawdled as I stood there debating, and even if I somehow caught him, what would I say? You swore an oath—please keep it? Show me to your superiors so I can turn in my cohorts, and please don't hang me? I could even head to the baron, appeal to the highest secular power in the land to extricate myself from the whole thing. But that idea lasted only long for me to remember the gurgling, screaming guard strapped to a table, his face soon to be flayed apart if it wasn't already. There was no untangling this mess.

I tried to convince myself I accepted this commission because it was an opportunity to witness something unlike anything else I'd ever see, so far removed from ledgers and revenues, dowries and upjumping. But the truth was I was the worst kind of upjumper. I took the job for the most mercenary reasons of all—fame and fortune. Attaching my name to something large and grand and extraordinary and milking that association to better my own status.

But there was nothing large or grand about the things happening here. They were small and shadowy, punitive and bloody, occurring in the middle of one of the busiest centers of trade in the world, and yet unknown to all but a few key players who seemed intent only on deceiving or destroying others. If this was how history was made, I was a fool to want to be part of it.

Leaning against a wall, I breathed deep, steadied myself, and tried to imagine what Lloi would do. And the answer was obvious. She would do what needed doing. That's what she would do. And as if acting of their own volition, my feet were carrying me back to the Grieving Dog, where I would do just that.

ACKNOWLEDGEMENTS

Countless people helped *Scourge of the Betrayer* along its winding way here. So if you were one of them and I neglected to mention you, hit me up for a beer later.

There were several folks who saw the earliest iteration of the manuscript and cheered me on, despite probably being tempted to suggest ice sculpture (or ice dancing) as alternate pursuits. So thanks, Josh Stevens, Eric Gubera, Kris Choma, Doug Folger, and Grant Keiser for excessive tact.

Many thanks to my agent, Michael Harriot, for believing in fantasy more intimate than epic, and for invaluable advice and feedback. Jen Brown uncovered countless gremlins lurking in the text and exterminated them with extreme prejudice. The posse at Night Shade Books also deserve special praise: Jason Williams, Jeremy Lassen, Ross Lockhart, Liz Upson, Amy Popovich; and surely others who contributed in ways I'm completely oblivious to. I bombarded them all with far too many questions and suggestions, and they handled them all with aplomb as they kept me from having panic attacks.

The artist, J.K. Woodward, and designers, Federico Piatti and Victoria Maderna, killed it—they did an exceptional job on the cover and really captured the spirit of the book. While we're talking aesthetics, Gabriel Macintosh also built a great website despite my incessant waffling.

And to my lovely wife, Kristen… more gratitude than I can ever say, for putting up with my tempests, moods, and the Moose Pants Depression, and steadfastly encouraging me all the while. She is truly my better half, and inspires me to try to keep pace every day.